SHE'S A WILD ONE

THE WILDS OF MONTANA

KRISTEN PROBY

&
Ampersand
Publishing, Inc.

She's a Wild One

A Wilds of Montana Novel

By

Kristen Proby

SHE'S A WILD ONE

A Wilds of Montana Novel

Kristen Proby

ACKNOWLEDGMENTS

Writing a whole series in one year isn't an easy feat, and I would be a big jerk if I didn't take a moment to thank everyone.

In 2023, I was feeling pretty burned out. I knew that I needed to take my writing back to a place where I felt at home, to a place where I knew the readers would love to come with me, and thus Bitterroot Valley, Montana, was born. This little town isn't unlike the real-life town I live in, with mountains and lakes and a great big sky. But it's the people who live in Bitterroot Valley that make it truly magical, and they've certainly embedded themselves in my heart forever.

First, I have to extend a huge thank-you to you, the reader, for coming on this wild journey with me. When we announced this series, you didn't hesitate to come with us, and I can't tell you how humbling that is. Thank you for taking a chance on something new and loving it so much that you've shouted it from the mountaintops. Whether you've been with me since *Come Away With Me* in 2012 or if *She's a Wild One* is your first foray into my creative mind, I'm so grateful that you're here!

My assistant, Crystal Eacker, is a powerhouse, who has been just as excited, if not more so, about the Wild family as I am. Crystal, your work ethic is incredible, and I know that without you, *The Wilds of Montana* wouldn't have been as amazing as they are. Thank you for every little thing you do for me (trust me, they're not so little) every single day. For the long hours of plotting with me, the late night "but what if..." texts, and generally being a wonderful friend. You're stuck with me, babe.

To my agent and publicist, Georgana Grinstead. You are...I can't even put into words what you mean to me. You are my ride or die, my fierce warrior. I love you from the bottom of my heart.

To the whole Valentine PR team, Kim, Kelley, Josette, Amy, Meagan, Ratula (who is the boss at helping me with blurbs!), Sarah and everyone that I might be forgetting, THANK YOU for the many hours of work that you put into every single release. You are all incredible!

To my Pam. Pamela has been with me since 2012. You're so much more to me than the one who makes me beautiful graphics for every release, Pam. You are a confidante, a cheerleader, my comic relief, and one of my very best friends. I love you so much! Thank you for every single thing you do for me.

To Rachel, who is my newsletter, online shop, and website guru, you're the best there is. But as a friend? No one compares. Thank you for all of my last-minute changes and for being someone I trust and lean on. I adore you!

I have to extend a huge thank-you to my editor, Jaime, who knows all the things that I don't and keeps these manuscripts looking beautiful. Thank you so much for all your many hours of hard work!

And to my proof team: Tiffany, Renee, Yvonne, and Katrina, thank you for all the giggles in our text thread, and for making sure we find any of those last-minute errors that every book has. I appreciate you so much!

Hange Le is not only my friend, but a mastermind when it comes to cover art. Thank you for the many hours we spend together, not only creatively, but for your friendship, too. I'm honored to work with you. Here's to many more projects together!

Katie Robinson at Lyric Audio is a patient, compassionate, amazing producer, and I'm so grateful for the hours of brainstorming who would be the perfect voices for each of these characters. Thank you, Katie! And thank you to every narrator who gave their immense talent to the series.

Last but never least, to my husband, John. This year went from "I think I'll write less in 2024" to "I can't stay away from my desk, the words are pouring out of me, please don't ask me to do anything else." You took it all in stride with understanding and patience, and I am so incredibly grateful to you for taking care of me so I can focus on make-believe. I love you more than all the stars in the sky.

xo,

Kristen

CONTENT WARNINGS

You can find a comprehensive content warning list at the following link:

https://www.kristenprobyauthor.com/potential-trigger-content-warnings

Kristen

PROLOGUE

HOLDEN

Eight Years Ago...

It's been the best fucking month of my life.

I've spent every spare minute with Millie Wild and all her young, innocent beauty since I ran into her at the farmer's market four weeks ago. She's home for the summer from college, and like a moth to an inferno, I couldn't stay away from her.

She's too young for me. All my instincts scream that at me daily.

She may be an adult, but I'm pushing thirty, and I should stay away from her. At nineteen, she's *too young*.

Not to mention, she's the only daughter and youngest child of John Wild, my father's arch nemesis. Our families have a hundred-year-old feud to maintain, so the likelihood of either of our parents sitting back and agreeing to this match is less than zero.

But I'll be damned if I can stay away from her.

"I don't want to go back to college," Millie says with a sigh. We're not on either of our properties, on the off chance we get caught. Instead, we're sitting on a pile of blankets in the back of my truck at my good friend Brooks Blackwell's ranch. The sun has gone down, and the stars are starting to come out.

"We still have a week," I remind her. Her head is in my lap, and I'm brushing my fingers through her long, soft chestnut-brown hair that feels like silk against my skin. "We'll do whatever you want before you go. Name it."

"Except we can't actually go on a *date*." She narrows her eyes up at me. "This family feud shit is stupid, Holden. Who cares if our great-great-grandparents hated each other? Everyone needs to get over it already."

"I couldn't agree more." I drag my fingertip down the bridge of her nose. A coyote howls somewhere off in the distance.

I can't stop touching her. For a month, it's been impossible to keep my hands to myself. Whether I'm holding her hand or touching her hair or sitting like this, memorizing her gorgeous face, I need to be in constant physical contact with this incredible woman.

But I haven't slept with her. Because once we do that, there's no going back, and I don't want to push her too far before she's ready. I don't ever want to do anything that might make her pull away from me or run in the other direction.

"Holden?"

"Yes, Rosie?"

That makes her smirk. She told me a couple of weeks ago that her favorite flower is a wild rose, and now, that's how I think of her. My little wild rose. It's appropriate, given that her last name is Wild.

And when I want to see that sweet smile, I call her Rosie.

"I'm not going to see you for a while, am I?"

I sigh, not wanting to think about what's going to happen after she returns to Bozeman to go to school next week.

"I wish I could come out there every weekend to spend a couple of days with you, but I have to be here for my sisters."

She nods, understanding shining in those amazing hazel eyes as she stares up at me. "I know you do. I'm sorry that your dad's so mean to all of you."

She doesn't know the half of it. I shudder to think what would happen to my four little sisters if I wasn't here to run interference.

"But I'll see you when you come home for holidays," I remind her. "And I'll talk to you every day. We can video chat before bed."

"Yeah, I'd like that." She sits up and moves to straddle me, planting her knees on the blanket on either side of my hips.

And just like that, my cock is on high alert.

"Mill—"

She covers my mouth with hers, so gently, so sweetly, that it tugs at my heart.

"Millie," I try again, stilling her hands when they roam over my shoulders and kiss them both. "Baby girl, if you keep this up, I won't want to stop."

"Who said anything about stopping?" She grins and leans in closer, pressing herself against my hard-on, and I can't help the groan that slips out of my throat. "Holden, I want this, especially before I have to leave and not see you for *months.* That's going to be torture."

I cup her face, and then my hand glides down to her cheek and over her jaw until I'm holding on to her throat —gently, but still holding.

"You need to be completely sure."

Her tongue pokes out to her lip, and with her eyes boldly on mine, she lifts her sundress over her head and discards it to the side.

Jesus Christ, I can't look down. She's not wearing a bra.

My girl is mostly naked, straddling me in the middle of nowhere, offering herself to me with utter love and trust shining in those golden eyes, and it's almost more than I can take.

"Holden," she whispers as she tips forward and rests her forehead on mine. "Make love to me, okay?"

And that's all I can take. Christ, who could say no to this sweetness?

I take her lips, kissing her the way I've learned she

loves, and then I pick her up and move her so she's lying on her back on the blanket. My eyes haven't left hers.

"Before I look at all of you, I want you to tell me how you like to be touched."

She frowns and bites her lip. "Uh, what do you mean?"

"How do you want it?" I ask and drag my nose up her cheek.

"I don't know." She swallows hard, and I pull back so I can see her face in the waning light. "I've never done this before."

Fuck me sideways.

"Oh, baby." Jesus Christ, I'm gonna go to hell for what I'm about to do.

And I don't fucking care.

"But I'm *really* sure," she assures me and grips on to my T-shirt, tugging it high on my torso. "I want to see you."

"Me first."

For the first time since she stripped off that dress, I let my eyes move down, and my mouth goes dry.

My cock has never been so hard.

Her skin, all smooth and bronze from the sun, feels like velvet under my hands, and her nipples are already hard little nubs, just begging for my mouth.

I have to remind myself to be gentle. For this first time, at the very least, I have to go easy on her. Get her good and ready for me.

"Do you trust me, Rosie?"

She nods, but I cover her throat with my hand again and lean in to press my lips to her ear.

"I need your words, baby girl. Do you trust me?"

"I trust you." Her throat works under my palm as she swallows hard, and the pulse under my thumb is strong and fast. "More than anyone."

"Good. We're going to take this nice and slow."

"Or, we could hurry."

I smile against her skin as I make my way down her body, kissing her *everywhere*. She's so damn perfect. Every inch of her. "No, I'm not about to rush this incredible moment. No way."

She arches her back as I take a nipple into my mouth, wanting more. Those hips are moving, her long legs scissoring, and I loop my thumbs in her little pink panties and pull them down her legs, tossing them onto her discarded dress.

"Gorgeous," I groan, but she moves her knees together almost shyly, and I shake my head. "Open those pretty thighs for me, baby girl."

She takes a deep breath and lets it out slowly, but she does as I ask, letting her thighs fall to the side as her gorgeous eyes never leave mine.

I press my hand to her chest bone, then slowly drag it down. Her breath shudders when I reach her pubis, and I pause.

"You can stop this at any time."

"No stopping," she says breathlessly, her chest rising and falling. "Do not stop, Holden."

I grin, dragging my hand lower, and when I cup her already soaking-wet pussy, she moans.

"I'm the first one to touch this pretty pussy?" I drag my fingertip through her swollen lips, up around her hard clit, and back down again, reveling in the sounds coming from her mouth.

"Yes." Her hand dives into my hair as I shimmy down to nudge my shoulders between her thighs.

With one long stroke, I lick her from her glistening opening up to her clit, and her hips arch up off of the blanket.

"Holden!"

"Easy," I croon before licking her again. "Easy, baby."

She's fisted the blanket in her hands, her head moving frantically back and forth.

"Look at me, Millie."

Instantly, she follows that command. My girl is good at taking orders, and it only makes me want her more. I want to pound into her and brand her as mine.

But first, I have to make sure I won't hurt her.

I press one finger inside of her, and she moans low in her throat. And when I fasten my lips to her clit and rub my fingertip over that spongy spot, she comes undone, bucking against me.

Not able to hold myself in check any longer, I find the condom in my wallet and toss it next to her hip, then strip out of my shirt and jeans, thankful that Millie and I both took off our boots when we got here. Her hands reach for me, gliding down my abs, and I grin at her.

"Like what you see?"

"You're so sexy. Holy abs, Batman."

She licks her lips again, and I grab the condom and slip it on, then kiss up her gorgeous body—Jesus, I've never seen anyone more beautiful—and kiss her hard as I lay the head of my cock against her.

"Inside me," she says, holding on to my shoulders. "Please. Please, Holden."

"We'll go slow," I promise her, easing just the tip into her. It takes all of my strength to hold back and not just pound into her, taking what I've wanted for weeks.

"Oh, God." Her eyes close, and I grip her throat.

"Up here, baby. Eyes on me."

She complies, and I ease in more. One inch at a time, watching her face as she takes me.

"You're so fucking amazing." I kiss her lips lightly, breathing in her gasps. "You're so beautiful. And all mine."

"Yours," she agrees, and I push the rest of the way in until I'm buried balls deep, and I pause here, as if I can freeze this moment in time.

"Mine," I say again as I begin to move. "God, Rosie, you're so snug. You're so fucking good."

And she's all mine. No other asshole has been here but *me.* And no one will be. I'll make fucking sure of that.

"Oh, God," she says, her eyes widening in alarm, and I feel her start to ripple around me. "Oh, I can't. This is too much. It's too much, Holden."

"Baby," I whisper against her lips. She's starting to tremble, to contract more around me. She's about to have her first orgasm like this, and I fucking love it.

"Listen to me. Listen to my voice. It's okay. Let go, Mill."

She looks so worried. It's adorable.

"Trust me," I remind her, and then her whole body erupts under me as the orgasm moves through her. She throws her head back, her nipples are hard, and her whole body is tight with pleasure.

It's the most amazing thing I've ever seen in my goddamn life.

And I can't hold back anymore. I follow her over into the most intense climax I've ever had, and I know that my life will never be the same.

Suddenly, she's giggling beneath me.

"You think that's funny, wild rose?"

She laughs again, and it makes me groan because her muscles pulse around me.

"Holy shit, we did it." She's smiling up at me so big she could light the night sky. "I'd like to do it again."

"Give me a few to recover, and we'll see what we can do."

It's the best night of my life, lying out here under the stars on this hot summer night, making love to my girl.

My girl.

My Millie.

My little wild rose.

And when the sky begins to lighten with the promise of dawn, we get dressed, smiling softly at each other.

"I'll see you tonight?" she asks. "At the usual spot?"

"Of course." I take her wrist and tug her against me, kissing her hard. "Wouldn't miss it."

"Have a good day at work," she whispers against my lips. "I'll miss you."

WITH NOTHING but Millie and our amazing night together on my mind, I hop out of my truck and start toward the small cabin that I live in here on the Lexington ranch. I moved out of the family home years ago, but I wanted to be close by for my sisters.

"It won't happen again."

I stop short and scowl, my hands fisting when I see my father sitting in the one chair on my porch.

"What are you doing here? We don't start morning chores for an hour."

"You won't be with her again," he repeats. His voice is hard and mean, just like it always is. "The fact that you've been fucking around with a *Wild* is not acceptable."

"Dad—"

"Shut the fuck up," he snaps as he stands to his full height. He might be getting older, but he's still fit from ranch work, and he's tall. "Whatever the fuck you've been playing at is over. You won't see that whore again."

Hot blood rushes through my head. I want to fucking kill him.

"I'm an *adult*," I remind him through clenched teeth. "There's not much you can do about it."

"Oh, no?" Now that sick, evil grin slides over his face,

and I know I'm fucked. "If you don't stop seeing that cunt, I'll kill Charlie."

My heart stutters. My mind spins. Jesus Christ, he can't be serious.

"I know she's your favorite. There are a lot of places to hide a body on this ranch. Animals will take care of it for me. Girls get taken all the time."

"You're insane."

"I'm not fucking with you," he says, losing the smile. "No son of mine is going to so much as sniff at a Wild. You keep it up, and I'll kill everything you love, starting with that sister of yours. And then I'll kill that little Wild bitch."

Terror claws at my throat.

"Charlie's your *daughter.*"

"Who the fuck cares?"

He smirks, walks down the stairs to the truck that I didn't notice when I pulled up, and drives away.

When he's out of sight, my knees give out, and I lower to the top step of the porch, covering my face with my hands.

He would do it, too. He's not bluffing.

God*damn* it.

CHAPTER ONE

MILLIE

"How many grandmas do you have?" I press my phone to my ear and scowl as I lean my hip against the counter and absently wipe a rag over it. "Because this is the *sixth* one that's died in the past six months, Shelly."

"Uh, well—"

"And don't forget that we live in the same small town, and I've known your family longer than *you* have."

"Millie—"

I roll my eyes, listening as the sixteen-year-old stammers through a bunch of excuses. Shelly is notorious for calling out, whether it's because she claims to be sick or because a mythical grandmother has sadly crossed to the other side.

I'd have fired her sooner, but I'm short-staffed.

Looks like I'm even *more* shorthanded now than before.

"Shelly," I interrupt her tirade about why she needs

to spend more time with her boyfriend. "I'm too busy to do this with you. I get it. You're not coming in tomorrow."

My one and only day off.

"But," I continue, "you won't be coming in at all. This is the last straw for me. Good luck to you."

I hang up and sigh. I am *not* giving up my day off tomorrow. And since I no longer have the second staff member for the day, I'll have to close down the shop.

It's not my favorite solution, but damn it, *I'm fucking exhausted.* Not to mention, I have plans for the whole day that I can't shift.

"You okay, boss?"

I turn to Candy, the one employee that I can count on for literally anything, and sigh.

"Shelly's done. Which means I need to close down tomorrow."

"Cool, I can use the day off," she says with a smile. "But it sucks for you. I have a couple of friends who are moving to town and might need jobs."

"A *couple* of friends?" I ask her. Candy's in her mid-twenties and has worked here since she was in high school. She's a total ski bum in the winter and a sun goddess in the summer.

"Yeah, they want to be here for the summer, and they're coming early."

"But that means they probably won't be here long term."

"Maybe they'll love working for you as much as I do, and they'll never want to leave." Candy bats her eyelashes at me, making me laugh. "At the very least, it'll get us through the summer rush."

"You have a point." I push my hand through my hair, remembering that I need to put it up in a ponytail. "Okay, have them come see me. They'll need references."

"No problem." Candy turns to take a customer's order.

"I'll be right back. I have to grab more medium cups."

Hurrying to the stockroom, I make a detour to pull a scrunchie out of my purse and throw my hair up into a high pony, then I grab some sleeves of cups before returning to the dining room, smiling at Beckett Blackwell, who happens to be placing an order right now.

"Hey, Beck," I say with a smile as I stow the cups away. "How's it going?"

"Can't complain," he says with that easygoing smile. Of all the Blackwell brothers, Beckett is the most laid-back. He's just a big ol' sexy-as-all-get-out teddy bear. "How are you, Mill?"

"All in all, things could be worse." I wink at him and turn to make his coffee.

I love it when my shop is bustling like it is right now. Not just because it means that I'll have a profitable day, but because I enjoy seeing the people from my town that I love so much. I know that Bitterroot Valley is growing, but the connections from my childhood are still here, too.

Just after I pass Beckett his cup, I turn and find Holden Lexington standing on the other side of the counter, and my heart jumps into my freaking throat.

Jesus. Fucking. Christ. Warn a girl, will you?

It's been eight years, and still, every time I lay my eyes on this man, my entire being longs for him. And after the shit he's put me through, that just pisses me right off.

"Hey." *Good, Millie. Keep your voice neutral. You've got this.* "What would you like today?"

"My usual."

"And that is?" I know exactly what it is. Medium roast, black, one sugar. But I'll never let him know that I remember his drink. He doesn't get even that much from me.

He narrows those blue eyes, and my stomach flutters.

Stop it.

"Coffee. Black. One sugar." I hate it when he watches me with those eyes that see too fucking much. Eyes that used to look at me as if he loved me. As if he couldn't get enough of me. As if I hung the goddamn moon.

Of course, that's ancient history.

"Ah, yes, that's right." I tap his order onto the screen of the computer. I always feel so awkward with him. So, I try to fill the silence with small talk. "What are you up to today?"

"Headed to the lawyer's office." He taps his card on the screen, paying for his coffee, and I can't help but watch his hands as he pushes the card back into his wallet. I know from experience that Holden has *really good* hands, and he knows what to do with them. "Will reading."

That brings my gaze back up to his, and I can't help

but soften toward him just a bit. I can't imagine losing my own dad. I know that Holden was not as close to his father, but still, I'm not a complete ice witch. "I'm sorry, Holden."

"Yeah, well. Have to get it over with." He shrugs as if it's nothing, but I know it's not nothing by the way his whole body just tensed up.

I might despise this man, and the wounds still ache, even though it's been so many years since he broke my heart—or, you know, tore it out of my chest and set it on fire—but I still know him.

And that's its own special, horrible hurt.

"I was sorry to hear about your dad." My voice is softer, and I can tell by the way Holden's muscles relax a bit that he believes me. He simply nods again, and I take that as my cue to turn and get his coffee ready.

I know *exactly* how he likes it. He doesn't just want one sugar. It's more like one and a half. After stirring it, I snap on the lid and turn to give it to him.

"Thanks."

"You're welcome. Good luck."

He turns away and walks out, and I have to take a long, deep breath to get my body to calm the fuck down.

He doesn't want you, you idiot. He made that crystal clear. You have got *to let this go.*

Thankfully, we're busy the entire day, which makes the hours pass quickly. Before I know it, Candy has locked the door and we're cleaning up the espresso machine and mopping the floor, and I've counted the till and stowed the cash away in the safe.

"Well, boss, have a good day off tomorrow," Candy says, after looping her purse across her body. "I'll see you in a couple of days."

"Have fun," I reply with a grin and walk the short two blocks home to my apartment.

I like my place, and it totally suited my needs in the past, but lately, I've been feeling like I've outgrown it, so I've decided to move. I'll be renting Polly's house just a few blocks over. I need tomorrow to get most of my stuff moved and settled in so I can clean the apartment for the next tenant.

I grew up on a ranch twenty minutes outside of town, and once I was old enough to make those kinds of decisions, I knew that I didn't want to stay that far away from civilization.

I'm a town girl. *Not* a ranch girl.

Don't get me wrong, I do love our family ranch. The mountains are spectacular, and I like helping with branding and vaccinations on the calves in the spring.

But I do not want to live out there.

"Hi, Hazel." I offer my elderly neighbor, Hazel Henderson, a wave as I unlock my door. That woman is *nosy as hell* and always pokes her head out the door to see who's out here whenever I come home, and I'm going to miss her after I move.

"Hi, Millie. Did you have a good day, dear?"

"It was fine, thank you. How's the corn on your foot?"

I shouldn't know about Hazel's corn, but she likes to tell me about *all* of her ailments.

"What's that?"

She must have her hearing aid turned down, so I point to my own ear, and she hurries to adjust her volume.

"How's the corn on your foot?" I repeat.

"Oh, I went to the podiatrist yesterday. They took it out. It's sore today, but I'm fine. Thank you for asking."

"Well, you go take it easy, Hazel. I'll see you later."

I let myself inside and toss my keys and purse on the floor by the door, kick out of my shoes, and walk straight past all the packed boxes to my bedroom, where I strip out of the clothes I've worn all day and then flop down on the bed, naked.

I like being naked. Not in a pervy, exhibitionist kind of way, but I don't like tight clothing, and when I'm at work, I have to wear jeans and T-shirts, and they feel like straitjackets. I can't wait for summer, when I can wear loose summer dresses on my days off.

If I get any days off.

After throwing my arm over my face, I start to feel guilty about closing up the shop tomorrow. It's a Friday, and I should stay open. It's not quite tourist season yet, so we're not swamped, but still.

It's not exactly a good business decision to just close up on a Friday. But damn it, I'm ready to move to the cute little house just a couple of blocks away.

I knew when I bought the coffee shop almost two years ago that it would be a big undertaking. That it would mean long hours and that it's not easy to keep workers year-round in a ski resort town. But man, I didn't realize that it would be *this* hard. I hope Candy's friends work out, because if they do, I'll be covered for the summer.

"Okay, no more work." I rub my hands over my face and blow out a breath. "You're taking the next thirty-six hours off. You're going to be productive. You're going to finish selling the rest of the furniture and get all the boxes moved over, and then you're going to clean the fridge."

I wrinkle my nose. I don't want to clean the fridge.

I must fall asleep because the next thing I know, I open my eyes, and I'm *cold.* I have goose bumps all over my body because I didn't crawl under the covers after getting naked and throwing myself onto the mattress.

Deciding that I need a shower anyway, I pad into the bathroom and start the water. Thirty minutes later, I'm warmed up, my face is clean, and I'm no longer super tired.

I hate napping late in the day. I'll be up all night now.

"I need a drink." Staring at myself in the mirror, I brush on a little mascara and lip gloss, brush out my hair, and then pull on a white blouse that I like, along with a pair of dark-wash denim.

I'm taking myself out for a drink.

Typically, I wouldn't want to go alone, but I know that all four of my best friends, who happen to be married to my brothers, are busy tonight. They all have kids, and they can't just leave at the drop of a hat. Sure, my brothers wouldn't mind, but it's not considerate of me to just call them up and be like, *Come on, bitches, let's go get hammered.*

So, a night out alone it is.

I'll inevitably see someone that I know anyway, and we'll have a beer and chat, and then I'll walk home, and all will be well.

After sliding my feet into a new pair of Adidas and grabbing my bag and keys, I lock the door behind me and walk the couple of blocks to The Wolf Den.

Surprisingly, I recognize most of the faces here, and I can't help but grin when I belly up to the bar where Brenda, a gal I went to school with, waves at me excitedly.

"Hey, Mill," she says. "What can I getcha?"

"Tequila. Straight up. No training wheels."

Her eyebrows climb into her bleach-blonde hair. "It's like that, is it?"

"Oh, yeah. It's like that. Hook me up, Bren."

"You got it." She pours the drink and passes it to me, and I swallow it in one gulp, then pass the glass back to her. "Another. I'll sip this one."

She pours again, and I turn on the stool to look around the bar. The Wolf Den is the hot spot in town, where locals and tourists alike come to eat, drink, and socialize. I love it when the five of us girls come and order just about everything on the menu to help soak up our huckleberry margaritas.

We'll have to arrange for a girls' night out soon.

Suddenly, someone laughs to my left, and I'd know that laugh *anywhere.*

I turn my head, and sure enough, there he is. Holden, drinking a beer and laughing at something another guy has said. He nods and takes a pool cue to the table and takes a shot.

And misses.

He already looks a little drunk. He also looks delicious in a black Henley, sleeves pulled up his forearms, showing off the tattoos on one muscled arm that he didn't used to have, and tight jeans.

Of course, he's wearing dark cowboy boots. The man is *always* in boots. And tonight, rather than a cowboy hat, he's in a backward baseball cap.

Fuck me.

Why does he have to be so…*beautiful*? Just why?

I set my untouched second drink aside, already deciding that I'd be helping Holden get home tonight. I would usually scoff at him and call him an idiot for being out and acting like a moron.

But his dad recently died, and they had the reading of the will today. It was likely hard on all of them. And while the Lexingtons aren't my favorite family in town, I don't hold the ill will for them that my ancestors did.

The rivalry is just stupid, if you ask me.

Of course, Holden is my least favorite, but I don't wish anything *horrible* for him. Maybe he could lose his dick to a flesh-eating bacteria, or he could trip and fall and break his nose, ruining all that handsomeness, but I don't want anything *catastrophic* to happen.

I snort and turn back to Brenda. "You know what? Let's switch to Coke."

"You sure?" She lifts an eyebrow, and I nod.

"Yeah, a Coke will be fine. Thanks."

She fills a glass and passes it to me, and then I turn to watch Holden some more. He's pounding another full glass of beer, and in the past ten minutes, his steps have only gotten sloppier. It's almost as if getting hammered was his whole goal in life tonight.

Not that I can blame him. It was going to be my goal, too. No judgment here. And I *really* try to judge Holden Lexington as much as humanly possible.

Because he's a first-class ass.

And he *has* a first-class ass.

"For fuck's sake," I mutter before drinking my Coke. With one ear on what's going on in Holden's corner, I turn back to the bar. I'll just sip my drink and hang out until he's ready to go home. Because there's no way in hell that he's driving out to his ranch like this.

I would hope that he'd call one of his sisters, but I want to make sure.

Why do I feel responsible for him? Why do I have this ridiculous soft spot for him?

Because I'm a masochist, apparently.

"Millie?" I turn and frown at the sight of Bridger Blackwell. Not because I don't like him, but because *what* is he doing here? "I thought that was you."

"You never come out," I say as he takes the stool next to me. "What are you up to? Where's Birdie?"

"My mom's with her," he says on an exhale, and when Brenda approaches, he orders a beer. "She and Dad are in town for a couple of days, and I needed an hour away."

"I get it." I clink my glass to his when Brenda slides his drink to him. "How is she?"

Bridger's young daughter has had a lot of medical issues over the past year, and I know it's been really hard on him. For quite a long time, I helped him out by staying with her when he had to work at night.

"She's doing better. I'm not really sure that they've figured her out completely, but the new medication seems to be working."

"Good. I'm glad to hear that, for both your sakes."

Bridger nods and swallows his beer. He and I have been friends for a long, long time. There's never been anything besides friendship between us, which is too bad because the man is hot as hell, and on top of that, he's the fire chief.

I mean, hello, hot man in uniform.

But it's just never been like that for us. He's one of my best friends.

"What are *you* doing out?" he asks, making me sigh.

"I just needed a drink and didn't want to be in my apartment alone. Which sounds really, *really* pathetic."

"No, it doesn't." He grins over at me and then nudges me with his shoulder. "It sounds pretty normal. Next time, call me. I'll go with you."

"You have a daughter. I'm surrounded by a bunch of parents." I sigh into my Coke and ignore the feeling of longing as my biological clock lets out a little *gong*. "You're no fun."

"I will have you know that I'm a *lot* of fun," Bridger replies with a mock scowl. "Just ask my daughter."

I laugh at that, and then the hair on the back of my neck stands up when I feel eyes on me.

Not just any eyes.

Stark blue, intense, *Holden* eyes.

I glance over, and sure enough, he's watching us with his jaw clenched and his eyes hot, and it almost makes me laugh.

Instead, I let out a deep sigh.

This man is so damn confusing. He doesn't get to be territorial when it comes to me. He made it clear that he didn't want me.

But apparently, he doesn't want anyone else to want me, either, because he's convinced that Bridger and I have a thing going, but we don't. And I refuse to tell Holden that because it's none of his goddamn business.

For the next hour, Bridger and I chat and laugh, and finally, he tosses some bills onto the bar and stands up.

"I'd better get home," he says and leans in to hug me tight. Bridger gives the *best* hugs. "You okay?"

"Oh, yeah, I only had one drink, and you know I don't live far. I'm glad I got to see you."

"Same goes." He pats my shoulder and then leaves, and when the door closes behind him, I feel Holden standing next to me.

"What the *fuck* is going on between you two?"

And just like that, my back is up, and I regret not drinking more and feeling responsible for this asshole.

Slowly, I turn on the stool and look up at him, my gaze raking over his torso, neck, and then his face.

He's so...*broad.* Muscular. Tall. Strong.

And such a pain in my ass.

"Hello, Holden."

"Tell me," he says, bracing one hand on the bar and the other on the back of my stool, caging me in.

"No." I push my empty Coke glass away. "I don't think I will. Are you about done drinking for the night?"

"Why, baby? You want to go home with me?"

My heart stutters at that, and I feel the goddamn blush move over me, effectively embarrassing the shit out of me.

Fuck. This. Shit.

"I was trying to be nice," I grind out through clenched teeth. "Because you had a hard day, and you're drunk, and I was going to stay sober and help you home. But you know what? Shame on me for dropping my guard for even *one fucking minute* when it comes to you and your bullshit. You're such a piece of shit, Holden. Find your own way home."

"Shit, I'm sorry, Ro—"

"Don't you fucking dare." I get in his face now, glaring at him and ignoring the heat coming off of him. "You will never call me that again. Do you understand me?"

He swallows hard, clearly more sober than when he walked over here, and nods.

"Yeah. Got it."

Without another word, I turn away from him, hop off the stool, and stomp out of this fucking bar all the way home.

My heart is going to come flying out of my chest at

any moment, it's beating so hard. I haven't heard that name roll off his tongue since that morning in the field, when I was ready to pledge my undying love to him and beg him to marry me.

He will *not* do that to me ever again.

Fuck Holden Lexington.

CHAPTER TWO

HOLDEN

Someone is trying to kill me by jackhammer to the goddamn head. My whole body hurts, and it tastes like I ate a skunk.

"Fuuuuuuck."

"Wake up."

Suddenly, I'm sprayed with cold water, and I slit one eye open. Staring back at me with a frown on her face is my former favorite sister, Charlie.

"Stop it." I think I said those words, but it might have just been a grunt.

"What the hell did you do last night?" she demands before spraying me in the face again.

It actually feels kind of good.

"Not a cat," I remind her before scrubbing my hand over my face.

"I woke up to my brother sacked out on my couch, smelling like beer and bad choices. Tell me you walked here."

"Yep." I try to pull myself onto the edge of the couch in a sitting position, but then fall back over on my side. "Kill me. Please. If you ever loved me, just fucking kill me."

"Aww, poor baby." She squirts me again, and I just snort. "Get up. Who did you drink with last night?"

"Don't know." I bury my face in a throw pillow, but Charlie wraps my hair around her fingers and yanks me up. "Hey! Stop that."

"You deserved a night of debauchery. I should be glad there's not a naked woman draped all over you."

That makes me snort again. I've never done that to my baby sister.

"But now debauchery time is over, and you need to sober up."

"Don't wanna."

"Too damn bad. Come on, I'll make you coffee and some pancakes to sop up the leftover beer. Jesus, go take a shower, will you? You smell like a dumpster."

"Don't wanna."

I can hear her rolling her eyes as she storms away, and I decide that a shower doesn't sound too horrible. On my way over here last night, I had the foresight to grab my go-bag out of my truck. I pick it up and take it into the bathroom with me, and thirty minutes later, I'm sitting at Charlie's table, scarfing down pancakes and coffee.

I might still be just a little drunk.

"We have to talk about it," Charlie begins, and I close my eyes. "If you say *don't wanna*, I'll punch you in the face. You're too hungover to fight me off."

"You didn't used to be this violent. I raised you better than that."

"And you didn't used to be this *drunk*. God, I don't think I've ever seen you this wasted."

Because I don't usually drink more than two beers at any given time. My dad was a filthy drunk, and I won't go down that road.

But I needed it last night. And I don't regret it.

Wait.

An image of Millie, her eyes full of hurt and anger, flashes through my mind, and I clench my jaw, hating myself as my stomach twists into freaking knots.

I guess I have *one* regret.

"Holden, we have to talk about the terms of the will."

"It just is what it is, Charlie. I'll figure it out and make sure you four get the money that's coming to you. We all know that the ranch should be split five ways."

"No, it shouldn't."

Her eyes soften when I glare at her.

"Holden, the four of us have moved out of there. We don't work the ranch, and none of us really has a desire to. *You* do. Hell, you've done more out there than Dad ever did for *years*. You hire the guys, and you keep the cattle healthy. *You are the ranch*. The only reason it's worth a dime is because you didn't let Dad ruin it."

Because I didn't want to see it fail. I didn't want to watch a hundred-year-old legacy go into the shitter.

"Doesn't matter. It should be split five ways, and Dad was a prick for what he did to you four."

"Dad was just a prick. Full stop." She shrugs a shoulder and pops a bite of pancake into her mouth. "Do you really have to get married? That feels so...dramatic."

And at that thought, I push away my plate, no longer hungry.

"If I want to keep the ranch and make sure you're all taken care of? Yeah. I do."

She sighs and pushes her fingers through her blonde hair. "Holden, it's not that we don't all want to see you settle down with someone awesome and have a million babies. We totally do. But there is no way that we want you to marry some random girl just for the inheritance."

"She's not random." The words slip out before I can keep my mouth shut, and Charlie's eyes widen.

"Who the hell is she, then? I didn't know that you were dating anyone."

I shake my head and stand up from the table. I can't tell my sister my plan. It wouldn't make any sense to her. Hell, it *barely* makes sense to me.

And the woman in question very well might tell me to go fuck myself.

In fact, that's likely how this will go, so there's no use in getting anyone's panties in a twist.

"I have a plan, okay? You just have to trust me." And I might as well get this plan underway, since I'm still a tiny bit buzzed, and if ever there was a time to do it, it's now.

Before I lose all the liquid courage I worked so hard for last night.

"I hate being out of the loop." Charlie lets out a forlorn sigh. "So, tell me everything as soon as you can."

"I can do that." I kiss her on the head as I pass by, heading toward the front door. "Thanks for letting me crash here last night."

"I didn't even know you were here," she reminds me. "I woke up to you passed out on my couch."

"Thanks anyway." I toss her a smile and then leave, headed for Bitterroot Valley Coffee Co. to try to have a conversation with the most beautiful woman in the world.

She'll probably kick me out on my ass after what happened last night. How was I supposed to know that she was waiting around to give me a ride home? Millie avoids me like the plague. As Dad got older and sicker, I got braver, flirting with her and bringing her flowers when she bought the coffee shop. Little things.

And every once in a while, she'd drop her guard enough to laugh or smile.

But then those walls would slam back into place, and I'd be iced out again.

Then I go and fuck up a kind gesture from her because I was drunk and horny and way more clever in my head than what came out of my mouth.

Fuck.

When I pass by my truck, still parked outside of The Wolf Den, I toss my bag into the back seat and then keep going on foot to the coffee shop.

But when I get there, there's a sign on the door.

Dear Customers:

So sorry, we are closed today. We will be back tomorrow!

-Millie

What the fuck? What's wrong? Jesus, did something happen to her last night after she left the bar? Is she hurt? An image of my girl hurt, in a hospital bed, flashes through my mind, and I'm now stone-cold fucking sober.

I head off toward Millie's apartment. I've never been inside, but I've been sure to know everything there is to know about my wild rose over the past eight years.

I've simply done it from a distance.

Taking the stairs up to her apartment two at a time, I pound on her door with the back of my fist.

There's no movement inside as I pace back and forth outside of the door, so I bang again.

Where *is* she? Shit, I could call the hospital. I can't call her brothers; they wouldn't tell me. I'm lucky they didn't kill me eight years ago. They would have, if Millie had confided in them.

Finally, I hear the deadbolt turn, and Millie opens the door, looking sleep rumpled, with messy hair and a crease down her cheek from her pillowcase. She's wearing a silky pink robe held closed by just a small silky belt.

I've never wanted anyone as badly as I want this woman.

"There is not enough coffee or fucks for this." She scowls and scratches her head. "What the fuck are you doing here? Wait, is this a nightmare?"

The door next door opens, and a gray-haired woman pokes her head out, scowling at me.

"Hi, Hazel," Millie says with a forced smile. "Everything is fine here."

Hazel gives me the stink eye before she closes her door.

"Well?" Millie demands. "What do you want?"

"Can I come in?" Every nerve ending is on high alert. Do I want to go into Millie's place, where I'll be consumed by her smell, her essence? No. Not really. It'll be just another slash to my heart.

But I have to talk her into helping me. For the sake of my sisters, I don't have a choice.

"That would be a *fuck no.*" She moves to close the door, but I prop my hand on it, stopping her.

"Please. I just need ten minutes, and then you can kick me out on my ass."

She rolls her eyes and steps away from the door, walking barefoot through her living room, wrapped only in that robe sent from heaven.

But I stop just inside the closed door and scowl.

The living room is full of moving boxes. There's no furniture in here at all, just the boxes marked *Kitchen* and *Linens* and *Lingerie*.

I linger on the lingerie box for a second and then focus on the woman in the kitchen.

"Where the hell are you moving?" I demand, watching as Millie pops a coffee pod into her coffee maker and presses a button. My voice isn't raised, but even I can hear the steel in it.

"Nunya," she says with a yawn and pulls some cream out of the fridge, giving it a little shake.

Nope. Not acceptable.

I march through the small living space until I'm on the other side of the island from her and lean on my hands.

"Where. Are. You. Going?"

She keeps that bland look on her beautiful face, but I see her pulse pick up in her neck as she turns, and her eyes find mine.

"Holden—"

"Goddamn it, Millie, answer the question."

"Not that it's any of your goddamn business, but I'm moving into Polly's old place a few blocks away. Jesus, I'm not *going* anywhere. Calm yourself." Her coffee finishes brewing, and she turns to pour some cream into it, takes a sip, and closes her eyes. "Someone should be here in about thirty minutes to pick up my bed. Sold it."

"You sold your *bed*?"

"Hmm." She takes another sip. "I only want to move boxes. Now that we've had this charming early-morning conversation, would you please explain to me what you're doing here, waking me up at this ungodly hour on my day off?"

"I thought someone was coming to get the bed in a half hour?"

"*Holden.*"

I've reached the end of her patience, so I hold my hands up in surrender.

"Okay." I blow out a breath. Jesus, I didn't practice what I was going to say. My stomach is suddenly in my throat, and every word I know has vanished from my brain.

"Whoa, are you in trouble?" Her voice has softened, and she's watching me warily, and I feel like an absolute asshole.

I don't deserve her. I don't deserve for her to agree to help me. I don't deserve even *one word* of kindness from her after the shit I did to her.

But I have to ask her.

"Kind of," I admit and start to pace in front of the island. "Listen, I don't know how to do this, so I'm just going to lay it all out on the line, tell you everything, and hope to God you don't try to cut off my balls."

"No promises." She presses her lips to the rim of her mug and sips her coffee. I've never wanted to be a mug so badly in my life.

"We had the will reading yesterday, as you know." Her eyes narrow as she sips more coffee. "My asshole of a father left my sisters each ten thousand dollars."

"*What?*"

"And the rest of everything else to me. With some conditions."

"What conditions?" She's openly scowling now, listening.

"Well, one condition, really. I have to get married."

"Man, sucks to be you. Wait, he can do that?"

"And I have to stay married for one year."

"I don't know why you're telling me all of this." She shakes her head. "I don't really have any single friends to hook you up with."

"*Millie.*" She frowns at me, and I want to kiss the fuck out of her. "Let me finish."

"Okay."

"I have to stay married for a year, at which time everything fully transfers to me, and I can finally make things right for my sisters. I can divvy up the money, give them land, all of that stuff. But I can't do any of it until after the year is up."

"Ooooookay," she says, drawing out the word. "I mean, that's pretty harsh. All of it. I'm sorry for your sisters. I actually like them. But I don't see—"

Her eyes widen.

The blood drains out of her gorgeous face.

I have to rush around to grab the mug before it goes crashing to the floor.

"No." Jesus, she sounds horrified. Not great for my ego, but also not a surprise.

"Listen—"

"Have you lost your *mind*?" She's shaking her head, pacing away from me in that thin robe. Is she naked under there?

Jesus, my heart can't take this.

"Under no circumstances did you just show up here to ask me if I'd help you out with your inheritance by *marrying you.*"

"I know it's not exactly a romantic proposal."

"Oh, my God!" She flings her arms out, and the belt of her robe comes a little untied, and yep.

She's fucking naked.

She hurries to cover herself and glares at me. If she could shoot fishing knives out of her eyes, I'd be a dead man right now.

"You fucking *crushed* me, Holden Lexington. You destroyed me, completely shredded me. You were mean and cruel, and I've hated you for years. And now, you want me to help you by marrying you?"

I prop my hands on my hips and lower my head, looking at the floor, feeling each of those words like a jab to the heart.

I know it. I *know* I did those things to her, but for fuck's sake, it was to protect her. To protect Charlie. I didn't have a goddamn choice in the matter, and she wasn't the only one that was destroyed because of it. Not that I could tell her that.

"There is no one else in this world that I would even consider marrying," I admit softly before lifting my gaze back up to hers. "There is no one else, Millie."

Her jaw drops. Her gorgeous eyes are round, and that pulse in her throat is beating the tempo of "Mambo Number Five."

"And if it wasn't for my sisters, I would never ask you."

"This isn't fair," she whispers, her voice cracking as a tear slips onto her cheek. Christ, I don't want her to cry. Rail at me, hit me, but don't cry. "To put this on me. It isn't fair."

"I know." I shake my head, wanting nothing more than to pull her to me and hold her, to tell her how sorry I am, and explain everything that happened all those years ago, but I know that my touch wouldn't be welcome right now, and I don't know that she would believe the story anyway. "It's not fair, not even a little bit, but it's the only chance I have to take care of them. Please don't say no right now. Don't give me an answer right away. Think on it, Mill."

I hold my hands out, and her eyes cut over to my arm. I'm in a T-shirt today, and the sleeve has moved up on my biceps.

Higher than she's seen in, well, years.

On purpose.

Her gaze sweeps up the grayscale tattoos on my arm until they freeze on the pink flower high on my biceps.

My stomach drops.

Her eyes narrow.

The flowers are the only thing in color, standing out from the rest of the grayscale tattoos on the sleeve.

"Holden." The tears have dried up, but her voice shakes, and I know this isn't going to be good.

I swallow hard. "Yeah."

"Is that—" She breaks off, and when tears fill her eyes again, she blinks and swallows. "Is that a—"

"Wild rose? Yeah. It is."

"Get out of my house." Her face is mutinous, angrier than I've ever seen her. This was not the reaction I was expecting.

There's a knock at the door before I can say anything else, and Millie rushes over and yells, "Hold on! Be right there!"

Then she jogs around me, on her way to what I assume is the bedroom.

"I want you out of here," she says, pushing the tip of her finger into my chest. "Now."

Once she's closed the door of her bedroom, I turn to leave. There's no way she's going to agree to help me. As much as I see some longing in her eyes, some of the chemistry we'll always share, there's also contempt and anger. So much fucking anger.

I'm going to have to figure out another way. Maybe I can hire my own attorney to contest the will. I don't know if it'll help, but I can try.

When I open the door of the apartment, I find Bridger Blackwell standing there with a smile. When he sees that it's me, that smile fades. His oldest brother, Brooks, climbs the stairs behind him.

"Hey, Holden," Bridger says with a confused frown, just as rage begins to course through my blood. "What are you doing here?"

"I'd like to ask you the same fucking question."

CHAPTER THREE

MILLIE

Holy. Shit. What in the hell kind of alternate universe did I just wake up in?

I have to lean on the door of my bedroom, hand pressed to my chest as I will my galloping heart rate to slow down. Bridger and Brooks are waiting for me, and I'm hiding in here, having an existential crisis up against this door.

"I don't have time for this." I march over to the last open moving box and pull out the clothes I set aside to wear today, dump my robe inside of it, and close the flap.

After I dress, I brush my hair and tie it up in a loose messy bun, wash my face, brush my teeth, and then toss all the last-minute toiletry items into yet another box.

After pulling my sheets and comforter, along with the pillows and cases, off of the bed, I put those into a tote, planning to wash them at the new place, and then take a moment to pull in a deep breath.

Holden Lexington just asked me to marry him. I don't think I dreamed that. He stood in my apartment and asked me to marry him, *and* he has a wild rose tattoo on his freaking arm.

A tattoo. For me.

I want to touch it and examine it and ask him all the questions.

Essentially, all of my nineteen-year-old fantasies just came true, except he's eight years too late. I can't stand him, and he asked simply because he wants me to help him keep his property.

Not because he loves me.

I snort at that thought. Of *course,* he doesn't love me. If he loved me, he wouldn't have been so cruel all those years ago. But he was cruel, and I learned my lesson about trusting Holden Lexington. I need to remember that. Marrying him is preposterous.

With that decided, I step out of my bedroom and frown at the crazy amount of testosterone filling the living room.

Bridger and Holden are practically toe-to-toe, both with their hands fisted, jaws clenched, ready to duke it out. They really are a sight to behold. Both so tall and broad. Muscular. Tattoos, tanned skin, thick hair.

And there's Brooks, scowling, also hot as hell, hands on his hips.

"Enough." My voice is hard. "I don't know what either of you is trying to prove, but *enough.*"

"I want to know why he's here," Bridger says without sparing me a glance.

"Same goes," Holden adds, and Brooks pinches the bridge of his nose, closing his eyes. The Blackwell brothers and Holden have been friends since way back.

But Bridger is Brooks's brother.

What's a guy to do?

"Brooks and Bridger are helping me out today," I say at last, turning my eyes to the ceiling in frustration. "And Holden is just...here."

I'm not going to blab about Holden's personal life. As much as I want to strangle him, that's not my story to tell.

"Are you going to load my bed up in your truck or what?" I demand, staring at Bridger. "For fuck's sake, stop it with the dick-measuring contest. I'm not sleeping with either of you, so just stop it."

Holden's shoulders relax, his fists loosening.

And Bridger does the same.

Bridger is maybe the only person in the world who knows the whole story of what went down between me and Holden. Several years ago, when we had some drinks and were really talking, the story just came out of me, and he listened without judgment. I needed a friend right then, and I know that Bridger considers Holden a close friend, too.

Which is why this is so freaking weird.

"Guys, we don't have time for this. I'd really like to have all my things moved over by noon so I can work on getting unpacked and settled before I have to go back to work tomorrow. So, please, for the love of all that's holy, stop the staring contest. I'll talk to you later, Holden."

"If they're helping," Holden says as he points at the guys, "I'm helping."

I can't help the sigh that escapes me.

"You don't have—" But he glares at me, and I just don't have it in me to fight with him. If he wants to invest time and energy into moving all of my shit for me, so be it.

It doesn't mean anything.

"Fine," Bridger says with a resigned sigh. "Help if you want to help, but lose the fucking attitude."

Brooks pats Holden on the shoulder as he walks past, headed for the bedroom.

"I just have stuff in the bedroom and in here. Everything is packed up and ready."

Bridger moves for the box marked *Lingerie,* but Holden growls and scoops it up before Bridger can get his hands on it.

"I'll go grab my truck. Be back in ten."

He stomps out the door, box in hand. I can't help but smirk. I should probably tell him that there isn't really lingerie in there, but this is too much fun.

"Why is he such a dick sometimes?" Bridger props his hands on his hips and then frowns at me. "Oh, yeah, because you won't just talk to him and tell him that you and I are just friends. For fuck's sake, Millie."

"It's none of his business." I sniff, lifting my nose in the air, and reach for a box as Brooks calls out from the bedroom.

"Bridge! Get your ass in here and help me with this bed."

It actually went really well. The four of us got all the boxes moved over to my new place in less than an hour. When I told the guys that they could go, they all shook their heads and dug in, opening boxes and helping me get settled.

"So, you bought Polly's old furniture?" Brooks asks me.

"Yeah, it's nice stuff. Mine was getting old, and I didn't want to move it anyway, so I sold it. The beds are both new. Well, the mattresses are, anyway." I shrug and smile as I look around the place. My brother had the whole thing renovated when he and Polly were still dating, and I absolutely love it.

Holden and Bridger have finished bringing the last of the boxes in from the trucks, and Holden's holding four cold waters. He tosses one to each of the guys and then crosses over, holding one out for me after he breaks the seal of the lid.

"You need to hydrate."

I accept the bottle. I want to ask where he found four cold waters, but I don't. I can't help but glance at his arm and see the little bit of pink peeking out at the bottom of the sleeve of his black T-shirt.

Goddamn it, it turns me on, and that's what pisses me off the most.

"I ordered sandwiches from Mama's Deli," Holden adds. "They'll be here in about twenty."

“I could have done that. You all are doing the hard work. I should buy you lunch.”

His gorgeous blue eyes never leave mine as he smirks, his lips tipping up in a half smile. “No way. You don’t need to buy me shit. Now”—he searches the area and lifts the box marked *Lingerie*—“I’ll go unpack this one.”

“Help yourself,” I reply with an innocent grin. “It’s the bedroom on the right.”

“I’ll find it,” he says, walking past me.

“Shall we unpack the kitchen?” I ask Brooks, who’s watching me with shrewd brown eyes. Bridger is currently unpacking my bathroom.

“You bet.” He finishes his water, tosses the bottle into an empty box, since I don’t have garbage or recycling set up in here yet, and then grabs two stacked boxes marked *Kitchen*. Just when I’ve unwrapped some mismatched glasses and started to organize them in a cupboard, Brooks asks, “So, where are your brothers today?”

“They’re busy,” I murmur, feeling an ache in my breastbone. “They all have jobs and families now, with kids and property to take care of. I appreciate that you and Bridger are close by and are willing to sacrifice your morning for me.”

“We’re always happy to help,” Brooks agrees. “Anytime, you know that. But, sweetheart, your brothers will drop whatever they’re doing at a moment’s notice to come help you. You know that, too.”

I feel tears burn the backs of my eyes, so I bite my lip, keeping my eyes down on the Montana State University mug in my hands.

"I know," I whisper.

The truth is, I miss them all so much. But now that they're all settled down, doing their own things, I feel like an outsider. I don't really fit in anywhere, and I don't want to feel like an obligation or a pain in the ass.

"Where do you want the plates?" he asks with a sweet smile.

"Just right there." I motion to the cabinet next to the stove. Then the doorbell rings, and Holden comes jogging out of the bedroom.

I can't help but bite my lip again, but for another reason entirely. I wonder if he opened the lingerie box.

"Hi, Jeanie!" I call out, waving at the manager of Mama's Deli, who smiles widely and waves back.

"It's moving day," she says happily. "How fun. This is such a cute little house. It'll be perfect for you."

"You can keep the change," Holden says with a wink.

"You're sweet. Thank you. Don't work too hard." Jeanie waves again, and then Holden closes the door, carrying the sandwiches to the kitchen.

"Hungry?" he asks.

"Fucking starving," Brooks answers, and Holden tosses him a wrapped sandwich.

"Is that lunch?" Bridger asks as he joins us, and Holden tosses *him* a sandwich. "Nice. Thanks, man."

"I'm still pissed at you," Holden says, glaring at Bridger, but his words have less bite than before, and Bridger just grins when he takes a bite out of what looks like turkey on wheat. Holden turns to me, his expression softening, and smiles at me. Goddamn it, he needs to take that smile elsewhere. "Here. I got you the Italian."

How can he push my world off of its axis with a fucking sandwich?

"Thanks." I blink and accept the sandwich. He remembered my favorite.

Because, of course, he did.

That son of a bitch.

I keep my face neutral as I unwrap my lunch and take a bite. It's damn good.

"So, your lingerie is interesting," Holden says, and Bridger smirks. "Shoes. A computer cord. Playing cards. A night-light. I believe there was a spider in there."

"There was not!"

He laughs. "Why'd you label it that?"

"To get a rise out of the guys." I'm smug when I take another bite out of my sandwich. "Looks like it worked. Besides, I'm not really a lingerie kind of girl. I sleep naked."

I shrug a shoulder as Bridger and Brooks both choke on their food.

Holden stops chewing, his eyes hot on mine. They journey down my body and up again, as if he's undressing me with those gorgeous blue orbs, and my freaking nipples betray me by tightening under his scrutiny.

Of course, the jerk doesn't miss *that*. He smirks and takes another bite of his sandwich.

"I'm going to haul the empty boxes out of here," Brooks declares, brushing crumbs off his hands before he starts to gather the cardboard. "Looks like we got most of them unpacked."

"You guys were a huge help, and I'm grateful." I break myself out of Holden's spell and set my lunch aside so I can help the guys gather the empties, break them down, and set them by the front door.

Finally, when pretty much everything is done and good to go, the Blackwell brothers each offer me a hug.

When it's Bridger's turn, he whispers in my ear, "Call me if you need me."

I ignore Holden's growl as I smile up at my friend. "Always. Thanks, guys. Tell Birdie I said hi."

They wave, and then they're gone, and I'm left with the one man on this earth that I do *not* want to be alone in a room with.

He watches me as I wrap up half of my sandwich and set it in the fridge. I pull out a plastic garbage bag and line the can before setting it under the sink, and then I tug a couple of Clorox wipes out of a tub and wipe down the countertops.

"Are we done talking, then?" he asks softly.

"I'm honestly talked out," I reply. I just want him to go so I can relax and let my mind start to unravel everything that has happened today. After tossing the wipe in the trash, I move to the back door and open it, then step out onto the patio.

I love that there are screens that lower with a remote, closing in the patio so I can avoid bugs in the hottest months. I walk to the edge of the stone surface and wrap my arms around my middle, taking a deep breath.

I feel him join me, and from my peripheral vision, I see him step up beside me, crossing his arms over his chest, taking in the fresh air.

Being near him shouldn't be this easy. It should be awkward as fuck, and I should scream for him to get out.

That's what I *should* do.

But I don't.

And we stand like this, quiet in the spring afternoon, listening to the birds. I want to lean into him, so I lean away, and he sighs beside me.

Suddenly, he reaches up and tucks my hair behind my ear, the way he did back then.

And just like then, it sends a jolt right down my spine.

"You could destroy me." I didn't plan to say it out loud, even in a whisper, and heat floods my cheeks.

"Same goes, Millie." He drops his hand, not touching me anymore, and without another word, he leaves. I can hear his footsteps through the house and then the front door closing.

I wait until I hear his truck start and then the engine revving as he drives away before I lower myself to the swing and drop my face into my hands, finally letting the tears come.

God, I can't possibly entertain the notion of marrying him. My body is humming, begging for him after just a couple of hours in his presence. And I hate myself for it because that means that if I agree to this insane idea of his, I won't be strong enough to pretend that it's not real for me.

I won't be able to keep my heart safe from him.

Because despite all of it, I want to give in. Over the past couple of years, Holden has softened toward me. He brings me flowers, stops into the shop to chat, and always has a smile or a wink or something nice to say.

At first, it shocked the hell out of me.

Then I started to get used to it, even though I tried my best to be mean to him in return.

There have been moments when I've caved and laughed at a joke or smiled at him. When he brought me roses and sunflowers—my second favorite, next to the wild roses—the day I officially took over ownership of BVCC, I thought I was going to melt into a puddle. He told me he was proud of me. His eyes were so sincere, and I had to bite the inside of my cheek to keep it together until he left.

Damn him.

I hate what his dad did to his sisters. They don't deserve that. And I respect that Holden is doing what he can to make that right. Because I know how much he loves *his girls*, as he calls them.

He adores them.

He's protecting them.

But he's trying to use me to help him do that.

"Jerk," I mutter when I sit up and tip my head back as I brush the tears off my cheek. "Swoony jerk."

The look in his eyes this morning when he told me that there's no one else he'd consider marrying almost brought me to my knees.

There's no one else.

I'm so fucking confused!

Without overthinking it, I grab my bag and keys and march out to my SUV before heading out toward the Lexington ranch. It just happens to be near my family's ranch, since they have property that borders each other.

I've never set foot on Lexington property before, and I don't know where Holden's living out there, but I'll find it.

If I get lost, I'll turn back and come home because I don't have his number.

I deleted that a long time ago.

I pass the turnoff for the Wild River Ranch, and about four miles later, I turn onto Lexington Ranch Road. I follow it until it curves and winds around to a small grouping of buildings, one being a big farmhouse.

But Holden's truck isn't parked in front of that. I can see it back a ways, in the trees, over by a smaller cabin with a tiny front porch, and I frown.

I guess he didn't want to live in the farmhouse.

It's not long ago that if I'd been caught setting foot on this property, I might have been taking my own life in my hands. Literally. Holden's dad was an ass, and he made it no secret that he wished all of us Wilds dead.

What a jerk.

I park next to Holden's truck and then stumble to a stop, staring at the second truck parked by the cabin.

The old, two-toned Ford that he drove forever. I lost my virginity in the back of that Ford, and standing here, looking at it, brings back all kinds of memories that have my nipples puckering and my thighs tightening.

"Get it together, Millie."

Before I lose my nerve, I walk up to the door and knock.

I can hear footsteps inside, and then he swings the door open, and his face drains of color.

"We're going to set some ground rules."

CHAPTER FOUR

HOLDEN

Get. Her. Out of here.

I do not want Millie anywhere close to this ranch. She can't be here, not under any circumstances.

"Let's go back to town." My heart is hammering as I step outside. It's not that I'm embarrassed about where I live. I just don't want her here. Not here, with all the ghosts that could still hurt her. "We can sit on your patio and talk."

She scowls at me as if she's wondering if I've lost my mind. "No, I'm here now, and I want to just get this out."

"Millie, let's go somewhere else. Anywhere else."

"Jesus, Holden, I don't care if your house is messy. So what?"

"That's not it." I shake my head. My stomach is jittery, my palms sweaty, and every molecule in my body is screaming at me to get my girl the fuck out of here. "I just don't want you here."

"For fuck's sake." She rubs her fingertips over her

forehead, and if I'm not mistaken, she looks hurt. Jesus, that's the last thing I want. I've inflicted enough pain on this woman to last a lifetime. "If you've changed your mind about the whole thing, that's great. I'm off the goddamn hook."

She turns to leave, but I grab her elbow, stopping her. As much as I don't want her here, I don't want to fuck this up, because I think she's going to say *yes.* "I haven't changed my mind. That's not what this is about."

"You're not making any sense," she says as she turns back to me. "I just want to talk."

"I know, but I don't want you *here.* On this ranch. Not today or any day."

Her eyes soften, and she doesn't pull her arm away. "Holden, no one is going to hurt me out here. He's dead."

"Don't care." God, is that *my* shaky voice? "Let's get off of this property. Please."

"Okay, okay." She swallows hard, still frowning. "There's a scenic overlook about a mile up the highway. State property. Let's go there. I'll meet you."

"I'm right behind you."

I climb into my truck as Millie slips into her SUV, and I'm ten feet behind her as she makes her way down the long driveway to the highway. And when she finally turns right, off of my land, I let out a long, shaky sigh of relief.

Seeing her out there made me panic. If Dad were alive, she'd be dead by now. I *never* want her there.

She drives up to the turnout I know and pulls in,

making room for me to park behind her, and then we both get out of our vehicles.

This is a great viewing spot for tourists driving through. The mountains are tall and proud in the distance, with pasture in the foreground, full of black cattle. This is Lexington property, and those are my cows. And I fucking love those mountains.

"Okay," Millie says as I approach, and we both sit on the rock wall, turning to face each other. "We're on neutral territory. Better?"

"Yeah." I lick my lips and have to remind myself not to reach for her. Whenever I'm within twenty feet of her, I want to yank her against me and bury my nose in her hair.

Old habits die hard.

"I see you still have that old Ford truck," she says, trying to sound nonchalant. She doesn't look me in the eyes.

"Of course, I still have it. It needs a little work. I'm taking it in to Brooks this week, and he'll tinker with it when he has time."

She nods and shoves her hands in her pockets.

"You said something about ground rules?" I ask as my system slowly evens out.

"I have several," she confirms. "And they're firm. Deal breakers."

"Let's hear them." This should be good. It seems my life is full of conditions right now. I cross my arms over my chest, and her eyes dip down, watching the motion.

Her tongue runs over her bottom lip as she eyes my biceps, and I can't help but smirk at that.

Yeah, baby, I'm hot for you, too.

"One," she begins, raising her index finger. "I get my own bedroom. I'm not sleeping in the same room as you."

Fuck that. I just raise an eyebrow, and she keeps going.

"Two." Her middle finger joins the first. "This has an expiration date. *One year.* I'll help you keep your inheritance and make sure your sisters get their share, and then I'm out."

Like hell.

"Three." Another finger. "No swoony bastard."

"Excuse me?"

"No swoony shit from you. No looking out for me, bringing me flowers, or tucking my hair behind my ear. This is a contract, not a real marriage."

Now I'm getting pissed.

"Four." She tucks her thumb against her palm. "You will *not* call me Rosie. Or wild rose, or baby girl, or any of those pet names."

She hears the growl that escapes my throat, but she swallows, ignoring it, and that thumb pops up.

"Five."

"How many are there? Should I be taking notes? I forgot my legal pad at home."

"Just one more," she says calmly, those golden eyes holding mine. "No sex."

"No." *Absolutely fucking not.*

"I know you." Her chin raises, but her voice has more shake in it now. "And I know that if I say no, you won't push me. The only reason I'm agreeing to this certifiably insane idea is because, despite everything else, I'm physically safe with you."

Physically safe.

Damn it, she's right. I'd never force her to do something she doesn't want to do. I'd take my own life first.

"Fine." My jaw is tight as I grind my teeth together. I should have expected this. I didn't think she'd agree at all, but on the slight chance that she did, I should have known that she'd have stipulations. "And what do you get out of this, Millie? Do you want money?"

She recoils as if I hit her.

"Come on, sweetheart, no one gives up a year of their life for nothing. Not out of the goodness of their heart. Especially when you can't even stand the sight of me. So, what do you want? How much?"

She swallows hard and looks out over the view. Her eyes skim our mountains, over my land, my cows.

Does she want some of my property? I'd give it to her. I'd give her whatever she wants, as long as it's mine to give.

She's so fucking beautiful. Her hair is a rich chestnut brown in the sunshine, and her lips are plump and kissable. As if reading my mind, she bites down on that lower lip, making my stomach clench and my cock harden.

Christ, I want her.

And if this is the only way I can have her, so be it.

Because this isn't a one-year contract for me. I've been waiting eight horrible years for her.

I want her to be *my wife.* I want to make a life with Millie Wild, and if it takes all of those 365 days, I'll win her over.

I'll make her mine.

"I want—" she begins, but then she has to clear her throat. She lets out a humorless laugh and turns to me with tear-filled eyes. I hate it when Millie cries. She's so fucking strong, so badass, and seeing her vulnerable unravels me every time.

"What, Mill? Tell me what you want in exchange for this."

"I want to be able to move on." She lets out a shaky breath, swallows, and says it more firmly. "I *need* to be able to move on."

God damn. Of anything she could have said, I was not expecting this.

I'm such a son of a bitch.

My throat has closed, so all I can do is nod, but I have no intention of letting her move on from me.

"Seal it with a kiss?" I ask, and that has the desired effect because she laughs and shakes her head at me.

"Did you not hear the rules?"

"There was not a rule about kissing on your long list. Trust me, I was listening."

"Hmm." To my relief, she doesn't add that as rule number six and simply holds her hand out. "Shake on it."

I close my hand around hers and feel the electricity move up my arm. I know she feels it, too, because she gasps, just a little. Unable to resist, I bring her hand up to my lips, and I press a kiss to her knuckles, ignoring the way she narrows her eyes on me, as if she wants to toss me over this cliff.

"Thank you," I murmur as she slowly pulls her hand away from me. "Thank you for this, Millie."

"Do we have to live together?" she asks.

Fuck yes, we do.

"We have to be married for a year." I shrug a shoulder. "Married people live together."

She bites that lip again, and I can't resist reaching out to tug it free with my thumb.

"I don't want to live at your ranch," she admits.

"You won't set foot out there," I reply easily. "Absolutely fucking not."

"Tell me how you really feel." Her voice is dry with sarcasm, and she narrows her eyes at me. "Why?"

"Too many ghosts." I shake my head. "We'll live at your place."

"Just like that?"

"Sure. There are the required two bedrooms and everything."

"But that means you'll be commuting back and forth, making your days longer."

"Don't look now, but it sounds like you're worried about me."

I grin as she shakes her head in denial.

"Whatever. Do what you want. I prefer the house in town anyway." She lifts that chin, and I can't help but think, *good girl.* I love it when she's strong and stands up for herself.

"We'll go tomorrow."

"Where?"

"To Idaho. To elope. No waiting period for a marriage license, and we can get there and back in the same day. Easy."

She's shaking her head, panic suddenly in her eyes. "I have to work tomorrow."

"Have it covered, Mill. It's your wedding day."

I wink at her and then chuckle when her face goes pale.

"You did realize that getting married requires a wedding day, right? Even if it is before the justice of the peace."

"Well, shit."

Could there be a bigger *fuck you* to my father than marrying Millie Wild to get around his stupid conditions for getting the inheritance?

I don't think so. In fact, I kind of wish he could rise up out of hell just for a minute so I could toss it in his ugly, fat face.

I'm actually surprised that he didn't have it added to the will that I could marry anyone *but* Millie. That was an oversight on his part.

I know that he was relieved when all four Wild

brothers found women that weren't one of my sisters. I think the bastard was holding out on dying just so he could make sure that none of them ended up with a Wild.

Because even though he didn't give a rat's ass about his daughters, he still wouldn't have stood for them being part of that family.

I just returned to my cabin and am packing a few bags, getting ready for tomorrow because tonight is my last night out here for a long while.

And if I ever do come back to live on this property, it'll look *very* different.

I grab my phone and open the group text with my sisters and type out a message to them.

Me: FYI, I'm headed to Idaho tomorrow to get married. I won't be reachable for the day. Don't ask me who because I'm not telling yet. Also, if any of you want anything out of the farmhouse, you need to come get it. I'm tearing the fucker down next week.

It takes a millisecond to start getting responses.

Dani: WTF? WHO IS SHE? I don't want anything out of that house.

Charlie: SPILL IT! FFS, you can't just say that to us, Holden.

What does FFS mean? Why can't these girls just type the goddamn words?

Darby: Can I have Mom's china set? I think she got it from her grandmother.

Me: You can have anything. It's all in there.

Alex: We're all coming out there tonight. I'm bringing pizza.

I sigh and press my fingers to my eyes. I love my girls. I raised them since Mom died not a year after Charlie was born. I wasn't quite nine at the time. Dad didn't give a shit about the girls and could be really cruel to them, so I did whatever I could to keep them calm, happy, and quiet.

That's not easy to do with toddlers.

I'd never tell them that they can't come out here. This is theirs as much as it's mine, but I don't really want to see them tonight. I should have waited to send that text until tomorrow. But they have the right to know what's happening, and I really do want them to take whatever they want from the house.

Instead of tearing it down, I should burn it.

In fact, I think I will. I'll call Bridger and ask him for help to keep the fire under control.

I've just finished packing and loading the couple of bags into the back seat of my truck when Dani comes driving up, all three sisters with her in her Ford SUV. I motion for them to drive over to the farmhouse, and I set off on foot to meet them there.

I fucking hate this house. Most of my shitty memories are in here, and I only go inside when it's absolutely necessary.

I know the girls don't like it any more than I do. So, maybe it's good that they came out tonight, so we can just get it all over with.

"Hey," Charlie says, giving me a side hug. "You look considerably better than you did this morning."

I grin down at her. "Duh. Also, it's an improvement that no one is spraying water in my face."

I hug each of them and keep Alex by my side, my arm looped over her shoulders, as we walk to the porch.

"We'll eat pizza after," Dani says.

"Maybe we should eat it before," I reply. "Might not have an appetite after."

Hell, I don't have an appetite *now.*

"I hate it here," Alex says with a whisper and shivers as her eyes are pinned to the front door. "I hate everything about this house."

"I know. Me, too." I squeeze her to me and then feel Dani push her hand into my free one. "You know, you guys can just give me a list of what you want, and I'll pull it out for you. You don't have to go in. We can just go over to the cabin and eat pizza."

"We'll go in," Charlie says. "And get it over with. Then you can do whatever you want with it."

The front door isn't locked. Hell, even the wildlife steers clear of this house, as if it knows what kind of evil lived here. So, we walk right in, and the smell of must assaults my nose.

Dust motes filter through the air. No one has been in here since the son of a bitch died.

I was the lucky one to find him. Dead in that chair. Likely had a heart attack while watching TV, since it was still on.

That was too easy of a way for him to go out, in my opinion. Too fast. Too painless.

"I think that anything I want is in the kitchen," Alex says, moving quickly that way. "I want Mom's recipes and China."

"We should look for photos," Charlie suggests. "There are probably albums somewhere."

"Closet," Dani says, pointing to the hallway.

There are so many fucked-up memories already assaulting me. Dad throwing Mom down those stairs because she was wearing lipstick, and what the fuck was she doing wearing lipstick on a ranch? Who was she fucking behind his back?

Dad holding Dani's face under the faucet because she forgot to feed the chickens.

Dad backhanding me when I was six because I couldn't finish my dinner.

"Jesus," I mutter, wiping my hand over my face.

"I'm sorry," Darby says softly, her eyes full of tears as she watches me. "I know this is hardest on you."

"I'm fine." I eye the photo of Mom on her graduation day in Darby's hands. "Is there anything else you want to grab?"

"Did Mom have any jewelry to speak of?" Charlie asks with a frown.

"Maybe. Let's go see if there's a jewelry box upstairs," Alex says, but Darby's shaking her head.

"I'm not going upstairs," Darby informs them. "Never again. You can have the jewelry."

Darby is the next oldest, after me, younger by two years. The fact that his second child was a girl infuriated Dad, and he took it out on Darby as much as possible, almost on a daily basis.

"Do you want anything else?" I ask her, and she shakes her head no, so I take her hand and lead her outside. "We'll wait for them out here."

She takes a long, deep breath and lets it out slowly. "Whenever I'm in that house, it feels like someone is sitting on my chest. The energy in there is just *horrible*."

"I know." I rub a circle on the middle of her back. Before long, the other three come outside, carrying totes they found somewhere in the house full of what they want.

"We found the jewelry," Alex says. "She had some pretty things, so we just took the whole box and we can go through it later, and I grabbed what I wanted from the kitchen."

"I found the photos," Dani adds.

"And I grabbed a folder full of documents. Marriage license, death certificates, that sort of thing. We may never need them, but you never know. And I found Mom's diaries. I kept them. I don't know if I can read them, but we have them." Charlie swallows hard and then turns her eyes up to the house. "You're going to destroy it?"

"And everything inside of it," I confirm.

"It's a hundred years old," Darby murmurs. "And Dad ruined it for us."

"He ruined everything," Alex reminds her.

The farther away from the house we walk, the more relaxed we all become, and we get the things stowed in the back of the SUV.

Dani drives her SUV over to my cabin, and the five of us open the two large boxes of pizza and dig in, quietly chewing as if we're thinking about what we saw inside the house. Finally, it's Darby who speaks up.

"Who is she?" Darby asks, her pizza in hand, staring me down.

"You'll find out soon enough." I shove my crust into my mouth and reach for another slice. I'm hungrier than I thought.

"Are you embarrassed by her?" Charlie demands, and then her eyes go wide. "Oh, shit, is she a hooker?"

"What? Jesus Christ, no." I scowl at my sister. "Why the hell would you say that? Are there even hookers *in* Bitterroot Valley?"

"I mean, maybe you're paying someone," Charlie continues. "So it's more of a business transaction and not so personal."

"I know he's gross because he's our brother," Dani points out, making me glare at her, "but he's cute. He doesn't need a professional for something like this. Most women throw themselves at his feet when he breathes in their direction. Have you seen the reaction he gets when he *smiles*? It's kind of appalling."

I blink at her, stunned.

"I mean, he's okay," Alex says with a shrug.

"Gee. Thanks. I shouldn't have pulled you out of the swimming pond when you were six, saving your life."

Dani just rolls her eyes.

"She doesn't deserve you," Alex says, pressing herself against my side for a hug. "No one in this world is good enough for you."

The love these girls show me every day is humbling.

But Alex is wrong.

It's *me* who doesn't deserve Millie.

"I hope you know what you're doing," Darby says, shaking her head. "Because this could go really badly for you, brother."

"It's going to be fine." I have to keep telling myself that. "Everything is going to be just fine. Trust me."

"We trust *you*," Charlie reminds me. "That's not what worries me. It's the woman. Maybe she's a gold digger."

"Just trust me," I repeat and reach out to tweak her nose.

CHAPTER FIVE

MILLIE

It's a rainy spring day.

Not just a little sprinkle, either. Huge raindrops fall incessantly, Holden's wipers moving quickly to keep up as we drive on the freeway, heading to Idaho. The clouds are dark and low, casting everything in shadow. I look over at the man beside me, his hands firm on the wheel and gaze trained on the wet roads, fully alert.

I haven't been alone with Holden in a truck in the better part of a decade.

And if you'd have told me back then that I'd one day be on my way to marry him, I would have squealed with joy. I wouldn't have cared about the elopement. I've never had dreams of a huge wedding. I just wanted *him.*

Now, my heart is thudding for completely different reasons.

I have no business doing this. I know it. My family is going to freak the fuck out at me. My dad may never speak to me again. Marrying Holden *Lexington*? Oh, hell no. My father has held on tightly to that feud, and there's going to be hell to pay when I get home.

It already makes me sad.

The girls will want to know details, and they'll be happy for me. They're my ride-or-dies. My best friends.

But my brothers?

Oh, they'll for sure try to kill Holden where he stands, so we might want to show up armed.

I smooth my hands down the skirt of my white dress. It's not fancy at all. I bought it to wear to a BBQ last summer, so it has thin straps, a ruffled skirt that hits me right at the knee, and it's comfortable. I paired it with a denim jacket and some brown cowboy boots.

It doesn't look like I'm going for a bridal look, but even though this is a sham wedding, it is our wedding. It just felt right to wear white, especially since I have no intention of ever getting married again.

Holden's in a nice pair of dark jeans with black boots and a blue button-down shirt that's rolled up his forearms, and I saw him tuck his nice Stetson in the back seat.

I have to admit, it's nice that he dressed up a little. At least he's not in a ratty T-shirt and boots with cow shit on them.

Not that I think Holden would do that to me. He wouldn't.

I can't help but look his way again as we begin our ascent up one of the two mountain passes. The tattoos on his right arm are sexy. I admit it. I've seen glimpses over the years, because they come down his forearm and used to end at the wrist.

Until last year.

Last year, I noticed that he got ink on his hand, all the way down his fingers to the middle knuckles, and I have to assume that hurt like hell. And I'd never say it to him—in fact, I'd rather cut out my own tongue, but they're hot.

So damn hot.

I can't make out what all of them are. There's an elk head and other flowers, and I'm sure they all mean something to him.

But my mind keeps going back to the one currently covered high up on his arm, almost to his shoulder. The only one in color.

The wild rose.

I almost punched him when I saw it, and then I wanted to kiss the bastard.

Don't even think about it. Don't let his swoony ways get into your head because he was also cruel and hurtful, and that's the same man you're sitting next to.

"Sex doesn't mean forever, sweetheart."

"Jesus, grow the fuck up, Millie. I never promised you anything."

"What, did you think I'd marry *you? Not likely."*

"I'm not even convinced that you were a virgin. You didn't bleed."

Of course, I didn't bleed. I've been riding a horse since before I could walk.

So, yeah, he's a bastard.

Never forget that.

"You're thinking way too hard over there." His deep voice breaks into the silence.

"Just taking in the beautiful rainy scenery."

"Hmm." He flicks his gaze my way and then back to the road.

"Do you know where we're going? Do we just show up at the courthouse and *boom*, it's done?"

"Something like that," he confirms, his blue eyes jumping up to the rearview mirror. "Come on, you asshole, just wait and pass me after we get through this pass."

I look back and see that there's a sports car on our ass, but the pass is too windy to go very fast. He speeds up, hugs the back bumper, and then drops back, swerving to the side as if he's judging if he should go around us. Even though there are two lanes, there's a solid white line here because it's too tight for two vehicles.

Sports Car Idiot is going to cause an accident.

Holden doesn't speed up or slow down, but his jaw ticks as he looks in the mirror again.

"Motherfucker," he mutters as the car goes for it, swerving around us on the inside just as we come around a blind corner, but there's a huge semi-truck, flashers on, going about twenty miles per hour, and Holden has to slam on the breaks so we don't rear end it. "Fuck!"

I'm rocked forward, but the seat belt does its job, and I'm not hurt when Holden turns my way.

"I'm okay." My heart is hammering, and I know my eyes are wide, but I'm not hurt.

To my surprise, Holden snatches up my hand and pulls it to his lips, holding on tightly as he maneuvers us around the truck. We were already at the top of the pass, and if the driver had just had patience for three more minutes, he wouldn't have almost caused an accident.

"Holden." He tightens his grip on my hand. "I'm okay."

He's glowering, but he kisses me once more and then reluctantly lets me go.

"I'd like to follow that idiot and punch him senseless."

This man is way more intense than he was when I knew him. A little broodier. He's obviously seen a lot more life, and I don't think it's all been kind to him.

Not that I care.

Because I don't.

He's an ass.

But my hand tingles where his lips were. Stupid tingles.

It's not my fault that my body betrays me at every turn. Holden is a sexy man. Those are just the facts. He turns heads. He has a body that could have been sculpted from marble, a chiseled jawline, and blue eyes so intense they'll steal the breath from your lungs at twenty paces.

The sexiness is hard to miss.

But my body needs to calm itself down because we're not going there. No touching. No sexy time. Absolutely none of the above. Because if I give in to those things, there's no way that I'll be able to move on and shake Holden off when all of this is over.

"Again with the thinking too hard," he says next to me, sounding remarkably calm. "Are you ready to have me pull over so you can get out and run away?"

"Oh, I was at that point the minute I got in the truck." I nod slowly. "And have considered that idea at every mile marker since."

He glances at me, raising an eyebrow. Jesus, why does he have to be so sexy?

"But these boots aren't really made for hitchhiking, and it's cold outside, so I guess you're stuck with me."

"Cute."

"Are your sisters pissed off?" I ask him. "Did they try to talk you out of this?"

"Why would they be pissed?"

"Because it's *me*, Holden. Because my last name happens to be Wild."

"Only for another hour or so," he reminds me, and my heart stops.

Oh, shit.

"I didn't tell them that it's you. They know I'm eloping today, but I didn't say with whom."

"And they didn't ask?"

He spares me another quick glance. "Of course, they asked. I just didn't tell them. Why? Did your family get as pissed as I think they did? Are we coming home to a firing squad?"

I'm still mildly irked that he didn't tell his sisters about me, but then I sigh.

"I didn't tell them."

"Looks like we're even, then, aren't we?"

We're quiet while we enter into the outskirts of Coeur d'Alene, driving around the edge of the lake and into downtown. I've always thought this was a cute town. It's so green, and the lake is beautiful.

Maybe someday, I'll come stay at their big resort and have a relaxing weekend or something.

I snort out loud and then rub my finger under my nose.

"What was that thought?" Holden asks me.

"I was just thinking that this is a cute town, and I've always wanted to stay at the resort on the lake, and maybe I would sometime, but then I remembered that I don't take vacations because I run a business."

"Even business owners take vacations."

"Really? When was the last time you took one?"

He narrows his eyes. "When Bridger got married, a bunch of us went to Vegas."

My stomach drops at that. I remember Bridger telling me about that trip, and how some of the guys got stupid and ended up hooking up with a group of girls they met in the casino. He never said explicitly *who* hooked up, but just the thought of it being Holden makes me want to put my elbow through the window. I hate that I get jealous when it comes to him. He didn't want me. He cast me aside, so why should I care if he fucks his way through all of Vegas?

I don't know, but I do.

And that's stupid.

"I think it's right up here," he says, pointing to a building. Sure enough, it says *Courthouse* out front.

Holden pulls into a parking lot and eases the truck to a stop, cuts the engine, and unclips his seat belt, then turns to me.

"Millie, if you don't want to do this, I won't make you. I will turn around and go home right now. No hard feelings."

I scoff. "No hard feelings?"

"I'm not kidding. I understand what I'm asking you to do, and it's not like I'm just borrowing a cup of sugar or something here. So you tell me if this is *not* what you want."

This is not what I want.

But I made a promise. And for all the stupid, fucked-up reasons floating around in my head, I think I can make it through this with my sanity intact.

"Let's do this." I unclip my belt, grab my purse, and push out of the truck, walking quickly through the rain to the door. Holden holds it open for me, and we walk inside and find the counter marked *Marriage Licenses.*

I feel like I might pass out, but Holden presses his hand to the small of my back, keeping me upright, and just that small touch gives me a little extra confidence.

We both thought ahead to bring our birth certificates and all the documentation we would need to fill out the paperwork, and before I know it, we're walking back out again with a license.

"Now we walk over there," he says, pointing to a smaller building across the street that says *The Hitching*

Post. It's built to look like something out of the old west, and it actually makes me laugh.

"Okay, partner, let's go."

With our paperwork in one hand, Holden takes my hand with the other and leads me across the street. When we approach the door, the butterflies in my belly become murder hornets, and they're fighting to get out.

I might throw up.

"Hello, I'm Holden Lexington, and I have an appointment."

The older lady with silver hair curled tightly against her scalp, smiles up at Holden, and then her blue eyes widen in surprise. "Well, hellooooo. If she backs out on you, honey, I'll fill in."

I smirk, and Holden chuckles.

"Thanks, ma'am." He looks down at me. "You stayin'?"

"Planned on it."

"Well, darn," she says with a sigh. "I have you two set up in the western chapel. Is it just the two of you today?"

"Yes," we say in unison.

Before I know it, we're standing in a little room with the woman from the front desk as the officiant and a guy who looks like he might work maintenance as our witness.

The old-school traditional vows are recited, where I promise to love and honor until death do us part, and that makes me feel kind of guilty because I know that I'm not going to uphold *that* promise, but this old lady doesn't know that.

Holden's eyes are intent as he holds my hands and looks into my eyes as he recites his vows. His voice is low and sincere, and it almost brings tears to my eyes because it sounds like he means what he's saying.

What a jerk.

We slip plain gold bands onto each other's fingers. I was surprised when he whipped those out. I have no idea where he got them.

And I don't hate seeing it on my hand as much as I should.

Finally, I hear the words, "You may kiss your bride."

Holden's face descends to mine, he wraps his arms around me, and for the first time in eight years, his lips cover mine, and my eyes close, and I'm lost to him.

He groans and sinks into me, brushes his tongue over my bottom lip, and I eagerly open for him, all common sense flying out the window.

Holy fucking shit, this man can kiss.

We hear someone clear their throat, and Holden reluctantly pulls back, watching me with hot blue eyes, and I instinctively lick my lips, still tasting him.

"You're a beautiful couple," Old Lady says with a smile. "I hope you have a wonderful life together."

Don't bet on it, lady.

HOLDEN ASKED me if I wanted to stop for lunch before we headed home, but I said no. I'm not hungry.

I don't know what I am.

We've been quiet on the way back. And I'm staring down at the yellow gold band on my finger as Holden pulls into my driveway and cuts the engine.

"Millie."

I don't reply. For once, I don't have a witty or clever comeback. I didn't expect to feel so...*sad.*

"Millie," he repeats, and I turn my head to look at him. "Tell me what you need me to do."

I blink. Shrug. Look back down at the ring.

"Liquor," I say at last. "I think I need to get really drunk tonight. I have tequila, but if you want something else, you'll have to go get it."

"How much tequila do you have?"

"Two bottles."

"Let's go in."

He grabs his bags from the back, and I lead him to the door, where I key in the code and show it to him, since he's living here now.

Holy shit, Holden Lexington lives with me. And we're married.

"We'll have to share a bathroom," I tell him as we walk through the house. "But that's okay. You get the smaller bedroom, but it still has a king bed."

He walks into the guest bedroom and sets his bags on the floor, then eyes the master over my shoulder.

"That's *my* bedroom."

His eyes dart back to mine, and now there's some anger in them. Maybe some irritation.

"I heard your rules," he reminds me. "And I put my

stuff in the other room, so you can watch how you speak to me."

I sputter, but he moves in, lifts his hand to cover my throat, and drags the pad of his thumb over my jawline and down to my pulse point as he presses his mouth to my ear.

"*Wife.*"

Holy motherfucking shit.

He kisses my cheek, drags his lips to my mouth, and gently kisses me before pulling back and dropping his hand, and I almost fall into him because I'm leaning in.

He smirks. *This asshole smirks!*

"Come on, let's have drinks. We'll need some food so we don't kill ourselves from alcohol poisoning."

"I have a lasagna that I put in the fridge last night," I reply. "I'll pop it in the oven to warm."

Needing something to do with my hands so I don't just jump him, completely ruining my rules in the first six hours of marriage, I start the oven and take the lasagna out of the fridge.

"Where's the tequila?" he asks, and I point to the sideboard in the living room. "Got it."

"I don't have lime or margarita mix," I inform him, and he smirks at me.

"We don't need training wheels, babe."

I should tell him not to call me that. I said no terms of endearment.

But I don't have the fight in me tonight.

The light catches on my gold band, and I stare down

at it. It feels foreign on my finger. Holy shit, we actually did this.

We're married.

The murder hornets are back, and they're pissy.

"So, what happens now?" I ask Holden as I slip the lasagna into the oven and grab some shot glasses out of the cupboard. "Do you take the marriage license to the attorney as proof?"

"I'll do that tomorrow," he confirms and pulls the lid off the bottle and then pours two shots. He holds one up, and I clink mine to his. "Happy wedding day."

I nod, and then we pound the shot, and it burns going down. "Another."

"Yes, ma'am."

He pours us each another shot, and we pound that one, too. I don't want to get too drunk too fast, so I shake my head when he offers me another.

"I'd better space them out," I reply and wiggle out of my boots. "I'm going to put on something more comfortable."

"I will, too."

We move into our bedrooms and close the doors.

I think about locking mine and then shake my head at myself. There's no need to do that. I know him. He won't do anything I don't want.

But after that kiss in the hallway, *I want.*

Jesus, do I ever want.

Scowling, I stomp over to the dresser and grab my wide-leg yoga pants and a hoodie, along with some soft socks, and change. I brush out my hair and twist it up into a ponytail, and then I walk back out to the kitchen, where Holden is pouring himself another shot.

My mouth goes dry.

What he's wearing shouldn't be anything to write home about. He's just in loose basketball shorts. They're black, and they're obviously not new because they look soft and well worn, as if this is his usual loungewear every day after a hard day on the ranch.

But on top, he's in a red T-shirt that hugs his muscles in the most delicious way. The tequila is already hitting my brain because, holy shit, I want to run my hands over that cotton and feel every sexy ridge of muscle.

And then I want to peel it off of him.

Bad, Millie!

"Another?" Holden holds up the bottle and raises an eyebrow.

"Absolutely, yes."

CHAPTER SIX

HOLDEN

If my girl doesn't stop staring at me like she's starving to death and would like to eat me fucking alive, I'm going to break rule number five in about six seconds.

She's in those baggy pants and a big, oversized sweatshirt that hides all her curves, but I know how goddamn amazing her body is.

And I know that she's wearing those clothes for comfort because today was rough on her. When we were saying our vows, so many emotions swam over her gorgeous face, and I wanted to interrupt the old lady and tell Millie that everything would be okay.

I wanted to wrap my arms around her and comfort her.

And I likely would have had sharp nails raked down my face for it.

It's been a long, uncomfortable, exhausting day. And it's barely dinnertime.

Millie pulls the lasagna out of the oven and says, "It has to rest for a few. We can sit in the living room, if you want."

"Lead the way."

We each take a small glass of tequila with us. Millie curls up in a chair, pulling her legs under her, and I sit on the couch across from her. We watch each other quietly for a moment.

Jesus, I've wanted nothing but this exact moment for the better part of the past decade. To be alone in a room with her. To be able to talk to her, touch her. Hold her.

For now, talking is fine. *For now.*

"What time do you have to leave for the ranch in the morning?" She's not looking me in the eye. She's plucking at a string on the seam of her pants. She looks tense, her eyebrows pulling together, making little lines that I want to smooth out with my fingertips. Or my lips.

"Around five."

She nods and sips her tequila. You have to admire a woman who can fucking *sip* tequila.

"That's when I leave for work, too."

"That's pretty early."

She nods again and takes a deep breath. God, I hate seeing her be so fucking uncomfortable around me.

"I open at six. People want coffee on the way to work, you know? I go in around five, get ready for the day, and pick up the baked stuff from Jackie at the Sugar Studio. I actually really like the early mornings in there by myself. It's quiet, and I can think." She shrugs and sips. "Do you have a lot of animals at the ranch? Aside from cows?"

So, we're going to just limp our way through small talk this evening. It's fucking torture, and I'll need more tequila, but I can do that.

"No." I shake my head and cross one ankle over my knee. "We haven't had any other animals since the girls were young."

Because my dad would use those animals to torture my girls, so I put a stop to it. Made him think it was his idea, but stopped it, nonetheless.

"Why do I think there's a story there?"

I press my lips together. I don't want to tell Millie about the ugliness of my childhood. I didn't back when I was dating her, and I don't want it to touch her now.

"We live together, Holden," she says simply. "You can tell me stuff. I'm not a blabbermouth, and even though I don't particularly like you, I won't be a huge bitch."

I lift an eyebrow. "You won't refer to yourself as a bitch ever again."

She narrows her eyes. "I *can* be a bitch. I was raised with four older brothers. I can hold my own just about anywhere. But I'm pretty chill in my own house. So, why no chickens or pigs or goats?"

"Because my father was fond of torturing them to upset my sisters."

All the blood drains out of Millie's face, and I don't look away from her as I sip my liquor.

"Fuck," is all she says.

"Yeah. Fuck. He didn't hurt the cattle or horses because those are the bread and butter, and the girls were taught that they're not pets. None of my sisters have ever ridden a horse. It wasn't allowed. Also, no dogs or cats, either."

"No dogs or cats on a ranch," she whispers and shakes her head slowly. "No wonder my father hated him so much."

"What are your favorite animals?" I ask her, trying to change the subject. Jesus, we never had a hard time talking before. Never resorted to fucking *small talk.* It's torture.

"I always liked the chickens," she says with a shrug. "I've thought about getting a dog, but I'm not home enough, and I can't take a dog to a place where I serve food. Maybe a cat would be okay; they tend to be more independent. Maybe two cats, so they have each other. I don't know."

She checks her watch and then stands.

"Let's eat."

She dishes up the lasagna, and we stand at the kitchen counter to eat. I'm holding the plate up, leaning my hips against the counter, watching her.

"We could sit," she says around a bite.

"Sat all day," I remind her around mine.

"Exactly." Her eyes actually smile at me as she chews. "I eat like this most nights. Just stand here and gobble it down. Where do you eat?"

I shrug. "Wherever. This is good. You can cook."

"I'd like to take the credit, but Erin made it." She laughs a little, and it's a shot to my stomach. I fucking love her laugh. "My sister-in-law is an excellent cook, and she likes to stock my fridge because she knows that I work long hours, and she claims that she doesn't want me to starve. Not that I would because I'm a grown woman who can feed herself, but if Erin wants to make me delicious meals, who am I to turn them down?"

"So you *can't* cook?"

She grins. "If I say no, will you want a quickie divorce?"

"No." I narrow my eyes at her. "No, Mrs. Lexington, you're stuck with me."

The humor leaves her eyes, and she swallows hard at the sound of her new name. "Anyway, I can cook okay. It's nothing to write home about, but I won't starve."

She finishes her dinner and stacks both of our plates in the dishwasher, and just as she turns to cover the leftovers, her toe catches on the mat and she stumbles, but I easily catch her.

Millie gasps, and I instinctively pull her against me, wrapping her up in a hug, and plant my lips by her ear.

"Are you a little drunk?"

"No. Just clumsy."

She takes a deep breath, and after a long moment, she wraps her arms around me and hugs me back, and if I died right now, I would die a happy man.

There is *nothing* like having Millie Wild-Lexington in my arms.

"I don't like that we're so awkward with each other," she admits, so softly that if I wasn't twelve inches from her mouth, I wouldn't have heard it. "I don't know what to say to you, and we never used to have a problem talking."

She's basically saying my thoughts out loud.

"I know." I sigh and rest my lips against the crown of her head. "Maybe it's just because of the day, Mill. It was a weird one."

"But I'm not the only one feeling awkward, right?"

"No." I'll admit to anything if it makes her feel better. "I feel it, too."

"I can't talk about cats and my work schedule for the next year, Holden. I'll go crazy."

That makes me chuckle until she turns her gaze up to mine, and I see that tears are beginning to well in her beautiful eyes.

"Hey, don't cry, baby girl. It's okay." I tuck a lock of her soft hair behind her ear. "Thank you so much. For everything. I don't deserve you."

"I know."

My lips twitch. "I'll never deserve you. But I'm so grateful to you and, honestly, in complete awe of you because you're so fucking strong and good."

"Don't be nice to me." She shakes her head sadly and starts to pull away, but I hold on tighter. "I don't trust you when you're nice to me."

The wind is sucked from my chest. *Trust* is the one thing that we need, or this will never work. And I'm reminded that I have one hell of a hill to climb to earn hers.

I trust you more than anyone. Her words from years ago echo in my ears. In that moment, I felt like I could fly.

And I need to get there again. So, I'll climb that

fucking hill as high as it needs to go to make her see that she can trust me with anything.

"How do you want me to be, Millie?"

"Just be yourself."

"I am."

She shakes her head and then pulls the rest of the way out of my arms, and the magical moment is gone.

"I'm doing this for your sisters." I can't tell if she's reminding me or herself. "Charlie is actually my friend. I like her. I like all of them, although Darby always kind of gives me the side eye when she comes into the coffee shop, as if I've poisoned her or something, but on the whole, I think they're all good people. So, I'm doing this for *them*."

"Ba—"

"Rule number two." She points her finger at me as her eyes flash with annoyance. God, she's gorgeous when she's pissed. "Stop breaking the rules."

"Is it number two? Or was it number three?"

"Argh." She turns to stomp away. "Good night."

"Sleep well, wife," I call after her, and she flips me off before she disappears into her bedroom and lets the door slam shut behind her.

I sigh and drag my hand down my face before I finish tidying up from dinner and drinks, make sure the doors are locked, and head down the hall to my bed. I pause by Millie's door and can hear her moving around, getting ready for sleep.

I want to barge in and tell her that I'll be sleeping by

her side, and she won't argue with me about it. But she might try to smother me in my sleep.

So, I turn to the other bedroom, resolved that this will be the only night we spend apart.

"There are about to be some big changes around here."

We've just finished the early morning chores, and I'm standing in the barn with all three of my full-time hands, Vance, Levi, and Tim. I've worked with Vance and Levi for eight years, from the day I hired them.

Since the day that I pretty much took over running this ranch.

And Tim's been around for as long as I can remember. He worked for my dad, and he's stayed on with me, too.

"Good," Vance says, shoving his hands into his pockets. "You did it your old man's way for too long."

"Even though I ran things, he still held the purse strings." I shrug at that and don't let the anger seep in today. "But that ends now. I want to move some pasture. We've had the beef in the same fields for too long."

"Agreed," Levi says with a nod. "Where are you thinking?"

I lay out the plan for them, and when all three nod in agreement, I take a deep breath.

"This would make room for more head," Tim says. "You could expand, make more money."

"That's the goal this year." My horse, Peanut,

nudges my shoulder from his stall, and I reach back to pet him. Now that Dad's dead and gone, I can actually put the plans I've had for years into action. I know I can grow this business and do better than our ranch ever has before, now that my hands aren't tied by a tyrant. "We're going to start here. I have some other ideas, too, but I need to make some calls and do some research."

"This is a good start, boss," Vance says. "A damn good start."

We run down what we're all up to today, and then we head our separate ways. Just as I'm walking out of the barn, I see Bridger driving up in his big red work truck with the Bitterroot Valley Fire Department shield on the door.

I wave as he pulls up in front of me and then hops out.

"Thanks for coming out here," I tell him as I shake his hand. Bridger's been my friend since I was a kid. I was fucking pissed when I thought he might have something going on with Millie, and when I confronted him about it, he wouldn't confirm or deny.

Likely at her request.

I should spank her for that alone.

"No problem. Are you going to kill me and bury me somewhere out here just because I'm friends with Millie?"

"Not today." I give him a toothy grin, and he shakes his head with a laugh.

"You're an ass."

"Takes one to know one." I clap him on the shoulder. "I need to burn some shit down."

His eyebrows climb into his dark hair in surprise. "What shit would that be, exactly?"

"Every standing building on this property. Including this barn, but it'll have to go last because I need it until I can have something else built. We'll start with the farmhouse."

Bridger scowls and props his hands on his hips. "What the fuck, Holden?"

"Come on. Let's go have a look." I climb into the passenger side of his truck so he can drive us the quarter mile or so to the farmhouse. When he's behind the wheel, he glances over at me. "I'm not crazy, man. Just trust me."

"You sound crazy," he mutters, but drives us over to the house that haunts me every minute of every fucking day. When he's parked, we sit here for a minute, staring at it. "It's a fucking creepy house."

"It's about to be gone. We start here. I want this house, and everything in it, reduced to ash. Then we'll move on to my cabin and the other outbuildings."

Bridger looks my way. "Why?"

"Because my father ruined everything he touched. He killed my mother in that house."

My friend's eyes widen, and his jaw drops. "Holden, everyone was told it was an accident. *You* told me it was an accident."

I remember watching my mother fall down those stairs and shake my head.

"No. No accident. Not one square inch of this house holds anything good in it. The girls came and got whatever they wanted, and now it's time for it to go."

"*All* the girls?" He frowns over at me. "Even Dani? She's in Bozeman."

"She's moving back here," I reply, shaking my head and continue staring at the fucking farmhouse. "Now that he's dead, she feels safe to be in her own hometown again. It'll be good to have all my girls here, where I can keep an eye on them. Anyway, back to this. I didn't want to just pour some gasoline and light a match. I don't want to start a forest fire."

"I appreciate that," he says dryly, then rubs his hand over his mouth. His hand isn't altogether steady. "Why didn't you ever tell me?"

"If my dad had been *your* father, would you have told anyone? Even your best friends?"

"No." He shakes his head. "Okay, we can do this. You're outside the city limits, so you don't need a permit. We can use it as a training exercise for my guys. That would be great, actually."

"I'm down for that. Anything good that can come from this, I'm all for it. Can we do the cabin and the garage at the same time?"

Bridger climbs out of the truck, and I follow suit, and we stand side by side, looking out over the property.

"Yeah," he says slowly. "We could do them one after the other and simulate an accidental fire, where one blaze ignites the next."

"Good. When?"

"As soon as next week, if you want. Hell, I'll call some neighboring departments and see if they want in on the training. We don't get this opportunity often."

"I'll have my guys here, too. I wish I had another place to store the horses so they're not afraid of all the noise. I can move the cattle out a ways, so they won't be any the wiser."

"You can board the horses at our ranch," he offers without hesitation. "I'll call Beckett today. There's plenty of room in the barn."

Emotion runs through me. The fact that these men would help me after all the shit my father pulled means a lot.

"Appreciate it."

Bridger nods, biting his lip. I can tell that he's still running scenarios through his head, the best way to run the fires and what all goes into it that I don't know anything about.

"So, you *weren't* fucking my wife."

He doesn't turn to look at me for a second, and then he blinks and scowls, as if my words just penetrated his brain, and he spins to me.

"What the hell did you just say?"

"You weren't fucking *my wife.* I asked you, over and over, and you wouldn't answer me. Pissed me the hell off."

"I'm sorry. Who in the hell is your wife, Holden?"

I grin at him. "Millie."

"Do you need a hospital? Has all the stress finally tipped you over into *crazyland*?"

"Married her yesterday." I rock back on my heels. It feels fucking fantastic to tell someone, and I hold my hand up, showing him the gold band on my finger.

Bridger blinks at me, then his face goes red, and he makes a fist, and he punches me right in the jaw, but I move, so he only grazes me.

"What in the actual fucking fuck?" he demands. "You can't just fucking marry her. You weren't even dating her."

"I did marry her." I shrug. "So, you'll be careful around her."

"Jesus Christ." He shakes his head. "She's my friend, Holden. And *you're* telling *me* to be careful with her? You're the one who—"

He shakes his head, and I narrow my eyes. "The one who what?"

"Fucked with her head. You fucked with her head and then left everyone else to pick up the goddamn pieces, and now you've *married* her? Fuck!"

"You're still going to burn my shit down, right?"

"Oh, I'm going to do more than that. How did you... *why*?" He stares at me. "I'm out of here. I need to talk to her."

He rushes to his truck, climbs in, and kicks up rocks and dirt as he takes off for town.

I run my hand down my face. Maybe I could have handled that better.

But I didn't lie. She's my wife.

And she's going to stay that way.

CHAPTER SEVEN

MILLIE

Thank all the gods for busy mornings.

I didn't sleep worth shit last night. I kept thinking about the fact that a *very* sexy Holden was just mere yards away from me, likely not wearing much, and my body was on fire.

Stupid body.

And then, to make matters so much worse, after spending all freaking day with him yesterday, I actually miss the son of a bitch today. Like, truly, physically and emotionally, miss him.

What kind of fucked-up shit is that? I'm not supposed to like him. But damn it, I'm having a hard time resisting him already. Because he's been so *nice* to me. Like, sincerely kind. The way he was before...*before.* Before he tore my heart out and burned it to ash.

There's a quick lull between customers, and I yawn as I tie my hair up high on my head.

"You okay?" Candy frowns at me as I yawn again. "Not sleeping well?"

"Like shit," I confirm with a shrug. "I'll be fine. Thanks for covering yesterday."

"It was no problem," she assures me. "Plus, the friends I was telling you about? They'll be here next week, and they plan to come in to talk to you."

"Great." I grin at her. "I also hired a high school girl who wants some weekend work, and she starts Saturday. Can you help me train her? She's worked as a barista before."

"Of course, that'll be great."

The door opens, and the bell rings, and I look up to see Bridger striding in, and I smile.

But he doesn't smile back.

In fact, he looks good and pissed off.

"What's wrong? Is it Birdie? Oh, shit, do you need me?"

"No, she's fine," he says with a shake of his head. He looks around, seeing if anyone's close by, and then he leans in, and with an angry, low voice says, "Did you marry Holden?"

His eyes jerk down to my hand, but I took the band off this morning before coming to work.

"Who—"

"Yes or no, Mill."

I feel the blood drain from my cheeks. I know that Candy's standing nearby, and she can hear *everything*.

"I'm your fucking best friend, and you'd better tell me the truth."

"Yes." It's a whisper. "I'm not embarrassed or keeping it a secret, but we haven't told our families, Bridger."

"For fuck's sake!" His voice raises, and several heads turn our way, and he swallows and quiets again. "Do I need to remind you that your brothers might very well kill him?"

"No, they won't. They won't be happy, but they won't hurt him."

"Jesus Christ, Millie."

I reach for his hand and hold it firmly in both of mine, pleading up at him with my eyes.

"Please. Keep this quiet for now so I have time to tell them myself. Please, Bridger."

"Do you love him?" he asks, his voice still low. "Or did he force you?"

"Jesus, how would he *force* me?" I roll my eyes. "No, and no. And that's all I can say for now. I'm sorry you didn't hear it from me. Where did you—?"

I break off when the door opens again, and this time, it's Holden striding through. His eyes drop to where I'm holding Bridger's hand, and they darken; his jaw clenches.

And I'm suddenly breathless.

"I'll talk to you later," Bridger mutters, pulling away. "I can't do this here and make a scene in your shop."

"Later," I reply as he turns and stalks out, shoulder-checking Holden on his way. I huff out a breath. "Why are men so dumb?"

The man who's lived rent-free in my head all

morning calmly strides over to me, watching me with those hot blue eyes. In front of literally everyone in my shop, he reaches over the counter and closes his hand over my throat, then leans in and plants his lips at my ear.

"Hello, wife."

Jesus, Mary, and Joseph, I'm wet. Just like that. Why does that word turn me on?

"You told Bridger," I whisper as his thumb brushes over the line of my jaw before he pulls away and removes his hand from me altogether.

"It's not a secret, Millie."

"No, but I'd like to tell my *family*," I hiss at him. People are staring now. They're definitely looking and starting to talk, and I shake my head. "And now I have to call an emergency meeting. Right now."

"You go," Candy says kindly, her cheeks red, since she heard everything. "I can handle this."

"Are you sure?" I ask her.

"Totally. Go figure this out. And, uh, congratulations." She winks, and I blow out a breath and stomp back to my office, Holden hot on my heels.

When I get the door closed, I pull my phone out of my pocket and send a text to the family group chat. It has *everyone*, including the girls and my parents, and we use it for really important things like this.

Me: Hi, gang. I need an emergency meeting right now. Like, ten minutes ago. Do not take any calls from anyone in town before you talk to me. Please tell me everyone is available.

I chew on my bottom lip, very aware of Holden standing against the wall, his arms folded over his chest, watching me with those blue eyes that seem to see everything.

Why do I suddenly feel like I need a hug? I don't even like hugs. Sure, the one in my kitchen last night was nice, but I'm not really a hugger.

Or a toucher.

Within seconds, I get responses.

Dad: Come to the ranch.

Rem: Meet you at the farmhouse.

Ryan: Are you safe?

Okay, that one brings tears to my eyes.

Chase: Summer and I are headed that way.

Me: I'm safe. Just need to talk.

Brady: Abbi and I are at the property. We'll meet you there.

Me: No kids, if possible. Please.

Still biting my lip, I look up at Holden.

"I hate it when you cry." His voice is low and rough, which doesn't help the whole *needing a hug* thing.

"This isn't going to be fun."

"I'm sorry. I really am sorry for that, Mill."

I swallow hard and nod. I believe him. He sounds completely sincere.

After blowing out a long breath, I pocket my phone. "I guess I'll go handle this, then."

"No, *we* will go handle it."

I scowl at him. "There's no way you're going out to the ranch."

"There's no way I'm *not* going," he counters and moves forward, catching my chin in his fingers. "You're my wife. Where you go, I go. You don't have to do anything alone anymore."

I raise my hand to circle around his wrist, but I don't shove him away. His eyes narrow in on my finger, and he scowls.

"Where's my ring?"

"In my pocket."

"Why isn't it on your goddamn finger?"

I swallow hard, at a loss as to why all of this turns me on. Maybe because everything Holden Lexington does turns me the hell on. "Because we hadn't told anyone yet, and I didn't want everyone to talk and ask me questions that I wasn't ready to answer because we haven't talked to our families yet, Holden. Do I need to remind you that this is a *small freaking town*?"

He pushes his hand into the pocket of my jeans and

comes out with the ring, then takes my hand and pushes it back on my finger.

"It doesn't come off again, Mill. That's a deal breaker for *me.*"

"A rule?" I ask.

"Yep. A rule. Now, let's go get this over with."

"Do you have a gun in your truck?"

He smirks as he takes my hand and leads me out of my shop and to his truck, which is parked out front. He opens the door for me and makes sure I'm safely inside before he walks around and climbs behind the wheel.

I'm regretting some of my life choices right now.

Because while I knew that I'd have to come clean to my family, I didn't really let myself think about how this was going to go down.

How can I just bring Holden onto our ranch and announce that he's my husband?

What have I done?

As he heads out of town, Holden reaches over and takes my hand, brings it up to his lips, and kisses my skin, and it helps my stomach settle just a bit.

I mean, the murder hornets are way fired up, but this contact helps.

"I'm not really a physically affectionate person," I whisper, watching as he places another kiss on the back of my hand.

"You used to be." He glances over at me and frowns.

"Yeah, well. I used to be." But I don't pull my hand away when he sets it on his thigh and covers it with his own. As we get closer to the ranch, I feel more and more like I'm going to throw up.

So, I breathe.

And square my shoulders.

This is my *family*. They may not love the situation, but they love me, and I know without a doubt that, although it will be uncomfortable, it's going to be okay.

Everything is going to be okay.

"Why aren't you affectionate now?" he asks, clearly trying to distract me.

"I'm just not touched very often, so it makes me uncomfortable." I frown, not happy that I just shared that. "I hug the kids all the time, and family is fine, but for the most part, I'm not the touchy-feely type."

"Hmm."

Holden turns onto our road, and I punch the code into the gate, and it smoothly opens for us. When he pulls around to the farmhouse, I see that everyone is outside, sitting on the big porch on the front of the house, waiting for me.

And we're the last to arrive.

When they see the truck, everyone stands, and my dad's face reddens.

Oh, shit, I'm going to give my dad a stroke.

"Park there," I say, pointing at the spot next to Ryan's Aston Martin. We both climb out of the truck, and when I meet Holden at the front, I take his hand, and he gives mine a squeeze.

"What the fuck?" Remington asks, his eyes narrowed on our clasped hands.

"Uh, hi." I clear my throat and look up at Holden. He doesn't look nervous or scared at all. In fact, he takes his hat off and nods at all the girls.

"Ma'am," he says to my mom.

And she offers him a tentative smile.

"Hey, guys," Erin says, trying to sound happy. "What's up? What's going on?"

Chase is holding baby August, and he turns to Summer. "Here, Blondie, take the baby."

Once he's passed the baby off, all my brothers and my dad walk down the steps, while the girls stay up the five steps on the porch.

"John," Mom starts, but Dad holds up a hand, stopping her, and I frown. He *never* does that to her. Normally, she'd skin him alive.

"What the fuck are you doing on my property?" Dad addresses Holden, and I instinctively move in front of my husband to shield him from the shit storm about to come.

All my brothers notice. Ryan's jaw ticks.

But Holden gently takes my shoulders in his hands and moves me to the side, then kisses my temple, and I swear to God, Rem growls.

"I got this, Mill." I look up and see that he's smiling softly at me. His eyes are hard, but that's not for me, and my murder hornets take it down a notch. "We've got this. Don't worry."

"I'm worried about *murder*," I remind him with a hiss.

"Nah. Don't be." He turns back to my father. "Sir,

Millie and I wanted to come out here to announce to you all that we've gotten married."

There's a gasp.

Someone mutters, "Holy shit."

"Congratulations," Summer says with a bright smile, rocking her son side to side. "I want to know *everything*. This is so exciting."

But then her smile falls when literally no one else says a word.

Dad's gaze falls to me, then down to my finger where my ring sits before he looks me in the eye again. I've never seen him this angry. My hand reaches out for Holden's again, and I hold on tight as he rubs his thumb soothingly over my knuckles.

I feel like I'm going to throw up.

"I've never been so disappointed in you in my life." Dad's voice has never been this firm. So damn hard.

Chase moves forward with blood in his eye, and I've had just about enough, so I stomp my foot and scowl, making him come up short.

"Enough," I growl. "What in the hell is wrong with all of you?"

"Do you see who you're standing next to?" Remington asks, looking like he has homicide on the brain.

I look up at Holden, but he still looks perfectly calm. Although, I can see a little hurt in his beautiful blue eyes, and that just pisses me right off.

"Yeah." I turn back to my oldest brother. "I do. And you're all being a bunch of jerks. Holden is a *good* person.

He's not his father. He's done nothing but work hard, be good to his employees, and love his sisters. He raised his sisters. He's well-liked in this town, and there's no reason at all for you to treat him like he's a piece of cow shit on the bottom of your boot."

"He's a Lexington," Dad spits out, and I see red.

"Yeah, and guess what? I now share that last name, Daddy. That makes *me* a Lexington, too."

"Honey," Mom starts, but Dad shakes his head, cutting her off again.

"Let her speak, Dad, Jesus." Brady shakes his head and rubs his hand over the back of his neck in agitation.

"How dare you?" Dad's voice is lethal now, every word like a razor blade. "How. Fucking. Dare you?"

"Okay," Ryan begins. "Dad, that's enough. I know you're pissed, but come on. Holden *is* a nice guy."

"Yeah, let them talk," Brady adds, and I could kiss them with gratitude. "It's not that bad."

"He's not welcome here," Dad says, ignoring my brothers, and the murder hornets are back to being good and pissed off. Holden's grip tightens on my hand, as if he's silently telling me that it's okay.

But it's absolutely *not* fucking okay.

"If he's not welcome here, then *I'm* not welcome here," I reply, my voice softening. But there are no tears because I refuse to fucking cry. "Because where I go, he goes. We're a team. So, if that's really how you feel, we'll be going."

I let my gaze skim over the rest of my family. The girls all have tears in their eyes. Erin has to wipe her cheeks, and I can see the pain in her eyes. Polly mouths, *I love you.*

I grin at her.

"See you around."

I turn to leave, but Holden doesn't move with me, and I frown up at him.

"Before we go," he says without any hesitation in his voice, "I want to make it clear that any and all of you are always welcome in our home. Millie loves you. You're her family. This doesn't change that."

He nods and helps me into the passenger seat, and then he climbs into the truck, starts it up, and with all of those eyes trained on us, we pull away.

I can't help but watch in the side mirror as my home gets smaller and smaller until we turn the corner toward the highway.

When Holden turns off of Wild property, the floodgates open, and I let the tears come.

"Th-that was so much w-worse than I expected."

"Hold on, baby girl," he says as he turns away from town, toward his property.

"I'm so fucking pissed! How dare *I*? How dare *they*! What a bunch of jerks! They're my family. They've always told me that they'd be here for me, no matter what. Well, what a bunch of bullshit that was. What a bunch of assholes. Where are we going?"

"To the only safe spot on my ranch," he growls, and takes me on a dirt road that doesn't get much use.

Finally, he comes to a clearing and stops, and I lose my breath.

It's the same view that I have on *my* ranch. My happy place, with a view of the mountains, and I cry even harder. Because this is exactly where I would go when I needed to be sad, and it's as if Holden just *knew*.

He jumps out of the truck and comes around to my side and opens the door, unclips my belt, and turns me sideways to face him, but he doesn't pull me out of the vehicle. With his hands on my thighs, he just watches me, and I lean forward and rest my forehead on his chest as I let the tears come.

God, I'm so angry and sad and disappointed in them.

I knew it wouldn't be great, but I wasn't expecting *that*. To see my dad stare at me with so much contempt, I don't know if my heart can take it. And I also don't know if we'll ever recover from it.

"Aww, Rosie," he whispers, and that just makes me cry harder.

I told him not to call me that.

But I can't get the words out.

"I'm so sorry." He's crooning to me as if I'm a wounded animal that he's trying to comfort. And I do feel wounded.

I feel wounded down to my soul.

"Please don't cry, baby girl. They don't deserve your tears." He kisses the top of my head and rubs his hands up and down my arms as I cling to his T-shirt and cry into his chest. "I'm sorry."

"It's not your f-fault," I manage to get out. "My dad was so mean. He's never, *ever* looked at me like that. And I l-l-love him so much."

"I know." He kisses my head again. "I know you do. He needs some time. That's all. This was a shock for him, and he just needs a little time."

I shake my head and take a deep, shaky breath. When I finally look up at him, Holden is staring down at me with hard blue eyes, and it makes me blink in response.

"Now, we need to get some things straight, baby girl."

CHAPTER EIGHT

HOLDEN

“We do?” She swallows and wipes at her tears, but her bottom lip is still quivering with the pain that her family just inflicted on her, and it’s all I can do to stay calm.

I wanted to rail at them. Scream at her dad. Demand that they apologize to her, and scoop her up and take her away where they can’t touch her.

But it wouldn’t have done any good, and it only would have hurt her more. And it’s now my mission in life to make sure that very little ever hurts this woman again.

“Yeah, we do. Number one, you won’t *ever* step in front of me again. You won’t shield me from danger. Not today or any other day.”

“They might have—”

“And I would have dealt with it, but you won’t be caught in the crossfire, Millie. You won’t ever do that again. Do you understand me?” I cup her jaw and face in my hands, holding her gaze to mine, and it's killing me that her lower lip continues to tremble.

"I just wanted to protect you from them." The admission is a whisper, and it softens everything inside of me.

"I know, but it's unnecessary. We stand together." I can't keep my hands off her, so I brush the hair off of her cheeks.

"Can I get out of this truck and get some fresh air?"

I step back and help her down, and she walks about ten feet away, wraps her arms around herself, and stares at the mountains.

"This is the one spot that he never ruined for me," I inform her and shove my hands into my pockets, gazing at my girl as she stares at my mountains. "It's where I come when I need to think and be alone."

"I have the same kind of spot over at our ranch, with the same exact view. You couldn't have chosen a more perfect place to bring me right now."

Thank God I didn't fuck this up.

"The second thing I need to say," I begin, and then I have to lick my lips and clear my throat, because she deserves to hear this, but I'm pretty sure I'm going to be met with white-hot anger.

"What?" She hasn't turned back to look at me again, so I join her and stand facing her.

"I need to apologize and beg for your forgiveness, all at the same time."

She scowls. "No, you don't. You were amazing back there, Holden. So calm and confident, and you totally made me feel better."

"Not for today," I counter, shaking my head. "For eight years ago."

She clams up and takes a step back, recoiling as if I just struck her, and the walls come slamming down over her eyes. *Fuck.*

"You defended me today," I continue, hoping to God that she's really listening to me. "No one in my entire life has stood up for me the way you just did. It was the most amazing, most arousing thing I've ever witnessed, and it humbled me. And I know that that's exactly what *you* needed from *me* eight years ago, and I couldn't give it to you."

"Holden." She closes her eyes, but I shake my head and cup her face in my hands again. She grips on to my wrists but won't open those beautiful eyes.

"Look at me, baby girl."

"Rule num—"

"I don't give a fuck about the rules right now. For this minute, let me just do this before I lose my fucking nerve."

She closes her lips and gives a tiny nod as she opens her eyes. "Okay."

"I know that if this is going to work out between us, I have to come clean about everything that happened before so we can truly put it in the past."

"I know what happened. You were a complete asshole. You got in my pants, and then you dumped me. It's really my fault. I was young and should have known better."

"Stop. Fucking. Talking. You have no idea what

happened after that night. After that amazing, perfect night." I close my eyes and walk away, letting the terrifying memory fill my mind, and suddenly, Millie's hand is on my arm.

"What happened, Holden?"

"My dad was waiting for me when I got home that morning." I swallow hard against the nausea. "I don't know how he found out about us, but he did. He ordered me to stop seeing you, along with a bunch of foul language that I won't repeat. Because of your last name. And if I didn't..."

I suck in a breath, and Millie rubs her hand up and down my arm soothingly.

"It's okay. You can tell me."

"If I didn't, he'd kill both you and Charlie." The words come out fast because otherwise, there's no way I'd be able to get them out. "Jesus, I've never said that out loud before."

She's very still, and I turn to look down at her.

"He wasn't serious."

"Oh, he was absolutely fucking serious. My dad didn't make idle threats. He didn't give a shit about the girls, but he knew that Charlie and I were particularly close. And there isn't anything in the world that I wouldn't do to keep you safe. So, I had no choice."

"You did, though. You could have told me. My God, Holden, I could have gotten my dad involved, and—"

"You don't understand." I turn to her again and brush her hair behind her ear. "I couldn't risk you, and I couldn't risk my sister. There was no choice for me. I had to make you hate me because there was no other way I could have stayed away from you, and he would have followed through on his threat."

"You didn't just say something like, *'You know, Millie, now that you're headed back to school, I think we should cool it.'* No, I would have been heartbroken, but I could have lived with it. Instead, you told me that I was a child, insinuated that you thought I was lying about being a fucking virgin, and told me I was one of many, and that there was nothing particularly special about me."

I swallow hard, hating myself all over again. Because she's right. I did say all of those things. And just like it did back then, it makes my stomach want to heave.

"You were so ugly to me," she continues, fury vibrating in every muscle of her body. "Are you telling me now that you didn't actually mean any of it?"

"Fuck no, I didn't mean it!" Her eyes widen in surprise when it comes out as a shout. "Jesus Christ, I was *in love with you!* I would have married you the next day. I was sick and furious and at the mercy of a man who would have killed *all of my sisters* if it meant keeping my dick away from a Wild. You have no fucking idea how terrified I was that he'd do everything he threatened to anyway, despite my promises to stay away from you. He terrorized me for eight more goddamn years until he finally died, and I hope he burns in hell."

She's silent, watching me with tear-filled eyes. The forest around us is also hushed, as if it also can't believe what I just said.

"That's really fucked up, Holden."

I push my hands through my hair and stomp away, then turn around and come back to her.

"Which part?"

"All of it. So fucked up. I can't even begin to count the ways."

I nod and swallow hard. "You deserved to know, and now that he's dead and gone, he can't hurt you. He can't hurt anyone ever again."

"Including you."

I look down and shake my head. "I'm not important here."

"Bullshit. Don't you ever fucking say that you're not important again, Holden Lexington." I love it when Millie gets all fiery. "Because you're wrong. You are. I'm still mad at you, but you are."

"You're *still* mad at me?" I can't help but smile at her.

"Yeah. You were really mean, and I was young, and I had just handed over my V card to you, and I could have saved it for someone who wasn't mean to me."

I narrow my eyes on her. No, she couldn't have saved it for anyone else.

I don't want to even contemplate the idea of someone else touching her skin. Pushing inside of her. Hearing her little moans and groans and feeling the way she pulses around a cock.

Fuck that.

"Be careful, wife."

"I'm just saying." She swallows hard. She likes it when I call her wife.

"Well, don't say that kind of shit."

"I won't if you won't."

Staring at each other, we both scowl.

"Come on," I say at last and take her hand. "I'm taking you out to eat."

"I look like a mess, Holden."

"You're always gorgeous, and you know it." I help her into the truck and then get in, start the engine, and head back toward the highway. "Where would you like to eat?"

"I could really go for a big burger from Snow Ghost up at the ski resort right now."

"I've never been. Let's do it."

Millie left her phone in the truck while we were talking at the ranch, which was for more than an hour, and she checks it now.

"Holy shit."

"What is it?" I glance down at her phone and see her staring down at at least twenty unread texts.

"Everyone has been texting and calling. Ryan has threatened to track my cell phone to find me if I don't call him back right away." She rolls her eyes at that. "He's so dramatic."

"You should call him."

"I don't know that I want to talk to any of them. They embarrassed me."

"He's your big brother, baby girl. You should call him."

She sighs and then gives in and taps the screen, sets it on speaker, and Ryan answers on the second ring.

"You can't just leave and not answer me, Millie."

"Uh, yeah. I can. What's up?"

There's dead air, and I can't help but smile behind my hand. Leave it to Millie to keep riling up her brothers.

"I don't know, I just thought I'd call and shoot the shit. See how your hobbies are going. Talk about the fucking weather."

"Cool." Millie smiles. "It's been so rainy, hasn't it?"

"Cut the shit, Millie. I'm worried about you. Dad was out of line, and it shouldn't have gone like that."

"It went pretty much the way I thought it would, Ry. There was no way to break the news gently."

"He was still out of line, and I'm sorry for it. Now, tell me the truth, and I'll know if you're lying."

She blows out a raspberry between her lips, and I'm still smiling.

"Fine. Yes, you were really adopted, and we've all kept the secret from you. I'm sorry, I should have told you sooner."

"You're a riot."

"Aren't I, though?"

"Are you really safe, Mill? Is everything okay?" His voice softens, and if I didn't respect Ryan Wild before, this would have pushed me square into it. "You're not there against your will or anything like that?"

"No." Millie's voice isn't teasing anymore either. "Ryan, I'm really okay. I'm hurt after what just went down, but I'll get over it eventually. I'm safe."

Damn right, she is.

"If you need literally *anything*—"

"I know, Ry. Thank you. I love you, too. Thanks for not being a jerk like the others."

He snorts out a laugh. "Talk to you later, squirt."

She hangs up and lets out a long breath. "At least they're not *all* dead to me."

"None of them are dead to you." I smile over at her. "It's going to be okay."

"Yeah. Sure. Feed me."

"I'm on my way to do that right now."

I drive her up to the ski resort, and with her instructions, I find the pub and restaurant called Snow Ghost. It's a weird time of the afternoon, definitely a little too early for dinner, but all the emotional trauma that we just went through will make a person hungry.

There are only a few others in the restaurant, so we're immediately shown to a table with a view of the slopes where the snow is still melting off, and Millie sets her menu aside.

She already knows what she wants.

I decide to just get the same thing that she's having and set my menu on top of hers.

"So." She leans forward on her elbows, but we're interrupted by the waitress, who takes our orders, leaves waters, and then bustles away.

"So?"

"When are you going to tell *your* family?" Her beautiful hazel eyes are vulnerable, and, without hesitation, I pull my phone out and pull up the group text with my girls.

Me: Hey, guys. Yesterday went well. I married Millie Wild. Well, Millie Lexington now. I'll tell you more about it later.

I set the phone aside and smile at Millie. "Done."

She scowls. "You told them in a *group text*?"

"Sure. They knew I was getting married. I just didn't tell them to who. Now they know."

"Through a text message, Holden."

"Listen, I'm out to dinner with my beautiful wife. I don't have time to call an emergency family meeting."

My phone, sitting on the table by my elbow, starts to light up with responses from my sisters. Rather than answer, I turn the phone on Do Not Disturb and slide it into my pocket.

Millie's mouth drops open.

"You're not going to at least answer their questions?"

"Later." I reach over and take her hand. "I told you, I'm having dinner with my wife. I do believe this is our first official date."

"Oh, no." She shakes her head adamantly. "Definitely not. We're not calling this a date."

"We're out at a restaurant. Together. Alone. Pretty sure that constitutes a date, Mill."

"No. Because I look like shit, I've been through the emotional wringer today, and I refuse to look and feel like this on our first date. You'll just have to try again another time."

She frowns as if she didn't mean to say that.

"Actually, this is a sham marriage, so we don't need to go on dates."

"Millie?" I squeeze her fingers until she looks up at me. "Shut up."

Before she can respond, her phone starts to ring, and I see that it's Charlie, so I snatch it out of Millie's grasp and answer it myself.

"Oh, my God, nosy Nelly, stop bothering her. We're out to dinner. Leave her alone, Charlie, I mean it."

"No, I need details. *Millie Wild*? Oh, my God, this is fabulous. I love her! But her dad is going to fucking kill you, Holden. You're not safe. You need to enter the witness protection pro—"

I hang up on her, and before I give it back to Millie, I enter my number, assign my contact, and then turn it on Do Not Disturb and pass it over.

"You should talk to her," she says, her eyes laughing.

"No way. I'll answer questions another time. So, now that our families know, we don't have to keep it a secret."

"I didn't plan on keeping it a secret. Jesus, I can't lie for a whole year. That's insane."

Try your whole life, baby girl.

But all I say is, "Hmm," and take a sip of my water.

She's right, dinner is delicious up here. The burger is some of the best beef I've had, and the onion rings aren't too oily.

By the time we leave the restaurant and make it down to the house, we're both damn tired, and it's not even six in the evening yet.

"If it wasn't so late, I'd take a nap," Millie says with a yawn as I unlock the front door.

"We can still rest," I reply. "Go take a hot shower and get cozy."

"Not gonna argue," she says and does exactly that.

While she's busy in the shower, I do my best not to think about her naked and wet, and instead, I change into relaxing clothes of my own and then find a bottle of wine on the kitchen counter and open it, pouring her a glass.

I pour myself two fingers of tequila and remind myself to pick up some whiskey.

I don't usually drink this much, but today was one of the most stressful days of my life.

When Millie pads out of the bathroom, my tongue sticks to the roof of my mouth.

She's not in the too-big sweats tonight. No, my vixen is in little blue sleep shorts with a barely there yellow tank top and a zip-up hoodie open in the front.

She's a walking wet dream.

"Oh, wine." She holds her hand out for the glass. "Good call. Now what should we do?"

I should strip you out of those pitiful excuses for clothes and fuck you six ways to Sunday; that's what we should do.

And she must see it in my eyes because she clears her throat and sips her wine.

"Holden?"

"Yes, Rosie?"

"You're going to call me that whether I like it or not, aren't you?"

"Probably."

"Fine." She rolls her eyes and pads over to the couch. "Let's watch something stupid on TV."

"Why does it have to be something stupid?"

"Because I'm brain dead. I can't follow something serious tonight. But maybe we can watch something funny."

"We can watch anything you want. But you're going to have to share the couch because I'll get a crick in my neck if I try to watch TV from that tiny-ass chair."

"It's a big couch." She shrugs a shoulder and scoots over, and I sit right next to her, my thigh against hers. And I rest my arm over the back of the couch, around her shoulder. "Holden?"

"Yep?"

"You're crowding me."

"Yep. Choose something to watch, wife."

She rolls her eyes, but her cheeks flush with pleasure as she picks up the remote and aims it at the TV. It doesn't take her long to find a Sandra Bullock rom-com, and then she holds herself stiff for a while, as if she doesn't want to relax against me.

So, I just tug her into my side, kiss her temple, and whisper into her ear, "Just relax, baby girl."

After three seconds, she does. She curls into me, and we watch this silly movie, and the day rolls through my head.

She defended me. To her family. She stood in front of me, which really pissed me off, but she only did it because she wanted to protect me.

God, I love this woman.

CHAPTER NINE

MILLIE

I feel like I'm floating.

In fact, as I blink my eyes open, it occurs to me that I *am* floating.

"It's okay. I've got you," Holden whispers before kissing my temple. He's carrying me and lowers me to the bed. I'm on top of the covers, but I don't care.

I'm so damn tired.

I feel his calloused fingers brush my hair off my cheek, and then he presses his lips to my forehead.

"This might be the best dream ever."

Is that my voice? All thick and husky and maybe a little needy. Holden chuckles, but then I doze again.

Until I feel the mattress dip, and then there's my favorite fluffy blanket—the extra big one—draped over me, and Holden is next to me, and I can't help but curl into his warmth.

Strong arms pull me in, and now I know that I'm

dreaming because there's no other explanation for Holden being in bed with me.

But I have to admit, it's really nice.

So, I sigh and lean into this sweet, comforting dream, where Holden holds me with his arms wrapped around me, and I nuzzle in, feeling more content than I have in a long time, and let sleep wash over me once more.

IT'S STILL DARK when I wake up and turn over to check the time. 4:45.

I stretch my arms over my head and then turn to push my face back into the pillow. When I smell Holden there, I pause.

Why does my pillow smell like Holden?

I think he carried me to bed. I remember that. Aside from the ride on a cloud, I don't remember much of anything else.

I was physically and emotionally exhausted.

After one more stretch, I get up and pad into the bathroom, and once I've done my business, put my hair up, and washed my face, I pull on my usual work clothes of jeans and a Bitterroot Valley Coffee Co T-shirt, then brush on a touch of mascara and lip balm before heading to the kitchen.

Holden's there. His hair is wet from a shower, and he's in faded work jeans that mold around his ass perfectly. His broad shoulders fill out that blue T-shirt, and I see that he has a flannel draped over the back of a kitchen chair.

When he turns, his devastatingly blue eyes narrow and sweep over me, as if he's memorizing me, and then he smiles.

"Good morning."

"'Morning," I reply. "Thanks for taking me to bed."

My eyes widen as I realize what the hell I just said.

"I mean—"

Holden laughs and lifts a coffee mug to his lips. "I know what you mean. You're welcome. You were out cold."

"What time did I fall asleep?"

"Before eight." His smile falls. "You were tired, baby girl."

"It was a crazy day." I shrug a shoulder and try not to think about my dad glaring at me and the silence from the rest of my family. My heart hurts.

"Would you like some coffee?" he asks.

"Nah, I'll grab some at work. I have some tumblers if you want to take it with you."

"We have a pot in the barn," he replies. "It's always full."

He crosses to me and brushes his fingertips over my jaw before he holds on to my throat in that way he does that makes my murder hornets start to buzz. He held me like this before, too. Like he's possessing me, claiming me, and I should probably pull away, but I can't.

"You okay?" His thumb brushes along the underside

of my jawline, and I can't help but stare at his lips. My husband has amazing lips. "Mill?"

"Huh?"

"Are you okay today?"

"Oh, yeah. My heart's a little bruised, but I hope my dad will come around." Honestly, it's more than bruised. I've always been a daddy's girl, and the way he looked at me yesterday broke my heart into a million pieces.

"He will. Like I said, he just needs some time. I have to get going, but I won't be late today. Do you have a full day?"

We're standing in my kitchen, having the most domestic of conversations, like any married couple. Except, his hand is wrapped around my throat, sending signals to my core that should *not* be sent, and I want to lick him from head to toe.

"Baby?"

"Sorry." His eyes are full of humor, and I can't help but scowl. He knows exactly what he does to me. I lick my lips, and all humor flees from his eyes as they lower to my mouth. At least this lust isn't one-sided. "I'm interviewing some girls today, but I'll be done around three."

He nods, then leans into me and brushes his lips over my cheek to my ear.

Oh, God, my knees buckle when he does this part.

"Have a good day, wife."

And with that, he lets go and walks away, grabs his boots and hat, and then the door shuts behind him, and I have to cover my chest with my hand to try to quiet down the murder hornets and my beating heart.

Why do I have to be married to a goddamn heartthrob?

Aside from our wedding day, he hasn't kissed me. Not *really* kissed me. He's touched me and flirted and brushed his lips over mine, but it's likely for the best that he's keeping his delicious, addictive lips to himself, although part of me is disappointed.

No kissing isn't one of my rules.

"Get over yourself," I mutter as I grab my bag and keys and then lock the house up behind me as I walk into town.

It's not supposed to rain today, and my coffee shop is only about six blocks away, so an early-morning, brisk walk feels good. Spring has definitely sprung, and the trees are budding with fresh green buds. Daffodils and tulips smile lazily from fence lines, and the air just smells good.

It's almost time for my favorite time at the ranch: branding and taking care of the spring calves. I love the hard work of it, getting out there in the pen, roping, and vaccinating.

My footsteps stumble when it hits me that I might not be invited out to help this year. Not that I've ever needed to be invited before. It's my home. It's who I am.

But I'm not welcome there anymore, and it makes the bruise around my heart ache. Did yesterday even really happen? Did my entire family stand there and stare at me with so much contempt and disappointment?

Okay, that's not fair. It was mostly Dad and Remington who were the worst. Chase wasn't a lot better. Mom was confused, if nothing else. And everyone else was...quiet. Brady and Ryan tried to be the voice of reason, but my dad is the patriarch of the family, and what he says goes.

And until yesterday, that was okay because he's always been a good, kind, strong, honorable man. And now, I'm not welcome at the only true home I've ever known.

"I guess I'll be helping Holden," I whisper and turn the corner on the block where my coffee shop is. It's quiet this early in the morning, and I'm the only one out and about this early.

I like it that way.

The other huge bombshell came after the conversation with my family, when Holden admitted the way things really went down after we had sex, when he was cruel in the way he broke things off with me. All these years, I thought I'd been a joke to him. I was humiliated and heartsick, and I hated him with every fiber of my being. I was cruel in return. And yet, there was always chemistry there, and I'd started to soften toward him over the past couple of years because I couldn't help myself.

But now I find out that he was *forced* to be horrible to me, to drive me away, all to keep me and his sisters safe.

Because his father was an evil, horrible son of a bitch.

And I don't even really know how to process that. Am I supposed to toss out everything that was said and done, fall back into love with him, and give him my whole heart and soul again? A huge part of me wants to do just that. But the memories of how he laughed at me, how he looked at me so coldly and sneered, and made me feel like I was *nothing* is still embedded in my core memories, and I don't know if I'm ready to trust that it wouldn't happen again.

I don't know if I'm ready to trust that my heart is safe with Holden Lexington.

I look up as the sun starts to lighten the sky over the mountains and feel my soul settle a bit. The mountains always settle me.

Bitterroot Valley is in my blood. My family, along with Holden's, settled this area well over a hundred years ago, and we're proud to be a founding family. I love my town. Even though I went away to college, I couldn't get back here fast enough. I've always known that this is where I belong.

Once inside, I immediately start to tidy up, although Candy is always great about leaving the shop clean, and then I get ready for the day. After a quick trip down to The Sugar Studio to pick up the day's pastries, I get the display case filled and then unlock the door to start the day.

"I'M SO glad that Andrea and Macy worked out," Candy says with a bright smile. "They're just the nicest girls, and this will be the perfect job for them."

"I'm glad, too," I agree. "And with Hannah helping on weekends, since she's still in school, and then more when her schedule loosens up, we should be covered through the summer. I'm going to look into what it would take for me to offer full-time employees benefits, to help entice more long-term employees. Being a small business owner in a tourist town isn't easy, and it's not easy to work in one, either."

"That would be amazing," Candy says. "But you know me. I'm with you no matter what, babe."

"You're the best." I wrap my arm around her shoulders and squeeze as my cell vibrates with a text. "Do you mind grabbing some more vanilla and caramel syrup out of the back?"

"You got it."

Candy takes off to the storeroom, and I pull out my phone.

> Husband: My sisters forced me into a family meeting this morning. Just wanted you to know that they're headed your way this afternoon. They're happy, so don't freak out.

I scowl at the phone. I didn't have Holden's number, and I definitely didn't assign *Husband* to his name. He must have done it yesterday at the restaurant.

First, I type out a reply.

Me: Thanks for the heads-up! Glad it went well.

Then I bring up his contact info and change his name to *Big Jerk*, just to make myself laugh.

An hour later, after the lunchtime rush, all four Lexington sisters walk into my shop, grinning at me.

Well, except for Darby. She's not watching me with open hostility, but she's kind of giving me the beady eye.

And that's okay.

"You're my *sister-in-law*!" Charlie rushes around the counter and throws her arms around me in a huge hug. "I can't believe it. I'm so *happy*."

"Hi, guys." I laugh, and then I'm swept up into two more hugs, which surprises me and would normally make me a little uncomfortable because I'm not a huge hugger, especially with people I'm not close to. And then Darby's eyeing me again.

"Oh, for fuck's sake," Alex says to her sister. "Don't be a brat."

"She's not," I say and hold my hand out to shake Darby's. "I get it."

Her gaze falls to my hand, then lands back on my face before she reluctantly reaches out to shake.

"If you hurt him, they'll never find the body. He's too good to be dicked around with."

My heart softens. "I will never intentionally hurt him."

After a few more moments of watching me, she nods once. "Okay, then."

"It sucks that you eloped," Dani says. "Charlie would have thrown you one heck of a party. Oh, and we brought you flowers. Every bride needs flowers."

Okay, that has my eyes stinging. My family threw us out, but *his* family welcomed me and brought me flowers.

Talk about emotional whiplash.

Charlie is the best wedding and event planner in the area, and I've seen what she can pull off, including my own brother's wedding to Erin. She's talented, and if I were to ever have such an event, I'd definitely want her in charge.

"Thank you." I set the flowers aside and see Candy smiling as she restocks cups, doing her best not to look obvious about her eavesdropping.

I should probably have a conversation with her, but everything has happened so fast, I haven't had time. I'll do it today.

Holden's sisters are beautiful. Like him, they have dark hair and blue eyes. Charlie is tall and thin, almost like a ballerina. Darby is shorter, with killer curves. And Alex and Dani fall somewhere in between.

When the four of them are together, they look like they should be on the cover of a magazine.

"We know you're working," Alex says with a smile. "But we couldn't *not* stop in to see you after our chat with Holden this morning."

I glance toward Candy again. I know that his sisters know that we got married because of the will, but

Holden and I haven't exactly talked about how we want to handle that piece of it.

So far, we've kept it between us.

Dani clears her throat. "Let's plan on a girls' night soon, and we can talk more. Welcome to the family, Millie."

"And there I go, getting choked up again," I say with a half laugh. "Thank you. And thanks for these beautiful flowers."

We say our goodbyes, and I turn to find Candy watching me.

"I know. I need to tell you what's going on."

"No, you don't," she says, shaking her head. "It's none of my business. I just hope you're happy."

"I'm...okay." I nod slowly, thinking it over. "I'm not unhappy, but it's complicated."

"Honey, I grew up here. I know everything there is to know about the famous Wild-Lexington feud. I'd be shocked out of my mind if it was anything but complicated."

I can't help but chuckle at that, and then I look to the door when it opens and feel my heart stumble when *my* girls walk in.

Erin leads Summer, Polly, and Abbi into my shop, and tears fill my eyes, and I feel my cheeks flush.

"We would have come to your place last night," Abbi says as she approaches, "but we figured you might need a minute since you didn't reply to any of our texts."

I can't keep my lip from wobbling, and Erin circles the counter to pull me in for another hug.

Jesus, everyone is touching me today, and I'm not even freaked out about it.

"I love you," Erin says. "We all love you. Nothing has changed."

"I'm going to lock the door and put a sign up that says we're closed for the rest of the day," Candy says quietly. "It's only thirty minutes early. You deserve privacy, Mill."

"Thank you," I whisper and let Candy handle it. "And you're wrong, E. Everything has changed."

"No," Polly puts in as the others shake their heads, "it hasn't. It's only your dad that's lost his mind. Even Remington asked him why he was being so cruel after you left."

"Rem doesn't *love* Holden," Erin agrees, "but even he admits that no one holds any animosity toward him."

"They don't hold whatever his dad did against Holden," Summer adds as she rubs a circle on my back. God, I love these girls so much. "Even Chase. He felt really bad last night. Couldn't sleep. He spent a lot of time in his workshop, sanding shit down."

"I'm just so mad," I murmur and wipe the tears from my cheeks. "I wanted them all to stand up for Holden like I did. I mean, maybe not *exactly* like me, but I wanted them to try harder."

"You might have given everyone the surprise of the century," Polly reminds me. "None of us knew this was even a possibility. We've seen the hot looks between you two, but whenever he comes around, you call him a jerk and tell him to fuck off. You wouldn't even talk about him, Millie."

"Yeah." I smile at that. "I did do that. Look, there's a story here that's too long to get into standing in my shop. It also requires a lot of alcohol. But I love you all for coming here. It makes me feel a little better."

"We love you, always," Summer says, reaching out to take my hand. "You're our family."

"Okay," is all I can say when the tears come again, and then I'm in the middle of a giant group hug.

"You're not kicked off of the ranch," Abbi says. "Never."

"If m-my husband isn't welcome, then I'm not either. You'd feel the same way."

"Who the *fuck* made my wife cry?"

CHAPTER TEN

HOLDEN

All of their heads whip up in surprise at the sound of my voice. Candy unlocked the door for me on her way out, and the first thing I heard was my wife talking through tears, and my blood immediately started to boil.

She's had enough tears to last her a fucking lifetime.

Millie's wet gaze finds mine as the others grin and shuffle their feet.

"Hi, Holden," Polly says with a little wave.

I nod in return, but I still want to know what the hell is going on.

"It's not a bad cry," Millie assures me as she crosses to me and cups my cheek in her hand, pulling my gaze down to her. Those gorgeous eyes are glassy, and it makes my stomach hurt. "They came to love on me."

And just like that, I feel the tension move out of my shoulders, and I nod before kissing her on the forehead.

"We wanted to make sure she's okay," Erin says. "How are *you*, Holden?"

I blink in surprise. "I'm great. Look at my wife. It doesn't get any better than this."

Millie's jaw drops, and Summer says, "Aww, that's so *sexy*."

"Mill, we need a girls' night," Abbi says as the girls begin to walk past us to the door. "STAT. Like, yesterday."

"I hear you, loud and clear," Millie says with a laugh. "We'll make it happen. In the meantime, go poison my brothers' drinks or something. Withhold sex. Slash some tires."

"Why are you trying to punish *us*?" Summer asks with a wink. "Don't worry. They feel like shit."

"Good," Millie grumbles. "Love you guys."

"Love you more," Polly says with a wave, and then the four of them are gone, and Millie locks the door behind them.

Her eyes drop to the box in my hand, and her brow furrows. "What's in there?"

"Oh, I forgot I had it with me. I grabbed you a cupcake from Jackie's store."

Her eyebrows climb in surprise. "What kind?"

"Red velvet."

Her eyes get glassy again, and I shake my head as I approach her. "No more tears today, Rosie. I can't take it. I just thought you could use a treat, and since you own the coffee shop, coffee was out."

"You got my favorite," she whispers as she takes the box from me and bites her lip. "I haven't had one of these in years."

"Then it's time." I grin at her as she sets the box on the counter and then blows out a breath and brushes her fingers over her cheeks, clearing away the tears. "How did your interviews go?"

"Really well. They'll both start tomorrow so Candy and I can get them trained and on a rotating schedule. That'll help a lot for the summer."

"Good." I reach out, unable to keep my hands to myself, and tuck a piece of hair that escaped her ponytail behind her ear. I slept next to her all night, and it was the best night's sleep I've ever had in my life.

And she doesn't even know it.

"I'm going to ask you a question," she begins, and then clenches her eyes closed and bites her lip.

"Okay. Ask."

"I kind of hate myself for it." Her voice is a little shaky, so I lace my fingers through hers.

"Stop judging yourself and ask."

She lifts her chin, and with her golden eyes on mine, she says, "Are you ever going to kiss me?"

My gut clenches, my dick hardens, and I have to take my hand away from her. Unfortunately, she takes that the wrong way and backs up, shaking her head.

"I'm sorry, that was stupid. Obviously, if you wanted to kiss me, you would. It's just that I didn't say you couldn't, and you—"

I brace her face in my hands and kiss her—not in a soft, sweet brush of the lips, but as though I want to consume her.

Because I do.

Jesus, she's the most beautiful, amazing woman I've ever met in my life, and I want her so much that I can't breathe. But I have to let her decide what she's ready for because I won't have her hating me later.

She whimpers deep in her throat and leans her stomach against my cock, and I let one hand drift down around her throat while the other one slides down to her ass, holding her against me.

God, she's everything.

She willingly opens herself to me, and I don't hesitate to push my tongue inside of her mouth, rubbing it against hers, drinking the moans that come from her.

When I come up for air and rest my forehead against hers, Millie swallows hard.

"You didn't have to do that," she whispers.

"Shut up, Rosie."

She grins, loops her arms around my neck, and I lift her so she can circle my waist with her legs, and then we kiss again as I carry her to the counter. I set her down so my hands can roam and cover one perfect breast, teasing the hard nipple through her shirt.

She slips her hand under the hem of my T-shirt, and my muscles ripple when her sweet touch glides over my stomach and up my ribs.

"Baby girl, I have to get you home," I whisper into her neck before I sink my teeth in and then suck.

I want to mark her.

I want everyone in the fucking world to know that this woman is *mine*.

"Mm," she agrees, but she doesn't pull away.

"Someone could see us," I remind her and kiss her cheek. "And while we *are* married, no one gets to see us like this."

She blinks up at me, as if she's trying to understand my words through a thick fog. Finally, she takes a long, deep breath.

"I wouldn't call myself an exhibitionist," she says with a frown.

"We got caught up," I reply. "And that was overdue. I just didn't want to rush you."

She brushes the tip of her finger over my bottom lip. "You're going to break rule number five, aren't you?"

"As soon as fucking possible."

She doesn't smile. With her eyes still on my mouth, she sighs, as if the weight of the world is on her shoulders.

"You have to talk to me, baby girl. I need your words here."

Reluctantly, she looks up at me, and I don't like the apprehension in her gaze. She swallows hard. "For eight years, the biggest regret of my life was the night we spent together."

She might as well have taken a knife and sliced me from neck to cock. I can't help the groan of despair that slips past my lips, and when I start to pull away, Millie frames my face in her hands and holds on.

"I didn't know, Holden."

"I'm so sorry. Because that night was the only bright spot in a world so dark, I thought I would die."

She kisses my lips softly, tenderly, as if she's comforting both of us.

"I know." Her voice is a whisper. "I'm sorry, too. I'm taking number five off the list because I can't make my body shut the fuck up."

I narrow my eyes at her. "And what is your body saying, Rosie?"

She doesn't answer. She bites that lip and pulls my hands around her until I'm hugging her and she's resting her head against my chest.

"My body says to give in and climb you like a tree."

Satisfaction fills me.

"But my heart—"

"It's okay." I press a kiss to the top of her head. "You can tell me."

"It says to be very careful."

I blow out a breath. "I understand."

That has her pulling back and staring up at me in surprise. "You do?"

"Of course. We're both carrying scars, Millie. There's still a lot to talk about. I want you so much that I ache with it."

Her eyes dilate.

"Hell, I spent the night holding you, and I wanted to slip inside of you so many times, but—"

"I *knew* it. My pillow smelled like you this morning."

I grin down at her. "I snuck out before you woke up. I don't plan to sleep alone again, by the way."

"At the end of this year, when it's over, just don't be cruel, Holden. That's all I ask."

I want to tell her that it won't be over. It'll never be over, because Millie is mine. She belongs to me, just like my heart belongs to her, and she'll never be rid of me.

Instead, I brush my lips over hers. "I'll never intentionally hurt you again, little rose. I promise you that."

She chuckles, making me frown.

"What's so funny?"

"I said pretty much the same thing to Darby when your sisters came by and she was glaring at me and threatened to kill me if I hurt you."

I'll be having a conversation with my sister about death threats.

"So, it's agreed, then. No intentionally hurting the other."

"I like that agreement."

Before I can sink into her again, her phone rings, and she scowls. She pulls her phone out of her pocket, and her eyes go wide.

"It's Jake." She taps the screen. "Hey, buddy, what's up?"

"Aunt Mill?" I can hear his voice on the other end of the line, and he sounds miserable. I know that Jake is the teenager that Ryan adopted not long ago. He's a good kid.

"Are you okay, Jake?" Millie asks as I step back to give her space.

"Yeah, I'm okay, but I ran out of gas and forgot my wallet at home. Are you in town? Can you help me out?"

"Of course, kiddo. Where are you?"

"I'm at the high school. I must have coasted in here on fumes this morning and didn't realize it."

"I'm on my way. I'll have to stop by the house to get a gas can, so give me like thirty, okay?"

"Thanks. And please don't tell my dad, okay?"

Millie smirks. "Sure thing. See you in a few."

She hangs up and looks up at me.

"Feel like rescuing a teenager?"

"Let's go. I'll follow you home."

"I was hoping for a ride. I walked this morning."

I pull her to a stop and glare down at her. "You *walked*? Jesus, why didn't you say something? I would have given you a ride."

"Because that would have been the opposite of what I wanted. I like to walk to work."

"Not at fucking five in the morning, Millie. Absolutely not."

She rolls her eyes at me, earning her a smack on the ass, and she gapes at me.

"Did you just *spank* me?" Her cheeks are flushed in pleasure, and I file that little nugget of knowledge away for later.

"When it comes to your safety, you won't defy me, baby girl."

"God, you're overbearing." She grabs her purse and leads me to the door. After she sets an alarm and locks the door behind us, she follows me to my truck, and I open the door for her. "So, about the spanking thing."

I tip up an eyebrow.

"Do it, and I'll hit you back."

I lean into the truck and press my lips to her ear. "Challenge accepted."

After clicking her seat belt into place, I shut the door and walk around to my side of the truck.

"I have a gas can in the back," I inform her. "No need to stop at the house."

"Handy."

Jake is the last kid parked in the lot when we pull into the high school. He's sitting on his open tailgate, looking at something on his phone, and looks up when he hears us approaching.

He looks surprised to see my truck, and when we get out to join him, he immediately offers me his hand.

"Hey, I'm Jake. I heard you married my aunt Millie."

I take his offered hand, impressed with his firm shake. "I did."

Jake smiles at Millie. "Congratulations. I think everyone is pissed that you eloped."

"Why do you say that?" she asks as Jake gives her a hug.

"Because they look pissed, and I can't think of any other reason for it." He shrugs, and Millie's eyes fill with tears, and Jake looks at me in a panic.

"Shit, don't cry. I don't think they're that mad. I take it back, Mill. *Please* don't cry."

"You're the sweetest boy in the whole world," she

says as she folds him into a maternal hug that tugs at my heartstrings. She rocks him back and forth. "Just the best kid ever. You're my favorite nephew."

"You always tell Johnny that he's your favorite. And August, too, when you're holding him." Jake winks at me, and I grin back at him. "So, which is it?"

"You're all my favorite," my girl replies as she sniffles. "And you give the best hugs. So, I guess I'll do you a solid and not call your dad."

Jake winces. "This is the third time I've run out of gas, and I'm pretty sure Dad's annoyed. He doesn't yell or anything, but I can tell."

"I have an idea," I say, getting the teen's attention. I pull my wallet out of my pocket. "Take this forty bucks and tuck it into the glove box, like in the owner's manual or something. That way, if you forget your wallet again, you're not stranded. You'll always have some cash on you."

"Oh, you don't have to—"

"Take it," Millie says. "And put some gas in your truck. The fuel we brought with us should get you out to your ranch and back."

"You're the best," Jake says and hugs her once more. "My favorite aunt."

"You say that to all of us."

Jake grins and then shrugs. "I cannot confirm nor deny that."

"Brat." She pulls on a lock of his hair. "You can always call me, by the way. For anything. I'll always come get you."

"I know." He's so happy and sure in that answer that it makes me smile. "Welcome to the family, Mr. Lexington."

"You can just call me Holden," I reply, oddly moved by his words. "And thank you very much."

I get the gas poured into his tank, and then he's off. Millie and I sit in my truck for a minute before I start the engine to go home.

"That's what it should have been like for you yesterday," she says before swallowing hard. "The same as what your sisters gave me today."

"Babe, I'm okay."

She turns to me and bites her lip. "I'm not. I'm not okay with it at all."

"Let's go home," I murmur and start the truck, then drive the few blocks to the house. To my surprise, Millie's mom is sitting on the porch, looking absolutely miserable.

"Mom," Millie says in surprise.

As soon as I stop, Millie hops out and runs to the porch, where her mom stands and opens her arms for her daughter.

They hold each other tightly as I get out of the truck and then walk up to the house.

"Mrs. Wild." I tip my hat to her, and she nods back at me as she releases her hold on Millie. Before my girl can speak, I continue. "Mill, I'm going out to the ranch for a while. I have a mare that's going to foal any day, and I want to check on her. I'll be home in a couple of hours."

"Thank you," Millie says and reaches for my hand to give it a squeeze. "I'll see you later."

I return to my truck and look back to see both women going inside. I'm glad that Joy came to see Millie. I could tell that everything that happened yesterday was as devastating for her mom as it was for Millie.

Family politics are the worst on the best days. Add in days that don't feel great, and it's way worse.

I hate that my marriage to Millie has her family upside down. It's the best thing that's ever happened to me.

When I get to my barn, I see that Vance and Levi are at the stall of the mare about to give birth.

"Anything happen yet?" I ask them.

"Nope," Levi says. "Tim just ran to get us dinner. I think we'll be out here all night, but we'll take shifts."

My guys live in a bunkhouse that I had built for them about five years ago, against my dad's wishes and with my own money. It didn't make sense for these bachelors to live in town and commute back and forth.

"I appreciate it."

"I thought you left for the day," Vance says.

"I wanted to check in on her. She looked scared this morning."

"You're a softie, boss," Levi says with a big, shit-eating grin.

"Fuck you."

They laugh, and then I turn for the office at the end of the building.

"I'll be in the office for a while, catching up on some paperwork. Let me know if anything changes with her."

"Will do." Vance nods and turns back to the stall, and their conversation picks up where it left off.

I'd rather be at home with my girl, picking up where we left off at the coffee shop, but she needs this time with her mom, so I'll wait a while.

I've already waited eight years. What's another two hours?

CHAPTER ELEVEN

MILLIE

"Give me another hug." Mom pulls me in, wrapping her arms around me and holding me close, and although I've had a lot of support from Holden, his sisters, and *my* sisters of the heart, I really needed this.

A hug from my mom.

"I'm so sorry," I whisper into her ear. "I knew Dad would be mad, but I didn't expect *that.*"

"Come on. Let's sit and talk. Do you have tea?"

"In the kitchen."

Mom leads the way and takes control of filling the kettle and finding the mugs. I pull out the tea bags and honey and set them on the counter for her.

"Your father is a good man," she says after turning on the burner under the kettle. "A wonderful man. But he's human, darling, and even I don't know everything that went down between him and Holden's father. I know snippets, but John was always adamant that I be shielded from him."

Now that I know more about what kind of person Lawrence was, I understand more. Mom turns to me with shrewd eyes.

"Do *you* know some of what he did?" she asks.

"Some," I confirm and blow out a breath. Jesus, I need to confide in someone, and my mom has always been that person for me. "I guess I need to admit to something, and I really need to talk this out."

"That's why I'm here." She smiles softly, but her eyes are sad. "You never used to keep secrets from me. We don't have that kind of relationship."

The kettle starts to whistle, and we take a minute to make our tea and then move to the small, round kitchen table and sit facing each other.

"I hate keeping secrets. I'm not good at it."

"You usually just say whatever's on your mind, unapologetically. I've always admired that about you."

I take a deep breath, let it out, and start at the beginning.

"I was nineteen," I begin, and Mom leans in, listening intently. I tell her *all of it.* How much time Holden and I spent together that summer, how sweet he was to me, how tender he was with me. So many emotions flit over her pretty face, from concern to swoon to anger when I get to the end and tell her how he spoke to me, how he drove me away. "I was so heartbroken."

"Of course, you were." She reaches for my hand. "I remember that year. You became so distant when you went back to school, and I thought it was just because you were consumed with classes."

"I was consumed, but it wasn't with classes." I shake my head and drink my tea. "I was so confused. His whole personality just did a one-eighty, and I didn't trust myself with people after that. I didn't trust my own judge of character."

"It wasn't your fault." She squeezes my hand, and I hold on tightly. It feels so good to share this with her.

"I know that now." I'm not going to tell her why Holden came to me about this fake marriage. Not yet. I haven't discussed with him how he wants to handle that part, and it's his family business. "Over the past couple of years, I started to soften toward him. He's been flirty, and nice, and since his dad died, he's sort of back to himself, the man I knew during that month before it all fell apart. And then, after we went to the ranch yesterday, and Dad did what he did, I was so upset. So Holden took me to his special place at his ranch, with a view of the exact mountain *I* go to."

Mom's mouth tips up into a smile.

"And he apologized again and finally told me why everything happened the way that it did." Her eyes widen and then fill with tears as I relay the story of Holden's dad threatening his sister and me. And when I finish, she has to wipe tears from her cheeks.

"That poor boy," she whispers, shaking her head. "What a horrible man."

"That's too good of a word for what he was." My voice is full of anger, but I can't stop it. "He tormented those kids all their lives, Mom. Made them suffer. And I don't even know half of what he put Holden through, but I bet it was pure abuse, plain and simple."

"I suspect you're right." She sighs and presses her fingers to her forehead. "And now, after all this time, you've found your way back to each other."

Leave it to my mom to be the romantic.

"Yeah, I guess you could put it that way."

"I've always liked the Lexington kids," she says. "I know they're all adults, not kids at all, but I like them. And I really loved their mom. She was so much fun in school. She loved the drama club, and she was a cheerleader."

"I didn't know that you knew her."

"Sure, Barbara and I were in the same class. She was funny and full of life. And then she married *that man,* and we hardly ever saw her around town. I don't think she was allowed to leave their ranch much, and when I ran into her at the grocery or around town, she was kind, but the light was gone from her eyes. It made me so sad. Her husband...what an asshole."

I nod in agreement and let my mom talk it out. Obviously, she has a lot of feelings about this.

"When she died—"

"Wait," I put in. "How did she die? She was young."

"She was only in her thirties," Mom agrees. "Charlie was hardly walking, if I remember right. Officially, it was reported that she fell down the stairs."

I gasp and cover my mouth with my hands. "Oh, my God."

"Your father and I have suspicions, though." She sips her tea. "And I'm sure we're not the only ones."

"What kind of—oh, God, do you think he *killed her*?"

She stares into her cup for a moment and then looks up at me. "Yes. I do. In my gut, I do think that. I told your father, even back then, that I wanted to run over there and scoop those kids up and bring them home with me. Of course, there was no legal reasoning to do that, and I hated that they had to stay there."

My lip quivers. I wonder if Holden saw...I can't even think about it.

"Well, damn," is all I can say as I wipe a tear from my cheek. "I'm selfishly glad you didn't, because then I would have been raised with Holden as a brother, and... yikes."

She laughs at that and pats my hand. "Your father will struggle with this for a long time, my love. I hate that he took it out on you, and I told him as much. I saw the shame in his eyes, but whatever happened between those two men sparked an intense hatred and fierce protective instinct in your father. He's going to need a lot of time."

"That's what Holden said," I reply softly. "That he needs time."

"Your husband is smart." We're quiet for a moment, and then she adds, "He's also quite handsome."

I grin at her. "I know. Damn it, I tried to not be affected by his chiseled jawline and hot blue eyes, but I failed miserably."

Mom laughs again and sips the last of her tea. "No

one could blame you. Not at all. Now, you need to stop worrying so much and trust that all of this is going to work out."

I nod. "I hope so. I love my family too much to never see them again."

"Psh," she says, shaking her head. "It's been two days, Millie. Trust me, it's going to be fine."

"When should I try to talk to Dad? Should I give him space and let it fester or go confront him right away?"

"Your father loves you deeply. Don't ever forget that. I'd give him a couple of days, and then go see him. Maybe by yourself this time."

"Okay." I feel so much better. I needed this time with her. "I'm really glad you came over."

"Me, too. I wanted to run after you as soon as you pulled away from the house, but I had to settle everyone else down and help your father process some stuff. I think the bottle of whiskey he nursed all night did more for him than I did."

My eyes go wide. "He drank a whole bottle of whiskey?"

"He went for a second bottle, but I intervened and sent him to bed."

I blow out a breath. "Poor Dad."

"He'll be okay. You both will. Now, I'd better get back home." She stands and pulls me in for another hug. "Just be happy, Millie. That's all we want for you. If Holden gives you that happiness, you take it, and you hold on to it."

"Thank you, Mama." I kiss her cheek and then walk her to the door. "I love you."

"I love you, too." She pats my cheek, and then she's off, headed to her SUV. "Oh, I made you a meatloaf."

I can't stop the laughter that bubbles through me. "You didn't have to do that."

"I needed to do something, and being in the kitchen soothes me." She pulls an insulated box out of the back seat and brings it to me. "It's cold. I had it in the fridge all afternoon. Just pop it in the oven until it's heated through."

"You're the best mom."

She laughs and returns to her car. "Call me tomorrow."

I wave and watch her leave, then take the meatloaf to the fridge and put it away.

I have so many feelings running through me. I'm sad for Holden and his family, and relieved that I got to talk it all out with my mom. I'm not as tired as I was when I first saw her, and I feel like a big weight has been lifted, but I really need some air.

I could go for a walk. It's not dark out yet, and I could just take a nice, long walk through the neighborhood. But I know half of the people who live on this street, and I don't want to get stopped to chat.

Without overthinking it, I grab my keys and bag and get into my SUV. The drive out to Holden's ranch only takes five minutes longer than if I were going to my family ranch because the two have neighboring property lines, and I take the little dirt road to the spot that Holden took me to yesterday.

I pull up to a stop and get out of the car and stare at my mountain.

I've considered it to be *my mountain* since I was a little girl.

I take a long, deep breath, pulling in all the freshness and stillness around me, and then exhale, letting go of the hurt and pain.

I've carried sadness and hurt for a long time. Far longer than the past two days.

And it's time to let it all go and move forward.

Because the bad is just too heavy to carry.

CHAPTER TWELVE

HOLDEN

"Hey, boss." Levi sticks his head in the doorway. "There's something on the trail cam you should see."

I frown and immediately flip on a screen. "Which one?"

"Number six. North road. I don't recognize the vehicle. Could be someone who's lost, but they came pretty far in for that."

I page through until camera six comes on screen and feel a jolt of surprise work through me.

"That's Millie."

"Oh." Levi straightens. "Sorry, I don't think we know what your wife's car looks like."

"I don't plan on her being here much." I stand and push my chair in. "I'll go go see what she's up to. If I don't come back to the barn tonight, keep me posted on Sunshine."

"Will do. I don't think she's going to foal tonight, but I'll keep you posted."

I nod as I grab my keys and drive out to the spot I brought Millie to, relieved to see that she's still parked out here when I pull in beside her.

She turns, her arms wrapped around her middle, hugging herself. Her thick, chestnut-brown hair is down and blowing in the light spring breeze. She's not crying, much to my relief.

I've seen my girl cry way too much over the past few days. I want to see the fire back in her eyes, even if it means she tells me to fuck off.

She turns back to stare at the mountain as I approach her, my hands shoved into my pockets.

"I know you don't want me on your ranch." She swallows hard and shakes her head. "But—"

"You are always welcome to come here," I inform her easily. "Always."

"How did you know where I was?"

"We have cameras set up. Levi saw your car come in and told me someone was here." I want to reach out and touch her, but I can't exactly read her mood, so I wait. "How did your visit with Joy go?"

"Great." Her lips tip up into a small smile. "She knows everything now. I had to talk about it. The only thing I didn't tell her was why we got married."

She turns to me with a frown.

"We haven't really discussed if we're going to keep that just to ourselves."

“I’d like to, but if you’re not comfortable—”

“It’s fine,” she says with a shrug. “I don’t mind. My mom always puts things into perspective for me and makes me feel better.”

“I’m glad. Millie, I can’t read you right now. I need you to tell me how you feel and if I can touch you, because I need to touch you.”

She blows out a breath and turns to face me now, letting her arms fall to her sides.

“Relieved.” Her eyes—more green than gold right now—aren’t impassive anymore, and I can see the relief in them. “I just had to let a lot of shit go, you know? I needed to shake off the anger and resentment so I could just...live. Live my life and be happy, and I feel a lot lighter.”

“That was some conversation with your mom.”

She grins, takes a long, deep breath with her face pointed up at the sky, lets it out, and then looks at me again.

“About the second part of your question.”

I lift an eyebrow.

“Please, for the love of Betty White, touch me.”

That’s all the invitation I need. In two strides, I’m in front of her, her face in my hands and my mouth on her lips, and heat rushes down every nerve ending in my body.

Millie groans against my lips and pushes her fingers into my hair, fisting them there.

“Not here,” I whisper against her cheek as I kiss my way down to her neck, every instinct telling me to lean in, not back away, but there are cameras, and I won't do this out here. "I'm not doing this outside again because you deserve a bed, and once I get you naked, you'll stay that way for a while. And I won't make love to you *here*."

"At the ranch or at this specific place?"

"I'm working on exorcising the ghosts, but it's going to take a while yet." She wraps her arms around me, so sweetly that it makes my heart ache, and I do the same, pulling her in for a long, tight hug. "We need to go home."

"I wish we didn't have two cars." I can hear the smile in her voice. "I'd kind of like to give you a blow job while you drive. Not that I've given any blowjobs in my life, but I think it would be a good time."

Taking her by the shoulders, I yank her back and stare down into her smirking face. *Fuck me.*

"Thought that might get a rise out of you."

"In more ways than one." Jesus, I'm so hard. I have to reach down and readjust myself in these jeans. "Let's go. Now. Get in your fucking car."

"Okay, I'll meet you there."

"I'm following you."

Millie rolls her eyes. "You don't have to do that. I'll be perfectly safe."

"Less talking, more driving, sexy woman."

She giggles at that, and she's right. I do see the change in her compared to how she was just a couple of hours ago. Her shoulders are lighter, as if the weight of the world has been lifted from her, and that makes me happy for her.

It's twenty long minutes before we pull into the driveway. I'm at her car door before she can even open it and offer her a hand. When we get to the front door of the little house that we share, I punch in the code, and then we're inside. Her keys and bag hit the floor, and she launches herself into my arms, wrapping her legs around me and kissing me like she's a woman on a mission.

Everything she is wraps itself around me. She smells like honeysuckle and sunshine, and when I push my hand under her shirt, her skin is warm and soft over her ribcage.

"You're so fucking incredible." I carry her to the sofa and sit with her straddling me, and this amazing woman crosses her arms at her waist, grips her T-shirt, and pulls it over her head, dropping it to the floor, and my mouth goes dry. "Fucking hell, Mill."

"You, too." She's moved back on my legs so she has access to my shirt, clawing at it to get it off me, and I oblige her, pulling it over my head and casting it aside with hers. "*Holden.*"

With fire in her gorgeous eyes, her fingertips gently trace the tattoos on my right shoulder and down my arm, circling around the pink wild rose there. She licks her lips as my hands roam up her sides and then over to her fucking gorgeous breasts, where I tease her already tight nipples.

"I want to ask you so many questions about these," she whispers and then gasps and tips her head back when I pinch a little harder.

"You can ask me anything. Later." I sit up and take

her mouth, knowing that I'll never get enough of her. She's grinding on me, pushing her breasts against my chest, and I unfasten the elastic on her back, and she lets the bra fall down her arms. Without missing a beat, my mouth fastens onto one hard nub, making her arch her back as she holds on to my shoulders. "Baby."

"God, your mouth," she groans. "How did I live without your mouth on me?"

"We have to move."

"Not if it means you stop doing that."

I grin against her skin, fucking loving everything about her, and rake my teeth over her sensitive flesh, satisfied when she breaks out into goose bumps.

"I need to lay you out and see every glorious inch of you, baby girl. Goddamn it, I'm going to fucking *worship* you."

"Well, when you put it like that."

I stand with her still in my arms and walk down the short hallway to our bedroom, lay her on the bed, and unfasten her jeans. She lifts her hips, making it easier for me to slide them down her long, lean legs, and then she's lying here in nothing but some little blue panties.

There's a wet spot covering her pussy, and it makes me growl.

"Your turn," she murmurs, but I ignore her as I crawl onto the bed and take her thighs in my hands, spread her wide, and kiss her over that blue fabric, inhaling her. Millie's hands fist in the bedding as her whole body engages. "Oh, dear God."

"Jesus, look how wet you are. You're fucking perfect."

I grin up at her as I kiss my way north. Yes, I want to devour her pussy, but it's going to have to wait while I explore her.

Her stomach ripples under my lips, and I dip my nose into her navel.

So much about her is the same as eight years ago, but so much is different. She's grown up, become even more of a woman, and I can't fucking get enough of her.

"Why are you so good at that?" she murmurs. "Don't answer that."

I laugh and roll her nipple under my fingers as I kiss the other one. "We have to set some ground rules, Rosie."

"No more rules." She rolls her head back and forth, her eyebrows pulled together in a frown. "I'm so over the rules. We're already breaking the biggest one anyway."

"These are important." I kiss up her sternum and over her collarbone, and I absolutely fucking *love* the way her hips are moving under me, as if she's searching for my cock.

And she'll get it.

"Number one." I nibble at the side of her lips. "If at any time you want me to stop, or you aren't comfortable, you say so."

"Not shy, remember?"

I grin against her jawline. "Good. Number two." My hand grazes up her side, and my girl purrs.

Fucking *purrs.*

"There is nothing you can say or do while we're together that could ever turn me off or change the way I feel. You don't hold back, Millie. Do you understand me?"

"Hmm."

I take her jaw in my hands and make her look me in the eye.

"Tell me you understand."

"You got way bossier." I simply raise an eyebrow, and she grins. "No holding back. Got it. When are you going to take off your pants?"

"In a minute." She'll have questions, and this will stall, and I'm not ready for that. I'm going to make her come at least once before she sees the metal in my cock. "Number three."

"Holden?"

"Just one more, baby girl. One more." My hand drifts up her belly, between her breasts, and holds on to her throat, just under the jaw, the way I've always done. "As soon as we do this, you're *mine.* There's no going back from this. I'm going to erase the memory of anyone who has been here since me, and there will be no one after."

That has her golden eyes, so full of green now, widening.

"Holden." It's a whisper.

"Tell me you understand what I just said. I need the words."

She holds on to my wrist but doesn't pull me away. She licks her lips, lets her gaze fall to my mouth, and then flicks it back to my eyes. She suddenly looks nervous.

"Holden."

"Yes, baby?"

"There's been no one since you."

The world stops fucking spinning. I can't look away from her as my vision blurs. My heart is going to pound out of my chest.

"What did you just say?" My voice is ragged, raw with emotion as I cup her face.

"No one," she whispers, vulnerability heavy in those eyes as she confesses to me that the one and only time I was inside of her is the only experience she has with sex.

How is that fucking possible?

She mistakes my silence for something bad because the shutters start to come down over her eyes, and I lean in to kiss her tenderly.

"Don't you dare." I brush my lips over hers twice more as my hands drift down her arms. "You stay here with me. Don't you shut me out. I'm just so...fuck, Millie."

"Yes, fuck Millie."

I chuckle against her lips, still trying to process this new bit of information.

In the eight years since she was with me, there's been *no one.*

Not one single motherfucker has had his hands on her. His cock inside of her.

"I hate it when you're quiet," she says, pulling her fingers down my cheek again. "I should have told you I fucked dozens of men, then you wouldn't have slowed down."

I narrow my eyes and kiss her softly and slowly.

I don't deserve this. There is no universe in which I deserve everything good and wonderful about this woman.

"*Millie.*"

She smiles so softly, so sweetly, that it makes me ache. Her gaze lifts, and she watches her own fingers brush my hair off my forehead.

"Holden, I'm going to need you to break this really long dry spell I've had. Okay? We can get emotional and talk about our feelings later. Right now, you need to keep doing what you were doing because you're really good at it, and I need you inside of me."

She leans up to kiss me, and that's all it takes for my head to get back in the game. She's right, we can hash this out later. Much later.

Right now, I'm going to fuck my girl senseless.

"You're so goddamn sweet," I murmur as I kiss my way to her ear and my hands resume their exploration of her body. "Do you have condoms in here?"

She looks up at me like, *really?* And it makes me smirk.

"Been on birth control for a long time," she says and then scowls at me. "If some skank gave you a disease—"

I laugh again, continuing to kiss her, pressing her down into the mattress.

I can't stop kissing this woman. I will never stop kissing her until the day I die. She's my life force. My reason for everything.

"No diseases, baby girl." Now, I make my way down her torso, back to that little wet spot inside of her panties. I want to devour her, lick every inch of her, and make her scream my name.

"Take your pants off."

I shake my head and nibble on her navel. "After you come on my mouth, and not a minute before."

"Holden—"

"Number four," I interrupt, pinning her in my hot gaze, satisfied when her eyes widen. "You're not in charge here, Rosie. That's me. Now shut up and let me fucking worship you."

She plants her teeth in her bottom lip, her eyes go glassy, and I take that to mean that she likes it when I take control.

Good. I'll be doing it often.

Once I've nudged my shoulders between her legs, I hook my finger in the side of her soaking-wet panties and tug them out of the way so I can stare down at her glistening slit.

"Baby, you're so goddamn wet for me."

She moans, watching me with hot eyes as I lean in and lick her, from her opening to her clit, and she falls back to the bed, gripping the bedding in her fists.

"Holy fucking shit."

Now, it's time to get to work. I flick my tongue over her clit and then down to her lips and pull them into my mouth, pulsing around them.

Millie's hands dive into my hair and hold on tight.

"So goddamn beautiful," I whisper before I lick up again and insert a finger into her, then groan when she squeezes around me like a vise.

Jesus Christ, she's going to kill me.

Her hips are moving in circles, encouraging me to move, to continue giving her the best time of her life.

And nothing could make me stop now.

I add another finger and crook them up, rubbing that rough patch that makes her thrash her head from side to side, incoherent thoughts coming out of her beautiful mouth as she continues to squeeze around me.

"That's right." I replace my tongue with my thumb for just a second, wanting to talk to her. "Give into it, baby girl. Don't you hold back on me. Lose control, Millie. Give it to me. God, you're fucking gorgeous."

"*Holden.*"

"Give it to me. Come on my mouth."

I cover her again, licking and sucking, pushing my fingers in and out of her. She starts to contract, her legs start to shake, and she screams out as the orgasm moves through her, and I can't lap her up fast enough.

She's breathing hard and moaning softly as I place wet kisses on her thighs, at that junction of her leg and core, and finally, I pull her panties off and toss them over my shoulder, then lick my own fingers clean, wanting every last drop of her in my mouth.

"Get. Naked." Her voice is firm, demanding, and I grin up at her, not bothering to wipe my face off before I lunge up and cover her mouth with mine.

She lets out a startled moan, and then she holds on to my face, kissing me fervently, as I unfasten my jeans and work them down my hips.

Her hands move down my sides, and she cups my

balls, making me see fucking stars. Jesus, I'll do anything she wants. *Anything.*

Then that talented little hand moves up my hard, pulsing cock, and when she gets to the tip, her eyes fly open.

"What the fuck is *that*?"

CHAPTER THIRTEEN

MILLIE

"Let me see it." I try to scramble out from under him, but Holden holds firm, his blue eyes hot on me. Jesus, my body is on fire. He makes me feel things that I've never felt before. I didn't know it was possible to freaking feel like I'll combust if he doesn't fuck me. "Holden, let me at your cock."

"Fuck, I love your mouth." He bites my lower lip, then soothes it with his tongue. "I know you have questions, and I'll answer them *after* I fuck you, Rosie. After I'm inside of you, and I make you come again."

"Let me have a peek." I bite my lip, and his eyes fall to my mouth. "*Please.*"

He pushes up onto his knees and holds his big, hard dick in his hand, and I can't take my eyes off of the metal shining at the tip.

Two bars, one on top of the other, just under the head of his cock.

"Fucking hell, that had to hurt."

"That was the point."

I frown up at him, and he shakes his head. "Later. We'll talk *later*, baby girl."

He leans forward and rubs himself through my wet slit, and I inhale sharply as pure electricity shoots through me. And when those metal balls rub against my clit, I'm pretty sure I see stars. I might even get a glimpse of heaven.

"I'm being rewarded," I mutter before I bite down on my lip, trying to catch my breath.

"What?" He laughs and tweaks my nipple as the head of his cock continues to do amazing things to my core.

"Rewarded. For the dry spell. Jesus Christ, Holden." I reach for him, and he covers me again, smiling down at me as he rests himself at my opening. "Please, I need you inside of me. Right now."

He kisses me, his tongue pressing inside my mouth as his cock slowly, ever so damn *slowly,* fills me up, and we both let out a long, low groan. He's finally here, and I feel like I could cry. Just sob and weep for all the years we've missed. He lowers his head and rests his lips against my own.

"You are the sexiest woman I've ever fucking laid eyes on."

And then he's moving in and out of me in the most delicious rhythm. My hips move with his, as if we've been doing this together for years, as if no time has passed between us at all, and he buries his face in my neck, his breath hitching.

"God, I missed you, baby girl." He nibbles on my skin,

just below my ear, and it pushes me closer to my own release. "You're so fucking incredible. So beautiful."

"Oh, shit." I feel it moving through me again. I may not have had sex with a man since Holden, but I've given myself orgasms over the years. Plenty, if I'm being honest.

But they've never felt like this.

"I'm gonna come. Oh, shit, Holden."

"Yes, baby. Come for me. Come all over me, my precious girl. My Rosie."

His voice, combined with the way that metal is massaging inside of me, and just *everything*, is my undoing.

I explode, clinging to him, my legs wrapped around him. I push and tighten and lose complete control of myself as I have the most incredible orgasm of my life.

"That's my girl," he croons, but his voice is tight, and I want him to go over with me. I want him to let go.

"Come," I whisper in his ear. "Inside of me."

His breath catches, and he thrusts three more times before he comes with a roar, rocking into me as he spills himself inside of me.

I *love* it when he collapses on top of me, breathing hard, giving me his weight, if only for a minute before he rolls to the side, bringing me with him. We're still linked, and I can feel the metal drag along my flesh, and it makes me tighten around him again.

"God damn," he mutters, tracing my lips with his fingertip. "Are you okay?"

"Am I *okay*?" I look up at the ceiling, taking stock.

"No. I wouldn't use that word at all. Not okay. I'm...well-fucked. I'm...humming. I'm really happy."

His smile is bright and proud, and he kisses my nose and then my lips. "I'm going to clean you up before we make an even bigger mess."

He pulls out, making me whimper as my nerve endings wake up once more, and with a smirk, he walks out of the room, giving me a stellar view of his impressive ass.

When he returns moments later, he has a warm cloth with him, and he gently wipes me off, then tosses the cloth into my hamper, and we snuggle down under the covers.

"Questions," I begin, and he chuckles.

"Hit me with them. I'll answer anything, you know that."

I curl into him, my head on the crook of his shoulder, and wrap my arm around his middle, and he presses his lips to my forehead. His fingers drag up and down my spine, and it makes me want to purr. Lying next to him, naked, feels luxurious, and I take a second to just soak it in.

"You're not asking," he murmurs before pressing his lips to my forehead and leaving them there.

"There's no rush." I nuzzle his chest. I know that I'm not typically super affectionate, but I can't seem to keep my hands and lips off this man. It's...comforting, being here in his arms. "You know I'm going to ask about the piercings."

"I figured." His fingertips drag up and down my spine

again and then into my hair, and I push into his fingers, as if I were a feline.

"And the tattoos. You've done a lot to your body since I last saw you naked, Holden."

"Hmm," he agrees. "How deep are we getting here, Rosie?"

"You were just so deep inside of me that you practically pierced a lung, so I'd say we can get pretty personal."

That makes him laugh, and then he rolls me to my side and kisses me softly and slowly.

"You're funny," he murmurs softly, nuzzling my nose. God, cuddly Holden is awesome. "You've always been funny."

I love lying here like this, with just the soft glow of the bedside light on, under the covers with this man. It feels so sweet and intimate, and I hope we do it often.

"You don't have to tell me if you don't want to." I cup his face, and he turns to press a kiss to my palm.

"It started with the wild rose tat," he begins as he takes my hand in his and links our fingers, then holds them close between us. I can't get enough of how his inked skin looks against my untouched flesh.

"When did you do that?"

"About a month after I ended things with you."

My eyes widen in surprise. "Holy shit, Holden."

"I was missing you, and it hurt. So, I decided to get something that hurt *physically* so I could try to mask the pain in my heart. And that's how it went for eight long years."

I swallow hard, trying to will away the tears.

"Every time the missing you got to be too much, I'd get another one. And another, until the sleeve was finished."

I'm tracing the ink with my free hand, listening intently. He did all of this because he missed me?

"Why the piercings, Holden?"

My gaze finds his again, and he looks so unbearably sad that it takes my breath away.

"The first one was when you graduated college, and I couldn't celebrate with you. During the month we were together, I'd decided that when you graduated, I'd take you wherever you wanted to go. Europe, or somewhere tropical. I didn't care. It was about you and what you wanted."

"We were together before my sophomore year, Holden."

His eyes just hold mine, and my heart aches a little more.

"And the second?" I ask when he doesn't answer.

"When you bought the coffee shop. I was so fucking proud of you, Rosie. *So* proud. I wanted to throw you a big party and make a fuss, and I had no right to do that. It wasn't my place. And that fucking killed me."

"You brought me flowers," I whisper, unable to look him in the eyes. "Beautiful flowers, and I called you an asshole."

"Hey." His fingers are under my chin, and he tips my face up to look at him. "Baby, don't do that to yourself."

"I was so mean," I whisper. "And you were so nice to

me. But I was confused, and I didn't trust it. And even though it happened years before, I still wanted to punish you for being such a jerk."

"I deserved it." He kisses my lips tenderly, and I can't help but think that he *didn't* deserve it. I just didn't know any better.

"And the hand?" I ask when he pulls back. "Your sleeve used to end at your wrist, until last fall."

"I thought you were fucking Bridger." It's said so simply, I have to pause and take in the words.

"You got your hand inked up because you thought I was fucking someone else?"

"Yes." His blue eyes don't leave mine. He doesn't look away or flinch or waver. I swallow hard.

"Holden, let me get this straight. For the past eight years, you've purposefully inflicted pain on yourself because of *me*?"

"No." His hand rests on my throat, so gently that that alone brings tears to my eyes. "I did it as a punishment for what I put you through and as a way to dull all the other horrible shit in my life."

"Your father."

He narrows his eyes. "He was a huge part of it, yeah."

"God, I feel so guilty." I move into him, wrapping myself around him in a tight hug. I can't get close enough to him.

"Shh, baby. No, don't feel guilty. It was all my own doing."

I shake my head and pull back to look up at him. "I

flirted with you like crazy at that farmer's market. I basically made you take my phone number."

"Are you under the impression that I don't know how to say no when I'm not interested in a woman?" His eyebrow lifts, but it doesn't make me feel better. "Millie, I knew going into it that my father would be pissed. We both did, but we did it anyway. And I wouldn't change it. Well, I *would* change how it ended and what he did. But I can't."

"I'm so sorry." I take his face in my hands, desperate to make him see how much regret I have. "That you went through all of that. I'm *so sorry*, Holden."

"Baby girl." He kisses me and then simply pulls me against him, his hand covering the back of my head as he hugs me close. "Please don't. I'm okay. I'm here with you, and that's all I ever wanted."

"I want to kill him," I admit into his neck as I shudder with pure rage. "Over and over again. He should have to suffer, for what he did to your sisters, to you, to *us*. Jesus, I'm so fucking pissed."

Holden sighs and kisses my temple so tenderly. "We need to move on, Millie. We can't stay stuck here."

"I know. It's really not healthy." I plant a kiss on his neck and then his jawline. "I do have a confession, though."

His eyes narrow. "I'm listening."

"Although I don't love the reasoning behind the ink and the piercings, they're hot as fuck."

That devastating smile spreads over his lips, and I push him onto his back, covering him with my body.

"Now, enough serious stuff for a minute. I have some time to make up for."

He doesn't argue. In fact, he doesn't say anything at all as I kiss over his shoulder and down his pecs. My hands roam over his washboard stomach and down to the perfect V that makes up his hips.

I may not be experienced, but I'm not a kid, and I'm not shy with Holden.

He's already hard again, that silver metal winking at me as I take his cock in my hand and press the tip against me, then lower myself onto him.

His hands span my hips, and when I start to raise and lower, he guides me effortlessly.

"Fuuuuck," I moan, loving the way it feels from this angle. So deep, hitting places that he hasn't before, and I can't help but let my head fall back as I ride him.

"You're a goddamn goddess," he growls as one hand cups my breast, rolling the nipple between his fingers. "Look at you. My God, just look at you."

His words only make me feel sexier, and I move faster and reach down to cover my clit with my fingers, and his eyes go black.

"That's it, baby girl, fucking touch yourself."

I clench around him, and he bares his teeth.

"Good girl. Oh, baby."

I love it when he talks to me when we're having sex. It makes me hotter. Makes me move harder and faster, and suddenly, he sits up and wraps his arms around me and kisses me as we make love, sitting up in the middle of the bed.

"Go over," he whispers against my lips. "Come for me, baby girl."

I couldn't deny him if I wanted to. This orgasm rolls through me like thunder rumbling lazily in the sky, and Holden's eyes close as he rests his forehead on mine and follows me into his own climax.

Just when we've settled back into bed, and we're about to fall asleep, my back pressed to his front and his arms wrapped around me, he whispers, "I have a question for you, Rosie."

"Okay." My voice is soft, and I sound very satisfied. "Ask me."

"Why no one else?"

I don't tense up. I don't try to come up with excuses. A week ago, I would have done both of those things, but too much has happened for half-truths or evading.

"Because they weren't you."

His arms tighten around me, and I catch another glimmer of metal in the moonlight.

Our wedding rings, where our hands are linked together.

"Sleep well, husband," I whisper.

"Goodnight, wife."

I WAKE UP TO AN ORGASM.

"What the fuck?" My hips buck, and my hands instinctively reach for Holden's hair. His face is planted in my core, licking and sucking on my clit, and his fingers are already inside me, and I don't even know how we got here.

"Good morning," he growls against me. "Time to wake up, baby girl."

"*Fuck*."

"Oh, we will." He grins up at me as his fingers work faster, and then he's crawling over me, easily slipping inside. When he's balls-deep, he kisses me long and slow. "Had to make sure you were ready for me."

"I think that's a yes."

He's moving in long strokes, filling me up and pulling away, over and over again, and the friction from his metal is delicious.

He takes my hand and pins it above my head on the mattress, and, using that as leverage, he moves faster and harder.

"Mine," he growls in my ear. "Tell me you're mine."

"Yours." I swallow hard, so lost to him I can't think straight. "Always."

After just a few more thrusts, we're both coming apart at the seams, and then he picks me up and takes me to the shower.

He's quiet as he washes me, and then himself, and rinses us both before lifting me against the tile and fucking me again. I'm so sore all over, but I can't tell him no because he's looking at me as if he can't get enough of me.

As if I might vanish.

"I'm right here," I assure him, framing his face in my

hands and kissing him gently as he continues to thrust into me against the wall. "I'm *right here.*"

He groans and kisses me hard, rocks against my clit, and sends us both over into another climax.

"We're going to be late," he says, but he's leaning on both hands flat against the wall, breathing hard and staring down at me.

"Don't pull away from me." I frown up at him. "I feel you shutting down, and I won't have it, Holden."

"I'm not." He pulls me to him and hugs me close as the hot water continues to spray against us. "I promise, that's not it. Last time, the morning after was my worst nightmare, and—"

"Never again." I shake my head emphatically. "It'll never be like that again. You'll see me later today. I promise."

He kisses the top of my head and then my forehead before sighing and letting me go.

"Thank you." He turns off the tap and reaches for a towel, making sure that I'm dry before he uses the same damp towel on himself.

Before long, we're dressed and ready to leave the house for the day.

"Are you planning to walk to work?"

"Yes." I lift my chin, almost defiantly, at my husband. "It's a nice day out there."

"Then I'll drive beside you and make sure you get there safely."

"You're not going to drive three miles an hour next to me."

He puts his hat on his head and smirks down at me. "Watch me."

"Holden—"

"I don't think that's my name anymore."

I frown at him. "Are you having a stroke?"

"I think I liked the other word better. Right before we fell asleep."

I blink, thinking back, and then sigh. "*Husband*, I'm perfectly capable of walking to work."

"No." He kisses me hard and then shoos me—*shoos me!*—out the door to his truck. "Humor me, baby girl."

"You're really overbearing, you know that, right?"

He just shrugs, and then we're on our way to my shop. He pulls up to the curb out front, and before I can jump out, he grabs my hand and tugs me to him, kissing me hard.

"Have a good day, wife."

I grin against his lips. "You, too. See you later."

After one last peck on the mouth, I hop out and unlock the door. Once I'm safely inside, Holden pulls away, headed for the ranch.

My body is *sore*. I'm not used to any of what we did last night, but it's not a bad sore. It's...satisfying. I even have rough spots inside my thighs from Holden's scruff, and while it's not exactly comfortable, it's a fun reminder of what he was doing down there.

I take two steps farther in and then stop. The hair on the back of my neck stands up.

Something isn't right.

Immediately, I pull my phone out of my pocket and

call my brother. Chase is a cop in Bitterroot Valley, and I know he'll be here ASAP.

"Millie?"

"I know we're not great right now, but something isn't right at my shop."

"Two minutes," is all he says, and then disconnects.

Should I call Holden back? That seems silly, since I don't even know for sure if anything is wrong. It just feels *off*.

I open my phone and discover that *Big Jerk* has been replaced with *Your Husband*, and it makes me grin. Quickly, I shoot him a text.

Me: Hey, something's weird here. Chase is on his way. Just wanted to tell you.

As soon as that's sent off, Chase is standing at the door, dressed in his uniform. He must have gone to work early today.

"Hey," I say as I open up for him. "It's probably nothing."

"What's wrong?" His eyes are already skimming the area. "Is something out of place?"

"I don't know. I got three steps in, and it felt weird, so I called you. I know that's lame—"

"It's not," he interrupts and kisses me on the forehead. "Always trust your gut, Mill. I'm going to look around, okay?"

I nod, grateful that he's here.

"Thank you."

I wait for him by the front door, and after about five

minutes, he returns, shaking his head. "I don't see anything out of order. The back door is locked. Did you see anything on your cameras?"

He insisted that I have security cameras installed at the front and back doors when I bought this place.

"No, nothing was triggered. It's probably all in my head." I take a breath, and then I can't help myself. I hug him. "I'm sorry, Chase."

"No, *I'm* sorry. I should have called you before. I'm just too stubborn."

"I don't know how Summer puts up with you."

He chuckles and lets me go. "Me neither. Are you okay?"

Suddenly, there's knocking on the door, and I whirl around to find Holden there, eyes dark, his whole body tense.

"Oh, I texted him," I say as I hurry over and let him in. "It's nothing. Chase looked around, and there's nothing wrong."

"Are you sure?" Holden asks my brother, who just nods soberly. Holden turns to me and frames my face.

"I just had a weird gut feeling after you left, but I was wrong. You didn't have to come back."

"Baby girl, you texted and said that something was wrong, and you called your brother, the cop. Do you think I wouldn't immediately get my ass over here?"

I bite my lip. "Well, yeah, I guess you're right. I shouldn't have texted."

Chase laughs behind me, and I turn to scowl at him.

“Good luck with her,” Chase says as he walks past us to the door. “She’s a wild one, you know.”

“Thank you for coming,” Holden says.

“She’s my sister, dude. Of course, I came. I’ll see you later.”

He waves, and then he’s off, and Holden is still tense as he stares down at me.

“You can go to the ranch.”

“You scared me,” he says softly. “And before you say something stupid, *yes*, you should have called me.”

“Aww, that’s sweet.” He narrows his eyes, and I laugh, then boost myself up on my toes and kiss him. “Now, you go to work so I can, too. Everything’s fine here. Nothing even tripped the cameras. It’s just my crazy imagination.”

“First, I’ll have a look around.” I start to object because Chase just did that, but Holden shakes his head and glowers at me. “You stay here.”

“Okay. Overprotective much?” I mutter as he walks away. I prop my hands on my hips and nibble my lip. I kind of love that he rushed back here after my text. It makes me feel...cared for. After just a couple of minutes, Holden returns, more relaxed now.

“I didn’t see anything.”

“Told you.”

“You’re my wife,” he says as he pulls me into his arms. “I’m glad your brother came right away, but I’ll always make sure that you’re safe, Rosie.”

“Maybe it was an excuse to get your fine ass back here so you’d kiss me some more.”

He grins against my lips and obliges me, dipping me back and devouring my mouth, making my head freaking spin.

"Mmm. Yeah, it was totally a ploy," I murmur, making him chuckle. "Now, go to work, babe, before I take you into the back room and have my way with you."

"I don't know who *babe* is." His eyes narrow on me, smoldering in a way that makes my thighs clench with anticipation.

"Holden."

"Try again." He cocks an eyebrow.

"Big Jerk."

His lips twitch, but he shakes his head *no.*

"Husband, you need to go to work now."

He growls and kisses me again, and when he pulls away, my head is spinning even more than before.

"Go." I point him to the door and give him a little push. "I'll see you later."

"Call me if you need *anything.*"

"Yes, yes, I will." I make a motion with my hands, shooing him out. "Have a good day."

"I'm going to spank you later, just for that."

"You can try, husband. You can try."

CHAPTER FOURTEEN

HOLDEN

It's been a week and one day since she married me. It's been the best fucking week of my life. Millie is my wife, she's all mine, and she's the most amazing, gorgeous creature on this planet.

Now, I need to finish tearing down what my father loved so I can move forward with her.

"Thanks for letting me board the horses here overnight," I say to Beckett Blackwell, shaking his hand. "I didn't want to scare the hell out of them today."

"Understandable. You're burning it *all* down?" he asks, raising a brow.

"Everything I can," I confirm. "I can't burn the barn until I have a new one built, so that's the next project."

"Do you need more help out there today?" he asks as I rub my horse's cheek.

"Bridger's bringing our fire department and a couple of guys from surrounding areas who want to train. I'll have my ranch hands there, too, so I think we're good."

"Well, just call if you want us to come help," he says. "And don't worry about these guys. They're safe here."

The Blackwell property, called the Double B Ranch, has always been a safe place for me and my sisters.

And today is no different.

"I appreciate it. Mind if we come get them tomorrow?"

"Whenever the fire's out and you're ready for them, just come get them. You don't need to call ahead."

Nodding, I hop into the truck with Levi, who's already in the driver's seat, ready to drive back to the property.

"I'm glad they're safe here, especially that tiny foal," Levi says.

Sunshine finally gave birth a couple of days ago, and it's a little thing.

"Agreed."

While Levi drives, I shoot a group text to my sisters.

Me: Good morning, girls. FYI, I'm burning everything down today. Just wanted to let you know.

Before I can put the phone away, responses come flooding in.

Charlie: We should have a party.

Dani: It's about time!

Darby: Do you need us out there?

Alex: I could bring some marshmallows.

I chuckle and reply.

Me: No need to come out. No party or marshmallows today, but maybe later this week at our place in town. Love you guys.

Lots of heart emojis come in, and then I shove my phone into my pocket.

"You're ready for this?" Levi asks me.

"Beyond ready."

"Can I be frank?"

I turn to look at his profile. Levi's a couple of years older than me. I've known him a long time.

"I prefer it."

He nods. "I'm glad you're burning it all to the ground. Your dad was evil enough that he's soaked into everything out there, turning something that was once beautiful into a dumpster fire. If you erase all of that and start new, it could be something really great again."

I swallow hard and stare out the windshield. My voice is rough when I say, "Yeah. That's my plan. I need that son of a bitch gone, once and for all."

"Then let's go get the fucker gone."

When we pull in, Bridger and his men are already here, their trucks parked strategically about, ready to direct the fire if they need to.

Our primary goal today is to burn this safely, without lighting the nearby trees on fire, too.

"We're soaking those evergreens," Bridger says by way of greeting, shaking my hand as he joins us. "And you want to start with the farmhouse?"

"Yeah. I do."

"Great, let's get started. You're sure you don't want to pull anything else out from inside the structures?"

"No. Torch it all."

Bridger grins at me. "This is going to be fucking fun."

We work as a team, getting a couple of wooden pallets, loaded with a combination of diesel and gasoline, into the center of the building. I don't look around, don't give the goddamn memories a chance to assault me as I keep my head down and focus on what we're doing. We move through the house, opening all the windows so there's plenty of oxygen to fuel the fire.

"We want these here in the center of the first floor," Bridger says as we set them down. "We also want to tear some of this drywall out so we expose the beams and get things moving more evenly and quickly."

"I'll get a sledgehammer," I reply.

An hour later, I'm standing behind Bridger as he lights the wooden pallets with a blowtorch, and then we back out of the house and wait for the flames to spread.

"The guys are going to train on the house, and we can get the other structures ignited. They're smaller, so they won't take as long. Mind if I take my guys for this?"

"Go ahead," I reply with a nod. I wanted to be the one to make sure that the farmhouse was decimated first and foremost.

The flames are louder than I expected. Glass breaks. It's amazing to see how quickly fire can spread.

At the sound of tires approaching, I turn and feel my eyebrows wing up when I see that it's Remington Wild pulling in.

He parks a safe distance away and then strides to me, his eyes on the house now engulfed in flames.

"You okay, Holden?"

I nod and hold my hand out to shake his, which he immediately takes.

"It's a planned burn. I'm sorry, I should have given you a heads-up. You probably saw all the smoke from your place."

"I did. Thought I'd better check in. Can I ask why?"

He lifts an eyebrow at me and gestures to the fires with his chin.

"Because I want anything and everything that my father ever cared about to die with him."

Remington swallows, looking around again. "Understood. Mind if I stay, in case you need the help?"

I narrow my eyes at him and shove my hands into my pockets.

"You want to *help*?"

Rem lets out a breath and shuffles his feet. "My wife thinks I owe you an apology. I usually do whatever Erin wants because she's the best thing in this world, and if she wants it, she gets it."

"I know that feeling."

He narrows his eyes at me. "I've never had an issue with you. I *do* have an issue with you marrying my sister without a word to any of us first, as if it was a big fucking secret. That's my beef. I don't give a rat's ass what your name is. That's my dad's deal, and I can't speak for him."

"Understood."

"So, this might be one of the few times that I don't give my wife what she wants," he continues grimly. "Because I can't apologize for wanting to protect my sister. I suspect you'd do the same for yours if the roles were reversed."

With my eyes on his, I think it over and then nod slowly. "Yeah, I'd likely break your face."

"Exactly. Now, do you want me to stay and help or not?"

I suspect that in the grand scheme of things, this is going to be as close to an olive branch as Remington and I will ever share.

And I'm not going to pass it up.

"You're welcome to stay. We're also lighting up the garage, the shed, and my old cabin, just over there."

"That's a big day," he says with surprise.

"The other departments are on their way," Bridger says as he joins us. "Then we can light the others on fire, and we'll have plenty of teams to keep things under control. Hey, Rem."

"Bridger," Remington says, shaking the other man's hand. "This is...interesting."

"You said it." Bridger grins and then hurries away again, and Remington and I stand side by side, facing the farmhouse. The flames are rolling through now, lighting it up from the inside out.

I can hear the screams that only exist inside my head. My mother sobbing. The girls crying out in pain when Dad would hit them, the terror of the animals when he tortured them.

My mom's last gasp as she tumbled down those stairs and broke her neck.

It's as though the screams and cries are carried up with the smoke, high into the sky.

"What will you do with this once it's all cleaned up?" Rem asks as we walk around to the far side of the house, continuing to watch as the structure is destroyed.

"I'm going to turn it into a pasture and let the cows shit on it."

We're quiet for a moment, and then Remington lets out a startled laugh. When I turn to him in surprise, he continues to laugh, and I can't help but smile back at him.

Suddenly, I hear my name being screamed, and my heart stumbles in my chest as my blood runs cold.

CHAPTER FIFTEEN

MILLIE

"You've been looking *very* happy the past few days," Candy says as I slip past her to make an Americano. "Like someone who's been getting lucky."

"The luckiest." I wink at her and then smirk when Macy looks back at us, her eyes wide, before turning back to take an order from the next customer. "Thanks for noticing."

"Girl, it's impossible to miss. I'm happy for you. Love looks good on you."

Love.

My heart stumbles a bit at that. Do I love him? Absofuckinglutely. There's no denying it, even to myself. If something were to happen and I couldn't be with Holden anymore, my world would stop spinning.

He is my whole heart.

But we haven't said the words yet. Eight years ago, I was young and inexperienced and completely bold with saying those words to him.

And now, despite everything we've been through, the words are the piece that I hold back. However, every single night, we make love and fall asleep wrapped up in each other, as if we never want to let go.

It's the fucking sweetest.

And, I'm becoming a *hugger*.

Which is just weird.

I've just slid the Americano across the counter and called out *Jeff* when Jackie Harmon walks into the shop.

"Did you guys hear?" Her eyes are wide, and I suddenly have a very bad feeling. "There's a big fire out at the Lexington Ranch. I hear it's a rager. I sure hope no one's hurt."

"Go," Candy says, nudging me along. "Get out there. We've got this, no problem."

I look at her, unseeing, and she takes my shoulders in her hands. "Millie. Go to the ranch. Right now. Go."

"Oh, God." My voice breaks, but I run out the door, grateful that it was chilly this morning and that I brought my car to work. I pull my phone out of my pocket as I run.

With my heart in my throat and tears threatening, I dial Holden's number, but he doesn't pick up. It just rings and rings, and when I get the voicemail, my voice is trembling.

"Husband, you better call me right now. RIGHT NOW!"

I toss the phone into the passenger seat and head off for the ranch, driving way faster than I should, but I know this road like the back of my hand.

I could drive it blindfolded.

And I kind of am because I'm blind with fear. Absolute terror.

What if he's hurt? My God, what if—

"No, don't do that," I lecture myself and brush tears from my cheeks. "He's fine. Everything's fine. Deep breaths, Mill. He's fine."

I breathe deeply, but then I choke on a sob.

If he was okay, he'd answer his phone. Or call me back.

Why hasn't he called me back?

I turn onto the main ranch road, and I can see the smoke. God, there's so much smoke. This is a huge fire. And when I get closer to the old farmhouse and Holden's old cabin, there are so many firetrucks, I can't get through.

So, I stop the car, slam it in Park, and don't bother to turn it off or shut the door behind me as I bust out of it and sprint to where the smoke is coming from.

There are so many people. Someone calls out, "Hey, you can't—"

But I ignore them.

"Holden!" God, I can't see him. I only see firefighters. So many firefighters.

"Millie." A strong arm wraps around my waist, pulling me off my feet and stopping me just before the roof of the farmhouse caves in, and I start to scream.

"HOLDEN! HOLDEN! Oh, my God, where is my husband?"

"Millie, you have to stop—"

But then I see him. Oh, God, I see him! He's running, *sprinting,* toward me, and I shake off the person holding me and run to him, jumping into his arms and wrapping myself around him as I weep.

"Oh, God. You're okay. Oh, Jesus."

"Hey, I'm fine. I'm right here, Rosie. I'm fine."

He's holding me and squeezing me, kissing my face, but I can't stop crying. I look up in time to see men with huge, long poles pushing the outside walls of the house toward the middle, as if they're stoking a fire.

Which, I guess they are.

And I can't stop crying.

"I th-thought." I swallow hard as I press my face into his neck. "Fuck, Holden."

"Baby girl, listen to my voice." His lips are at my ear, and he's carrying me away from the fire. I can't take my eyes off of it. Oh, God, what if he'd been inside? "Do you hear me? I need you to listen to me, wife."

Wife. God, I love it when it says that word.

I give a tiny nod.

"I am safe. No one has been hurt. *No one is hurt, Millie.*"

"Y-you can*not* be hurt," I insist through the shudders moving through me.

"Baby. Hear my voice." He sits on something and sets me in his lap, dragging his fingers down my cheek. "Look into my eyes, Rosie."

I do, and it's the first moment that I start to calm down.

"I'm right here." His hand moves to my throat, and

his thumb brushes over my jawline, but I can't help the tears that won't stop. "Ah, baby girl, please don't cry."

"You didn't tell her?"

I frown and look over my shoulder, stunned to see Remington here. His thumbs are in the loops of his jeans, and my mouth opens, but no sound comes out, and I have to try again.

"Am I dead?" I ask.

"Don't you ever say that again," Holden growls into my ear.

"No, really. My brother is standing on Lexington property. You can see it, too, right? What in the alternate universe is going on here?"

"This was a planned fire, Millie," Holden says, pulling my gaze back to his. "Bridger and his guys are using it as a training exercise, and I get to rid this ranch of the last of my father."

"You didn't tell me." The words are a whisper. I'm so *mad.* And still in the middle of a panic attack. "I can't breathe."

I stand up and pace away from him, willing my lungs to fill, and then I finally look around and see that it's not just the farmhouse that's on fire.

The shed.

The garage.

Holden's cabin.

All lit up in flames.

"Oh, my God." I cover my mouth with my hands and spin back to where Holden's standing next to Remington. "What have you done?"

"I'm exorcising the last of the ghosts. We'll talk about the why later." Holden crosses to me and tips my chin up so he can look me in the eye. "Just trust me."

"Jackie came into the shop and said there was a huge fire, and I was *not* prepared for that, Holden Lexington! I panicked. Jesus, I'm still panicking."

"Millie." Remington's voice is the same tone he's taken with me since I was little, and it kind of pulls me out of my head. "Stop. Everything is okay."

"Don't you *ever* run toward a burning building again," Bridger snarls as he walks past me, scowling and pointing at my chest. "Do you hear me?"

"You're not the boss of me, *Chief*!"

"There she is," Holden murmurs and kisses my forehead. "My fierce wife."

"Your wife is about to be even fiercer, Holden Lexington."

"Who's that?" He lifts an eyebrow, but I scowl at him.

"I am in no mood for this game today."

I hear more footsteps behind us, and Holden's eyes narrow as he looks over my head at who's approaching.

When I turn, my heart stumbles in my chest.

All *four* of my brothers are standing there, looking around, then turning to me with concern.

"Everything okay here?" Brady asks. "We saw the smoke from the barn and thought we'd better see if you need help."

Holden swallows hard, and I grin at them through the tears that still roll down my face.

"Was this fire *today*?" Chase asks, making me frown.

"You knew about this?"

"I thought everyone knew about this," Chase replies and then shrugs when we all stare at him. "I do have conversations with the fire department, you know."

"Thanks for telling me," I mutter and then glare up at my husband, who watches me with impassive eyes. "I'm not leaving."

"Okay," Holden replies easily. "But you'll stay out of the way."

"I shut your car off and closed the door," Ryan informs me before he reaches out and pulls me out of Holden's arms so he can wrap me up in a hug of his own. "Don't worry, okay?"

And that just makes me cry again.

What the fuck is wrong with me? Suddenly, I'm this hugging, crying *person.*

"Oh, God, you broke her," Brady says, and then I'm passed to him, and he rubs his big hand up and down my back. "You know we hate it when you cry."

"I'm not crying."

They laugh at that, and then I pull out of Brady's hug and scowl at all four of them before zeroing in on Remington.

"I'm sorry," he says, surprising the ever-loving shit out of me, because my grumpy oldest brother never apologizes. I feel my eyes widen, and the tears dry up, and all I can do is stare at him. "I should have done better."

"*Damn it.*"

Now Rem hugs me, kisses me on the head, and then I pull away and wipe my face on his flannel shirt.

I should blow my nose in it, too. He deserves it.

But I don't.

"I don't like fighting with you guys." I sniff, swallow, and then look at Holden, who's watching me with narrowed eyes. His hands are in fists. The sexy muscle in his jaw ticks.

He doesn't like to see me cry, either.

"Did he take a swing at you?" I ask my husband.

"Dude, we *just* got here," Ryan reminds me.

"No, him." I point at Rem, and my oldest brother just grins at me. "You did not!"

"No, I didn't." He crosses his arms over his chest.

Finally, I turn into Holden and wrap my arms around his middle, bury my face in his chest, and breathe him in, not caring in the least that my brothers are watching.

He smells like a campfire, but he's alive and not hurt.

"Do you need us?" Chase asks.

"We have a lot of people here," Holden replies. "You don't have to stay. The firemen are using this as a training exercise, and they'll be here until everything is cold."

I don't pull away. I just close my eyes, wrapped in his arms, and listen to my husband and my brothers talk as I will my heart to slow down and my breathing to return to normal.

I never want to relive this day again. Not ever.

"We'll head out, then," Brady says. "We're breaking in a new horse. But we can come back if you need us."

"Appreciate it," Holden replies. I can feel him move and let go of me with his right arm so he can shake their hands.

"Bye, guys," I call out. "Love you!"

"See you, Mill," Brady replies, and then I hear them walk away.

"I'll go, too," Rem says quietly. I feel him run his hand down my hair, and it brings tears back to my eyes. "Call if you need me."

I nod, unable to speak, and then his footsteps leave, and I'm left with my husband.

"My brothers just walked onto this ranch as if it was nothing."

Holden kisses the crown of my head. "Yeah. I liked it."

"Holden." I look up into his eyes and feel the tears want to well again. "Holy shit, I've never been that scared in my life."

"Everything is okay. We'll talk about it later tonight, but I have to be on hand here until it's over. Do you want to go home and wait for me? Or go back to work?"

"I told you, I'm not leaving you. If you could just carry me around like a koala on a tree, that would be perfect."

He grins and presses his lips to my forehead, giving me a little squeeze. "I don't think that'll work. You stay here, sit on this log, and do *not* go near any of these burning structures."

"I was only running for the one that looked like it might have you in it."

His eyes soften, and he presses his lips to mine. "Never do that again, either."

"Fine, I'll let your ass burn."

Holden rolls his eyes, then points at me. "Stay."

It's a long day. I heard someone say that because of so many structures being in play, it takes a long time to get everything done that they want to. Bridger leads drills that I don't understand. Around lunchtime, I go into town and get about twenty pizzas for anyone who's hungry, and within twenty minutes, they're all gone.

I guess they were hungry.

Finally, just when the sun is starting to set, some of the men start to climb onto firetrucks and pull away.

Bridger and his team of about five guys are the last to go. There's no more steam coming up from any of the piles of ash, and he assures Holden that it's all cold to the touch.

"I appreciate it," Holden says, shaking Bridger's hand. "I owe you."

"We're good." Bridger looks over at me. "Don't scare me like that again."

"I thought my husband was being burned alive." I have to swallow hard after saying that. "You tell me that you wouldn't do the same."

He mutters something about being a dumbass and stomps away.

"Let's go home," Holden says, holding his hand out for mine.

"Where's your truck?"

"Out at the barn. I'll get it tomorrow. For tonight, I want to ride home with you."

I slip my hand into his, and he laces our fingers together before bringing them to his lips, and then he guides me to where someone relocated my car so it was out of the way for everyone to leave, I'm sure, and he puts me in the passenger seat.

When he lowers into the driver's side, I'm still trying to push my seat belt into the buckle, but my hands are still shaky, and I keep missing.

Holden takes it from me and clips it into place, perfectly calm.

"Are you okay?" he asks me, holding my gaze with his.

"Let's just get home."

He nods, starts the car, and then drives us into town, to the little house that we rent from my brother and Polly.

Without a word, I cross through the house to the shower, strip down, and get into the hot water, washing away the day. When I'm dressed in sleep shorts and a tank, with my wet hair twisted up on my head, Holden gets in the shower to do the same.

Usually, one of us would either make a comment about joining the other in the water, or we would just help ourselves.

But neither of us is in that mood at the moment.

I've just poured Holden a shot of whiskey and myself a shot of tequila when he comes walking out in a pair of gray sweatpants and absolutely nothing on top. Jesus,

Mary, and Joseph, this man is beautiful. With all that ink, those muscles, and the scruff on his face. That dark hair.

Did I mention the muscles and the ink? For fuck's sake, he looks like he should be in a movie. Or on the cover of a magazine.

Hell, both.

"I can't talk to you when you look like that."

He cocks an eyebrow. "Like what?"

I wave my hand in a large circle, indicating *him*. "That."

My husband smirks and reaches for the whiskey. "I arranged with Bridger a week ago to burn all the buildings at the ranch."

My eyes go wide as I lean against the kitchen counter across from where *he* leans against the sink. "Why?"

"Still getting those ghosts cleared out of there," he replies. He's almost too calm, as if it's taking everything in him to fight the emotions running through him.

"Why didn't you tell me?"

He blinks and frowns down at his whiskey. "Because when I'm out there, taking care of business, I don't think of you at all."

Arrow, right to the heart. I can't help the small gasp as hurt moves through me, and suddenly he's against me, holding me, those blue eyes intense.

"I didn't mean it how it sounded. I can't think of you when I'm out there because it makes me panic." That tightly reined-in control is slipping now. His eyes are hot, his hands tremble as he drags his fingertips down my cheek. "Because I have so much fucking baggage from that son of a bitch that when I think of you even considering stepping foot out there, I have a goddamn panic attack. He would have killed you, Millie, without thinking twice. Jesus."

"But he can't kill me now."

He pushes away and prowls around the kitchen as if he wants to punch something. His muscles ripple, his hair is wet and still dripping a little down his back, and he's magnificent.

He's *mine.*

"Holden—"

"That's not my fucking name."

Those blue eyes are fierce as he watches me, his chest heaving, and I boldly cross to him and take his face in my hands.

"Husband," I say softly, loving the way his scruff feels in my hands. "You have to tell me these things."

"Why?"

"Because I'm your wife."

CHAPTER SIXTEEN

HOLDEN

She's soothing me. Trying to calm me. It's as though the last of the anger and fear that I've carried my entire life is moving through me, finally being exorcised with the smoke from earlier today, and I can't control my emotions or my body. I just know that I need her.

"I'm your wife," she says again, her golden eyes begging me to listen. "We're a team now, Holden. That ranch isn't your father's anymore. It's yours. It's *ours.* And if you're going to set the whole thing ablaze, I need to know because—"

Her lower lip quivers, and I can't take it. I lower my forehead to hers, soaking in her sweetness. "Don't cry, little rose."

"Because I was blindsided," she continues after a breath, "and I thought I might lose you, and I literally got you back three minutes ago."

Without another thought, I back her up against the

counter, drag my hands down to cup her ass, and sink into her, groaning as everything in me focuses on this woman in my arms, and my only instinct is to get inside of her as quickly as humanly possible.

She moans when my tongue laps at her lips and then presses into her mouth, and she pushes her stomach against my already hard and swollen cock. And that's all I need to know that she needs me just as much.

I rip away her little tank top and toss it aside before I bend over to pull her nipple into my mouth, and her fingers dive into my hair.

"*Husband*," she moans, and with just that one word, my control snaps.

Her shorts are gone in a flash, and I cover her pussy, push my two middle fingers into her, and press the heel of my palm against her clit, giving her a little shake.

"Fucking hell," she groans, leaning her forehead against my shoulder.

"This isn't going to be soft and slow, baby girl," I warn her. "I'm going to fuck you hard and fast. Stop me now if you're not okay with that."

"Never."

I grin and kiss her neck as she pushes my sweats down my hips and takes my cock in her hand.

I spin her around. "Hands on the counter."

I drag the head of my cock up and down her slit, watching as it glistens in all of that wetness. And then I'm inside her, my hands on her hips, pulling her roughly onto me, fucking her fast and hard, just like I promised.

Jesus fucking Christ, I can't get enough of her. I can't stop this constant wanting for her.

"When you ran toward that fire today..." I shake my head as I relive it, terror clutching at my chest. "God, you fucking scared me."

I slap her ass hard, and she gasps in surprise and then groans.

"And it was the sexiest fucking thing I've ever seen."

I pull both of her arms behind her and thread my own arm through her elbows, arching her back as my free hand moves down her belly and finds her hard clit.

"Husband!" She's shuddering, and I know she's so close to coming, so I stop rubbing that hard nub and bite her shoulder.

"You're not going to come yet."

"What in the hell?"

"Not yet," I repeat with a growl, and she groans as I slide out of her.

She fucking loves the metal in my cock. Which is good because I got them for her.

Before I can boost her up onto the counter, this incredible woman falls to her knees, wraps both of her hands around my cock, and sucks the tip into her sweet, pink mouth, then pushes her tongue over the piercings, and my eyes cross.

I have to lean over her, onto the counter, when my knees threaten to buckle.

"Baby girl."

She moans, moving up and down on me, taking me so far into her mouth that I hit the back of her throat.

Then she relaxes her muscles and pushes down even further, and I can't resist plunging my hand into her hair, guiding her gently.

She's going to make me come, and I'm not ready for that, so I take her by the shoulders and pull her up.

"Hey, I wasn't done—"

I kiss her roughly, her jaw in my hand, and then boost her onto the countertop and press my hand on her breastbone, urging her to lie back.

With her eyes bright and on mine, her chest heaving with hard breaths, I bring her legs up to my shoulders and slip back inside of her, making us both moan.

"Oh, God." She covers her own breast and pinches her nipple, and I feel her tighten around me. I kiss her calf and then her ankle, press my thumb to her clit, and *fuck her.* "Oh, God!"

"Who do you belong to, wife?" I can't slow down. I slam into her, over and over again, making her tits shake and bounce, and she arches her neck and grips my arm as if looking for an anchor. "Answer me."

"You. I belong to you."

"That's right. You're mine. God damn, you're so fucking beautiful. So fucking amazing."

"I'm going to come. Please, can I come?"

With a grin, I press my thumb to her harder. "Go over, my love. Do it."

She is a goddess when she comes. She cries out, arches her back, and squeezes my dick so hard I see stars, and she pulls me right over the edge with her.

As we catch our breath, I plant kisses on her legs,

then slip out of her and pull her up to sitting and kiss her sweet, swollen lips.

"Do you feel better?" Her question is whispered against my lips, and I wrap my arms around her and hug her close. "After everything today, I mean, not just this."

"*This* made everything much better," I confirm and press my lips to her forehead.

"I want a tattoo."

I frown at the simple statement and then pull back so I can look down at her.

"No." I shake my head and drag my hands down her arms. "I don't want you to ever feel pain, baby girl."

She lifts an eyebrow. "It's just a tattoo, you know. You have a million of them."

"And you know why."

Her eyes soften as she traces the lines of the rose on my arm, then down to my hand, and brings it up to her lips before covering her heart with my palm.

I've never loved anyone or anything more than I do my wife in this moment.

"What would you get?" I ask her softly, brushing her hair off her cheek.

"Our wedding date." She swallows hard. "On the inside of my left wrist."

Staggered, I tip her chin up and look into those beautiful eyes. "Millie."

"Because," she continues, her voice growing softer, and I have to lean in to hear her. "Even if this is only for a year, it'll be the most important year of my life."

The breath leaves my body as I lower my forehead to hers. The vulnerability in that one sentence is staggering.

"I'm not letting you go in a year, wife. I'm not letting you go in a hundred years. I belong to you, heart and soul. You're the reason for everything I fucking do."

She wraps her arms around me and hugs me so tight that it seems she wants to crawl inside of me.

And I can't blame her because inside of *her* is my favorite place to be.

"If you want the ink, you should get it," I whisper into her ear. "Maybe I'll do the same."

"Matching tattoos?" She smiles up at me. "How fun. Where will you get yours?"

"Over my heart, of course." I kiss her softly and then help her to her feet. "We need to clean up. Are you hungry?"

"I'm starving. There are leftover taco fixings in the fridge."

"You go put on clothes that aren't ripped, and I'll take care of everything else." I run my hand down her hair as she walks away and then use the next couple of minutes of alone time to clean the cum off the floor, wipe myself off, and then heat up the taco meat for the leftovers.

By the time she comes back, my system has leveled out.

"Hey, I have a question," she says as she ties up her hair into a bun.

"Ask away." I lick some queso off my thumb and turn

to look at her, then freeze with my thumb still in my mouth. "What the fuck are you wearing?"

She frowns and looks down at the white T-shirt that's so thin, I can see the outline of her pretty pink nipples as clearly as if she was naked.

"Just a ratty old shirt. This might be the most comfortable thing I own."

"Jesus, wife, you're a walking wet dream."

The grin that spreads over her face is full of satisfaction. "I still have a question."

"The answer is yes." I can't take my eyes off her tits. "Absolutely yes, whatever you want."

Now she laughs and reaches for a tortilla chip. "You're such a *man*."

"Never claimed otherwise."

"Hey, my eyes are up here." She bends to catch my gaze in hers, still grinning. "Don't be rude."

"I'm not being rude. I'm admiring my wife's amazing body."

"Dude. We *just* had sex two seconds ago. Focus."

"I am focused."

"Holden."

Now my eyes find hers and narrow.

"Husband, I have a question."

"Fine." I sigh and go back to work building a taco. "What's up?"

"When do you guys brand and castrate at your ranch? Isn't it almost time for that?"

I frown over at her. "Yeah, it's actually on Thursday."

"Like, three days from now?"

"Yes."

She blinks. "I want to help. It's my favorite time of year."

Stunned, I stare at her. "You want to help?"

"Of course, I do. I'll have to go get my horse. I've been wanting to do that anyway. I miss her. I know that Lucky and the kids are taking good care of her, but this is the longest I've gone without seeing her. Anyway, what can I do to help before Thursday? Do you have the food tent ready to go?"

"What food tent?" My head is spinning. My wife wants to help me on one of the most important days of the year on my ranch. I always have the Blackwells come help, and a few other neighboring families, but never the women.

My dad would have blown a gasket.

"The food tent." She frowns at me. "Don't you feed all those hungry cowboys?"

"I usually order sandwiches or something." I shrug, suddenly feeling like I've been missing something important.

"Okay, I'll handle the food. Erin and Summer will come do that. I'll be working with you, though. I'm a cowboy, not a helper."

I raise an eyebrow at her. "You're a cowboy?"

"Hell yes, I am. Just wait and see. You know, you should invite your sisters out to see what it's all about. I assume if they weren't even allowed to ride horses, they weren't allowed to help on the most fun day of the year, either."

I raise my eyebrows. "I guess I should invite them."

"I'm going to offer to teach them how to ride."

Stunned, I push my plate away and cross my arms over my chest. "Why?"

"Because they grew up on a ranch, and they never got to enjoy it. They're going to now, if I have anything to say about it. Actually, Jake is really great at teaching people to ride, and they have a bunch of awesome, gentle horses at Ryan's ranch, so I'll see if your sisters want to go out there. It'll be fun."

She takes a bite of her taco, and, oblivious to the fact that she just keeps saying all the things that make me fall even more in love with her, she keeps going.

"What time should I have everyone come out there?"

"Huh?"

"What time do you start on branding days?"

"Around eight, I guess."

"Easy peasy." She licks some salsa off her hand. "I'm excited. I hope I can help at my family's ranch this year. My dad might not let me."

"No, your dad won't let *me*," I remind her gently. "You can go, baby girl."

"Not without you." She frowns down at her half-eaten taco. "I'll talk to him."

In a daze, we finish eating, tidy the kitchen, and then head for bed. It's after nine, and we both have early mornings.

Not to mention, I want to make love to her once more tonight.

So, in the dark, after she's shed her lounge clothes

and we're under the covers, I roll over her and nestle myself between her thighs.

"Now it's going to be soft and slow," I whisper against her lips. "I'm going to make love to you, wife."

"Oh, that sounds nice."

She grins, and I slip inside of her, wiping that sassy smile off her delectable lips.

With long, slow thrusts, I move inside of her. "You're so incredible."

"*You're* incredible." Our voices are hushed in whispers as we make love in the quiet.

She wraps herself around me, holding me to her, and I bury my face in her neck.

"Can't get close enough," I murmur.

"I want all of you." She kisses my cheek. "Give me all of you."

"You have it. You've always had it."

She clenches down on me, and I come just as hard as before, rocking into her wet heat.

Later, after we've cleaned up yet again and are curled around each other, we lie still; the only sound in the room is our breaths.

Suddenly, in the quiet, I hear her whisper, "I love you so much."

My throat closes, and I have to swallow hard before I tug her close, tip her chin up, and in the moonlight whisper back, "I love you, too. So much."

Her eyes widen. "I thought you were asleep."

A chuckle escapes my throat. "You only whisper

sweet nothings when I'm asleep? I'd better start staying awake longer."

"It's not nothing." She cups my cheek in her little hand. "It's the biggest thing."

Full of emotion, I kiss her palm and then her lips. "It's everything."

CHAPTER SEVENTEEN

MILLIE

I'm pissy today.

I can totally admit it. My mood is dark. First of all, I've barely seen my husband since Monday night. He's been up and out extra early the past two mornings because he has to get ready for branding day, and he's cleaning up from the fires. He worked an eighteen-hour day yesterday, not getting home until almost midnight, and then he was up and out again before four this morning.

I freaking miss him.

On top of that, I overslept after he left this morning, so I didn't get to work until ten minutes before opening, which is not enough time to get ready. Thankfully, because I have to leave for our monthly Iconic Women's Collective luncheon today, I have Candy, Macy, *and* Andrea all here to work the whole day, so at least I don't have to worry about Candy being here alone.

They'll all be here tomorrow, too, so I can be at the ranch.

I'm so glad that I found some good, reliable help for the summer.

"Gladys!" I set the mocha on the counter as a middle-aged woman approaches to take it and smile at her. "Have a good day."

"It's busy today," Andrea says with a smile. "I love it."

"And I'm glad that you do." I sigh and try to shrug off the attitude. I'm the only one suffering from it.

But just as I'm about to put myself into a brighter, sunshine mood, I hear, "I wouldn't mind getting set up with Holden Lexington."

I narrow my eyes and turn my head to look at the three women sitting at a nearby table, drinking coffee and gossiping.

"Right?" a blonde says. "He's one hot cowboy. I'd like to ride him."

"You know," the original voice, a brunette, adds as the bell above my door rings with an incoming customer, "my sister knows *his* sister. I bet I could get introduced. I'd rock that man's world. Those tattoos! I want to lick them."

"I want to lick him all over."

"Holden's wife probably wouldn't approve of that."

All three heads whip around at the sound of my voice, their eyes widening as they look at my face.

I'm sure it's fucking mutinous. It's a good thing this counter separates us because I'd be pulling them out of here by the hair.

"He's not married," the blonde says with a scowl, and I hold up my hand, showing them my ring.

"Yeah, he *is* married. To me. And I don't appreciate the way you're talking about my husband. Trust me, if I ever find out that any of you tried to lay so much as the tip of your filthy tongues on my husband's tattoos, it would be the last thing you ever tasted before I ripped them out of your heads."

"Jesus, no need to be a bitch," the brunette snarls. "We're just talking about a hot guy. Calm down."

"Fuck that. He's *my* hot guy, and because I also own this business, you'll get your dumb asses out of my chairs, march out of here, and don't ever come back."

Their jaws drop, but I just snarl at them, and when I watch them start to walk out, I see the man himself, standing near the entrance, smiling so widely at me, it's blinding.

"Don't fucking look at him," I yell at the girls. "Don't even breathe in his direction! Do you hear me?"

Finally, they're out the door, and my husband crosses to me and lays the flowers on the counter before sliding his sexy, tattooed hand up my throat and brushing my jaw with his thumb. He plants his lips by my ear.

"You just made me harder than I've ever been in my entire fucking life, wife. I can't wait until tonight, when I can fuck you so hard and for so long that you'll be screaming my name."

I swallow hard and press my thighs together in anticipation, and then his lips are on mine, hungry and possessive, and I hear the round of applause around us.

I laugh when he pulls away, staring at me with hot, blue eyes.

"Bravo," Candy says, clapping the loudest. "Bravo!"

"I guess you didn't like what they were saying?" Holden asks.

"No. I didn't. That'll teach them to talk about another woman's man that way. Also, why do you have to be so hot? Is this going to be my life from now on?"

"Oh, baby girl, the things you do to me." He kisses me again, lingering on my lips, before he pulls back and retrieves the flowers. "These are for you. I haven't seen much of you, so I wanted to swing in and say hi."

"And we're all glad you did," Andrea assures him with a laugh. "Now I need to find a boyfriend because that was the hottest thing I've ever witnessed."

"Thank you." Ignoring her, I bury my nose in the red roses and sunflowers. "They're beautiful."

"What do you have going today?" he asks, leaning on the counter and giving me his undivided attention.

I run my fingers over the pink rose on his arm.

"I have an IWC lunch in just a few minutes, and then I'll be heading home. I want to plant some flowers."

That has his eyebrows climbing in surprise. "Really? What kind?"

"I don't know. I need to spend some time in the yard, plotting my strategy. I'm not sure what gets shade and what gets full sun and so on. So, I'll be home early today."

"Unfortunately, I won't be." He sighs heavily.

"Should I come out to the ranch instead and help? I don't mind at all."

"No." He shakes his head. "Enjoy the yard. I have a lot of help out there. Brady and Rem are even coming by for a couple of hours this afternoon."

My eyes widen at that news. "You're kidding."

"Nope."

"Wow. Well, that's good."

"I'd better go." He kisses me once more and then heads for the door, slapping his ball cap onto his head. "Have a good day, baby girl."

"You, too."

"Oh, trust me, the whole town has heard what happened at BVCC this morning," Erin says with a grin as we help Summer put flower arrangements on the tables at Snow Ghost, our favorite pub up at the ski hill, where we like to host our monthly luncheons.

The Iconic Women's Collective is a passion project, a *club*, for lack of a better word, that my sisters-in-law and I founded a couple of years ago. All five of us are businesswomen, and we wanted to find a way to support other women in business. To be hype girls for each other, network, and share tips and tricks for success.

Because at the end of the day, there's room for all of us to kick major ass.

Except for those three home-wreckers in my coffee shop this morning, that is.

"No one should talk about someone's husband that way," I insist and prop my hands on my hips as Summer and Polly share a grin. "You guys wouldn't like it if you overheard some broad saying that she'd like to eat your husband for dinner."

That makes Abbi scowl. "No. No, I wouldn't like that."

"See? Anyway, maybe they'll have better manners when they're out in public and save that kind of talk for private girls' nights, like a lady should."

Erin snorts at that. "Summer, these peonies are so gorgeous."

"I know. Feel free to take some after the meeting." Summer owns Paula's Poseys, the flower shop in town, and always brings fresh bouquets for the tables. "Erin, tell us about our guest speaker today. You said her name's Cora?"

"Cora's awesome," Erin replies. "I don't know her that well. Her family knows my family *somehow*, and she's from New Orleans. She was born into a killer tycoon-type family. She'll tell you all about it today, I'm sure. I happened to see her when Rem and I snuck away to New Orleans for Mardi Gras and asked her to come speak to us."

"I have a question," I say, waving my hand. "Is there literally anyone in the world who's famous and important that your family doesn't know?"

Erin taps her chin, narrows her eyes, and then grins. "No."

"Hey, that's good for us," Abbi reminds me. "We get

to have some amazing guest speakers at our meetings as a result."

"True that," Polly agrees, as people start to arrive for the meeting.

I always love seeing everyone. We have photographers and real estate agents. Attorneys and doctors, nurses, and a dog trainer.

It's such a diverse, amazing group of people that I'm always surprised by the turnout, even though I shouldn't be.

"There you are!"

I turn and grin as Charlie strides over to me, holding a glass of Coke.

"Hey!" She hugs me, and it doesn't even make me feel weird. "How's it going?"

"We're moving into wedding season, which means that it's fabulous and I'm busy, but I also never have time to catch my breath." Charlie shrugs a shoulder. "But it's all good, and I have zero complaints. But here's the real question. How are *you*?"

"I don't think we have time to go into that." I can't help but laugh. "But at the heart of it all, I'm also doing well."

"Glad to hear it. Now, who's talking to us today?"

I notice a redhead with a face of freckles and shrewd green eyes walk into the room, and I'm pretty sure that's our guest speaker.

"She's a kickass woman from New Orleans. That's really all I know, so I'm excited to hear what she has to say."

"Me, too." Charlie pats my shoulder. "I'll go find a seat. I'll talk to you later."

I nod and watch her go and then join my friends as Erin greets Cora.

"It's so good to see you again," Erin says with a smile.

"You, too. Holy shit, this town is gorgeous." I love her accent. It reminds me of warm, humid nights in the Bayou, and I've never even been to the Bayou. "I'll have to bring my cousins up here sometime."

"Oh, you absolutely should," Erin says with a nod. "That would be so fun."

We're all introduced to Cora, who seems incredibly friendly, and I can see in those green eyes a woman of high intelligence. I'm excited for her to speak.

Once everyone is seated with their lunch, Erin goes to the front of the room to introduce her friend, and we all take our seats. The five of us try to spread out through the room so we can also network and chat with the ladies.

"Hi, everyone," Erin says, grabbing our attention. "Thanks for coming to this month's IWC luncheon. Don't forget, we have our spring formal event happening in two weeks. We will be posting on socials and in the newsletter, so keep an eye on that."

That's right, it's coming up! Four times a year, we host a big, fancy party and invite spouses or significant others to join us to celebrate everyone's successes.

This time, I get to bring my husband as my date, and that makes the murder hornets wake up in my belly and do the cha-cha.

"Now, without further ado, I'd like to introduce my friend, Cora. She came all the way from New Orleans to be here with us today. Cora's family is in the shipbuilding business, and well, I'm going to let her tell you all about it. Give Cora a hand!"

As we applaud, the beautiful redhead in her pretty green dress takes the mic from Erin and smiles at all of us.

"Wow, this is an intimidating room to stand in front of. Erin has told me so much about what she and her besties are doing with your Iconic Women's Collective, and when she asked me to come speak to you, I jumped at the opportunity. Normally, I'm on the shy side, but I kind of wanted to come be a part of the cool kids' club."

There's some laughter in the audience, and Cora continues.

"My name is Cora Boudreaux, and Erin was correct when she said I'm from New Orleans. I have a big, loud, crazy family down there that I'm pretty wild about. My great-great-great-grandfather started building ships on the Mississippi River about a million years ago, and our company is called Boudreaux Enterprises. My father, Eli Boudreaux, is the CEO of the company, but I am interning with him because he'd like to eventually retire and spend the rest of his many years spoiling the hell out of my mom."

She grins when we chuckle again and settles into a rhythm of talking about the challenges of running a multi-billion dollar enterprise, one that's so high profile and important.

And I can tell that some of the women here are thinking, *But how can this help my small business*?

"I have a question," I say, putting up a hand. "How do you find ways to reach out to your community and help the local people that you employ?"

Cora grins at me. "Good question. Because although we are global, and pretty damn big, we're also committed to being involved in our local community."

Finally, she shifts to talking about what Boudreaux Enterprises does in New Orleans, and now I see more interest sparking around me.

I glance over at Erin, who mouths *thank you*, and I grin at her.

Two hours later, once everyone has left and we've cleared out the flowers and helped with some of the big cleanup, we walk out to our vehicles.

"That was awesome," Polly says with a sigh. "Also, we keep upping our guest speaker game. That was impressive."

"Also, *also,* when she said that her uncle was a baseball player, and her cousin is currently a pro baseball player, it made me want to know more about their family. They sound like yours, Erin," Abbi says.

"They're pretty cool, yeah." Erin grins. "Hopefully, Cora will bring them out here for a visit, and we'll have a big party at Ryan's house."

"We're in," Polly says. "Okay, ladies, I have to get home to the bambino. Lottie should be waking up from her nap anytime."

"Same," Summer agrees. "August is teething, and

he's moody. But we'll see you tomorrow, Millie. We're all coming out to help at your ranch. Joy's going to watch all the kids for us."

I blink at her, surprised. "You're *all* coming?"

"Of course," Erin says, patting me on the shoulder. "It's branding day."

She winks, and then everyone gets into their vehicles to go home. I climb into mine, too, so full of gratitude and emotion, I have to pause before pulling out of the parking space.

For generations, it's been a firm policy that the Wilds and the Lexingtons do *not* help each other out on their ranches. Other neighbors do, but not those two rival families.

Never.

But now that that evil man is dead and buried, and Holden and I are married, things are changing, and I love it so much.

"It's about time things start to change. Now, if my dad would just come around."

I start my car to leave, but my phone rings, and I frown when I see that it's Bridger.

"Hey, what's up?"

"Hey, are you busy for the next few hours?" I hear the fatigue in his voice. He needs a sitter for Birdie. I can feel it in my bones. Since his parents moved to Florida, the poor guy can't catch a break when it comes to help with his sweet little girl.

"Not especially. What's going on?"

"I had to go to a meeting in Missoula, and my childcare for the rest of the day has fallen through. Do you mind going to watch Birdie until I get home? It'll be around eight when I get back to town."

Well, there goes garden planning, but that's okay. I love that little girl.

"Sure, of course. Where is she? And do you mind if I take her to my place?"

"I don't mind at all." The relief in his deep voice is real. "She's at home with the only babysitter I could find, but she's just bailed on me."

"Okay, don't worry about it. I've got her. Just swing by when you get back to town."

"Thanks, Mill. I appreciate it."

"Drive safe."

I hang up and head into town, bypassing my house and driving a couple of blocks farther to Bridger's place on the edge of town. His house is cute, with a well-kept yard, but it's a total bachelor pad. There are no flowers, no patio or porch furniture. No wind chimes. And I know that the inside is just as simple. He and Birdie have all the conveniences, but there are no pictures on the wall or extra pretty pillows on the couch. It's so... *bland.*

He's such a man.

I pull into the driveway, and a teenager that I don't know comes running out the door toward me.

"Are you picking up Birdie?" She sounds way too excited at the prospect of being rid of the kid.

"Yes. Who are you?"

"Shayna," she says, as if I should just automatically

know. "Sorry, I just can't stay the rest of the day. I have stuff to do."

"But you took the job."

"Yeah, because have you seen Bridger? But then I realized that he wasn't even here. It's just the kid, and that's such a drag. I have a party to go to. See you!"

And then she runs to her car and zooms out of here so fast, I'm surprised there isn't smoke coming off her tires.

Birdie and I stare at each other for a minute, and then I can't help but laugh.

Birdie grins and plays with her little dark braid.

"Hi, sweet girl."

"Hi, Aunt Millie. She didn't like me."

"Oh, you're pretty much impossible to dislike. I think Shayna just had a crush on your daddy and didn't think this through. You wanna come hang with me at my new house?"

She jumps up and down, so excited, and I'm suddenly glad that my day took an unexpected turn. I haven't spent much time with this little one lately, and I've missed her.

"*Yes!*"

"Good. Let's go in and grab you a few things, and then we'll go to my house. I'll fix you something to eat. How have you been feeling?"

Birdie's been dealing with an illness that no one seems to be able to pinpoint. She has good days and bad days, more good recently, which is a huge relief.

Some doctors think that it might be something that

she just grows out of, but it would be better if we knew what in the hell it was.

"I feel fine. Kind of sleepy."

Being lethargic was the biggest culprit. Keeping this kid awake has been a chore for the better part of a year.

"Do you need a little nap?"

"Not right now." She slips her little hand into mine as we go inside. "I want to see your house."

"Okay, baby. Let's do that."

CHAPTER EIGHTEEN

HOLDEN

I haven't been inside of my wife in two fucking days, and that's about to change *right now.* My guys and I worked our asses off today to finish cleaning up from the fires and get everything ready to go for branding tomorrow, and that means that I'm headed home in time for dinner.

And for dinner, I plan to spread her wide and eat my fill of Millie.

Hearing her cuss those women out in her shop this morning was fucking sexy. I have no idea what got my girl so riled up, but after watching her claim me, show them her wedding ring, and then throw them out on their asses, I wanted to boost her up on that counter and sink inside of her right then.

She's beautiful when she's pissed.

I pull into the driveway and am walking through the door when I announce, "You have ten seconds to get nak—"

I stop cold when I see a little dark-haired, brown-eyed girl staring up at me, and all my plans for the evening immediately shift.

"Uh, hey, Birdie."

"Holden!" Birdie jumps up and runs to me, throws her arms around my waist, and squeezes. "You're here!"

"I am." I laugh and bend over to kiss her head. "I live here."

"With Aunt Millie?" She frowns. "Why?"

"Because we're married, sweetheart. Where is she, by the way?"

"She just went to the bathroom." Birdie takes my hand and leads me to where she was sitting on the couch. "I'm watching *Paw Patrol.* Come sit with me."

"Give me a minute, okay?" I get her settled and kiss her head again and then go in search of my wife. "Millie?"

"Back here." I hear her muffled voice in the bedroom and find her in the closet. "I'm hanging laundry. Do you want your T-shirts hung or folded?"

My heart stops and then starts to hammer in my ears. Jesus Christ, no one woman should have the audacity to look like this.

She's in shorts, the kind that barely covers her ass, and a white tank top. Her hair is piled in a messy knot on her head, and she's hanging laundry out of a basket.

I'm not a misogynist. I do not expect my wife to do my housekeeping, cook my meals, and be at my beck and call.

But holy fucking shit, I want to fuck her.

Instead, I stalk over, frame her face in my hands, and kiss her like I'm starving for her, because I am.

She moans in surprise and then melts against me in that way she does, wrapping her arms around my waist.

"Laundry turns you on?" she asks when I come up for air.

"You turn me on." I tuck her hair behind her ear. "You don't have to wash my clothes, baby girl."

"I'm doing it anyway." She shrugs as if it's no big deal. "And my plans were kind of changed because of Birdie. Speaking of which, I need to check on her."

"She's fine. She's watching TV. What happened there?"

"Childcare fell through, and Bridger called me. It's no big deal." She brushes her fingers down my cheek, and I take her hand and press my lips to her palm. "You're home sooner than I expected."

"I worked my ass off so I could spend some naked time with my wife."

Her eyes widen, and then she sighs. "I'm sorr—"

Before she can complete that thought, I cover her lips with my own and then hug her close. "Don't be. I'm still at home with you, and we can get naked later."

"Deal."

"Where are you?" Birdie calls out as she walks down the hall.

"In here, baby," Millie calls back and grins up at me. "Are you hungry?"

"I'm starving," Birdie says, and then giggles when I

pick her up and toss her over my shoulder. "Hey! I'm not a sack of potatoes!"

"Yep. You are. I'm going to fry you up and have you for dinner." I tickle her side, making her giggle. "Come on, let's cook dinner while Aunt Millie finishes the laundry."

"Can we have nuggets?"

"Honey, you can have whatever you want."

I lower the little girl onto the kitchen counter so she can watch me bustle about the kitchen. After washing my hands thoroughly, I open the fridge. I took a shower at the ranch before coming home. I had a shower installed at the barn just for that.

"Okay, half-pint, it looks like there are, in fact, some nuggets in the freezer. But if I'm going to make those for you, you have to agree to eat some vegetables."

Birdie wrinkles her adorable nose. "Ew. I don't want vegetables. They're bad for you."

I grin at her, and she does her best to look innocent before she breaks down in giggles.

"You're trouble, you know that?"

"Yeah, that's what Daddy says, too."

Bridger's headlights pull out of the driveway, and I turn to where Millie's curled up asleep on the couch.

She and Birdie fell asleep, watching a Disney movie. Neither of them woke up when Bridger arrived to pick up his little girl.

After I lock up, I lift my wife into my arms and carry her to the bedroom, get her tucked into the bed, and then take off my clothes and climb in with her.

Tonight didn't go as planned at all, and there will obviously be no sex tonight, but I don't really mind. For years, all I wanted was to be with Millie, just like this. Curled up together, holding her tightly in my arms, without any fear that my touching her could hurt her.

She murmurs in her sleep as she burrows down against me, sighs, and I kiss her hair before I follow her into dreamland.

"She's good." Vance is standing next to me at the fence line, our boots on the bottom rung, watching as Millie rides her horse in the pen, roping a calf.

She's not just good. She's fucking amazing.

I had no idea she could do this. How is it that literally every single thing this woman does turns me on?

My ranch is a hive of activity. The calves are in one pen, with their mamas in one next to them to help keep them calm.

I have all five Blackwell siblings here, my four sisters, all the Wild brothers with their wives and ranch hands, and several other families, as well.

Millie was good to her word, and her sisters-in-law have been manning the food tent all day, which they brought with them and set up from scratch, serving hot meals to all the cowboys.

Rem's and Brady's kids, along with Birdie, are running about, helping more than getting into trouble.

Hell, even Jake is in that pen, giving vaccinations.

"I had no idea that some ranches operate like this," I say to Vance, who snickers next to me. "Why didn't you say something?"

"Because it wouldn't have done any good," he says, shaking his head. "Your dad was stuck in his ways, and even though he didn't have much to do with this part of the ranch anymore, there's no way he would have stood for this kind of operation. Even if it did make his life easier and make the day go by faster. He wasn't exactly worried about being part of the community, Holden."

I let out a frustrated sigh and then look over to where my sisters are watching. They're standing side by side, their eyes wide as they take it all in, and I can't get what Millie said the other day out of my head.

They grew up on a ranch and never got to enjoy it.

I cross over to them and grin. "Are you ready to bolt yet?"

"No," Dani says, shaking her head. "This is actually really cool. Millie explained a lot to us when we got here."

"I'm on my way to help out with lunch," Alex adds. "I don't love hearing the babies cry."

"It only hurts for a minute," I assure her before I pat her shoulder.

Dad always tortured Alex the most with the animals because she was the softest at heart.

The prick.

"I can't stay all day," Charlie adds with a sigh. "I have too much work, but I wouldn't have missed coming out for the world. Thanks for having us."

"It's your ranch, too." I wink at her and then notice that Dani walks over to where Bridger's tying Birdie's shoe.

"Hey," she says, getting Bridger's attention.

He looks up, and his jaw tightens, but his eyes brighten when he sees it's her. "Hey, Dani."

"I just rented out the house across the street from yours. So, we're neighbors now."

"Oh, Dani," Alex mutters next to me.

"Your brother told me you left Bozeman," Bridger says with a nod as he rises to his full height. Dani shoves her hands into her pockets and looks down at the ground, then smiles up at my friend.

"I did. Since Dad died, and I had to come back here anyway, I decided to stay. I'll be a teacher at the elementary school this fall."

"Congratulations. I'm happy for you." He smiles softly and reaches out to pat her shoulder, and Dani just shrugs, as if it's no big deal, when I know for a fact that it's a big fucking deal.

"Thanks. Well, I'm sure I'll see you around. And I'll see Birdie at school." Dani grins at the little girl. "Are you having fun today?"

"Yes!" Birdie does a little hop, making Dani laugh.

"I'd better get back to work," Bridger says, but winks at my sister before walking away, and Dani returns to us.

"And you think that's not flirting?" Alex asks her twin sister.

"We're just friends." Dani lifts her chin, gives me the side-eye, and then turns to leave. "I'm going to see if they need me at the food tent."

When she and Alex leave, I turn to Darby. "Do I have to kill Bridger?"

"Nope. It's your sister that's the problem."

I scowl at my sister. "Why is she a problem?"

"Because Dani has put Bridger in the friend zone, and I'm pretty sure he'd like to be *out* of the friend zone."

"*Darby.*"

"What? It's the truth. Dani's just too blind to see it, even though she's crushed on him for years. Bridger lights her fire, if you know what I mean."

She winks at me, waggles her eyebrows, and then stalks away, and I want to find something to stab in my eye.

"Come on, baby, let's go," Millie says, talking to her horse and catching my attention once more. Jesus Christ, she's sexy on that animal.

The day goes so much smoother than normal. Within a couple of hours, we have all the calves branded and vaccinated, and then we're herding them back out to the pasture. I ride up next to Millie and pass her a bottle of water.

"How do you always have water on hand?" She twists off the top and takes a sip. "It's like magic or something."

"Or something. I have to make sure you're hydrated, baby girl."

"Hey, Millie!"

We turn our heads when Levi rides up next to her, his eyes all shiny with appreciation, and I stare my man down.

"That's Mrs. Lexington to you, Levi."

He blinks fast at my hard tone, swallows hard, and then lets out a nervous laugh. "Sorry, boss. I just wanted to show your wife that the tiny calf she was worried about earlier is fine. See, she's with her mama, safe and sound."

"Oh, good. She's *so small*," Millie says quietly, watching the calf. "I was hesitant to vaccinate her. But she seems okay."

"She'll be fine," I agree, enjoying having Millie by my side. I've only had a few moments of panic, wanting to get her off of my land to protect her, but they've been fleeting.

Maybe setting everything on fire actually did the trick after all.

"No need to get territorial," Millie mutters when Levi rides away. "I'm not going to run off with one of your ranch hands, you know."

"I'd murder him if you did." Her gaze whips over to mine, and then she laughs. "I'm not kidding, Rosie."

"You're intense, husband."

"You're mine. The sooner everyone remembers that, the better."

"You're welcome to come over to our ranch next week," Remington says as he sits next to me at the bonfire. To my shock, when everything was cleaned up and put away, people didn't automatically clear out.

They stayed for more food, music, and to laugh and hang out.

Hell, the Wilds even brought the little babies over to hang out, and Millie's holding Ryan's daughter, Lottie, kissing her little head.

I've never had so many people at my ranch for so long in my life.

And I don't hate it.

"I appreciate that," I reply to Remington. "But until I have a conversation with your father, out of respect for him, I'll sit this one out. But please include your sister. She'd be devastated if she couldn't go, and I know she's going to say that if I can't go, she won't either, but we'll talk her into it."

He's quiet for a minute, staring into the fire.

"You love her."

"More than anything in the world."

I meet his gaze head-on.

"My dad will come around, man. He's just being stubborn."

"He refuses to speak to Millie." I sigh, watching as Millie laughs at something Lottie does. "She's tried reaching out, but he won't take her calls. She doesn't deserve that."

Rem shakes his head. "I'll try to talk to him. In the meantime, what are your plans out here? Now that you're actually in charge, what do you want to do with your operations?"

"I want to add more head to the herd. Beyond that, I'm not sure."

He nods thoughtfully. "If you ever want to brainstorm it, I'm around. Not that I have all the answers, but we don't do too bad."

I narrow my gaze, thinking it over, and an idea starts to take root in my mind.

"You know, I might just take you up on that."

"Good. Do. My wife's flagging me down, so I'd better go see what she needs."

He stands, and I do the same, looking for my own wife.

I find her, wearing one of my flannel shirts, standing with Summer, who's holding baby August.

"I found this shirt in your truck," Millie informs me. "I was cold. I hope that's okay."

"Doesn't bother me at all."

I fucking *love* seeing her wear my clothes. She can have all of them if she wants them.

"Hey, hold him for me," Summer says, pushing the baby into my arms as she dances in place. "I have to run to the bathroom real quick."

She hurries off, and I stare down into the somber eyes of the cutest little boy, with big blue eyes and dark hair.

"Well, hi there, little man." I settle him against my shoulder and bounce him a bit.

"Why are you so good with babies?" Millie asks, watching me closely.

"I raised four of them," I remind her as I kiss August's head. I grin at him, and he smiles back. "You're cute, aren't you? Are you gonna be a cowboy someday? I bet you are."

"Holden." I glance at Millie, whose cheeks are now flushed, and the pulse in her neck is throbbing faster.

"Are you okay?"

"I think my ovaries just exploded."

I narrow my eyes at her and lean in, still holding the baby close as I whisper into her ear.

"Rosie, there are dozens of people here. Your brothers are watching, and I'm holding an infant. I can't exactly fuck you up against the nearest surface right now, so stop looking at me like that."

She licks her lips. "Can't help it. Holy hell, you're hot with a baby. Your tattoos as you hold his little head? My clothes are about to fall off. Seriously, this should be illegal."

I smirk. "Get it together, Rosie."

"I'm trying." She swallows hard. "Holden?"

"Who's Holden?"

She narrows her eyes, but I know she loves it when I do that.

"Husband?"

"Yes, wife?"

"Do you want kids someday?"

I kiss August on the head and sigh when he rests his little cheek on my chest. "I never thought so. I couldn't imagine bringing any children onto this ranch where my dad could get to them, but now that I have you...yeah. I could see myself with some babies. I could see *you*, round with my child. What about you?"

"Yeah. I mean, not today. I'm not in a hurry or anything, but...someday."

I grin and lean in to kiss her sweet lips. "Someday."

"You're being a bad influence on my kid." Chase approaches and holds his hands out for his son, and I pass him over. "Come on, August, you don't need to be subjected to that smut."

"Whatever. You make out with his mom every chance you get," Millie calls after her brother, who just laughs as he walks away.

"Today was amazing." My voice is rough as I pull Millie against me and wrap my arms around her, burying my nose in her hair. "Nothing like how we usually do things out here."

"It sounds like it used to be really boring." She leans her chin on my chest and stares up at me. "This is way more fun."

"It is that. And there's less cleanup after when everyone chips in to help."

"You used to clean up alone?"

"Sure."

"Nah, that's not how we do things anymore. This is better."

I cup her cheek in my hand and brush my thumb over her skin. "You just waltzed in here and shook everything up, didn't you?"

I'm not just talking about today. She's completely turned my life upside down, in the best ways possible.

"I—" She frowns. "If you want me to stay out of it, I will. I'm sorry. I just got excited because I like it so much, but I didn't mean to take over. This is your operation, Holden."

"Stop." I tip her chin up and kiss her hard. "You didn't do anything I didn't want you to. In case you hadn't noticed, I love having you here for this, and I never thought I'd say that because the idea of you being here used to terrify me."

"Things are changing." She shrugs and then grins up at me. "In a good way."

"Yeah, in a very good way."

"Hey, Holden," Jake says as he approaches us. He's got his arm looped around the shoulders of a young redheaded girl his age, who smiles up at him dreamily. "Thanks for having us out today. It was fun."

"Thanks for helping." I shake his hand and smile at his girlfriend. "Are you two out of here?"

"I have a curfew," she says with a little shrug. "It's annoying."

"It's okay," Jake assures her and then turns back to me. "I can come back if you need more help."

"I think we've got it. Everything is pretty much done. Thanks again."

"You bet. Bye, Aunt Mill."

"See you later, cutie."

The young couple walks away, and I notice that she has her hand in his back pocket.

"Uh, Ryan's had the talk with him, right?" I ask my wife.

"God, I hope so. They've been going together for more than a year, and they're so cute, but there's no way they're not having sex."

"Hmm." I kiss her temple, and much to my relief, it looks like Jake's departure is the beginning of everyone else deciding to head out, too.

"Today was fun," Beckett says with a grin. "Good job, buddy."

"It was all her," I say, pointing to Millie, who preens under the accolade.

"Good job, Millie." Beckett winks at her before walking away.

Eyeing Brooks gathering up his stuff, I figure now is as good a time as any to talk to him.

"I'm going to go catch Brooks before he leaves," I say to Millie, kissing her head. "Give me a minute."

"Take your time," she replies. "I'll say goodbye to your sisters."

Brooks looks up at me as I approach. "It went well today."

"Yeah, it did. Thanks for helping. How's the truck coming along?"

I haven't heard anything about it since I dropped the old Ford off to him the day before we lit the ranch on fire.

"It's a mess, man." He shakes his head and lets out a half laugh. "It's going to be a few months before it's done."

"I'm not in a hurry. I appreciate you fixing it up for me."

I'll never get rid of that truck, no matter what. Millie gave me her virginity in the back of it.

When everyone has gone, and my ranch hands are off to their bunkhouse, I lead Millie to my truck and help her inside, then climb into the driver's seat.

"I desperately need a shower," she says with a sigh.

"We'll get one." I take her hand and kiss her knuckles. "And then I'm going to make love to you for about three days straight."

"I'd better hydrate and eat something, too."

I laugh and kiss her knuckles again. "Good idea."

CHAPTER NINETEEN

MILLIE

The hot water is heaven.

I don't do much ranch work anymore. It's just once a year that I spend a few days with everyone, because it's a lot of work, and we need all hands on deck. It always reminds me that I both miss the ranch and that I'm happy owning my own business in town.

Because holy shit, muscles that I forgot were there are already singing and making it known that they're not at all impressed with working so hard today. But it's also a satisfying ache because it was on Holden's ranch, and for the first time in his life, my husband saw how it's supposed to be.

I could tell that he was a little overwhelmed, but he was his usual calm self, looking fucking hot as hell on that horse.

I've just finished washing my body and am about to lean back to wash my hair when the door opens, and my husband's gorgeous blue eyes travel lazily down my body. He steps in with me, and without a word, I drop my arms and he takes over.

With my hands on his hips, Holden ensures that my hair is wet before he murmurs, “Step.”

He moves back, and I take a small step forward, my hair out of the water, as he pours some shampoo in his hands and then starts to massage it through my long hair.

With a sigh, I close my eyes and enjoy the way it feels when he takes care of me. The steam billows around us, circling us in a warm cocoon, and even though he’s now seen every inch of me, made love to me, *fucked* the hell out of me, it’s moments like this that are the most intimate.

When he’s tender and quiet.

A little intense.

I can’t really tell what he’s thinking, but that’s okay because he obviously needs this moment with me, and I’ll happily give it to him. To us.

His strong fingers against my scalp and sliding through the wet strands could put me to sleep. After a moment, he says, “Back in.”

I oblige and tip my head back under the water, and he rinses the suds away, and then we repeat the process with conditioner. He’s careful to make sure that there are no tangles before I step back under the spray for a final rinse.

Before he can get me out of the shower and towel me off, I reverse our positions and grab a clean washcloth and his soap and start to wash him. God, his body is beautiful. He's broad of shoulder, with lean hips and muscles for days that scream for my touch.

He's quiet, his hands at his sides, watching me with those intense eyes as I take my time with him. When I've washed every inch of his skin, I pull the nozzle off the wall and rinse him off. I want to return the favor of washing his hair, but he's too tall.

I narrow my eyes.

Holden smirks and then lowers to his knees before me, and it brings tears to my eyes.

Before he can tip his head back to wet his hair, I lower my lips to the top of his head and plant a kiss there as his hands move up my thighs to my ass. His fingers dig into my flesh, holding on, as he presses a sweet kiss just under my navel.

"Be good," I warn him as I urge his head back into the water and then grab some shampoo. I massage his scalp and scrub his hair, and Holden's eyes close as he simply holds on to my hips and lets me wash him. The suds slide down his shoulders, sluicing through the hills and valleys of his body, and it's so freaking hot, it's all I can do to stay on my feet.

Once he's clean all over, he kisses me again and then stands and shuts off the shower.

"You're so quiet, husband."

He tugs me against him and holds on tight, kisses my wet head, and then murmurs, "There are no words for this."

My heart aches at the tenderness in his voice. At the

love. And I can't resist framing his face in my hands and kissing him softly.

We dry each other off, and then, with my hand in his, he leads me to our bed. He lifts me right off of my feet and gently lowers me to the mattress.

"You're so goddamn beautiful." His voice is rough as he covers me, giving me his weight. His elbows are on either side of my head, his hands buried in my wet hair, and his mouth hovers just an inch over mine. "I've never been prouder of anyone than I was of you today."

I drag my hands down his back, enjoying the feel of him over me, around me.

"Same goes."

His eyes flick down to my mouth. I can't resist bite down on my lower lip, and with a growl, he covers my mouth and kisses me fucking senseless.

He's not rough. He's not impatient.

But he's thorough, and as I spread my legs wider, hitching them higher on his hips, I feel the long, hard length of him against my core.

"Need you, husband."

His eyes open, and he brushes his nose over mine. "Say that again."

I lift my hips, loving the way he slides through my wetness. "I *need* you. Husband."

He lowers his forehead to mine, draws his hips back, and pushes into me with one long thrust, filling me so completely it makes me gasp.

God damn, that metal drags against my walls, sending electricity through me.

"*Yes.*"

"Is this what you need, baby girl?" He nibbles on my lips and over to my ear. "Do you need my cock?"

"I need everything."

He stills for just a heartbeat, and then he's no longer calm and gentle. He starts to move fast, thrusting hard, and when his hand closes over my throat and his thumb rests over my pulse point, I moan in happiness.

"Oh, baby, your pulse is fucking hammering. I want you to come on me." His voice is a growl in my ear that only ignites me further. "I want you to give me everything you have to give, little rose. Do you hear me?"

"Jesus Christ."

"Give it to me." He pushes hard, rubbing the root of himself against my clit, and stars erupt behind my eyelids. "Look at me, wife."

My eyes fly open. He's staring down at me with so much love, so much intensity, it sends me over, convulsing and contracting around him as the orgasm washes over me.

I don't even realize that I'm crying until he brushes his thumb over my cheek, catching the tears there.

"You destroy me when you cry, baby girl."

But I can't help it. With my arms and legs wrapped around him, I cling to him, giving him everything I have to give.

"You are my heart," I whisper through the tears. "You are everything."

He pauses, and then his hips jerk, and he comes with

a roar before rolling over and pulling me with him, still connected, until I'm lying flat on him.

For such a hard man, he's quite comfortable.

We're quiet while our breathing evens out and our heart rates return to normal. After a while, he kisses my head and then rolls me to the side so he can clean us up.

And then he joins me, facing me in the moonlight. Lightning flashes outside, and then thunder rolls, and I grin.

"I love storms."

"How come?" He brushes a lock of my hair off my face, and then the backs of his knuckles slide over my skin, as if he can't stand not touching me.

"It's like Mother Nature's throwing a fit. All loud and dramatic. It's kind of fun."

"Hmm."

"What about you? Do you like them, or do they scare you?"

He frowns, and a shadow passes through his eyes, so I reach for his hand, kiss it, and then tuck it with mine under my chin.

"You can tell me."

"My sisters didn't like storms." His voice is quiet. "And he thought that was funny, so he'd lock them outside so they had to sit in the middle of it."

Without a pause, I wrap my arms around his shoulders and pull him against me, and he buries his face in the crook of my neck, clinging to me.

"God, Holden."

"But now I have this memory with you. And it won't be so awful anymore."

"How did you all survive it?"

He sighs and kisses my shoulder, then my cheek, and we go back to lying on our pillows, facing each other.

"I had to survive it because I had my girls, Millie. After Mom died, I was the only one who cared about them. So I had to figure it out for them. But there were times, like during storms, that even I couldn't keep them safe from his sick and fucked-up ways. He was much stronger than me."

We're quiet for a moment as more lightning and thunder roll around us.

"You know, a few weeks ago, if you'd have told me that we'd be here like this, married and talking about love and all that mushy stuff, I would have stabbed you in the heart."

He smirks. "Mushy stuff?"

"We're totally mushy. And I don't usually *do* mushy." I swallow hard and frown. "I'm going to say some stuff, and I don't want you to run away from me, okay?"

"Nothing you could say could make me leave you, Millie." His eyes are serious, never leaving my gaze. "Never."

"I used to hate you." I swallow again, almost choking on the words that feel so wrong now. "Like, truly hated you. I was so resentful whenever you'd pop up around town, and even worse, when you'd come to my rescue. Do you remember a couple of years ago when I was in the bar, and those stupid tourists decided to be assholes, and you punched the biggest asshole of them all?"

"He fucking touched you. He's lucky he's still breathing."

That gives me pause. My husband can be intense, and I have to admit, I kind of like it.

"I think I was angrier about the fact that you stepped in than I was at the idiot tourist. I would have punched him. I would have taken away his ability to father children."

"I have no doubt. I got this tat after that night." He lifts his arm and points to a roaring mountain lion. "Because you were a little hellcat that night. And I wanted to take you out of there and protect you from anyone who even thought about hurting you. But I couldn't."

I swipe away a tear that drops from the corner of my eye.

"You just wouldn't stay away from me, and every single time, I wanted to swipe at you for it. I *did* swipe at you. I said horrible things to you, and I thought even worse things."

"Baby girl, you have to stop beating yourself up." He brushes away the tears.

"Why wouldn't you just leave me alone? Why did you keep coming back for more of my wrath?"

"Because I couldn't stay away from you." There is no pause in his reply. No moment to reflect or think about it. "Because I was selfish, and I needed to see you like a fish needs water. Even if you were telling me to go fuck myself, at least I could hear your voice. If you were glaring at me, mentally planning my demise, at least I could see those amazing eyes. I knew that I deserved everything you dished out, and if you hurting me was the only way I could see you, so be it."

"You've had too much pain, Holden." I frame his face in my trembling hands. "More than any one person should have in their whole life. You don't deserve that, and it stops *now*. Do you understand me?"

"Oh, baby, it stopped the minute you agreed to marry me. Nothing can ever touch me again as long as I have you."

Sobbing, I burrow into him, and he wraps his arms tightly around me, rubbing his strong hands up and down my back as he murmurs words of love into my ear.

Later, when we've quieted and we're all tangled up together, we fall asleep.

"How did you manage to get today off?" We're sitting on the bed, eating takeout burgers for lunch. I'm in one of his T-shirts, and he's in those gray sweats that make me crazy, and we've barely left this room all morning.

"I'm the boss, baby girl." He smirks and opens his mouth when I offer him a french fry. "How about you?"

"Same." I shrug. "I should have gone in, since I was gone for the branding yesterday, but they have it under control, and I feel like I've barely seen you this week. We're newlyweds, after all."

He narrows his eyes at me. "We need to go on a honeymoon."

I smirk. "No, we don't."

"That's something that newlyweds do."

"I would say that our marriage has been anything but traditional." I finish my burger and set the wrappers on the floor by the bed. "I don't need the rock and the dress and the trip."

His gaze drops to my finger at the mention of a rock, and I shake my head.

"I *like* my band. I work with food, so a band is the most sanitary anyway. Seriously, I have no complaints. How did we even start this conversation?"

I want to change the subject. I don't want him to think that I need anything more than what he's already given me.

"I should try to go see my dad this afternoon." I sigh and scrub my hands over my face. "He's not answering my texts or calls, and he can't avoid me forever. He's my dad. So, I'm going to take control and make him talk to me."

I eye my husband, who's watching me with shrewd blue eyes.

"I should go alone."

"I agree. But I'll be at my ranch, just five minutes away, if you need me."

I love that Holden is always ready to jump in to help me, defend me, love me. It's the best feeling in the world to know that all I have to do is ask him for help.

We get dressed and take separate vehicles out of

town. I turn off first, onto Wild River Ranch Road, and Holden continues up the highway to his place.

I stay to the right when the road forks, headed to where my parents live in a newer, smaller house than the farmhouse that we all grew up in. Remington and his family live in the big house now, as it should be.

I notice that Dad's big white truck is parked in the driveway, so he should be home.

Once I've parked, I pick up my phone and see that Holden has sent a text.

Your Husband: You've got this. ❤️

Why is he so perfect? I shoot back the kissy face emoji.

Stashing my phone in my purse, I climb out of the car and walk up the two steps to the front door. I've never knocked on my parents' door in my life.

Never.

But this time, I do, and it feels so weird, I want to cry. However, I've done enough crying in the last couple of weeks, and I'm determined to keep it together for this.

Mom answers the door, and her eyes go a little wide before she tugs me to her for a big hug.

"Hello, my brave girl."

"Hi. I need my daddy."

She sighs as she pulls away. "I know, baby. He's in the backyard."

I nod, squeeze her hand, and then walk through the

house to the sliding back door, open it, and walk through.

There's my dad, with his back to the house, his hands on his hips, looking out at the mountains beyond. He's a tall man, like my brothers, with wide shoulders. He hasn't lost his muscles with age, likely because, although retired, he still works his ass off out here on the ranch.

"I thought you were about to go volunteer at the hospital." He doesn't look back, and his voice is rough. It's clear that he thinks I'm my mom.

"I don't have time for that. I have to set things right with my dad."

He whips around and takes me in with wide, startled eyes. He looks like he wants to hug me, so I just cross to him and wrap my arms around him, hugging him tight, the way I've done for as long as I can remember.

"I need my daddy," I tell him firmly. "And I know you're mad, but damn it, I love you so much, and I know you love me, too, and this whole thing is ridiculous."

Finally, he hugs me back and kisses the top of my head, and I can sigh in relief.

"I do love you." His voice is rougher than before, and if I'm not mistaken, it sounds like he might have tears in his eyes, but I can't stop hugging him. "I love you more than I can ever tell you, and you know it."

"But you won't talk to me. You won't listen, and you *ignore me*. You know I can't stand that, Dad."

"Hey." He takes my shoulders in his hands and urges me back so he can look in my eyes. "I'm fucking pissed as hell. I've never hit you in anger, but I want to paddle your ass."

My dad may swear, but never at me.

"You've made that clear." I frown at his chest. "You can't go the rest of my life angry and not speaking to me."

"Are you going to divorce him?"

"Absolutely not."

"Then yes, I fucking can."

He turns to walk away, and I storm after him, anger boiling through my veins now.

"*Dad.* You're being unreason—"

"You don't know the half of it." He spins to me, pinning in his hot, angry gaze. "You have no idea why I feel the way I do and why I won't bend on this. No Lexington will ever be a part of my family. They will not set foot on my property."

"Dad." It's a whisper, and I shake my head. "Why?"

"That's none of your business."

"No, that's bullshit." I prop my hands on my hips and raise my chin. "If my own father is willing to pretty much disown me, I deserve to know why."

"*Deserve*?" He stares at me like I've just told him I'm moving to Russia. "You deserve to know why. After you snuck off and eloped and then showed up here, parading that man around in front of our faces and pretty much demanding that we just roll over and show our goddamn bellies?"

"That's not—"

"There was no goddamn discussion, Millie. No one

came and asked me for your hand. Your mother didn't get to fuss and do whatever mothers do when their only daughter gets married. So don't talk to me about what you deserve, little girl. Because we sure as fuck deserved more respect than what you were dishing out, and you know it."

"You're right." I blink at him, and then my shoulders fall. "I didn't handle it well. No one handled it well at all. It was a huge clusterfuck."

It doesn't matter that this marriage started out as a sham. It's real now. I love him more than anything, and I'll be damned if I'll walk away after a year.

Not a chance in hell.

"I'm not getting divorced. If you don't want to see my husband"—he flinches at that word—"that's fine. We won't come here. But you're my father. You've always loved me and protected me so fiercely that I refuse to believe that you'll have nothing to do with me. You are the first man I ever loved, and that won't change. But you said that you were ashamed of me, and I'm here to tell you that I'm ashamed of you, too. Because you don't know everything, and you refuse to listen. You're so stubborn, Dad."

"Hello, Pot."

"Argh!" I can't help it. I stomp my foot on the ground and fist my hands in frustration. "I love you. When you're ready to be reasonable, you know how to find me. And when I need another hug from my dad, I'll come find you."

"All right, then."

I shake my head and walk back to the house, but he says my name, stopping me.

"Yeah?"

"I love you, too."

"Stop being so stubborn, old man."

"I will when you will."

I feel a little better when I drive off of the ranch and then head for Holden. But nothing with my father is resolved. I don't know what to do or say to get him to talk to me about why he's so against my marriage to Holden. I know he hates Holden's father, but my husband never did anything to him. As far as I know, they've never said three words to each other.

Loving people is complicated.

I'm out of sorts when I drive up to Holden's barn on his ranch. The property looks so much different than it did that first time I ever drove out here. And it feels like a weight has been lifted, from the land itself and from the man who owns it.

My husband saunters out of the barn door, his eyebrows climbing when I get out of the car.

"How did that go?"

I take a long, deep breath. "He's so fucking stubborn."

"I'm sorry." He doesn't stop walking until his chest is flush against mine, and his arms wrap around me in a tight hug. "I'm so sorry, Rosie."

"Yeah, well. I'm stubborn, too, and he'll snap out of it eventually. I need to go for a ride on Betty."

He leans back and frowns down at me. "I'll go with you."

"It's okay." I shake my head, and when he tightens, mistaking my mood for pushing him away, I frame his face in my hands. "I just need an hour by myself with my horse, husband. It's nothing personal."

He exhales and tips his forehead to mine. "I don't like it."

"Nothing can hurt me here, remember? That's all gone. This doesn't even look like the same place, and it definitely doesn't feel like it did. I'm safe."

Holden's serious blue eyes roam my face until, finally, he nods once. "Okay."

With a grin, I boost onto my toes and kiss him on the lips. "I won't be too long."

I pull my phone out of my pocket and shoot a text to Remington.

Me: Hey, FYI, I'm going for a ride and will probably cross from Lex to Wild property. It's just me. Don't have one of the cronies shoot me.

I smirk and push the phone back into my jeans as Holden lifts a brow.

"I had to let Rem know that I'll be roaming around."

Side by side, we walk into the barn, and I take my time saddling up my girl. I love the entire riding experience, including the prep and the cleanup when we're finished.

It soothes me, being near Betty. She's been my horse since my sixteenth birthday. We've grown up together.

"Has she been happy out here?" I ask, sensing both Holden and Levi not too far away. "I should come check on her more often."

"She's settled in well," Levi assures me. "No issues with the other horses."

"She's a social girl." I kiss her nose, and she nudges my shoulder in return. "Any bear sightings lately?"

"No, ma'am," Levi replies, and I turn to see why Holden hasn't said anything. He's just staring at me, his arms crossed over his chest, those eyes hot and narrowed as he watches my hands move over my horse. "No bear in a couple of weeks. There was a mountain lion a few days ago on the south perimeter."

I frown. "Mama?"

"We didn't see any cubs," Levi returns. "You know your shit, Mrs. Lexington."

"This is in my blood, Levi. Of course, I know my shit. I have bear spray, but I don't have a rifle. Do I need one?"

"No." This is from Holden now, and he crosses to me and kisses the top of my head. "Nothing's going to hurt you, little rose."

I smile softly. "Okay."

"There's no cell coverage on the east border," he continues softly. "Stay away from there, just in case. I want you to be able to call me at all times."

I nod and then frown. "Wait, your east border is the Wild west border, and I planned to wander between properties."

"Do it towards the north side, and you should be okay. That blind spot worries me, and we need to put a tower over there."

"If you stay north of the creek," Levi adds, "you'll be golden."

I nod and swing up on my girl, rubbing her neck as we settle. "North of the creek. Got it."

Holden's big hand rubs up my thigh and then over and down Betty's flank.

"Be careful, wife."

I nod and then urge Betty out of the barn. Once we're in the warm spring sunshine, we take off in a gallop, headed for the north side of the property through the trees.

CHAPTER TWENTY

HOLDEN

"Boss, I'm going to say something, and I don't want you to cut my dick off for it."

My eyes don't leave my wife as she rides through the pasture toward the tree line. "Say you think my wife is sexy, and you'll not only be fired, I'll take your fucking eyes out."

I hear him gulp, and then he laughs in earnest. "I forgot what I was going to say."

He pats my shoulder and then walks away as I watch Millie's horse slow as they disappear into the evergreens.

She *is* sexy on that horse. Hell, she's sexy doing anything at all, but in my barn, taking care of her animal, it's almost more than I can take.

It's obvious that the visit with her father knocked her off her stride, and needing a little time alone to settle her nerves shouldn't hurt my feelings.

But for just a second, it did.

And that's ridiculous. We can't be attached at the hip

twenty-four seven. It's normal for people to take a moment for themselves if they need it.

But I had eight fucking years to myself, and I'm over it.

Shaking my head, I walk back into the barn and return to the chores I was doing while Millie was gone. Everything that I have to do here can be handled by my men. If I had to take a month off, my ranch wouldn't suffer for it.

However, I enjoy being out here, working. It soothes me, the way being on her horse calms Millie.

So, while she works out whatever's going on in that gorgeous head of hers, I'll stay here, waiting for her. She has one hour, starting now, to get her pretty little ass back here, before I go searching for her.

CHAPTER TWENTY-ONE

MILLIE

"It's so pretty back in here," I say to Betty as we discover another beautiful meadow full of wild flowers. Purples, reds, and yellows flutter in the breeze, and when I inhale, the scent of them surrounds me.

It's fun to explore new property. I've been on every square inch of my family's land, probably hundreds of times. I know it like the back of my hand. So, to be out here, exploring by ourselves, is fun.

And helps to clear the frustration from the conversation with my dad.

"We haven't done this in a long time, have we, baby?" I rub Betty's neck as we walk through the field. "Just you and me, wandering around. There's the creek they told us about."

I judge where the mountains are and urge Betty to the left.

"We have to stay to the north."

I check my phone, and I still have a signal, so we're

going in the right direction. I know Holden doesn't want me to be without a signal, and that's the last thing I'd want, too.

The air is cooler around the creek. Refreshing. I pull Betty to a stop beside it and swing down so I can let the water run over my hands. It's still ice-cold from snow runoff, but it feels good.

I glance to the right and see a little family of deer standing about thirty yards away. The spotted fawn is drinking from the water while two does watch me, their long ears twitching.

I grin but don't make any noise as I turn away from them. I don't want to scare them and send them off into the woods.

I'm on their turf.

Betty takes a drink of the water, and when she's finished, I hop back into the saddle, and she trudges easily through the current to the other side and climbs up the bank.

We wander for more than forty minutes. Just meandering around, taking in the scenery, enjoying the shade from the tall evergreens, and then breaking into the sunshine to warm up. I didn't realize just how beautiful the Lexington property really is.

Something makes me glance up to the trunk of a tree, and then I grin. There's a trail camera. I wonder if Holden's watching me right now, and I wave, just in case.

And then I blow him a kiss.

CHAPTER TWENTY-TWO

HOLDEN

Grinning, I lean both hands on the desk, watching as my girl waves at the camera and then blows me a kiss and gives me a sassy wink. Blood surges through me, right down to my cock.

I haven't been watching her every move as she's made her way through the property. I've given her privacy. I just happened to have this camera pulled up on the monitor, and the movement on it caught my attention.

But I'm glad to see that she's enjoying herself and seems to be just fine.

My shoulders relax.

Checking the time, I see that she's been out for almost an hour, but since I can plainly see that all is well, I'll leave her be for as long as she wants. She's north of the creek, like I asked her to be, so I don't see a reason to worry.

Betty and her beautiful rider move out of sight, and I leave the office.

CHAPTER TWENTY-THREE

MILLIE

We're on Wild property now. There was a gap in the fence that I need to tell the guys about so they can come out and fix it, but it worked out well for me and Betty. I recognize where I am. There's an old, sealed-off gold mine nearby that my brothers and I used to play around when we were kids.

My dad *hated* that we played out here and had the mine sealed up so we wouldn't get hurt. Not to mention, it's so close to Lexington property, and he didn't want us out this far.

And now, here I am, just aimlessly wandering back and forth between the two pieces of land, as though there never was a feud that could have ended a man's life. Probably *did* end someone's life a time or two, back in the day. And it feels really good to know that that piece of history is over.

Because as far as I'm concerned, it was just stupid.

Both families had more than enough land for their businesses to be successful. Hell, they still do.

There was just no reason for so much hate and ugliness.

"Good girl," I croon to Betty as we make our way south. I know that Holden said there's no cell service here, but I check my phone, and I have one little bar. If something happened, I could reach someone. Maybe it's just on his side of the line that it goes dead, because we've never had an issue before.

I want to make a big circle, and by the time I cross back over to Lexington property, I'll be back in the good cell coverage. It'll be fine.

My mountain looms so high and proud before me as Betty and I ride along. Aside from the deer earlier, I haven't seen any other wildlife.

But then I glance down at the ground and see the bear scat.

"Hmm." I narrow my eyes as we pass by. "Looks like a couple of days old. Not fresh. They're likely long gone by now."

Betty doesn't seem worried at all, but I pull the bear spray out of the saddle bag and clip it to the saddle to have it closer, just in case I need it.

"We've seen our share of bears," I remind us both as my eyes move back and forth. "But there's no need to be stupid."

"Millie?"

I spin as Betty shifts on her feet and see Brady and Bruiser riding not too far away.

"You scared me!"

"What are you doing out here?" My brother frowns over at me as his horse slows near mine. Bruiser hangs back just a little.

I think Bruiser used to have a crush on me, but because he works for my family, he never asked me out. He's always kept a respectable distance. And I like him. He's *huge*, at well over six and a half feet tall, but he's just a big teddy bear at heart.

And if I hadn't been in love with my husband since I was nineteen, I might have pursued something with Bruiser.

"I'm riding my horse. Duh." I roll my eyes, and Brady scowls at me while Bruiser hides a smile behind his hand.

"Why?" Brady asks.

"Because I wanted to go for a ride. Holden and Remington both know what I'm doing. I texted Rem before I headed out."

Brady's shoulders relax a bit at that. "He's in town, and I haven't seen him. You're okay?"

"Yeah, just more arguing with Dad, and I needed to clear my head."

Brady nods, his mouth set grimly. "I get it. I saw you on one of our trail cams, and I wanted to make sure you're okay, since you didn't answer your phone."

I scowl and look down at my phone and see that I don't have a signal.

"I must have been out of range for a minute. Sorry

about that. I'm just wandering, but don't worry about me. I have bear spray, and this isn't my first ride."

"Oh, I know you can handle yourself," Brady says with a wink. "Just making sure because I'm your brother, and that's what we do."

"Yes, I've had overprotective brothers my whole life." I soften and offer both men a smile. "Thanks for checking on me, though. I really am okay. I'm going to ride about two miles south and then cut back over to Holden's property and make a circle back to the barn. Should be there in less than an hour. It's a nice day for a ride."

"Text me when you get back, okay? Just so I know that you're safe."

Not wanting to cause anyone any undue stress, I nod. "I will. Thanks for checking on me. Go talk to Dad and tell him he's being an asshole."

Bruiser coughs, and Brady shakes his head. "I'd like to live, thanks. Have you ever considered that he has a good reason for the way he's acting?"

"Sure, but I asked, and he won't talk about it. Anyway, let me get back to finding my Zen. I love you. Kiss Daisy for me, and tell Abbi we need a girls' night."

"I'll do both." He turns back to Bruiser and nods. "We're good here."

"See you, Miss Millie," Bruiser says, tipping his hat at me, and then the two men ride off, back toward the way they came.

"We're surrounded by overbearing, super-alpha, overprotective men, Betty." I rub her neck softly as I watch the two men disappear. "It's infuriating. Do you want an apple?"

I hop off her to give her a break and pull an apple that I brought with me out of the saddlebag, and she gently takes it out of my hand, happily crunching away.

"You're my best friend. My best girl." I kiss her cheek, and I see the love in her brown eye shining back at me. "I know, you love me, too. I'm going to come out and ride you at least once a week, like we used to. Okay? You and me, Bets, we're gonna ride all summer."

She snorts and nods, and I grin.

She likes that idea.

"Okay, let's circle back, shall we? It's almost dinnertime." I launch myself back onto her, already feeling the pull of muscles in my thighs and butt, up into my back, that haven't been used lately. "Maybe we'll make something special for Holden for dinner. I'm pretty decent at fried chicken. I wonder if he likes fried chicken. He must. I mean, who doesn't, right?"

I'm singing a country song about *chicken fried* as we wander down the fence line to where it meets Lexington property again, and with a break in the fence, we easily march right through.

"There's a lot of downed fencing from winter," I mutter, shaking my head. "If we can get through, so can other animals and cows. I'll let the guys know. I haven't ridden fence in five years or more."

I never hated ranch work. In fact, it's honest, hard work that is damn satisfying. But I never loved being out in the hot sun all summer long. It zaps me.

We've come around a bend, still near the property line, and find the creek again, along with another fence. The property line must zigzag a bit over here.

"Want a drink, baby?"

Again, I hop down, and Betty gets a drink.

She doesn't really *need* to drink this much, but she's not working today. She's my friend. And I'm in no hurry.

As she drinks, I walk over to examine this fence. It looks older than the other one, and since we're about twenty yards from the actual property line, it doesn't make sense for it to be here.

"Maybe it's just a really old property line fence," I murmur as I approach. "Maybe an original piece, and it's still standing for sentimental reasons."

And then the world falls out from under me.

With a scream, I fall, landing hard on my right ankle, into the soft earth below. I scramble up, but because my ankle is hurt, I have to lean on the wall of dirt. There are roots sticking out, hanging down, and I don't even want to *think* about the bugs that are crawling around me right now.

Oh, God, the bugs!

I pull my phone out, but there's no signal.

No fucking signal.

When I flip on the flashlight and shine it around me, I yelp at the sight of the bones of a critter that died in here at some point. Maybe a raccoon or a possum.

"Ugh, that's so gross."

The hole isn't big. It's maybe six feet wide, square, but it's at least ten feet deep. I can't reach the top with my hands, even if I jump, which I can't because of my ankle.

Panic wants to set in, but I take a deep, earthy breath and let it out slowly, trying to hang on to my sanity with my fingernails.

"Okay," I mutter to myself, looking around. "Maybe I can hold on to the roots to pull myself out."

I pocket the useless phone and grab on to a handful of roots, and, ignoring my screaming ankle, try to climb the side as if it's a rock wall and I'm Alex Honnold, free soloing El Capitan.

"Yeah, because I could do that in any lifetime," I mutter, but then give it a shot and find myself flat on my back, staring up at the blue sky overhead and the broken roots in my hand. I scramble back to my feet. "Shit."

I try to roll the ankle and let out a whimper when the pain doesn't go away.

"Not broken, but definitely sprained." I sigh, looking up, and then the severity of the situation starts to wrap itself around my neck and tighten, stealing the breath from my lungs. My heart hammers, and blood rushes through my ears.

I'm at the bottom of a deep hole, on Lexington property, with no cell signal. I can't call for help. I'm at least a couple of miles away from Holden's barn, and farther than that from my family.

"Betty?" I call out, my voice sounding like sandpaper. "Betty! Come here, girl."

God, I don't want her to fall in, but maybe I could

reach her reins if she lowers her head. I hear her footsteps overhead, and then they get farther away.

Not closer.

"Go find help, Betty!" I scream it, hoping she not only hears me, but understands. "Go find help, girl!"

Now the panic is settling in, seeping into every pore of my body. I've never had a panic attack before, but if a racing heart, shortness of breath, and your life flashing before your eyes is what it feels like, then I'm there.

I hold my phone up as far as I can, but there's still no signal. I would have sworn that I had a tiny one when Betty was getting some water.

But apparently, at the bottom of a scary-as-fuck pit of despair, service isn't a thing.

Why is this hole even here? For wildlife? Why would they want to trap wildlife?

This is so weird.

"Help!" I scream, hoping someone can hear me. Maybe the trail cams have audio and they'll hear me in the office. "HELP!"

But I yell until my throat screams in rebellion, and there's no sign of anyone nearby. No footsteps, no voices. I can hear the water of the creek and some birds. And that's it.

I needed a couple of hours of alone time, and now I might die here in this fucked-up grave, alone for all eternity.

"Well, that's a lovely thought," I mutter, willing my heart rate to slow down. I don't want to sit on the dirt. I *do not want to.* But my ankle is killing me, and I can feel it swelling in my shoe, making it almost unbearably uncomfortable. So, I shine my flashlight again and make sure I'm sitting as far away from those bones as I can get and prop my foot up on a clump of dirt. At least, I hope it's just a clump of dirt and not something buried there.

"Jesus. Okay, calm down. Breathe in for three seconds, hold for three seconds, let it out for three seconds."

Is it three seconds you're supposed to do? Or four? I don't know, I heard it somewhere, and it's not helping.

"Stop," I whisper, and look up again. My neck is already sore from looking up. "When I don't come back to the barn, Holden will come find me."

Holden will find me.

Oh, God, he has to come find me.

"Don't be silly, he totally will. When I don't come back by dinnertime, he'll send out a big search party, and they'll pull me out of here, and it'll be a story we tell our grandkids someday."

My heart stills at that thought.

Our grandkids.

I close my eyes and let out a long breath. I know that neither of us wants our marriage to end after a year. We've both voiced it. And although we've only been married for a few weeks—and literally the day before that, I might have stabbed him in the neck for looking at me sideways—I can admit that I don't think that I ever stopped loving him.

It's like he just wormed his way inside of me and never left.

“Come on, husband. Come find me.”

According to my phone, I’ve been down here for over an hour when the rain starts. I tip my head back and stare up.

“Of course. Because sitting in mud will make this more pleasant,” I mutter, pulling my good leg up to my chest and wrapping my arms around it. Then lightning flashes and thunder booms, and a jolt sparks through me, making me jump at least a foot off the ground. “Seriously?”

I didn’t realize that we’d be getting thunderstorms this afternoon, but it’s spring in Montana. We almost always get afternoon storms in the spring.

I just thought I’d be home well before now, safe inside, making dinner. Maybe I’d vent about my dad, and then Holden would distract me with something flirty and sexy, and we’d end up having hot, crazy sex.

Water fills my eyes, and the tears fall, mixing with the rain as it pours in on me. It’s as if a faucet has been turned on, and I’m sitting in an outdoor shower.

Or a really dirty outdoor bathtub.

Where the hell is Holden?

CHAPTER TWENTY-FOUR

HOLDEN

I can hear the thunder off in the distance, and so far, there's been no sign of Millie. With a scowl, I open my phone and try to call her, but it goes straight to voice mail.

"Fuck," I mutter. "She's in a dead zone."

"Boss!" Vance comes running out of the office, and the panic on his face has me scowling and dread filling my stomach. "Boss, you have to see this."

I run behind him, into the office. "Talk."

"Right here," he says, switching to a different camera angle. "That's Betty, and she doesn't have a rider."

No.

My lungs seize, and my brain feels like it's going to explode, and then I launch into go mode.

"Get the others and saddle up. Now. I'm calling the Wilds."

Vance runs out of the office, calling for the others as he goes, and I immediately dial Remington's number.

"Hello."

"I need every man you can spare."

He's quiet for a heartbeat, and then, "What's wrong?"

I explain about Millie going for a ride *three fucking hours ago* and seeing Betty on the monitor.

"I can't reach her by phone. Wherever she is, she doesn't have a signal."

"Brady said he saw her out by the old gold mine," Rem says, his voice hard. "He and Bruiser went out to check on her, but that was two hours ago."

I curse a blue streak as another wave of terror moves through me.

"We'll find her. Let's call in Beckett and any of the men he can spare, too, since they're not too far away. You search your side, we've got this side, and the Blackwells can do both."

"On it. Jesus Christ, Rem—"

"We'll find her," he repeats, his voice harder this time. "She's fine. Might be hurt, but she's fine."

"I'm taking the walkies," I inform him. "Channel nine. The service is too spotty for phones."

"We'll do the same. Let's do this."

He hangs up, and knowing that Millie's brothers and their men are headed out to look, I immediately call Beckett.

"We'll all come help, and bring our walkies, too," he says, five minutes later. "I even have Blake out here today. On our way."

He hangs up, and I hurry out to find my guys, with four saddled horses, waiting for me.

"We spread out," I begin, talking through the lump in my throat as we each clip a walkie-talkie to our belts. My voice wants to crack, but I swallow hard. "I want one of you to find Betty and bring her back here right away. We don't know how far that horse has wandered away from Millie, but maybe not far. I've got the Wilds and the Blackwells helping, too."

I outline the rest of the plan, and my guys all nod in agreement. They're sober, a little scared, and if I'm not mistaken, *pissed.*

We all want my girl found, in one piece, immediately.

"We got this, boss," Levi says with a nod. "I'll go get Betty and bring her back here, then head north."

"I'll head south," Vance adds.

"Tim." I look at the older man who's been here for many years, going back to when I was a kid. "I want you to stay close by here, in case she comes sauntering out of those woods with the story of the year. Watch the cameras, and call us if you see anything we can use."

"Got it, boss," Tim says, immediately walking to the office.

Lightning and thunder boom around us, and the sky opens up, pouring rain in huge drops.

"Shit," I mutter.

She's out there, maybe hurt, getting soaked.

I grab an extra blanket, rolled into a waterproof cover, and toss it on the back of my horse, then lift myself into the saddle. "I'm headed east. Right into the dead zone. If she's not answering me, that's where she is."

That has to be where she is because the alternative is that she can't answer, and that possibility—I can't even think about it.

I can hear the Blackwells pulling in with their huge trailer full of horses.

Bridger is the first one out of the truck and comes running my way. "Any idea where she might be?"

"None." My voice is hard, and no one misses the fear in it. My heart is somewhere out there, in trouble, and *I don't know where she is.* "We fan out. The Wilds are doing the same on their side."

"We dropped Blake and Brooks at their barn on our way over here," Beckett informs me. "Two of us there, two here, and Billie's at the farm with Birdie."

"Thank you."

"Thank us later, after we get her back. Let's go," Bridger says, and we all set off, headed in different directions from the barn.

The rain is incessant, and I feel better about the lightning when we're all in the cover of the trees. I don't need anyone getting struck by lightning.

I head straight for the east border. I don't think she would have spent much time there, since we were clear that it wasn't safe, but she might have just been passing through, not thinking anything of it. Or maybe she got lost.

Jesus, I never should have let her go alone. She

doesn't know this property well enough for her to be off on her own.

I'm a goddamn idiot. I should have gone with her, shown her everything there is to see, so she'd at least know where she was going.

Over the next hour, the rain dies down, and the lightning stops, but thunder continues to boom from far away.

I get check-ins from guys all over the two properties, all saying that they don't see her.

"This is Levi," a voice says through my speaker. "I have Betty and am taking her to the barn, then I'll head south. She's not hurt. Over."

"Copy that," I say into my radio. I'm relieved that the horse is fine, but *what in the fucking hell is going on?*

I'm riding along the east border and notice that there's a spot in the fence that needs mending. She might have come through here. It's not far from the creek, and it would make a good passageway from the Wild ranch onto mine.

Suddenly, something has the hairs on the back of my neck standing up, and I stop the horse, cocking my ear, listening.

The sound of the creek might have drowned it out, but then I hear...*singing.*

I'm off my horse in a flash. "Millie? *MILLIE*?"

"Holden!"

Relief like I've never felt washes through me, almost bringing me to my knees, but then she shouts something that sends a chill through me.

"BE CAREFUL! DON'T FALL!"

I stop moving, my hands out wide as I frantically search the ground.

"Fall where?"

"In this huge hole I'm in!"

With my heart in my throat, I turn in a circle, and then I see it. Over by an old fence, a big hole in the ground, and I sprint over to it and lie on my stomach, staring down, relieved to see my wife staring up at me with wide, wild eyes.

"Oh, thank God." She starts to cry, and I've never felt so helpless in my life.

"Millie." My voice is firm, and I don't know how I'm keeping it together, except that I need her to focus so I can get her out of there. "Listen to me. Listen to me, baby girl."

She gulps and swallows, her eyes never leaving my face.

"It's getting dark," she cries.

"I know, but I'm here now, and we're going to get you out of there. Are you hurt?"

"My ankle." She stands and winces. "I sprained my ankle. Otherwise, I'm just freaked out. Get me the hell out of this pit, husband."

I unclip the radio from my belt and bring it to my mouth.

"Holden here. I have her, but she's fallen into a hole, and I don't think I can pull her out myself. It's deep and muddy."

The soft ground beneath me starts to shift, and I'm terrified that it'll collapse onto her, so I scramble back.

"Don't you *dare* leave me!"

"I'm right here," I tell her. "I'm not leaving."

I swallow hard and keep talking into the walkie.

"We're just over the property line, about ten yards in, roughly a mile north of the old gold mine. Over."

"Brady here," the response comes. "Roger that. We saw her there earlier and know where you are. We'll all meet you there. Over."

"I need Blake for a sprained ankle. Over."

"Blake here, I'm on my way. Over."

"Everyone on the Lexington side is headed your way, too. Over." That is Levi's voice, and I'm relieved to know that the cavalry is coming our way.

I approach the hole from a different angle and look down.

"If I reach down, can you grab my hand?"

"I can't jump," she says, starting to look panicked. "Holden, I need you to get me out of here."

"If you can't jump, I can't pull you out." Jesus, she's starting to shake even harder, and her face crumples. I *need* to get to her, to comfort her.

So, I do the only thing I can think of and jump down with her.

"Holy fuck." She wraps herself around me, desperately shaking, unable to catch her breath. "I didn't know you had booby traps set on this property, h-husband."

"Neither did I." Grimly, I take her dirty face in my

hands and plant my lips on hers. I can't stop touching her, running my hands over her to make sure she's really okay. "Baby, listen to me."

"Oh, my God." She's moving right into a panic attack, so I lean my forehead to hers.

"Millie. Look at me. I'm here, my love. I'm right here, and you're okay. We're gonna get out of here. Take a deep breath."

With her eyes on mine, she pulls air into her lungs. Tears continue to fall down her cheeks, leaving trails in the dirt on her skin, and it's enough to break my damn heart.

"But now we're *both* stranded down here."

"No, everyone's coming. They'll help me get you out of here. I just couldn't stay up there while you had a meltdown. It's better if we have a meltdown together."

"Were you scared, too?"

"I've never been that terrified in my fucking life." Wrapping my arms around her, I hold on tight. "I'll never let you go again. Jesus, Millie."

We're ankle-deep in mud from the rain, and I don't like the way the side leans in, as if it wants to give way at any moment.

If that happens, we're fucked.

"How did you find me?" Her face is pressed to my chest, and she's holding on to me desperately, as if I might disappear, leaving her down here to fend for herself.

"We spotted Betty wandering around." I fill her in on

the last two terrifying hours of my life, and when I've finished, she's clinging to me even harder. "Betty's safe in the barn. Jesus Christ, I'm so sorry, my love. I never should have let you go by yourself."

"*Let me*?" She laughs softly and cups my cheek in her hand. "Oh, husband. Are you under the impression that you can boss me around?"

"Hell yes, and you'll fucking listen, or I'll spank your ass."

"Kinky." She kisses me, and then her face crumples, and she starts to cry again, and I simply pull her against me, holding her tight. "I want to go home."

"I know, baby. The others are on their way over here. I want Blake to look at you before I put you on a horse."

"Blake?" She frowns at me, the surprise pausing her tears. "Who's been out here searching?"

"Your whole family, my guys, and the Blackwells. And if I didn't find you by dark, I'd have called in all of Bitterroot Valley. Make no mistake, little rose, I will find you anywhere."

"Holden!"

"Over here," I call out in reply. "Be careful! Don't fall into this fucking hole and kill us!"

Suddenly, about eight heads lean over the top of the hole, staring down at us.

"What the fuck is *this*?" Ryan demands, glaring down into the hole.

"I don't fucking know," I growl back at him. "But I'll find out. Now, get us out of here."

"Holden, can you bend down and get Millie on your shoulders, and then we can grab her hands and lift her out?"

Without an answer, I do exactly that, ignoring the spray of mud from her shoes as I stand with her on my shoulders.

"Reach up, Mill," Chase says, his voice hard as he reaches down for her. "Grab me with one hand and Bridger with the other."

"My hands are wet and slippery," she says, tears in her voice.

"It's okay, we've got gloves," Bridger replies. "We've got you, baby. Come on."

Suddenly, she's lifted off of me, and I look up to see her disappear over the side of the hole.

Levi has a rope in his hands and peers down at me with Ryan and Remington. "I'm going to lower this, and my horse is going to help you climb out, okay, boss?"

"Excellent."

He tosses the rope down, and I grab it. I'm able to easily climb the wall with the help of the horse pulling me.

Immediately, I drop next to Millie where she sits on the ground, and Blake is already sitting beside her, his first aid kit open at his side.

"Hey, Mill." Blake is the doctor in the Blackwell family, and he's smiling at my girl. "I hear you got hurt."

"My ankle," she says, lifting her right foot that's caked in mud. "I think it's just twisted. Hurts like a bitch."

I hear Remington and his brothers talking, but I ignore them and concentrate on Blake's hands on Millie.

If he wasn't a doctor and a friend of mine, he'd be losing those hands.

"It's swollen," he murmurs as he peels off her sock and shoe, revealing white skin under all that wet dirt. "Pretty bruised up already. Definitely looks sprained to me."

He moves it around, making her wince, but he seems satisfied.

"No break here. Keep it elevated with ice and ibuprofen for a couple of days. Try to stay off of it so it can heal up." He quickly checks her over, looking for any other injuries. "You didn't hit your head?"

"Not hard."

I growl down at her, and she shakes her head.

"The second time I fell—"

"There was a *second time*?" I demand.

"I tried to hang on to the roots to climb out, but they gave way, and I fell back. Not far. Hit the dirt, but didn't see stars or anything. I'm fine."

"I'm not," I growl and tighten my hold on her.

"Any other places that hurt, Millie?" Blake asks, ignoring me.

"My throat hurts from screaming and singing. I have a bruised ass, and I'll probably have a little PTSD for a while, but I'm okay. Mostly, I just got cold from the rain."

"Singing?" Chase asks with a smirk. "Were you trying to scare away the wildlife?"

"You're a riot in a crisis. I bet your coworkers love

working with you. I knew that I had to make noise if anyone was going to hear me." She clears her throat. "And screaming is really exhausting."

"Baby girl," I whisper, kissing her head.

"Take her home, get her cleaned up, and let her rest for a few days," Blake says to me, his shrewd eyes all business. "If you want a list of therapists, I can get that to you."

Out of all the shit I've been through in my life, *this* might be the thing that sends *me* to a therapist.

"Are there more of these holes along the property line?" Brady demands as I help Millie to her feet.

"I didn't know this one existed," I remind him. "I've been all over this ranch a million times, and I've never seen anything like this."

"Us either," Levi says, shaking his head.

"We know this land by heart," Vance speaks up. "I've never seen anything like this."

"It's not a wildlife trap," Rem murmurs, staring down.

"Yeah, well, it could be one because there were bones down there." Millie shivers as I stand and then simply lift her into my arms, as if I'm about to carry her over the threshold. "And it's fucking creepy as hell."

"I'm so sorry, little rose." I kiss her temple and then her cheek.

Then my eyes move up, and sitting on a horse on the other side of the property line fence is John Wild.

"Millie," I murmur, getting her attention, and then

gesture with my chin to her father as she tightens her hold around my shoulders.

"Daddy, why are you over there?"

"I won't set foot on that land." His voice is hard, but it looks like he has tears in his eyes.

"Dad, for fuck's sake," Ryan begins, shaking his head, but John just glares at his son and then turns his gaze back to us.

"You've done nothing but hurt her," he says, his eyes on mine. "And that's all you're going to do until she's dead and gone."

"*DAD!*" Millie's voice is hard and loud as she shouts at her father. "Stop it. Stop it right now. This was an accident."

"That hole didn't magically appear there by accident," John says, narrowing his eyes. "I'll bet everything I have that his fucker of a father dug that hole, hoping something like this would happen. Looks like he got that wish."

I swallow because I can't dispute what he says. My first thought was the same thing.

And Tim and I are going to have a long conversation, because the old man would know if this is something my old man did.

"If you think," I begin, cutting off whatever Brady was about to say so I can address their father, "that I let Millie ride her horse out here, alone, hoping that she'd fall in here and break her neck, you're fucked up in the head, Mr. Wild. Respectfully, of course."

John's lip curls up in a sneer, and I keep talking.

"She needed some time alone with Betty because she was beating herself up over her conversation with *you*. So, you go ahead and tell me exactly who's hurting your daughter."

I narrow my eyes, but he doesn't respond to me.

"That's what I thought."

"Jesus Christ," Chase says. "We'll get some men out to scout for other holes."

"I'll do that," I reply more calmly. "I have the men for it, and it'll be handled first thing tomorrow."

"If you need help," Remington says, ignoring the scathing look from his father, "let us know. We have the men, too."

"Appreciate it."

"Please stop, Daddy," Millie says, her voice soft and pleading. "This wasn't the fault of anyone here. He's long gone."

"Yeah, and he's still fucking with my family."

With a shake of his head, John turns his horse and rides off in the other direction.

"I think it's going to take a while for your dad to like me," I murmur against Millie's hair, making her choke out a laugh. "It's okay, I'll win him over."

"That's the spirit," Blake says with a laugh as he climbs onto his horse.

"We'll see you at the barn, boss." My guys head out.

"Want help getting her up there?" Ryan asks.

"Yeah. I don't want to hurt her."

It takes three of us to get Millie up on the horse,

ensuring that we don't hurt her ankle. I pull the blanket out of the waterproof sheath and then wrap it tightly around her to warm her up. I jump up behind her and take the reins before looking at all my friends and Millie's family.

"I don't really have the words—"

"This is what family does," Remington says with a shrug, then tips his hat and rides away.

Just like that, I feel like the wind has been knocked out of me again as the others nod and also ride away.

"Did he—?"

"Yeah," Millie says, wiggling back to rest against me, pushing her perfect little ass against my crotch. "My dad's an ass, which is something I never thought I'd say about my dad, by the way. Everyone else seems to be just fine, babe."

"I'm sorry." I kiss her head as I carefully maneuver the horse in the direction of my barn. The adrenaline is wearing off, and I feel the exhaustion wanting to settle in as darkness begins to seep in around us. She must be fucking decimated. "I don't know this *babe* person."

"Holden."

"Nope."

"Honey." I can hear the smile in her voice.

"Who?"

She chuckles softly. "Husband."

"There she is." I kiss the top of her head. "Sleep if you want, wife. I have you. I might not ever let go of you again, let alone let you out of my sight."

"I was so scared." Her voice is so small it breaks my

heart. "The only time I've been that terrified is w-when I thought you were in that building—"

"Shh." I wrap an arm around her shoulders, pressing my forearm across her chest, and hug her close against me. I can feel her heart hammering, and it fucking tears me apart. "I'm right here, baby girl. I'm going to get you home, and you're going to stay there for a few days, resting."

"I have the shop."

"We'll either have your people handle it or close the shop for the week."

"What did I say about you being the boss of me?"

"Do you have any idea how fucking out of my mind I've been today?" My voice is a growl against her ear as all the emotions of the day swamp me again. "How terrified? I saw Betty on that camera, and I swear my soul left my body. So, if you think that I'm not about to come unhinged and keep you in bed for at least a week, you don't know me very well, Rosie."

"I think you're obsessed with me." There's humor in her voice, as if she's trying to lighten the mood. But she has no idea just *how* obsessed I am with her.

"Are you just now figuring that out? And here I thought you were the smart one in this marriage."

She snorts out a laugh and then leans her head back on my shoulder.

"Fine. Be obsessed. I guess I kind of like you, too."

I smirk and kiss her hair, and then the barn comes into view as we exit through the trees.

The Blackwells have already gone home, but I see the

lights on in the barn, telling me my guys are still inside, waiting for us.

"I'm going to set you in my truck, and then I have to talk to the guys really quick, okay?"

"I need a shower, Hol—husband."

I grin at the almost slip of the tongue. "I know. I just need two minutes, and then we'll go home and get cleaned up."

I lead the horse to the truck and slide down, then I lower Millie into my arms and get her settled in the front seat.

Levi and Vance are immediately at my side, the reins already in Levi's hand.

"Is she okay?" Vance asks with a scowl.

"Yeah, she's going to be fine. I need Tim."

"He's still in the office." Levi licks his lips. "What do you need us to do, boss?"

"If you could get the horse cleaned up and put in its stall, that'd be a huge help. There will be a lot of work starting tomorrow."

As we walk to the barn, I outline the search I expect them to do to see if there are other holes.

"He was a sick fuck," Vance says, shaking his head. "But I didn't think he'd do something like that."

"Don't just look for holes. Look for any kind of booby trap, and be careful, in case he set fucking bear traps. I wouldn't put anything past that son of a bitch. Keep me posted. I'll be home with her for the week while she recovers."

When I walk into the office, I find Tim sitting at the

desk, his head in his hands, and when he looks up at me, he looks…haunted.

"I didn't remember it," he says immediately. "Your daddy had us dig those holes thirty years ago. Most of them collapsed in on themselves from rain and snow."

"But you knew they were out there."

"*Thirty years ago*," he repeats.

"By the Wild property line."

"He hated that family and was convinced that they came onto this land. For what, who knows? He wanted to catch them."

"He wanted to kill them."

"That was never a secret," Tim says with a sigh.

"So, let me get this straight. My *wife* went out for a ride by herself today and fell into a thirty-fucking-year-old hole that my dad dug so he could trap and kill her family." The fury has a life of its own as it courses through me. "I'm lucky that it didn't cave in on her!"

"Jesus, Holden. Jesus, I'm sorry. Like I said, none of them held up longer than a year. I didn't know it was still there."

"What other booby traps did he set?"

Tim shakes his head. "None that I know of, but he was sneaky, and he didn't trust anyone, so he might have done other things that we didn't know about."

"The three of you are going to ride every fucking square inch of this ranch and find anything that might so much as give her a hangnail." I lean in, glaring at the older man. "Understood?"

"Got it, boss."

"Good." I storm out of the barn and climb into my truck. Millie's sleeping peacefully, not even stirring when I close the door.

Maybe her dad is right. Maybe being with me is still a threat to her, even with the fucker dead. She wouldn't have gotten hurt today if it wasn't for me.

I shouldn't hold her to the terms of the marriage.

But I'll be fucking damned if I can let her go.

CHAPTER TWENTY-FIVE

MILLIE

God, who knew that everything in my freaking body would hurt so bad? I feel like I got hit by a semi and then was dragged behind it for about seventy miles.

I even discovered some road rash on my elbow that I didn't know I had because it was covered in mud.

"Burn the clothes," I say to Holden as he gingerly helps me into the shower. "All of them. The mud won't come all the way out."

"I'll trash them," he confirms as he steps in with me. "I wish I had a stool for you to sit on and get off of that ankle."

"I'll lean on you." I sigh as I plant a hand on his chest and let the hot water run over me. "Holy shit, that feels good. I don't even want to know if I have spiders in my hair."

"Uh, I don't think you do." I open my eyes and find

him watching me with serious blue eyes. "How are you, baby girl?"

"Meh." I shrug a shoulder and close my eyes again, but he takes my chin in his fingers and makes me open my eyes, focusing on him. "I'm going to be fine."

"Let's set some ground rules for this week, wife."

I sigh, but he keeps talking.

"Number one, when I ask how you are, you tell me the truth, even if you think it's not what I want to hear or it'll hurt my feelings."

"Fine. I hurt, I'm tired, and I might be a little grouchy."

He nods and helps me soap up my hair.

"Fair enough. Number two, unless it's in the shower or standing up from the toilet, you don't walk. I carry you."

"Hol—"

"I'm not asking, Rosie. I'm telling." Those eyes flash again, and the muscle in his jaw twitches.

I bite my lower lip. He's being unreasonable, but he's also being protective and so sweet and gentle, and I kind of love it.

"Number three." He urges me to lean back so he can rinse my hair, then he works in some conditioner, and as that sets, we get to work cleaning the rest of me off. This is not a lingering shower. This is just to get us both clean and rid of that hole. I grab a rag and some soap and start washing him off, too, enjoying the way the suds run down his tattoos. I really should ask him to tell me more about them. I wonder when he got this one of a willow tree. "Are you listening?"

"Hmm."

"Baby girl."

My eyes raise to his. "I'm listening, husband."

He pulls in a breath and lets it out slowly.

"God, baby." His hand covers my throat, and his thumb drifts down my jawline. "God."

"I'm *fine.*" Circling his wrist, I drag his hand down to my chest and flatten it over my sternum, pressing my palm over his hand. "Feel that? It's beating strong, and it's slowed down. I'm right here, in this moment, with my fucking gorgeous husband, who's pampering me and washing away a really horrible experience. Stay here with me, okay? Don't go back there."

He exhales, his eyelids flutter closed, and he shuffles close to me so he can lower his forehead to mine.

"I love you so much, Millie."

I grin and drag my hands down his sides. "I know. I love you, too. Now, keep going with the rules, and let's rinse off so we can snuggle in the bed. I'm really looking forward to that part."

His lips tip up into a soft smile, and then he shuffles back so we can continue washing each other.

"Where was I?"

"Number three." I drag the cloth down his hard-as-hell belly and down his cock and then smirk when it stirs. "I'm in no shape right now, but give me a few hours to gain my strength, and I could probably take this for a ride."

"Cute." He chuckles low in his chest, and it vibrates through me, spreading more heat and tenderness into me. "I'm not going to fuck you tonight."

"Party pooper. What's number three? The suspense is killing me."

"I don't know yet," he admits with a soft sigh. "It'll come to me."

"I think you're tired, too. You have to be. I think we're pretty clean now, so let's dry off and get you in bed."

"It came to me." He grabs the handle of the showerhead and takes it off so he can rinse himself, including his hair, and then hangs it up again. "No worrying about me."

"Yeah, okay. I've already broken that rule, husband."

His eyes narrow, but I bat my eyelashes at him, and he just shakes his head.

It takes a little longer than usual to get us dried off, me into loose sweats and a T-shirt, and settled into the bed, but we make it.

And I can't decide if I'm more tired or hungry.

But then Holden wraps his arms around me, pulls me into his side, and my eyes close.

I guess I'm more tired.

"I'll take the ice pack off of your ankle in about twenty," he murmurs against my hair.

"You put an ice pack on me?" I frown against him. I didn't even feel it.

"You're so tired, baby." He kisses me lightly. "Go to sleep. I've got you."

He said that on the horse, too. *I've got you.*

God, I love that he has me.

"It's a love language, you know."

He squeezes me and kisses my forehead. "What is?"

"*I've got you.*" My voice is so sleepy, so quiet, I hope he can hear me. "It's a really great love language. You speak it well."

He sighs and turns to wrap both arms around me in a hug. "I'll always have you, little rose."

"You guys are two of my favorite sisters-in-law." I pop a french fry into my mouth and grin at Charlie and Dani, who happened to stop by with lunch. I've been in this house for two days, and I'm starting to feel better. Not great, definitely not ready to go back to work, but I'm improving.

And, as much as I love Holden, I needed a couple of hours without him. He hovers. And he made me promise that I wouldn't get up from this couch until he came back from the ranch.

He's so freaking bossy.

"You say that to all the sisters-in-law," Charlie replies with a laugh before biting into her burger. "I wonder what The Wolf Den does to these burgers to make them so freaking good. Do they add crack? It's crack, isn't it?"

"Or, you know, garlic," Dani says with a grin.

"Same thing," Charlie decides. "I know that literally everyone and their dog has asked you this a million times in the past two days, but how are you doing, Millie?"

"Sore. Tired. But never bored because between *your* huge family and *my* huge family, I'm never alone. I have a revolving door of visitors, which is honestly nice. It makes Holden a little twitchy because he thinks that I should be left alone, but I'm not a television lover, and I can't just sit here, twiddling my thumbs all week, you know?"

"You don't like television?" Charlie asks. "Not even reality TV?"

"Not really," I confirm. "So, that's me. What's going on with you two? Tell me everything. Give me all the dirt. Tell me some gossip."

"I start working at the elementary school in August," Dani says with a smile. "It's not gossip, but it's exciting. I'll be teaching kindergarten, and that's my favorite age, so I'm excited to dig in. In the meantime, I'll find something in town to get me through the summer."

"You're hired." I point at her, surprising her. "I'll need more help this summer. If you want a job, I'll give you one."

"I'll take it," Dani replies in surprise. "Thanks."

"I'll also need help with weddings," Charlie reminds her sister. "So between the two jobs, we have you covered."

"Well, I don't know why I was worried." Dani winks at me and eats a french fry while Charlie starts to tell us all about her biggest bridezilla of the season so far.

But ten minutes in, there's a knock at my door.

"I'll get it," Charlie says, making sure I stay where I am. "Holden's orders."

"Bossy man," I mutter as she walks to the door and opens it.

"Hi," Birdie says with a bright smile. "I'm here to cheer up Millie."

"Come on in," Charlie says with a big wave of her arm.

"I'm sorry, we didn't know you already have company," Bridger begins, but then stops talking when he sees Dani. He immediately grins. "We can come back another time."

"That's lame." I roll my eyes, making a mental note to ask him what his deal is later. If he has a thing for my sister-in-law, why don't I know about it? "Come in here and love me."

"I made you a card," Birdie announces as she sits on the couch beside me. "See? I drawed it by myself."

"You drew this?" She passes me a folded piece of plain paper. On the front are two stick figures, one tall and one short, but both with long hair, and they're holding hands. The tall one is wearing a cast on her foot.

When I open it, it says, *Love, Birdie.*

"Daddy helped," she whispers and smiles over at her dad, who's hovering by the front door as if he wants to run away as fast as possible.

"Thank you. It's gorgeous, and I'll treasure it." I kiss her cheek, and Birdie wraps her arms around my neck, hugging me.

"Do you want me to kiss your owie?" she asks when she pulls back.

"It's on my ankle." I point to where my foot is propped on a pillow on the coffee table. "You can kiss it. I'm sure it'll feel much better."

Being very careful, Birdie leans over and presses her sweet, tiny lips on my leg, giving it a kiss.

"There."

"It feels better already." I reach for her and pull her next to me, then grin at Bridger. "Sit. You're making me nervous."

And his daughter catches sight of the food.

"Can I have some french fries?" she asks.

"Of course, you can." With a smug smile, I offer her my pile of food, and Bridger rolls his eyes and then sits in the chair across from me.

I glance over at Dani and see that she's nibbling on her lip, as if she's suddenly nervous.

Interesting. This is the kind of information I was asking for earlier.

Charlie has started telling Bridger about the wedding she's planning for one of his guys, and I can tell by the look on his face that he *does. Not. Care.*

Which makes me smirk.

Birdie's helping me with my food, chattering away, when suddenly, Dani stands and closes the lid on her food and licks her lips.

"You know, I think I'd better head home. I'm glad you're feeling better, Millie. Call me if you need anything."

Her face is flaming when she smiles at Birdie.

"Have a good day, sweetie."

Birdie waves happily as Dani flees the room, closing the door behind her.

"Well, she's my ride, so I'm out, too." Charlie stands with a laugh. "See you guys later."

The door closes again, and I glare at Bridger, who's currently staring a hole through the front window as if it personally offended him.

"What the hell is going on? Do you have a…*thing* for Dani?"

He rubs his hand over his mouth but doesn't answer me.

"I like her," Birdie decides as she takes a bite of my burger. "She's pretty, and she always says nice things to me."

"I agree." I kiss the little girl's head and narrow my eyes at her father. "Dani is very nice. Did you know that she's Holden's sister?"

"She is?"

"Yep."

"Cool."

I'm still watching Bridger, but he won't look me in the face.

"Don't do it," he mutters.

"Do what? Pump you for information?"

"It doesn't matter. Obviously. She can't stand being in the same room with me, so it clearly doesn't freaking matter. Let's drop it."

"Okay." I look down at Birdie. "Is your daddy grumpy today?"

"No, he wasn't. We were laughing in the car on the way here."

Now my eyebrow wings up as I look at him, and he just shakes his head.

What in the hell happened between Bridger and Dani? Is there some gossip about my best friend that I don't know?

And how do I *not* know it?

Deciding to leave him alone, I point to the kitchen.

"Hey, grumpy man, would you please fetch me an ice pack out of the freezer? I'm forbidden from walking."

He doesn't say anything, just walks to the kitchen, grabs the ice pack, and, despite his bad mood, lightly lowers it onto my ankle.

"Thanks. You okay, buddy?"

"Yeah." He lets out a long breath, rubs his hands over his face, and then smiles at me. It's only halfway forced. "Yeah, I'm good. How are you?"

"Not bored." I take the offered french fry from Birdie and pretend to bite her finger, making her laugh. "I'm sore. Had some nightmares last night. But, all in all, I'm lucky."

"Very lucky," he agrees. "Is Holden still beating himself up about it?"

"Yeah. He's at the ranch now, talking with the guys. They've been scouring the property, but I don't think they've found anything else. It's hard for him to accept that I happened to find the one and only trap left out there."

"It's like finding a needle in a haystack," Bridger agrees. "Highly unlikely. But you always were an over-achiever."

That makes me laugh. "That's me. Overachiever Millie. If there's a hole to fall into, I'll find it."

"You fell in a hole?" Birdie's face is stricken as she stares up at me.

"That's how I hurt my ankle." I kiss her head. "But I'm okay. I don't recommend it, though. It wasn't fun."

"I don't want to do that," Birdie decides.

"Good plan, baby. Good plan."

It's the middle of the night, and my husband is very warm and very naked, and I'm curled around him. I can't sleep, and not in a bad way. My body is healing, and I feel energized for the first time since I fell into the pit of despair, as I've come to think of it. I'm feeling so much better, in fact, that I think I'll bring up the subject of going back to work tomorrow. I know he'll want me to stay home for the whole week, but I can definitely put in a couple of half days here or there and come home when I get tired.

I look up at Holden and sigh happily. His face is relaxed with sleep, his jaw covered in that gorgeous, dark scruff that I love to feel beneath my hands, or between my thighs. Or anywhere else that he wants to kiss.

He's breathing deeply with sleep. The past few days have been rough on him, making him a little on edge and a little grouchy, which I can't fault him for. He's always gentle and sweet with me, but I've seen his brows drawn together with worry more than usual. All I've had to do is sit around and heal. Whereas he's been in constant contact with his guys, worried about what they might find out at the ranch. He also carries me around all day, making good on his promise from that first night that I won't walk without him, and takes care of me.

He's taken such good care of me.

It's been in these few days that I can see glimpses of the young guy he must have been, raising his sisters and caring for them. He's so tender and loving.

So precious to me.

And in return, life has kicked this poor man in the teeth, over and over again, and when I think about that, it fills me with so much heartache that it steals my breath away. I want to scream and hurt anyone and anything that tried to break this amazing man's spirit. He didn't deserve that. Not my man.

There hasn't been much that I could do to thank him for everything he's done for me since the accident. But as I lie here in the dark, against him, feeling his warmth, I know exactly what I'd like to do to show my appreciation.

If I caress his skin the way I want to, I'll wake him up. I'd love nothing more than to touch him and run my fingers over all that warm, smooth skin, but Holden isn't a super deep sleeper, so running my hands all over his rippling muscles and tattoos won't do.

At least, not until later.

For now, I simply scoot under the covers, finding it *so* convenient that Holden likes to sleep on his back with me tucked up to his side, and take his half-hard cock in my hand and into my mouth.

He instantly hardens, and a low groan escapes his throat as his legs shift, and I feel him wake up.

With a satisfied smile, I sink over him until he's pressed to the back of my throat, tighten my lips around his shaft, and pull up, all the way to the tip.

The covers are ripped off me, and I grin up at my husband, loving the heat in his eyes as one hand grips my hair.

"You shouldn't be—"

"Stop." I lick up the thick vein on his cock, then over the metal that I can't seem to get enough of. God, it's so damn sexy. "I'm fine, and my husband needs a blow job."

He growls as I sink over him once more, and then both hands are in my hair, urging me lower. I relax my throat muscles, taking him even deeper, surprised that my gag reflex hasn't kicked in.

When my nose is pressed against his stomach, he releases his hold, and I pull back so I can catch my breath and wipe the water from my cheeks, staring up at him.

"Fucking hell, babe. This is one fucking hot way to wake up."

I lift an eyebrow. "Who's *babe*?"

With his startled laugh, I sink down again, press my

hands to his, still in my hair, urging him to pull me down onto him.

"You like that, wife? You like sucking my cock way down into your throat?"

I moan and cup his balls with my free hand, loving it when they tighten under my touch.

"Look at me."

My eyes meet his as I pull up, circle the crown with my tongue, over the metal, then over the slit.

"You look so fucking beautiful with my cock in your pretty little mouth."

"I know." His eyes are proud and glazed with lust as I take him in again, and then he's pulling me harder, sinking into my throat even further, making me choke.

It's fucking glorious.

"Take my dick, baby girl."

I'm moving faster, up and down, both hands working him over, and I can feel by the way his stomach and leg muscles are quaking that he's about to come.

"You want my cum, Rosie? You want me to come in your throat?"

I nod, not stopping for anything. Hell yes, I want him to come. I love that he's losing control and that I'm the one that set it into motion.

"Shit, Rosie. Oh, God."

I moan, and his fists tighten in my hair, and then he's coming in my mouth, shooting me in the back of the throat, and I've never felt more powerful in my life.

I swallow all of him, my mouth working him over as he moans, and his hands tighten in my hair deliciously, tugging my scalp, making my own core tighten as I lick him clean. And when I'm done, I kiss up his stomach, his chest, and plant my lips against his neck, just under his ear as he pants, trying to catch his breath. And to my surprise, he rolls me onto my back, his fingers already deep inside of my pussy, and the heel of his palm against my clit.

"Hey, that was just for you."

He shakes his head, kisses me deeply, not seeming to care what was just inside of my mouth, and covers me with his big, hard body, nudging his way between my thighs and effectively setting me on fire.

"Never," he growls against my lips as his fingers start to move, curling to hit that spot that makes me come unglued. "It's *never* about me, baby girl. Haven't you figured that out? If you're horny enough to give me a gift like that, I'm going to pay it back tenfold. I'm going to—"

He breaks off when I pull his lips back down to my own. God, the things he says to me. I fucking love his dirty mouth.

His hand, oh, God, his hand is playing me like an instrument, and my legs have started to shake.

"Give it to me," he growls against my lips. "Come all over my hand, wife."

Jesus, I can't believe what he can do to me with just a few words. My body explodes, my pussy clenching around his fingers, and I see stars erupt around me.

"Husband." I don't know if it's a plea or a curse as my body rides out the orgasm, and then he's gently kissing me, petting me, making me feel so damn treasured that my heart feels like it'll burst. "Holy shit."

"You're perfect," he whispers against my skin as he tugs me back to his side. "Fucking perfect."

HOLDEN WAS STILL SLEEPING when I woke, so I quietly got up, dressed, and decided to head into town to check on my shop and get us a couple of coffees. I hardly have a limp at all. The bruising has started to fade on my ankle, and after that round of incredible sex in the middle of the night, I'm feeling damn good.

I want to let my man get some more sleep and then spoil him with his favorite coffee and maybe a sweet treat. Of course, I wanted to walk the few blocks, but I don't want to get into trouble for being foolish, so I'm driving in with all the windows rolled down. While I am feeling much more like myself, I don't want to push the ankle too far.

After parking right out front, I saunter inside and grin. Everything here looks fantastic. The place is clean and well-stocked, and I can see that my staff is entirely capable of taking care of things while I'm gone. And the *smell.* Goodness, I love the smell of coffee.

"Millie!" Candy practically screeches the greeting and runs around the counter to yank me into a strong hug. "Oh, my God, I've been so worried. Are you okay?"

"Much better," I assure her and smile over at Andrea, who's making an espresso. "Everything looks great here."

"We're just fine," Candy assures me. "I don't want you to worry about a thing. I hope you're not here to work because I'll kick your perfect behind right back out of here."

"No. I'm just going to grab some coffee and muffins to go for Holden and me."

"Your usuals?" Candy asks.

"Yes, please. Make it one chocolate and one huck-lemon muffin."

"You got it."

I lean against the counter and chat with the girls as they fill my order. It's such a different experience to be in here as a customer, and I must admit, I kind of love it.

My café is welcoming and bright, with white walls and black countertops. The artwork is local and pretty, and it just makes me happy to be here.

I wave at Brooks, who's just walked through the door. "Good morning."

He doesn't say anything; he just pulls me in for a big hug. "Scared us all, Mill."

"Yeah, me, too." I hug him in return, patting his back. Brooks is the eldest of the Blackwell brothers, and he's just so...*good.* A kind, gentle, good man, about the same age as Remington and Holden. "Thank you for helping to find me. I just love all you guys, and I appreciate you."

"I'm just glad you were found in one piece," he says, tapping my nose with a grin. "Because we all love you, too. Please tell me Holden knows that you're out on your own because he might get crazy if he knows you're on your feet without him."

I bite my lip and scrunch up my nose. "I decided to surprise him with coffee. I'm a grown-ass woman, Brooks. I can go to the coffee shop if I want to."

Brooks shakes his head and mumbles something about stubborn women as he shuffles up to order his own coffee.

I move to pull my phone out of my pocket and then realize that I left it at home. Ah well, I'm headed right back there anyway, so I can check my social media in a bit.

"Thanks, guys," I say when my order is ready. "Just call me if you need me."

"We won't need you," Candy says, waving me off. "Go heal up."

I grin at her and then return to my car. The drive home takes all of two minutes, and then I gather the coffee and muffins in my arms, climb out of the car, and nudge the door closed with my hip. The movement makes my ankle smart just a bit, but then it feels fine. I'll put it up with some ice while I drink my coffee with my husband.

I've just reached the top step of the porch when the door bursts open, and Holden's standing there, breathing hard, his eyes hot and fierce. His jaw is clenched. He's...*pissed.*

"Where the fuck did you go?"

CHAPTER TWENTY-SIX

HOLDEN

I'm so fucking livid, there's a red haze over my eyes. Millie's gaze is wide, her brows pulled down in a frown, and she's holding coffee.

"I just grabbed breakfast." She stares at me with one cocky eyebrow lifted until I step back to let her inside. She sets the tray on the coffee table, then turns to me, her hands on her hips. "What the hell?"

"*What the hell?*" Jesus, I want to shake her. I have to pace away from her, raking my hands through my hair. "I didn't know where you were, and you're fucking injured!"

"I'm feeling a lot better today, actually."

I spin and glare at her. She doesn't look sorry at all. In fact, she looks like she might laugh.

Fucking laugh.

"This is not funny."

"What? I didn't wake you so you could carry me into

the coffee shop, so now I'm in trouble? Jesus, Holden, calm down."

"That's enough." I cross to her and take her shoulders in my hands. "Don't you stand there and fucking mock me because I'm freaked out that I woke up to find my *injured wife* gone. I called. I texted. You didn't answer."

"I forgot my phone." She tips her chin up, not looking sorry or intimidated in the least, and I'll be goddamned if that doesn't turn me on.

What the hell is wrong with me?

"I laid down the ground rules, baby girl."

"You listen to me, *husband.* I'm not an invalid. I woke up feeling damn good and wanted to do something nice for you, so I did. I won't apologize for that. I didn't do anything wrong."

My heart is hammering. It hasn't stopped since I discovered her gone from the bed and realized that she wasn't inside this goddamn house.

I had a bad moment, forgetting that my fucking father is dead, and thought he might have—I swallow hard and let her go, stomping away from her.

"Listen, I know that you're obsessed, and—"

"For fuck's sake." I spin back around and stare at her. "You think I'm pissed because I'm obsessed with you? Christ, Millie, I'm not seventeen. I don't have to be attached to your hip just because I'm smitten. I was fucking worried. You're hurt, and I didn't know where you went."

"Well, now you know." Her voice is like ice, and she

shrugs as if she doesn't give a rat's ass, then shakes her head and reaches for her coffee. I have to take a long, deep breath to calm the fuck down. "Don't be a dick about it."

My eyes narrow, and I tilt my head to the side, my hands in fists.

Her gaze flicks down to my fists, then back to me.

"You won't hit me."

"FUCKING FUCK!" I yell and pace away, completely appalled. "Of *course,* I won't fucking hit you! What has happened in the last few hours, wife? We went from fun, middle-of-the-night sex to this?"

"I'm mad," she admits with a scowl. "And I don't fight fair when I'm mad. I'm mean, and I talk back."

"*You're* mad."

"Yeah, I'm fucking pissed."

"Looks like we're on the same page, sweetheart."

"Don't call me that."

"Don't call you sweetheart."

"No."

"Why?"

She's still scowling at me. "Because *you* don't call me that."

I'm a foot away from her now, unaware that I was slowly stalking toward her. She's not afraid of me because she hasn't backed away. My hand circles the column of her throat, my thumb pressed to her pulse point, which is thrumming hard.

"What do I call you?" My voice is quiet but hard, and

while her eyes are still spitting fire at me, she licks her lips.

"You already know the answer to that question."

My little spitfire. God, I fucking love her.

"You want to tell me to fuck off, don't you?"

"More than anything." She swallows hard, and the movement under my palm urges me on.

"Then do it."

"Go fuck yourself, *Holden.*"

My lips immediately tip up into a wide grin. God, I love it when she does that. She looks so angry, so brave.

But her pulse gives her away.

"I'd rather fuck *you*, little rose." I lean into her, not touching her anywhere but her throat, and she lets out a little whimper as I press my lips beside her ear. "My baby girl. My Rosie. My obsession."

My thumb drifts up over her jawline, and now my lips hover over hers.

"My *wife.*"

"Don't kiss me." There's no strength behind her words, and her eyes are pinned to my lips.

"You don't want my mouth on you, sweetheart?"

Those fierce eyes snap up to mine and almost knock me on my ass. "No, *honey.*"

"Too fucking bad."

She doesn't push me away when I cover her mouth with mine, urging her head to the side so I can devour her. No, she doesn't try to get away; she leans into me, grips my bare sides, and pulls me to her.

I'm still mad, and we'll be having a conversation, but first, I want her to submit to me.

I want all of her.

"On your fucking hands and knees, wife."

She blinks at me, her jaw drops, and I narrow my eyes.

"I didn't stutter."

She frowns and looks like she's going to argue, but then she smirks up at me and gets on the floor, on her hands and knees, her ass in the air.

Fuck me, she's gorgeous.

"I'm not taking my clothes off," she tosses over her shoulder, a smirk tugging at her delectable lips. "But you can get all the pervy satisfaction you want out of staring at my ass."

How did I go eight years of my life without this woman?

I shake my head and walk away from her, and when she moves to get up, I simply say, "Stay."

"Okay, Holden, that's enough."

"Stay," I repeat, glaring at her, and march into the kitchen, taking an ice pack out of the freezer, then a single ice cube from the bucket, and return to her.

"You're a bully."

"No, I'm a pissed-off husband, and you're about to be punished. Take your fucking clothes off."

"Fuck you."

"Oh, you will." I lean down so her ear is level with my lips. "I won't hurt you. I'll *never* hurt you. Take your clothes off, little rose."

She sighs, almost in relief, then takes off the cargo pants and panties, tossing them aside. Next, she pulls the sweater over her head and drops it onto her discarded pants.

She's not in a bra, and I have to swallow hard. I'll never get used to seeing her like this.

Naked and mine. She's staring at me defiantly, but there's trust there, too, and that fills me with satisfaction.

"Back where you were."

She moves back to her hands, and I carefully drape a hand towel over her ankle and then place the ice pack over that.

"This got a little swollen this morning."

She sighs, her shoulders droop, and I pop the single ice cube into my mouth before I kneel behind her and plant my face in her pussy, moving my cold tongue through her slit, and she jerks against me.

"Oh, God!" She pushes back against me. "It's too cold."

I don't reply. I just keep going, licking and sucking and nibbling. When the ice has melted, I don't slow down. I'm devouring her, making her crazy, and when I push two fingers inside of her, I can tell that she's getting close to an orgasm.

So, I stop, pulling away from her completely, not touching her at all.

Millie gasps and stares back at me, her mouth wide. "*Holden.*"

"That's not my fucking name." I push my sweats

down low on my hips, and my cock springs free. I palm it, gliding the crown through her slit and feel that it's still cool from the ice. When the metal brushes her clit, she groans. "I'm going to fuck you hard, wife."

"Yes," she says with a sigh, hanging her head and pushing back against me. "*Yes.*"

"And you won't come until I say you can."

"Holden."

"*That's not my fucking name.*"

Her face is flushed, her lips shiny and pink, and I push inside of her, not stopping until my hips meet her ass and she's moaning.

"Yes, husband. Fuck, yes."

"Good girl." Her pussy clenches around me at the praise, and my hips start to move. My hand glides from her ass, up her spine, and then fists in her hair. "You want to know why I'm so fucking mad?"

"Mmm." She's panting, rearing back against me.

"Wife, answer me."

"Tell me."

"Because I was *afraid.*" I pull out all the way when I feel her start to come, and she shudders, glaring at me over her shoulder. "I was fucking scared, and not much in this life scares me anymore. I couldn't find you. I couldn't get to you."

"It was j-just coffee."

"No." I lean over her and kiss her shoulder, sliding back into her. "It wasn't just coffee. It was my *world*. You are my center of gravity, the reason my heart beats, the only thing that matters. You, Rosie."

"Husband, please."

I feel her starting to convulse around me, and I won't stop her orgasm this time.

"I need you," she says, reaching back for me. "Please, let me see your face."

Pulling out of her, I gently turn her onto her back, then push back inside of her, and she cups my cheeks as I cover her, resting on my elbows at either side of her head.

"I'm sorry," she says with tears in her eyes as I turn my face and kiss her palm. "I didn't mean—"

I cut her off, kissing her hard as I reach down and cover her clit with my thumb, rubbing over that little bundle of nerves until she's writhing once again.

"Come for me, wife." I suck on one nipple, loving the way her fingers feel clenched in my hair. "Come, baby girl."

That's all it takes for her to go over, her pussy rippling around me. My balls tighten, and then I'm coming with her, pushing over and over again, riding her through my orgasm.

"I'm sorry," she says again, and when I open my eyes, I see that she's watching me with wonder. "I really just wanted to get you coffee."

"Next time," I kiss her lips softly, "leave a note, little rose. Please."

She grins and then laughs. "Yeah, I can do that."

"Where are we going?"

"This is the fourth time you've asked me that since we left the house." I open my mouth when she offers me a bite of a muffin and take the lemony goodness from her. "We haven't even made it through town yet. Impatient much?"

She smirks and takes a bite of her own sweet treat. She managed to warm up our coffees after we got dressed. How, I have no idea, but she's the coffee expert, so I don't really have to know.

"I don't love surprises. They're not usually good ones, honestly."

I glance over and notice that she's twisting the paper koozie on her cup, fidgeting.

"Hey, it's nothing bad. I'd warn you if it wasn't a good surprise. I don't like those either."

"Promise?"

I take one of her hands and lift it to my mouth, kissing that delicate spot on her wrist, just below her thumb. "Promise. I will tell you that we're going out of town."

"Like, to the ranch out of town, or to Sweden out of town?"

"I don't have my passport on me." I grin over at her. "You want to go to Sweden, baby girl?"

"Not really. It just popped into my head. If you could go anywhere, where would you go?"

"Maybe somewhere tropical in the winter." I lift a shoulder. "It always sounds like a good idea to go somewhere warm in January."

"That *would* be nice," she agrees. "Get some vitamin D, sit by the pool, eat my weight in fresh seafood, seduce the cabana boy."

Now I bite her wrist, making her laugh.

"Don't worry, I was picturing you as said cabana boy."

"Mm-hmm." I kiss her wrist once more as I pull onto the freeway.

"Are you really not going to tell me where we're going?"

"Guess."

She scoffs and shoves more muffin into her mouth, and when I glance over, her eyes are narrowed. "We're headed west, so...Missoula?"

I choke on my coffee. "How did you know?"

"I didn't, I just guessed. What are we going to do there? Are we staying overnight? I didn't pack a bag."

"Not overnight." I eye her and then turn my gaze back to the windshield. "Since you're a mind reader now, you tell me what we're doing."

"I don't know." She deflates against the door with a dramatic sigh, making me grin. "Maybe it should be a surprise."

Once my heart settled down this morning, and I made her sit with her ankle up on ice for at least thirty minutes, I told Millie to get ready to leave the house for the day.

She smiled like she'd won the fucking lottery.

I know she's been getting cabin fever. She's not used to being stuck at home for days on end. If she'd left a note or taken her phone so she could reply to me this morning, I wouldn't have been angry in the least that she went to get coffee. But waking up to a still, empty house, and not being able to find my wife, was a moment I don't want to relive any time soon.

"I think this morning is the first time I've seen you really pissed off," she says. There's no meekness there, no hesitation.

"I suspect that's the maddest I've ever been at you." I switch lanes, passing a truck. "It's probably as angry as I get."

"I was going to say, you're usually pretty even-tempered. Not much riles you up. Now I know what does."

I sigh, and Millie reaches over to lay her hand on my thigh, and I cover it with my own hand. "I have always been careful to keep my temper under wraps. My dad… well, there aren't words for what a piece of shit he was, but his temper was legendary, and I don't ever want to lose it the way he would."

"You are not that man." Her voice is hard. "Look at me."

I glance her way and see her jaw set and her eyes narrow. "I see you, wife."

"Listen, I probably would have been pissed, too, if the roles were reversed. Especially after what happened a few days ago. I still won't apologize for going out, because that wasn't wrong, but I *am* sorry that it scared you, and I promise that from now on, I'll make sure to leave a note and remember my phone."

"Thank you." I squeeze her fingers. "That's all I ask."

"However, I can't guarantee that I won't try to rile you up again, because you're intense when you're mad at me, and in a sexy way, so...take that as you will, husband."

My heart kicks up a notch, and I raise her hand to my mouth. "Are you just begging for me to find a back road out here in the middle of nowhere so I can make you come, Rosie?"

She snorts and pulls her hand away from me. "No. Ew. Some weird redneck would see us and get off on it, and that's disgusting."

"You have quite the imagination, you know."

She laughs and pulls her hair back from her face. "Oh, I know."

The drive to Missoula doesn't take long, especially on a beautiful, late-spring day, and just a few hours later, we're pulling into the parking lot of the place where we have an appointment.

"A tattoo shop," she says, and when I look at her, she's grinning, practically dancing in her seat. "Is this where you go?"

"Usually. Rich, the owner, has done 90 percent of my work."

"What about the piercings?"

I chuckle. "Yeah, those, too."

"Fun. Let's go."

She waits for me to open her door, and I lift her out of the truck and gently set her on her feet.

"I'd prefer to carry you."

"It's okay, caveman. It's not so bad today."

She grins when I narrow my eyes at her, but she takes my hand and threads her fingers through mine.

"Come on, let's go have some fun."

For the first time in my life, I'm walking into Rich's shop, Vintage Ink, when my heart isn't broken and I'm not looking for a way to hurt my body so I can ignore the organ pumping in my chest.

It's a completely different experience.

"Holden," Rich says with a smile. The man is forty-five and the size of a football linebacker, and aside from his face and scalp, he's covered in ink. He has a beard that a gang of bikers would be jealous of, and he looks like he could kill someone with his bare hands.

Because he probably could.

He's also the kindest man I've ever met.

"Is this her?" His eyes move from me to my girl, and his gaze doesn't leave her face. He doesn't leer at her or check out her body.

Because he's my friend, and he's not a piece of shit.

"If by *her* you mean his wife, yep. That's me."

Rich's gaze whips back to mine in surprise. "Wife?"

"This is Millie," I confirm with a nod. "My wife."

"Holy shit, that's a turn of events. Does this mean I just lost your business?"

Rich knows why I spent so much time under his needle, and I can't help but grin at him.

"Nah, I'll just be in here for different reasons."

Millie tucks herself against my side and gives me a squeeze.

"Well, slap my ass and call me Susan," Rich says. "Nice to meet you, ma'am."

"You, too. Holy cow, you are one big work of art."

Rich blinks at her, I frown down at her, and she shrugs.

"You are. Is that weird?"

Rich starts to laugh, and I join him, and Millie grins at both of us.

"What can I do for you, Mrs. Lexington?"

Millie's cheeks darken with pleasure, and it makes me want to puff my chest up.

"Well, I'd like to have both nipples pierced, please. Wait." She holds up a hand while my heart stutters to a stop. "Do you have a buy-two-get-one deal? Because if so, let's throw in the clitoral hood, too."

Again, he stares at her, and I lean down and press my lips to her ear.

"If you think this morning was intense, just wait until we get home, baby girl. Absolutely fucking *not.*"

Millie bites her lip and then busts up laughing. "It was too easy! The looks on your faces. I don't know, I've heard good things about the nipples, but—"

"*Fuck no.*"

She smirks and then turns back to Rich, who's folded his arms over his chest, watching us with a wide, amused grin.

"I just want a little heart with a date on the inside of my left wrist." She glances up at me, and then back to him. "With an H."

With an H.

"We can get that designed easily," he assures her before turning to me. "And what about you? You said when you called that you'll both be getting work."

"I want her name on my left ring finger."

"No." I stare down at Millie's horrified face. "No, Holden."

"It's *my* finger."

"They're *my* tits, and you won't let me pierce them."

Rich snickers. "I'm gonna go get the design going for your missus. You two work this out while I'm gone. Here, write the date on this for me."

Millie complies, and Rich saunters away. I close my hand over Millie's throat.

"I'm getting the ink, Millie."

"It's too much pressure." This comes out as a whisper, and I frown.

"What do you mean?"

She licks her lips. "My name on *that* finger. Forever."

Moving closer, my lips hover just inches over hers as she looks up at me with those gorgeous eyes.

"You're all over me, baby. Every single one is you. The rose was just the start. There is nothing on this arm that doesn't represent you."

Her jaw drops, her eyes widen. "What?"

"Every single image represents you or how I feel about you. So putting your name on me is nothing. Because you're permanently printed on all of me, including my heart."

"Fuck."

I grin and brush my lips over hers lightly before I sink

into her and hear her groan as she wraps her arms around me.

"Do you really want your nipples pierced?" I don't know how I feel about that. At the end of the day, it's her body, but I love it just the way it is.

"Fuck no. I hate needles. I can't believe I'm doing this."

Grinning down at her, I take her face in my hands. "I fucking love you."

"I know. I'm a brat."

"You're *my* brat."

"Okay, this is what I worked up," Rich says as he returns to the reception area where we've been waiting by the glass counter. He sets the paper down for Millie's inspection.

It's dainty. A simple, small heart with an H in the middle and the date is one side of the heart. There's even a little rose worked into the piece, and Millie's breath catches as she stares down at it.

"Oh, this is perfect, Rich. Can you make the rose pink, to match Holden's?"

"Duh." Rich winks at her and then turns to me. "Do you want the same font on the name as in hers?"

"Yep."

"Can do. Okay, come on back."

He gestures for us to follow him back to his workroom. A place I've spent many hours in. Millie has her lower lip caught between her teeth as she walks through the door, and I reach out to tug the soft flesh free.

"We're obsessed with sanitation here," Rich informs

her, busily putting on gloves, cleaning surfaces that he's already cleaned, and then unwrapping new needles and getting them ready in his machine. "Everything sparkles. I already put your art onto a transfer."

Millie sits in his chair and watches closely as he sets the image on her skin carefully, with her help to guide him exactly where she wants it.

I love that my girl isn't shy.

"Okay, go look in the mirror, move your hand around, and do all the things to make sure it's exactly where you want it because once we start, there's no moving it."

Millie nods and walks to the mirror. She holds her left hand down at her side and moves her hand around, watching the way it looks with the movement. Then she holds it up. Over her head.

Jesus, I can picture holding her arm over her head like that while I'm inside of her, staring at that tattoo.

I have to take a deep breath.

"Come here, Romeo. Let's get yours set, too." Rich smirks as I hold my hand out to him.

"Just above where the band goes. I want to wear both."

"Facing you, or facing out?"

I narrow my eyes, thinking about it. "Out."

He nods and carefully lays the transfer on my skin. As soon as he moves away and I look down, my heart stops.

I've been wearing the ring for weeks, but fuck, the ink makes it real.

She's mine.

Forever.

"I like it," Millie announces as she walks back to us. "I don't want to change it."

"Good deal. Have a seat, and we'll get started."

She follows his command, but I notice that her hands are shaking, so I take her free one in mine and sit next to her.

"I'm scared," she whispers softly.

"It's okay." I lean in and kiss her cheek. "Because I'm not. Rich is the best. It's going to sting, but he's quick. You don't have to watch if you don't want to."

"Okay."

Rich turns on the machine, filling the room with a loud *buzz*, and her wide eyes fly to mine.

"Deep breath, Millie," Rich says.

She takes that breath, and in the corner of my eye, I see him lower the needle.

"Oh." She frowns at me. "That's it?"

"That's it."

"Maybe I'll get my nipples pierced after all."

That makes us all laugh.

"Hurts about a thousand times worse than this," Rich informs her. "And takes months to heal. It can be the right thing for a lot of people, but it's not a walk in the park."

Millie wrinkles her nose. "I'm good. Wait, do you have yours done?"

"Of course I do, honey," Rich says with a chuckle. "I have just about everything done."

"Yikes. Do you love needles?"

"Can't stand 'em."

I grin at her, still holding her hand. God, I love her.

"How long did yours take to heal?" she asks me.

"Months. Hurt like a son of a bitch."

She smirks, squeezes my hand. "But so worth it on this side of things."

I lean in and press my lips to her ear. I don't really care if Rich hears me; I just like to whisper at her because it makes her shiver.

"Every moment was worth it, for you, wife."

"Aww, precious," Rich says, his voice dry. "We're almost done here, Millie."

"Already?" She looks down and frowns. "I don't mean to question your job skills, but it looks like a big, black blob."

"That's because I haven't cleaned it up yet."

"How can you even see what you're doing?"

"I've been doing this longer than you've been alive, little girl." He grabs a paper towel and sets to work cleaning her up. "I know what I'm doing. Maybe I'll come into your coffee shop and tell you how to make a mocha."

"You know that I have a coffee shop?"

"I know a lot." He winks at her and then says, "Have a look."

Millie looks down at her wrist. I've already stopped breathing. It's fucking gorgeous. But Millie starts to cry.

"Shit," Rich grumbles. "I hate it when women cry."

"It's so...perfect." She sniffs and then, to Rich's horror, launches herself into his arms and hugs him around the neck. "You're the best, Rich. This is so perfect. Thank you for being Holden's friend."

Tentatively, with his eyes on me to make sure it's okay, Rich gently closes his arms around her and gives her a little squeeze.

"I'm glad you like it, honey. Now, get your butt out of my chair so I can work some magic on your man."

"Okay." Before she can move away, he covers her ink with some plastic, and then we switch places. Millie takes my hand in hers. "Are you nervous?"

I chuckle and give her a squeeze. "Terrified. Hold me."

She laughs and presses a kiss over my tattooed knuckles as she clings to my right hand. My left arm is clean, no ink, until today when I'll get her name on my finger.

"This is gonna go quick," he tells me. "But the fingers hurt like a fucker."

"I remember." I nod. "It's okay."

The buzz starts again, and I turn back to Millie. Yeah, it hurts like a fucker, but I don't mind.

"Is it really bad?" she asks.

"I've had worse. Did *yours* hurt really bad? The inner wrist is tender. I figured you'd squirm more."

"I mean, it wasn't a walk in the park, but it wasn't too bad. Next time, maybe I'll do my shoulder."

That has me raising my brows in surprise. "Next time?"

"I've heard they're addicting. It seems that might be true."

"I didn't lose a client. I gained one." Rich grins up at me. "Score."

CHAPTER TWENTY-SEVEN

MILLIE

"We have barely seen you," Polly says as she clings to me in a hug that not long ago would have made me incredibly uncomfortable, but now just makes me happy. "With all the shit going on in your life, how have we barely seen you?"

"And never all at the same time," Abbi adds, smoothing her hand down my hair. I hold my hands out, and Erin and Summer take those, and now I'm in the middle of a big, weird group love fest.

"I know, I'm sorry," I tell them. "But it feels like it's been one thing after another every single day. Not to mention, Pound Town is a busy place to be a member of."

I grin as they all still, and then they start to laugh. It feels so good to be with my girls.

"I'm so glad we came early," Erin says as we untangle ourselves from each other. The IWC spring formal event is being held at Ryan and Polly's ranch, and our guys are off somewhere, looking at something that I didn't pay attention to.

I was too excited to see my girls.

"We needed some time together," Summer agrees. "Also, how hot are we?"

"Super-hot, of course," Abbi says with a laugh.

"One of the things you're going to tell us *now* is about that gorgeous tattoo," Polly says, gesturing to my wrist, and I grin.

"Happy to. Holden took me to his artist in Missoula, and we both had work done. He put my name on his ring finger."

"No pressure or anything," Summer says with a wink.

"That's what I said, but he insisted." I shrug and can't help but grin an my friends. "It was kind of sexy."

"It's a lot sexy," Erin says.

I love our seasonal events because we all get to dress up and bring dates. In the past, I never brought a date, but tonight I'll be on Holden's arm, and I can't wait to show off my sexy-as-hell husband. He's looking fine in his blue suit.

"This tent is great out here, Polly." There's even been a temporary floor brought in to lay under this massive tent, in the middle of their field.

The Wild River Ranch Event Center that my family runs was booked for a wedding this weekend, so Polly sweet-talked Ryan into hosting.

Not that he would ever tell her no to anything. My brother would burn down the whole world if she asked him to.

The grass is green, the wild flowers are in full bloom, and it's seriously so beautiful out here.

"We were happy to host," Polly replies with a grin. "And I didn't do anything. Charlie Lexington took this whole event under her wing and made it beautiful."

I grin as I take in the round tables covered with pretty flowers and linens, the party favors, the lights strung about that we'll turn on when it starts to get darker.

"My sister-in-law is kind of badass." I grin at the others and then reach out to take Erin's hand again. "I miss you guys. The truth is, I've missed you for months. I know that we're all busy, with men and families and businesses, but it feels like we've lost each other a bit in the past year or so."

"I feel it, too. But we're always right here," Summer assures me. "Always. We need to do better about seeing each other, not just when we have an IWC event."

"Agreed," Abbi says, nodding. "We can arrange for a girls' night once a month. We're not too busy for each other."

I feel tears threaten as I bite my lip. "Yeah, I'd like that a lot. I have so much to tell you guys. I know you get the highlights from my brothers, but—"

"It's not the same," Erin says, squeezing my hand. "It's not even close to the same."

"Okay, I actually put makeup on today, so no more getting mushy."

"People are starting to arrive," Polly points out, and we turn to see Jake giving carriage rides to the women of the Iconic Women's Collective and their dates, and suddenly, our guys join us, as if out of thin air.

"You must not have gone far," I say to Holden as he wraps his arm around my shoulders and kisses my temple. He's warm and strong, and I freaking love being in his arms. Not to mention, he turns me on with just a look or a touch. And he ravaged me before we came here today.

"Just the paddock," he confirms and kisses my hair. He smells fucking delicious. "Ryan just took in a couple of new rescue horses, and we wanted to take a look."

That's my brother, always taking in someone or something that needs a safe haven.

"I want to see them."

His blue eyes glance down at my shoes. "Not in those death traps."

I snicker and take a glass of champagne off a tray. "I'm in flats, husband. It's too soon for heels."

"They're not enough to protect your feet from mud and shit. But you'll love those horses. There's one girl in particular that's just a sweetheart."

"Maybe we should also rescue horses. And dogs. And...whatever needs rescuing."

He narrows his eyes at me. "You don't have time for that."

"Maybe just horses, then." I shrug a shoulder. "Unless you don't want my poor rescues on your ranch."

"We'll talk about this later."

Holden's sister joins us, all smiles.

"Wow, you clean up well, brother. I almost didn't

recognize you. Well?" Charlie asks, her hands on her hips as she takes a look at her handiwork. "What do you think?"

"I think it's absolutely gorgeous," I reply honestly. "You outdid yourself, Charlie."

"You killed it," Holden tells her and pulls her in for a hug. "I'm proud of you, sweetie."

Charlie's eyes mist over. "I think this is the first time you've seen one of my events."

"Best thing I've ever seen," he tells her and kisses her head. "You're incredible, darlin'. I couldn't be prouder of you."

"Don't make me cry." She half-heartedly smacks his arm but wipes away a tear. "You're the closest thing that any of us has had to a parent, Holden. So, having you here to see what I do is important to me. I love you."

His throat works as he swallows hard, and then he wraps her in one more hug.

"I love you, too."

"Oops, someone's talking in my ear." She points to the little device in her lobe. "I have to go put out a fire. Not literally, don't call Bridger. See you later."

She waves, and then she's off.

"That was incredibly sweet," I murmur as I take Holden's hand in mine. "They adore you, you know."

"Yeah, well, I love my girls. I'm glad they escaped with minimal damage. I need to be more mindful of being present for them. I should have seen her work before today."

I kiss his shoulder, and then we're pulled into

conversations, making our way through the crowd to mingle.

After an hour, we find our seats. We managed to get all ten of us around one table, and that makes me so happy.

Gazing around, I love seeing all four of my brothers with the women they love so much. They're all so smitten that sometimes it's disgusting. But there's no better feeling than knowing that their wives were my friends, first and foremost, and now they're my family.

Holden's hand settles on my thigh, and I smile over at him. Having my husband at this special party, as my date, is the best feeling in the world. We've been congratulated and shown so much love and kindness already today that my cup is full.

And I can tell that he enjoys being part of this community.

"You're fucking incredible," he whispers into my ear. "I knew this group was special, but seeing it in action? Outstanding. I'm proud of you, Rosie."

I smile up at him and accept his soft kiss without hesitation.

"Get a room," Chase says, but I just wave him off, making the girls laugh.

When we're served dinner, I notice that Holden's phone is on the table, so I snatch it and then hold it up for him.

"Unlock, please."

"It's not locked. I don't have anything to hide."

I swipe up, and sure enough, it's not locked. I'm not

snooping. I just want to change my contact in his phone, since he was sure to do the same in mine right away.

I never did change it from *Your Husband*. I couldn't bring myself to be a smartass and wipe that from my phone.

Opening his contacts, I page down, expecting to find my name. I can feel his gaze on me, watching me blatantly, and he doesn't say a word.

My name's not here.

No Rosie. No wife.

I frown up at him.

"Open the texts, baby girl."

I swipe up out of the contacts and open his messages, and right on top is one from me.

Obsession.

I press my lips together so I don't laugh out loud, and then I look up at him. "You've got to be kidding."

"Felt appropriate." He shrugs. "What were you going to change it to?"

"Your Wife."

"Same thing." He kisses my temple, and I lay his phone back on the table.

"Also, you only text four people?"

"I fucking hate texting. If someone needs me, they can call me."

I laugh and find Remington watching us. "What are you thinking about over there?"

"You're happy," he says simply.

"Yes. Don't ruin it."

He shakes his head at me as if to say, *Stop it.*

"Mom was saying that she misses having Sunday dinner with the whole family," he continues. "You two need to come to the farmhouse on Sunday. We'll grill something."

I blink at him, positive that I've misheard him.

"But, Dad—"

"It's my fucking house," he says, cutting me off. "*My* house. And I'll have whoever I fucking want in it. I want my family there."

The table is quiet, but Brady chimes in. "Dad'll be out of town, Mill. He's going to pick up a horse in Idaho."

"I don't care where Dad is," Rem insists. "If he doesn't like it, he doesn't have to come."

Holden takes my hand, lacing our fingers together.

"We'll be there," Holden says. "What can we bring?"

"Oh, we'll have plenty," Erin says. "This is so great. The kids will be so excited. They've been asking for you, Millie."

"Shit." I swallow hard, looking down at my plate as regret washes through me. "I should have been coming to get them more. Take them home with me."

"They're fine," Rem says. "But they will be excited to see you."

"It's time," Ryan adds, and the others nod. "It's time to get back to normal."

"It's obvious to anyone with a brain that you two love each other," Chase chimes in. "Dad will come around sooner or later."

"He won't have a choice," Brady agrees.

"Looks like we're coming to dinner on Sunday," I

reply, already excited about it. "I'm totally bringing dessert."

"I was hoping you'd say that," Summer says. "She makes the best cheesecake."

"Does she?" Holden smiles down at me. "I can't wait."

"TONIGHT WAS A SUCCESS." I kick my shoes off at the door, happy to be out of them. Even though they're just flats, they still pinch my toes a bit, and the cool hardwood feels good as I pad across it to the kitchen. "You were amazing, by the way."

"Me?" Holden lifts an eyebrow as he takes his jacket off. "I didn't do a damn thing."

"You looked like that." I gesture to him, my arm moving up and down. "Hot as hell. I really did marry some damn good arm candy."

He narrows his eyes on me. "I feel so used."

I snort a laugh and pull out a couple of glasses. "Tequila or whiskey?"

"Whiskey for me. I'm going to change out of this real quick."

"Go ahead. I'm going to sit on the patio for a bit."

Before he turns to walk away, he presses his hand on my hip and leans into me. "You are gorgeous in this dress, little rose. And if anyone was amazing tonight, it was you."

He presses his lips to mine, then walks away, and I have to take a second to catch my breath.

I don't think there will ever be a day that he doesn't steal my breath.

I pour our drinks and then pad outside and turn on the overhead fans. In a few more weeks, it'll be time to lower the screens to keep the bugs out.

So far, it's a little early in the season to be bothered by much.

I don't flip on any of the lights out here. I want to sit in the dark and listen to the neighborhood while I unwind from being around so many people. So much noise. We danced and laughed and had a great time.

I had no idea that Holden had moves on the dance floor. And he wasn't at all shy about it.

Within just a few minutes, Holden opens the glass door and slips out, dressed in his sweats and nothing else.

For fuck's sake, he should warn a girl when he's going to walk around like that.

He sits on the swing next to me, and I pass him his glass. We're angled toward each other, one leg bent on the seat, one arm resting on the back of the swing. Holden's rocking us with his toes.

It's the most calm and serene I've felt since we got married.

"I could tell that the women there tonight admire you." His voice is low out here in the quiet, and his fingertips brush my elbow, sending heat up my arm. "They ask smart questions. You listen to them, and when you answer or give advice, they pay attention. It's a testament to how well you run your business and how you treat people, Millie."

I bite my lip, staring down into my tequila.

"For a long time, I didn't know what I wanted to do. I felt a little lost." I take a sip. "I got that business degree in college, but only because I had to major in *something*. My brothers always knew what they would do. Rem would take over the ranch someday. Ryan's a business man, through and through, and we all know how well that's worked out for him. Chase is a total badass cop, and Brady's first love, until he met Abbi and Daisy, was to be on the back of a bull. They all had things they were passionate about."

I reach up and pull out the few pins that I popped into my hair to keep it tamed for the event, letting it fall, and brush it back behind my ears as I set the pins on the side of the swing.

"I knew that I had to come home." I glance at him and find him sitting still, watching me with those beautiful blue eyes. "I just wanted to be here, in Bitterroot Valley. I didn't want to live out at the ranch because I don't love ranch work."

His lips tip up on one side. "You're awfully good at it for not liking it."

"They don't have to be mutually exclusive." I stretch my foot out, looking at my toes as I spread them out. Holden sets our empty glasses on the ground and then takes my foot in his hands, gently massaging it. It shouldn't be sexy, but my girl parts decide to do the cha-

cha at the press of that thumb on my arch. "I love spring time at the ranch. All the babies and the branding and stuff. I always go out for that, and I always will. But the day to day?" I wrinkle my nose. "No. Not for me."

I sigh when he massages each little toe.

"So, I found the apartment in town, started working at the coffee shop, and it was kind of perfect for me. I like seeing all the people, and I'm good at memorizing what everyone's favorites are."

"Everyone except mine," he says with a knowing smile.

"Yours was the first one I memorized." I close my eyes and lean my head on my arm. "And every time you came in, it tore more of my heart apart."

"Rosie." It's a tortured whisper.

"But if you didn't come in, that was even worse. Anyway, we've been through this, and it's not why I'm telling you this story. A couple of years ago, when Marion came to me and said that she wanted to sell the shop, I didn't understand why she was telling *me*."

"Silly girl." He grins at me.

"It really didn't compute. I'm a worker bee. I'm not really a boss bee. But then I talked to Chase about it."

"You went to Chase first?"

"Yeah. I'm close to all my brothers, but Chase and I... we're kindred spirits. And he thought it was a great idea. Of course, I didn't have the kind of money it would take to buy a business like that. It wasn't cheap."

"So, you went to Ryan."

"Have I already told you this story?"

He pushes his hand up my calf. “No. Sorry, I won’t interrupt.”

“I went to Ryan. I knew he wouldn’t turn me away. He would have just bought the shop and given it to me as a gift if I’d asked him. He’s too fucking generous.”

“He loves you.”

“A lot, yeah. They all do, and that makes me a lucky girl. I made him set it up like a traditional bank loan, and I make payments to him. He refused the interest. In fact, he yelled at me when I told him to charge me interest.”

“I wouldn’t take that from my sisters, either, and I’m no billionaire.”

I shrug a shoulder. “It’s still nice of him. When I became close to the other four girls, we got drunk one night at The Wolf Den and decided to start this club for businesswomen. Because girls need to look out for girls, and there’s room for all of us to succeed. And now that we’ve been doing this for a little while, I honestly think that it’s the whole reason I was supposed to buy my shop, Holden. Because now I get to network and learn from all these incredible women, and they’re my friends. I guess my point of all of this is to say, I love that you’re proud of me. Like, *love* it. But I’m so grateful because for a long time, I felt lost. And now I’m not lost anymore.”

“Come here, baby girl.” He takes my hand, and I don’t even hesitate to crawl over into his lap and wrap my arms around him. He hugs me close, rubbing his big hand up and down my back. “You’re so fucking incredible, Millie Wild-Lexington.”

I *love* it when he says my whole name.

He covers my throat, drags his thumb over my jawline, and then his lips are on me, and I've never felt more cherished in all my life.

I shift, moving to straddle him, and press my already hot core against his hard length, and he groans against my lips.

I only have panties on under my dress, and that thin strap of fabric does nothing to cover how ready for me my husband is.

I rise up onto my knees and shimmy his sweats aside, unleashing him. But when I lower back down, I tug my panties out of the way and sheath him, not stopping until he's seated fully, and we're panting hard, staring into each other's eyes in the darkness.

"You said once that I'm your world." I kiss his lips. "Your center of gravity." Kiss his cheek. "The reason your heart beats."

"Jesus, wife." His hips move just a little, but it causes the most delicious sensation that has me tightening around him. "Yes, you're all of that and more."

"Same." My lips return to his. "And you were the final piece that made me feel found. Made me feel like I'm not lost."

"Baby girl."

I rock against him, taking it slow, keeping it so sweet. There are soft sighs and low chuckles. Breathless kisses.

I've never felt more loved than I do right now.

"You're everything," he breathes. "The beginning and the end. And you're mine."

"Oh, for sure." I tip my forehead to his and feel that

tightness fill me as the climax nears. "I've been yours all of my adult life, husband."

Later, long after our bodies have cooled and we've settled back in to rock in the darkness, Holden sighs.

"Everything."

"I'M SO glad Dani called us for help." I turn in my seat and smile at Holden, who's driving us over to Dani's new house. She's moving in today and called to see if we could lend her a hand with some of the heavy stuff. "I can't wait to see her place. I know which one it is, but I've never been inside."

"I have the boys coming in from the ranch to help, too," Holden replies. "It shouldn't take us long, and then we'll head to dinner at your brother's place."

I nod and grin at Dani as we pull up in front of her new house.

"Hi!" I hurry over to her and wrap an arm around her shoulders. "This is *cute.* Tell me the inside is adorable, too."

"It needs work," she admits. "But the owners said I could do some minor DIY projects to spiff it up."

"Dani, I don't want you living in a fixer-upper." Holden frowns at her, but Dani rolls her eyes.

"Yeah, yeah, okay. I can paint a wall, big brother."

She gives us a quick tour, and I take in a small kitchen and living area and then three small bedrooms and one bathroom.

It's tiny. It needs paint, new floors, and the kitchen could use a gut job, but it's clean. Everything else is cosmetic.

"You're not living here," Holden announces, his hands on his hips.

"Uh, yeah. I am." Dani mirrors his stance. "I already paid the money, and I have the keys. My stuff is here, Holden."

"Don't care."

"Okay, now you're being unreasonable," I say to my husband, who simply glares at me. "Seriously, it's a clean place, and she can make it her own."

"Exactly." Dani nods, and then Levi and Vance pull in, and Holden deflates.

"If *one thing* goes wrong in there, you move out."

"Whatever." Dani rolls her eyes again, and we all get to work carrying in boxes and small pieces of furniture.

"Whoa." Holden holds a hand up to me. "What do you think you're doing?"

"Helping."

"You're injured."

I laugh and boost myself up onto my toes to kiss his cheek. "I'm fine. I'm going back to work tomorrow."

"No."

"Husband." I cup his cheek and smile gently. "I love you, too. I'm fine."

"Where do you want this, Dani?" Vance asks, pointing to a lamp.

"Any of the bedrooms is fine," she replies.

Bridger's truck pulls in across the street, and I wave as he gets out, but he's ignoring me.

Birdie, however, isn't ignoring anyone.

"Millie!" She's all smiles as she walks to the curb, carefully looks both ways, and then hurries over to me.

"You're not supposed to cross the street by yourself," I remind her as I pick her up into my arms and give her a hug.

"You were right here." She hugs me back and then smiles at the others. "What are you doing?"

"Dani is moving in today, and we're helping her."

"I wanna help!" Birdie pushes against me, and I set her on her feet, and then she disappears inside.

When I turn back toward Bridger's, I find the man scowling from the opposite curb.

"Come on, grouchy man. Come talk to me. I'm not allowed to lift heavy things."

Dani jogs out of the house and comes up short when she sees Bridger cross the street. "Oh, hey, Bridge."

"Dani." He smiles at her, but now his eyes are a little more apprehensive, and I want to demand he tell me what in the *hell* is going on, but I know he won't. Because he's as stubborn as I am.

Dani grins, then reaches for a box in the back of the moving truck, but it must be heavy because she drops it on the ground with a loud *thud.* She's struggling to pick it up when Bridger walks up behind her.

"Let me get it for you."

"No, it's okay, I've got it."

He doesn't intervene, just stands behind her, his

hands on his hips, but she continues to struggle to lift it, until finally, he nudges her out of the way.

"Stop being stubborn and let me get it, Dani."

He easily picks up the box and carries it inside, and Dani worries her bottom lip between her teeth.

"Wanna talk about what's going on there?" I ask her.

Her blue eyes, so much like her brother's, shoot over to me, and she shrugs.

"We're just friends."

Some of the pieces start to fall into place. "Are you sure about that?"

Dani lets out a humorless laugh. "Trust me, Bridger made it very clear to me a long time ago that we'd only ever be friends. That's it. And that's okay because I really care about him, you know? He...well, he did a lot for me when I was a kid. Anyway, I'd better get back to work."

She rushes to pick up another box and carries it inside. Obviously, the subject is closed.

Interesting.

For the next hour or so, we unload the truck. Holden grumbles about his sister having too much shit. Bridger makes sure all the heavy stuff is taken care of before he takes Birdie home, and once the ranch guys have headed out, Holden turns to me.

"We'd better get out to your brother's for dinner."

"Thanks for your help," Dani says as she wipes some sweat off her forehead. "I never could have done that alone."

"That's what family does." I wink at her, and Holden and I head to the truck.

CHAPTER TWENTY-EIGHT

HOLDEN

We've been here for an hour, and I've never experienced so much amazing, organized chaos.

Children run around, yelling and playing in the yard. Babies fuss and are passed around from one set of arms to another. Jake and his girlfriend, Katie, are cozied up on a chaise lounge, talking and giggling together.

My girl is talking with her mama and two of the other wives, and I'm standing by the grill, nursing a beer, talking with Rem and Ryan.

"I know it's a family day," I begin, "but I'd like to talk business for a second, if you don't mind."

"I don't mind," Rem says and glances over at Ryan, then back at me. "Privately?"

"Ryan's fine. Hell, bring the other brothers over if you want. I don't have any secrets."

Rem turns the ribs on the grill, shuts the lid, then picks up his beer and gives me his attention. "Let's talk."

"You might think I'm insane."

Ryan laughs, and Rem just nods. "Probably. But it's okay."

I push my hand through my hair, look out over their property, and then back at Remington. "I want to figure out a way to combine our ranches."

Ryan immediately sobers, and Rem's eyebrows climb into his hairline.

"Why?"

I take a deep breath, and then I just start to talk. "I don't want to sell. I love my property, but there are still a lot of ghosts there, and I'm working on clearing those out. I'm almost there. I burned the buildings, and I've already made plans to move pastures around. Now we know that the asshole set traps, and those are gone. I'm not so sure that the property lines are correct anyway."

"We never stole—"

I cut Remington off with a shake of my head. "Not you. My father. His father. I'm sure they moved fences here and there, likely by a lot. Assholes."

"Is this one more *fuck you* to your dad?" Ryan asks.

"Oh, without a doubt. If he were alive, that fucker would kill me just for being here, let alone talking about merging my ranch with yours. It's not a financial thing. I have plenty of money. My operation is solid. It's really the principle. It needs a change. It's been over the past month or so, since Millie, that I've realized how isolated we are on our ranch, how much damage he did. It could be so much more."

"I actually don't hate this idea," Remington says,

rubbing his hand on the back of his neck. "Expanding and combining beef production could be huge. We'd be the largest cattle ranch in Montana. Not to mention, you have a lot more water on your land than we do. It would benefit the cattle."

Ryan hasn't said much, so I turn to him. "Thoughts?"

"If it's something you both want, I think you'd be stupid not to do it. It's too beneficial for both sides."

"I'd want to make sure that my men have jobs."

Rem frowns. "We'd be partners, Holden. I'm not going to fire your men, and you can't fire mine."

I blink at him. "Partners."

"Like you said, I'm not buying you out. We'd be merging."

I nod slowly, surprised that they're so open to this idea.

"I think we should have more conversations," Ryan says. "Speak with attorneys, get projections, that sort of thing, and go from there. Think it over."

"It's definitely not something to decide over Sunday dinner," I agree with a chuckle. "But I'm glad I brought it up. I've been thinking about it for a few weeks now."

"Definitely worth thinking over," Rem agrees.

Millie wanders our way, holding a fussy Lottie. "Ryan, I can't get your daughter to stop crying."

"Did you pinch her?" Ryan asks her as he takes the baby and bounces her against his shoulder. "Did Auntie Millie pinch Daddy's sweet potato?"

"No, moron." Millie rolls her eyes and then runs her

hand over the baby's head. "She was just sad. Weren't you, pumpkin? Don't be sad. Don't be a sad girl. Aww, you're so sweet."

She's smiling at that baby, making funny faces, and it makes my stomach clench. I want babies with this woman. I want to be here, with her family, and maybe my girls, too, with our kids playing.

I fucking want all of it. Everything I thought I'd never have in my life.

"Hi."

I look down and grin at a little brunette, who's missing her two front teeth and smiling up at me.

"Hi there. What's your name?"

"Daisy." I squat next to her so I can look her in the eyes. "Brady is my daddy."

"I knew that. How are you? Are you having a good day?"

"Yeah, it's always fun out here. We have a house on the ranch, too, but you can't see it from here. It's new. We just moved into it. Daddy got me cows."

"The black beef cattle?" I ask her.

"No, my *own* cows. Highland cows. Mini ones. Mom told him I could have *one*, but he got me *three*."

I grin at her. "Cows get lonely."

"That's what Daddy said. Anyway, you looked sad, so I wanted to say hi."

I frown at her. "I looked sad?"

"Kinda." She shrugs, and then Holly calls her name. "You can sit by me at dinner."

I grin at her and tug on her braid. "That's the best offer I've had all day."

She smiles that big, toothless smile again, and then she runs off.

"Well, that was cute."

I look over at Millie and find her smiling softly at me.

"You're just a chick magnet, aren't you, husband?"

Ryan smirks, and even Remington grins at me. I see that Millie's holding the baby again, and I cross to her, pat the baby on the back, and lean in to whisper in my wife's ear.

"I'm going to put a baby in you the first chance I get, wife."

Millie blanches, Ryan and Remington bust up laughing, and I simply grin at her.

"Geez, hold a baby for five minutes, and men start getting ideas. I'm going to find the girls."

She's not scowling when she walks away from us, and from the flush on her cheeks, I'd say she doesn't hate the idea.

"You know, I don't think I've ever seen my sister get as flustered as she does with you," Ryan says, clapping me on the back. "Way to keep her on her toes, man."

Remington takes the ribs off the grill, and before he can take them inside, we hear tires pull up at the side of the house.

Remington and Ryan share a frown, and unease moves down my spine.

"I'm about to get my ass handed to me, aren't I?" I ask them.

"No. This is *my fucking house*," Remington says, anger in his voice. Before he or anyone else can go see who it is, although we already know, John walks around the back of the building.

He grins, obviously happy to see everyone. He hugs the grandkids when they rush over to say hello before they run off to play in the treehouse that Ryan bought them last Christmas.

"Wait for it," I whisper.

And just then, he spots Millie. His face falls in surprise, but then his eyes narrow, and he skims the area. When he finds me, his face turns to stone. He straightens, snarls, and turns to leave.

"Dad!" Millie calls out, but he doesn't even look back at her.

"Enough," I mutter and hurry past her, squeezing her shoulders as I pass. "John. Mr. Wild."

"Fuck off."

"Stop. I've fucking had it with you hurting my wife."

I hear the gasp behind me, but I don't turn away from him. John stops and swings around to stare at me.

"You *what*?"

"All you're doing is hurting my wife, and I've had enough of that bullshit. So, let's have this out. Right now."

"You piece of *shit*."

"Dad!" Millie cries. I can hear the tears in her eyes, and when I glance over, I see that Chase is holding her, and I'm relieved to see that she's being taken care of. There's a crowd gathered, but aside from Jake and

Katie, the kids aren't around, and that makes me feel better.

"WHY DID YOU MARRY MY DAUGHTER?" John roars, getting within three feet of my face. "Of all the people in this town, why *my* baby?"

"Because I had no fucking choice!"

I rub my hand over my face and pace away from him. It's time to just come clean. To spell it all out. Because nothing will be resolved here if I don't, and Millie needs her dad.

"There are two reasons for that." I glance her way, and she nods, still crying against Chase. "The first one being that I fell in love with her eight years ago. It was sweet and amazing, and I would have married her then."

I push my hands through my hair, pacing.

"But my fucking father found out and threatened to kill her and my sister if I kept seeing her."

John growls. Joy cries out. There's more sniffling happening behind me.

With my eyes on John's, I continue. "He would have done it. You know it, and I know it."

"Fuck," John whispers.

"So, I had to break it off with her, but she's so damn stubborn, and she was young and sweet, and I had to hurt her. Fuck, I had to break her heart, and it destroyed me. But I had to hurt her to save her. She couldn't be anywhere near me."

Stomach roiling, I look at my wife again, and she's smiling at me through her tears.

"And then the son of a bitch died."

"So, you swooped in and took her," John says.

"No." I shake my head. "It's way worse than that. So much fucking worse. In the will, he added a clause that stated I wouldn't inherit the ranch unless I got married within sixty days of the will reading. He left my sisters *nothing.*"

"You got married to *my daughter* to inherit your fucking ranch?" John bellows.

"John." This is Joy, her voice hard. "Let that man speak, or I swear to God, you'll be sleeping with the chickens for a month."

"There is *no one* in this world that I would marry. No one. Except Millie. Jesus, I've loved her for the better part of a decade. And my sisters deserved so much more than what that bastard left them. So, I talked to Millie. I never lied to her. I never tricked her. I told her everything."

John looks to Millie, who nods.

"And she agreed."

"How much did he promise to pay you?" John asks her, his face bright red. "Because I'll fucking double it to get you to leave him."

"Dad," she says, wearily now.

"Are you telling me that you won't divorce him?"

"Of course, I'm not going to divorce him!" She comes down the steps toward him, so full of fire and indignation. "Jesus, I love him so much I might die. And this is not one of those *but Daddy, I love him* moments. Although, I do. But I love *you,* too! Why can't I have both of you in my life? What could he have done to you that makes you hate him so much?"

"It wasn't him," John growls, and the pit in my stomach grows as he turns to glare at me. "Your fucking *father* killed my cattle every chance he got. He wanted Joy back in the day, and when she said no, he threatened to rape her. Threatened to kill her."

"Jesus," Remington mutters.

"He set traps on *my* land," he continues, on a roll now. "He told everyone in town that I poisoned his cows. That I shot his animals. That I hit on his wife. Jesus."

Shaking my head, I shove my hands through my hair again. I believe every word.

"That's something he would do." I nod at him. "He killed my mother."

Dead silence.

"What was that?" John narrows his eyes at me and steps closer.

"Pushed her down the stairs. He did that a lot, liked to push her down the stairs. She wasn't even forty and could barely walk a straight line from all the tumbles she took. But the last time? Well, she broke her neck on the second to the last step. I heard it snap."

"Fuck me." I think that's Ryan.

"I was holding my infant sister, Charlie, at the time, feeding her," I continue. "Dad laughed. Told me to call someone to come clean it up."

Millie slips her hand into mine and holds on tight, and John's gaze falls to our hands, then back to my face.

"Do you think you can hate him more than I do?" I ask, still on a roll. "He beat the shit out of my sisters. Tortured their animals. Why do you think I only have horses and cattle? It was fucking physical and psychological *warfare* in that house, every motherfucking day. So, I'll ask you again, do you think that you can hate him more than me?"

John's breathing hard, and he surprises me. "And what did he do to you?"

"It doesn't matter—"

"Yeah, it fucking does. What did he do to *you*, Holden?"

"Anything and everything he wanted to. I was his punching bag. I was the one he threatened to keep the girls in line. I was the one who worked twenty-hour days because he didn't want to hire enough help. But in the end, *he took Millie away from me*. Because I couldn't have anything good, and it certainly wasn't going to be a Wild woman."

I can feel the wetness on my cheeks, but I don't care. I can't stop talking. I can't keep the secrets anymore.

"He left my sisters penniless. And he fucking *killed. My. Mom!* I buried her myself because he refused to pay to have it done. And when that asshole died, I burned it all to the goddamn ground, and now everything he thought he loved will be shit on by the cows he didn't even respect enough to treat with any kindness. I married the love of my life, and I'm finally in control of the ranch that I've been running for eight miserable years.

"Oh, yeah, after he made me give up Millie, he decided that I must have too much time on my hands if I had time to date. So, I did it *all* after that while that pathetic excuse for flesh did *nothing*."

"Why did you do it?" Chase asks.

"Because of his sisters," John says, his voice softer, the fight gone from his body.

"Yes, sir." I nod stiffly. "He always said, *it's really easy for girls to get lost. To be forgotten. Because no one gives a shit about them anyway*."

"Jesus." Millie leans her forehead on my biceps.

"But I give a shit. Those girls are my world. They're all sweet and good people, and if it meant I endured torment every day from the likes of him, it was worth it to keep them safe."

"You were a *child* raising those girls," Joy whispers.

"I was never a child." I clear my throat and then nod at her. "Ma'am."

John tips his head back and takes a long, deep breath, then lets his gaze fall to Millie before he looks back at me.

"Is someone going to feed us, or what?"

"Dinner's ready," Erin announces. "I'll go get the littles."

I hear the commotion of people shuffling away, but Joy joins John, Millie, and me and links her hand with her husband's.

"It's time to let this go, John," she says softly. "For yourself."

"I need to know one more thing," he says, turning to look at me. I'm surprised to see that his eyes are glassy. "You say you love her, but—" His lip wobbles. "I need to know that you'll never put a hand on her."

"Never." I hold my hand out to shake his, and he looks at it in surprise. "I swear to you, I would *never* hurt her in anger. I swear it on my mother, Mr. Wild."

His eyes bounce to Millie once more, and then he shakes my hand, and Millie dissolves into tears. I wrap my arm around her and tug her into my side, kissing her head.

"I don't deserve your daughter," I admit. "But she's the best thing that's ever happened to me, and I waited an awfully long time to make her mine."

"Come on," Joy says, tugging on John's hand. "Let's go eat. Let's go be with our family. Our *whole* family."

John nods and pats me on the shoulder as we follow the girls inside.

"Next time," he says gruffly, "bring your sisters with you."

I blink rapidly and then look over at him. "Sir?"

"John. Not sir. And if we're having family dinner, we'll have the *whole* family here. That's how we do things."

He winks at me, never cracking a smile, as he walks into the house and scoops up August, hugging the little boy close to his chest.

I have to take a minute to pull in a breath.

"Are you okay?"

Millie wraps herself around me in a hug, tucking her head under my chin. I hold her close and breathe her in.

"I'm...lighter." I'm fucking exhausted. I've been put through the emotional wringer. "And I think things are going to be okay with your dad."

"You told me you'd win him over." I can hear the smile in her voice. "You were right."

"I was only ever worried about winning *you* over, Rosie."

"Well, you've got all of us, husband. Take it or leave it."

I laugh and kiss the top of her head. "I'll fucking take it."

CHAPTER TWENTY-NINE

MILLIE

Two Months Later

"Brooks finally finished the old truck." We're bouncing around in it as Holden drives us to the far end of the property, where our favorite lookout spot is, to look at the mountains. "And it drives so much smoother."

"The body's the same," he says with a grin, "but the engine runs like new."

He backs into wherever he wants to be, cuts the engine, and turns to me. He drags his fingers down my face.

"You're fucking beautiful."

I feel my cheeks flush. "I'm glad you think so, babe."

His eyebrow ticks up, just like I wanted. "Who the fuck is *babe*?"

"Holden."

His eyes narrow.

"Honey."

"Try again."

I laugh and take his hand, planting my lips in his palm. "Husband."

"Hmm." He chuckles and shakes his head. "Come on."

We climb out of the truck, and I grin when I see that there's a pile of blankets and a cooler in the back. Holden spreads out the blankets, and we sit side by side, our backs against the cab of the truck, his arm around me, as we stare at the view that I've loved since I was a kid.

"I love this place," I whisper as he passes me a glass of tequila. "I feel like I can breathe when I look at this view."

"Good." He kisses my temple, then sips the whiskey he just poured for himself. "Because I'd like to build us a house, right here. With this view."

"What?" I stare up at him in surprise. "I didn't think you wanted to live on this ranch."

"Your brothers and I just spent two weeks moving fence," he says. "Next year, when I've fulfilled the terms of the will and everything officially moves into my name, we can move forward with the merger. I can pay my sisters their share and make sure they're taken care of. But in the meantime, we're going ahead with plans to consolidate the ranches."

I can't believe it's happening. A year ago, if someone had merely mentioned that our two ranches could someday be combined into one huge, successful operation, I would have laughed at the audacity.

And now, it's happening.

"When will we build the barn for the rescues?"

After seeing the horses that Ryan took in, and hearing that there are so many more who need love and help, I talked to Holden about having a small horse sanctuary on this side of the ranch, and he thought it was a good idea.

"We'll break ground on that next week," he says with a smile. "And then you can fill it up."

"Good." I sigh and enjoy leaning on my man while we watch the sun set over our mountain. "So, you want a house right here, huh?"

"I do. But there are going to be some ground rules."

I smirk and sip my drink. "Okay, husband, lay them out for me."

He tosses back the last of his drink, and I follow suit, and then he sets our glasses aside, and I straddle him so I can look into his eyes.

"You're missing the view, you know."

"No, I'm not." I kiss his lips softly. "Looking at you is the best view in the world. What are your rules?"

His hands move up my thighs and around to my ass, then back down again.

"Number one, we build what *you* want."

I frown at him. "No, it should be what we both want."

"I have everything, Millie. I have you. I want to build you the house of your dreams."

I sigh and tip my forehead to his. "You're so swoony sometimes."

"Number two, we're going to fill this house up with kids."

This isn't the first time he's mentioned babies, and it always wakes those murder hornets up in my belly.

"How many? Two?"

"Eight."

My mouth drops, and then I laugh at him. "Three."

"Seven."

"Husband." I kiss him and then drag my nose against his. "I can't have seven babies. That's too many. How about four?"

"Five, and that's my final offer."

"Let's see if we can have *one* and go from there. How many rules do you have, anyway?"

"A few more." His hand, that beautifully tattooed hand, journeys up my chest and circles the column of my throat, and his thumb presses on my pulse point.

I fucking love it when he does this. Thank God he does it every chance he gets.

"Number three," he continues, his voice getting rougher, "you need to wear this."

He holds something up between us, and my heart stumbles. Winking up at me is a beautiful solitaire diamond ring.

"I told you, I don't need—"

"I do." He slides it onto my finger, and it nestles right up against my wedding band. "I need it. We did everything so fast, and a little backward, before, and I want you to wear my ring. Besides, *I* have two."

He holds his hand up, and I grin at both the gold and the ink.

"I love your ring finger." I kiss it and then him. "Thank you."

"You're welcome."

"Any more ground rules?"

"Just one more. Number four, we always remember our anniversary and spend it like this."

I frown down at him. "Husband, today is not our anniversary." I hold my own tattoo up so he can see the date printed there. "Remember?"

"Oh, I remember. I'm not talking about that anniversary. It was nine years ago today that I had you in the back of this truck, and you gave me your virginity."

For the second time today, I swoon, and my jaw drops. "How do you possibly remember that date?"

"I never forget anything when it comes to you, little rose." He kisses me harder now, slipping his tongue between the seam of my lips to rub against my own. His hands have bunched my dress up around my hips, and then he pulls it up and off, tossing it to the side, the way I did all those years ago.

Except, this time, I'm not wearing any underwear.

"Fucking hell," he growls. "I'm one lucky son of a bitch."

"You're not lucky." I grind over him, then open his jeans and set him free, rubbing my hand up and down until I line him up with my entrance and sink over him.

"You're my soulmate, husband. There's no luck involved here."

"Rosie." It's a whisper on his lips as I wrap my arms around his neck, and his hands grip on to my hips, and we start to move. "Jesus, you're everything."

"And you're the reason my heart beats."

EPILOGUE

BRIDGER BLACKWELL

God, I'm fucking tired.

I'm coming off of forty-eight straight hours of being on call at the firehouse. As the chief, you'd think I would have a regular nine-to-five job, but that's not the case in this small department. I manage everything, *and* I fight fires.

But I'm also a single dad.

So I'm going to go inside and send my sister home for the evening, and tomorrow, my daughter and I are going to start gearing up for her first day of school.

Which starts next week.

Because I've been too busy and haven't had time to get it done before now, which really makes me feel like shit. Not that my daughter ever makes me feel guilty; I do a good enough job of that all by myself.

I park in the driveway and climb out of my truck, just as I hear a door open behind me, and I close my eyes. I can feel her before I even know for sure that it's her. Dani

Lexington, coming out of her house, to do what, I have no idea because it's past dark.

I turn around, and sure enough. There she is, with her long, dark hair, blue eyes, and killer curves that seem to star in all of my fucking dreams lately. She hasn't noticed me yet, and I take her in. She's in shorts that mold around her ass perfectly and show off her fucking amazing legs, and a V-neck T-shirt that dips only low enough to give me a glimpse at the very top of her cleavage.

That woman's curves set my teeth on edge, and I quickly adjust myself in my jeans.

Goddamn it, I've wanted her for half of my life, and I couldn't have her. Either she was too young or at college or...*something*. The timing was never right. Now, she's back in Bitterroot Valley, living across the fucking street from me, taunting me at every turn.

She glances up, then does a double-take when she sees me, and that tentative smile spreads over her lips. I miss the days of her giving me her bright, uncensored smiles.

"Hey," she says.

"Hey, Dani." I offer her a smile and wonder what it's going to take for her to realize that *friendship* isn't the only thing I want with her. "Did you have a good day?"

"I did, actually." She nods and tucks her hair behind her ear. "How about you?"

Fuck, she's beautiful.

"No complaints here. I'd better get inside to Birdie."

She bites her lower lip and frowns down at the

concrete beneath her bare feet. Then, right before my eyes, she squares her shoulders, swallows hard, and lifts her chin.

Good girl. Ask me to come back outside to sit with you. To talk. To put my hands on you.

But she seemingly decides to forgo whatever she was going to say, and I feel that familiar frustration fill my gut.

"I hope you have a good night," is all she says.

Fuck, living across from her is going to be torture unless I get my head out of my ass and do something about it.

"You, too, Dani."

I walk inside and close the door behind me, a plan starting to take shape in my head.

Are you ready for When We Burn, the first in The Blackwells of Montana series, featuring Bridger and Dani? You can order it here: https://www.kristenprobyauthor.com/when-we-burn

Turn the page for a preview of When We Burn:

WHEN WE BURN PREVIEW

BRIDGER

Her skin is velvet. Pure sin. Pure fucking everything. *Her big blue eyes shine as she bites that lower lip and spreads her legs, welcoming me to rest my pelvis between them. I'm so fucking hard, I can barely breathe as I rub my length through her already wet pussy, and she arches her neck back on a moan.*

"Bridger. Yes. Oh, God, yes."

Her fingers fist in my hair, but I grab her wrists, kiss them, and pin them over her head before I lick and suck on her already hard nipples.

"You like this, Dani? You want me to lick your delectable little body?"

She purrs, her hips lift, and her mouth makes a perfect O as I rear my hips back and rest the crown of my cock against her entrance.

"Yes. Please, Bridger."

I nip her jaw, lick my way over to her ear, and whisper, "I'm going to fuck you so good, sweetheart."

"Yes!"

I've wanted her for my entire adult life. She's a siren that I can't walk away from, and with her spread out, so hot and wet and needy for me, I can't resist her. I nudge just the tip inside of her, and she moans, and I can't hold back.

I slam into her. Her eyes go wide and glassy, and her legs lift, already begging for more. Her walls clench around me, as if she's already right there, on the edge of falling apart.

"Jesus Christ," I growl against her lips, licking along the seam of her lips, and she opens for me, giving me back as good as I give. "You're a goddamn temptress, you know that?"

She's so damn beautiful.

So perfect.

"Oh, Daddy!"

"Daddy!"

Oh, fuck.

I turn onto my side to hide my morning wood, courtesy of that sexy-as-fuck dream about a woman I've wanted for-fucking-ever, but a woman that I'll never have.

"Good morning, peanut."

Birdie, my five-year-old, giggles behind me. "You have to wake up, Daddy. We have to go shopping."

I reach over to tap my phone and scowl. "It's only eight, baby. The stores don't open for a while yet."

"You need breakfast."

I grin. That's code for *I want breakfast.*

"You're right. We need to eat. How about if I take a quick shower and then get started on the French toast, okay?"

She leans over so she can look at my face and pats my

cheek. Now that my nether regions have calmed down a bit, I roll to her and pull her in for a big hug.

"On second thought, never mind. We're not going shopping. You're not big enough to go to school. You're just a baby."

I bury my face in her neck and blow raspberries, making her giggle. She smells like her baby shampoo, and she's so sweet and small in her cute *Tangled* nightgown.

"I'm five." More giggles as I continue to kiss her cheeks. "I'm a big girl."

"No way. You're my baby." I hug her tight, and she wraps her little arm around my neck and hugs me back. "My tiny peanut."

She was *so small* when she was born. So little and sweet. But never fragile. Not my girl. Even with the medical challenges we've had over the past year, she's never been weak.

"I love you, Daddy."

I grin sleepily at her and kiss her cheek. "I love you, too, baby bird. Do you *really* have to grow up and go to school?"

"Yep. And I need clothes and shoes and notebooks. There's a list."

"Ah, yes, the list." I bop her on the nose. "You go get dressed and watch something on your tablet for a little while, okay? I'll get ready, too. We won't forget your list."

"Okay." She launches herself off my bed and runs for her bedroom, just down the hall from mine.

I sigh and drag my hands down my face. I came off a

three-day stretch last night, and when I got home, Dani was outside, wearing fuck-me short shorts and looking like a walking wet dream. No wonder I dreamed about fucking her.

The woman is gorgeous, with all that dark hair and blue eyes, and don't even get me started on her curves. Breasts and hips that would fit perfectly in my hands.

And there goes my dick again.

With a sigh, I get out of bed and pad into my attached bathroom, resigned to fucking my hand to get rid of this hard-on that only seems to happen when I see my sexy neighbor. Or even *think* about her.

I've known Dani Lexington since we were little kids. She's a few years younger than I am, and she and her siblings were staples at our ranch growing up. Her brother, Holden, the eldest of the siblings, is one of my best friends. I know that they had a rough childhood that fucked with all five of them. What they went through… well, their father should have been in prison. He was fucked up.

I'm sure that if I talked with Holden and told him that I wanted to date his sister, he'd be pretty cool about it. After he punched me, just for good measure.

I'd expect nothing less.

But Dani and I have been good friends through a lot of shit in her childhood. Then, when she became a teenager, I noticed that I didn't actually have *brotherly* feelings toward her, but I was eighteen, and she was a minor.

No way I was going to dick around with that. Literally.

So, I kept a healthy distance. She graduated and went to college in Bozeman, and I stayed here to be a firefighter.

And I met my ex-wife. And the rest, as they say, is history.

But now she's back, and although she's still put me squarely in the friend zone, I'm going to do my damnedest to make her see that we could be so much more than friends. I know I want her. I've wanted her for a long time.

But she's also been gone for a while, and I need to get to know her again. I'm not stupid. I can't just flash a smile, tell her she's fucking gorgeous—even though she *is*—and expect her to spread those pretty legs and tell me she can't live another minute without me.

It's going to take some time. And given her traumatic past, I don't want to scare her. I don't even know if I *would* scare her if I told her how much I want her.

Again, I need to get to know her better.

With the water running, I strip out of my T-shirt and boxers and get into the spray, my hand immediately wrapping around the base of my cock and moving up, with thoughts from my dream in the forefront of my imagination as I slide my fist up and down my length, until I come hard against the tile, then grab the handheld and wash it all away.

Jesus, this is ridiculous.

"Daddy, I'm hungry."

"Coming, peanut."

Between Birdie and a *very* full-time job of being fire chief of Bitterroot Valley, I have enough on my plate already, but ever since Dani returned to town, it's highlighted that something was missing from my life. I'm not lonely, per se—my life doesn't allow that if I'm honest—but on the quiet nights when Birdie is asleep in bed, there's been a noticeable absence of someone to spend that time with. I want to cuddle up with someone, feel them against me, talk about my day, and listen about hers. And I know that the only woman who appeals to me is Dani.

In some respects, it's always been her.

***

"If we're going to the pool party later, we need to go now." I'm holding the door open for Birdie, waiting for her to shimmy into her sneakers. The shoes I bought her at the beginning of summer are way too small now.

It's a good thing we're going shopping.

"Okay," she says after grabbing her sunglasses, which always makes me grin. She decided that because I wear them, she should, too, and hers are pink with green polka dots. "I'm ready."

I hear the lawn mower going as we walk out to my truck, and suddenly, Birdie is waving like mad. The lawn mower cuts off, and I follow my daughter's gaze.

There's Dani, standing behind the now-quiet mower, in cutoff denim shorts that barely hide her ass, a white tank that leaves absolutely fucking *nothing* to the imagination, her hair up on her head, and a sheen of sweat covering her dewy skin.

Fuck me.

"Hi, Dani," Birdie yells, still waving.

"Hi, Birdie," Dani replies with a sweet smile for my daughter. Then her gorgeous blue eyes shift to mine. "Hi, Bridger."

"Dani." I nod at her the way I always do and nudge Birdie toward the truck. "Let's go, peanut."

"We're going shopping for school," Birdie informs Dani. "'Cause it starts next week."

"I know," Dani says with a chuckle. "I'm going to be your teacher."

My heart stops. *What?* I knew that Dani would be teaching at the elementary school this year, but I didn't know that meant that she would be my daughter's teacher, which means I'll see her often, and *that* is a very good thing.

"You are?" Birdie asks, almost screeching with excitement. "Yay!"

Dani laughs now and nods. "I am. Your dad should have received that information in an email." Her gaze turns to mine again, with more humor in it now. "Along with the supplies list."

I take a deep breath and let it out slowly, willing my galloping heart to slow the fuck down. "I must have missed that part."

"Have fun shopping," she says and turns to start the mower again. It only takes her two pulls on the string before it fires up, waves, and then walks behind it, her hips and ass moving with every step, and I have to pry my eyes away.

Get a grip, Blackwell.

"Come on, peanut. We have a full day today."

***

"If you spent all day school shopping, you need a beer." Blake, one of my brothers, passes me a cold bottle, and I flip off the cap and take a pull. Yeah, I could use a drink, and not because of the shopping spree that I took my daughter on today. No, I need it because I just discovered that Dani is also at this pool party.

Which makes sense because it's being held at a friend's ranch, Ryan Wild, who Dani is now related to by marriage.

Of course, she's here. I should have realized that she would be. But I didn't think of it, and now here I am, sitting with a few of my brothers, Dani's brother, Holden, and a couple of the Wilds, watching as kids run around, swim, and play while a whole bunch of people drift around.

It's three families, and yet, it's chaos.

Because apparently in Bitterroot Valley, no one knows the meaning of having just a couple of kids and getting on with it. No, we're overachievers here in this town. Someday, I'd like to have more kids. Maybe not five, though. That's a lot.

"It actually wasn't that bad," I say to Blake. "I ended up getting her more shit than she needs, and we found everything on the supply list the school sent. She'll be set for a few months at least. Until she has another growth spurt, and I have to replace it all again."

"It's good that she's growing so well," Blake, the doctor in the family, says. "It means she's healthy, Bridge."

"I know. I'm not complaining at all. Hell, I'll buy her a new wardrobe every week if it means we keep her healthy."

I glance over to where Birdie is playing with a few other kids just a couple of years older than she is. She's laughing and running, and it wasn't that long ago that we didn't know if she'd be doing something so simple again.

No, I'm absolutely not complaining.

"How are things at the hospital?" I ask him. Blake is a doctor, splitting his time between the family practice clinic and the hospital. I always figured he'd move to a city and start a practice, but he came back to Bitterroot Valley, and I'm glad. He's a damn valuable asset to this town. I'm close to all of my brothers, but since Blake is only two years older than me, we've always been tight, not to mention that, given our career choices, we're like-minded, too.

"Busy. Always busy." He sighs and sips his own beer, which tells me that he's not on call today. And neither am I.

That never happens.

"Any good stories to share?" Brooks, our eldest brother, asks. "Anything particularly fucked up you've seen lately?"

Blake laughs and sits back, thinking. "Aside from a guy who almost tore off his face with a garbage can? Not really."

"That's disgusting," I say with a scowl. But I know exactly who that was. I was on that ambulance call.

"Dinner's ready," someone calls from the outdoor kitchen area. I get Birdie's plate made first and situate her with her friends at a little picnic table just for the kids at the side of the patio. She's thrilled with a hotdog, chips, and some watermelon, and then I go back to fill my own plate and sit back where I was before. I can see Birdie from where I'm sitting and can keep an eye on her.

Not that there aren't dozens of eyes on all the kids at all times, but I like being able to see her.

I also happen to notice that Dani's sitting with Charlie, her youngest sister, in one of the lounge chairs by the pool. They're eating, and Charlie's obviously talking Dani's ear off because Dani's just smiling that beautiful smile as she listens. She's in a different outfit this evening, some flowy white pants and a matching white button-down top that's open over a cropped pink tank. One side of the white top falls over a shoulder, showing off golden skin. Her hair is still up, with loose pieces hanging down around her face, and she isn't wearing any makeup.

She doesn't fucking need makeup. It's one of the things I like most about her. She's naturally beautiful.

It makes sense that she's not in a bathing suit. Who would want to be near the water after what she was put through? Fuck, it still affects me, remembering that summer when we were kids.

I-I-I forgot to get the eggs this morning, and when he said he was going to hurt me, I said n-n-no."

I've never felt so fucking enraged. *What sort of monster could do that to his little girl?*

Mentally shaking my head, I take a pull of my beer and turn my attention back to the conversation going on around me.

"Are you guys going to the hootenanny tomorrow?" Beckett asks. "I'll have a booth set up with milk and stuff for sale. Ice cream, too."

"Fuck no," Holden replies, shaking his head. "There are people there. I'll just come get your ice cream from your house."

"You're so social," Blake says with a chuckle. "It's for a good cause, you know. Several, actually."

"I'll donate money. I don't have to go there," Holden replies, his eyes scouting the area for his wife. When he finds her, his shoulders relax.

He married one of my best friends, Millie, months ago. They're stupidly in love, and it's mildly nauseating.

"I have to go," I reply. "I have to man a booth, too."

"In your firefighter gear?" Blake asks.

"Yeah, why?" My brother just grins at me, and I glare back at him. "Fuck off."

"You know you get more donations when you're in uniform," Blake says with a laugh. "Are you going to wear a shirt this year, or go without?"

"Are you jealous?" I tip up an eyebrow, and Blake only laughs harder.

"Fuck no. I think it's hilarious that you're a sex symbol. Women have no taste."

"He's so pretty," Holden adds, enjoying flinging me shit.

"Who is?" Millie asks as she joins us and sits in her husband's lap.

"Bridger," Holden replies.

"Beautiful," Millie agrees, and I flip her off.

"Now, don't make me kick your ass for disrespecting my wife." Holden's voice has no heat in it, and Millie's giggling.

"You're all a bunch of assholes. I'll be keeping my shirt on, thank you very much."

Suddenly, there's a splash, a scream, and my heart thuds as I kick into action. There's a second splash, and I run to the pool and take in what's happening.

Birdie—God, *Birdie*—is in the deep end, flapping around, and Dani has her, pulling her to the side of the pool. I meet her there and pull Birdie out and into my arms. She clings to me, wrapping her arms around my neck.

"Hey, are you okay? What happened?"

"I wanted to swim where it's deep." Her voice is small, and I can tell that it scared her, but she's not hurt.

I turn back to the water and see that Dani's having a hard time, her clothes now soaked and heavy, and her eyes are wide in terror. Before I can pass Birdie off, several of the guys

—Blake, Ryan, and Holden—have jumped into the water and are helping Dani stay above water, leading her to the shallow end of the pool and then out of the water entirely.

She sheds the sopping white shirt and lets it fall, but then her teeth are chattering, her eyes dilated.

Fuck. She's going into shock.

Or having a panic attack.

Maybe both.

Why did she jump in? She's terrified of water.

"Hey," Blake says as he takes a towel from Ryan and wraps it around Dani's shoulders, rubbing her arms briskly. We all know. We all saw what *he* did to her. It strikes me, again, that the way that bastard died was too good for him. "You're okay, sweetheart. I know you don't like the water."

Jesus, she's *terrified* of the water, and she jumped in to help my daughter.

"Can I swim some more?" Birdie asks me, and I kiss her cheek and then set her down, not taking my eyes off Dani.

"No, baby bird. Go wrap up in a towel and play with the other kids."

"But—"

"I said no."

She doesn't argue, and I'm thankful she's mostly so compliant. Yes, she loves to push my buttons—often—but she doesn't fight me when she knows I won't budge. Considering her mom's selfishness, Birdie's sweetness frequently amazes me.

My daughter runs off, and I cross to where Blake is consoling Dani.

Oh, kitten. I hate this for you.

"In through your nose," he says perfectly calmly, doctor mode obviously kicking in. "Out through your mouth."

"Sorry," she mutters and closes her eyes, her teeth chattering. "I d-don't like water."

"I know," Blake says grimly, and then his eyes find mine. He raises an eyebrow but doesn't say anything as he passes her to me.

I immediately wrap my arms around her and hug her close.

"Thank you, kitten," I murmur into her wet hair. God, I haven't hugged Dani in years, always careful to keep a safe distance, and I'm not sure that it's a good idea right now, but she's so scared, and she helped my girl. "Thank you for jumping in for her."

"It was too deep," she manages as she clings to me. "She scared the heck out of me."

I grin. Dani's always refused to swear. It's probably a good quality to have in a kindergarten teacher.

"Me, too." I rub my hands up and down her back. "You okay?"

She nods, and I look over her head to the crowd gathered around. "She's okay."

Holden's eyes catch mine. Hands on his hips, his face is grim. He shakes his head, and I can read his thoughts.

This will be bad for her.

So, despite the fact that I want nothing more than to

keep her with me, I let him hold her. Holden raised his sisters, kept them safe from a fucking tyrant, and she's *his* baby girl.

She's not mine.

Everyone resumes what they were doing before the fall into the pool. Birdie's completely fine, laughing with some of the Wild kids as she warms up in a big pool towel and they eat ice cream from Beckett's ranch.

About an hour later, when I'm about to get Birdie ready to go home, I spot Dani watching me from that same lounge chair as earlier. Someone gave her different clothes to change into, and her hair is mostly dry now. She doesn't look away when I meet her gaze like she usually would.

I have to know that she's okay.

So, I cross through the yard to where she's sitting by the pool and tap her lightly on the shoulder.

"Can we talk somewhere private?"

NEWSLETTER SIGN UP

I hope you enjoyed reading this story as much as I enjoyed writing it! For upcoming book news, be sure to join my newsletter! I promise I will only send you news-filled mail, and none of the spam. You can sign up here:

https://mailchi.mp/kristenproby.com/newsletter-sign-up

ALSO BY KRISTEN PROBY:

Other Books by Kristen Proby

The Wilds of Montana Series

Wild for You - Remington & Erin

Chasing Wild - Chase & Summer

Get more information on the series here: https://www.kristenprobyauthor.com/the-wilds-of-montana

Single in Seattle Series

The Secret - Vaughn & Olivia

The Scandal - Gray & Stella

The Score - Ike & Sophie

The Setup - Keaton & Sidney

The Stand-In - Drew & London

Check out the full series here: https://www.kristenprobyauthor.com/single-in-seattle

Huckleberry Bay Series

Lighthouse Way

Fernhill Lane

Chapel Bend

Cherry Lane

The With Me In Seattle Series

Come Away With Me - Luke & Natalie

Under The Mistletoe With Me - Isaac & Stacy

Fight With Me - Nate & Jules

Play With Me - Will & Meg

Rock With Me - Leo & Sam

Safe With Me - Caleb & Brynna

Tied With Me - Matt & Nic

Breathe With Me - Mark & Meredith

Forever With Me - Dominic & Alecia

Stay With Me - Wyatt & Amelia

Indulge With Me

Love With Me - Jace & Joy

Dance With Me Levi & Starla

You Belong With Me - Archer & Elena

Dream With Me - Kane & Anastasia

Imagine With Me - Shawn & Lexi

Escape With Me - Keegan & Isabella

Flirt With Me - Hunter & Maeve

Take a Chance With Me - Cameron & Maggie

Check out the full series here: https://www.

kristenprobyauthor.com/with-me-in-seattle

The Big Sky Universe

Love Under the Big Sky

Loving Cara

Seducing Lauren

Falling for Jillian

Saving Grace

The Big Sky

Charming Hannah

Kissing Jenna

Waiting for Willa

Soaring With Fallon

Big Sky Royal

Enchanting Sebastian

Enticing Liam

Taunting Callum

Heroes of Big Sky

Honor

Courage

Shelter

Check out the full Big Sky universe here: https://www.kristenprobyauthor.com/under-the-big-sky

Bayou Magic

Shadows

Spells

Serendipity

Check out the full series here: https://www.kristenprobyauthor.com/bayou-magic

The Curse of the Blood Moon Series

Hallows End

Cauldrons Call

Salems Song

The Romancing Manhattan Series

All the Way

All it Takes

After All

Check out the full series here: https://www.kristenprobyauthor.com/romancing-manhattan

The Boudreaux Series

Easy Love

Easy Charm

Easy Melody

Easy Kisses

Easy Magic

Easy Fortune

Easy Nights

Check out the full series here: https://www.kristenprobyauthor.com/boudreaux

The Fusion Series

Listen to Me
Close to You
Blush for Me
The Beauty of Us
Savor You

Check out the full series here: https://www.kristenprobyauthor.com/fusion

From 1001 Dark Nights

Easy With You
Easy For Keeps
No Reservations
Tempting Brooke
Wonder With Me
Shine With Me
Change With Me
The Scramble
Cherry Lane

Kristen Proby's Crossover Collection

Soaring with Fallon, A Big Sky Novel

Wicked Force: A Wicked Horse Vegas/Big Sky Novella
By Sawyer Bennett

All Stars Fall: A Seaside Pictures/Big Sky Novella
By Rachel Van Dyken

Hold On: A Play On/Big Sky Novella
By Samantha Young

Worth Fighting For: A Warrior Fight Club/Big Sky Novella
By Laura Kaye

Crazy Imperfect Love: A Dirty Dicks/Big Sky Novella
By K.L. Grayson

Nothing Without You: A Forever Yours/Big Sky Novella
By Monica Murphy

Check out the entire Crossover Collection here:
https://www.kristenprobyauthor.com/kristen-proby-crossover-collection

ABOUT THE AUTHOR

Kristen Proby has published more than sixty titles, many of which have hit the USA Today, New York Times and Wall Street Journal Bestsellers lists.

Kristen and her husband, John, make their home in her hometown of Whitefish, Montana with their two cats and dog.

Printed in Great Britain
by Amazon

59283580R00236